Praise for *Throw Like a Woman*:

"While, on the surface, this is a novel about a woman battling to make her way in the man's world of professional baseball, debut author Petrone presents a stirring and humorous story of a woman doing considerably more than that—trying to rediscover herself, provide for her family, and perhaps find a little love along the way."
— *Booklist*

"*Throw Like a Woman* is that rare baseball novel, both a paean to the game and a deeper exploration of character. Susan Petrone has a fan's heart and a scout's eye. Read it now. Don't wait for the movie."
— Stewart O'Nan, co-author of *Faithful* and *A Face in the Crowd*

"For baseball fans who yearn for a female Jackie Robinson, reading Susan Petrone's fun and absorbing novel *Throw Like a Woman* becomes a kind of prayer. 'Please, Lord! Give talent a chance. Let this dream come true!'"
— Mary Doria Russell, author of *The Sparrow*

"Someday there will be a woman who plays Major League Baseball. And when it happens, I suspect it will be an awful lot like Susan Petrone's fun *Throw Like a Woman*. Susan knows baseball and so the novel – and her hero Brenda Haversham – crackles with authenticity. You can hear the pop of the ball hitting the catcher's mitt."
— Joe Posnanski, author of *The Soul of Baseball*, NBC Sports National Columnist

"Petrone's storytelling is first-rate, and she weaves a credible baseball tale with well-defined characters throughout."
— *The Wave*

Throw Like
a Woman

·◊·

Susan Petrone

The Story Plant
Studio Digital CT, LLC
P.O. Box 4331
Stamford, CT 06907

Story Plant paperback ISBN-13 978-1-61188-219-3
Fiction Studio Books E-book ISBN-13 978-1-943486-16-8

Visit our website at www.TheStoryPlant.com

First Story Plant Hardcover printing: March 2015
First Story Plant Paperback printing: March 2016

Printed in The United States of America
0 9 8 7 6 5 4 3 2 1

Dedication

•◇•

For Mamie, Connie, Toni, Maria, Julie, Ila, Justine, Tiffany, Eri, Chelsea, Mo'ne, and every other girl and woman who ever decided she'd rather play baseball.

Acknowledgments
•◇•

Thank you to Dennis Lamp, who graciously shared his major league experience with me, along with the secret of why he had the best sinker in the majors. Thank you to Bob DiBiasio of the Cleveland Indians for giving me such an extensive tour of the clubhouse and the ballpark. Thanks to Becky Kyle, Stu Shea, Christopher Johnston, Nancy Marcus, Monica Plunkett, Bob Price, Toni Thayer, Jean Cummins, Catherine Donnelly, Jeanne Mallett, and Rich Bowering for reading and commenting on early drafts. Thank you to Joe Posnanski for helping out a fellow fan. Many thanks to Michael John Sullivan and Debbie Mercer for their assistance and friendship. A huge thank you to Josh Getzler for his spot-on editorial suggestions and to Jane Dystel for her kindness and professional expertise. My undying appreciation and thanks to Mary Doria Russell for her wisdom and humor. A biscuit to Juno and Mason for always keeping me company while I write. And most of all, thanks to Ella, for being the most encouraging, delightful, inspiring, creative little human I know, and to Mike, for holding the string of my kite.

Chapter One

•◊•

B RENDA HAVERSHAM'S FATHER TAUGHT HER HOW TO THROW A FOUR-SEAM FASTBALL WHEN SHE WAS NINE. The four-seamer is the go-to pitch when you need a strike. It is the heat, the pitch that makes batters tremble. The four-seamer should be gripped loosely, gently, to minimize friction between the hand and the ball and allow for the quickest possible release and maximum velocity. "You hold the ball like an egg, and it will fly out of your hand like a bird," her father would say in his slightly accented English. Brenda believed him and dutifully followed her father out to the park every weekend. Her sinker sank and her curveball curved, but she never managed to make the four-seamer fly. Without a team for a girl to play on, there was no reason to make it fly. She didn't find a reason until thirty-one years later, on a balmy day in March when Ed didn't show up.

The day had started out promising enough. Andy and Jon were waiting for their father at ten to ten, loaded down with their baseball gloves, bats, and a bag of balls in addition to Andy's ever-present mp3 player and Jon's equally ubiquitous DS. In the kitchen, Brenda decided to get a head start on the bills. She had a few other chores to do before meeting her best friend, Robin, for lunch. Undying love for her kids aside, she welcomed the break every other Saturday. Their bungalow was small enough that she could hear Andy and Jon fussing with each other in the living room as they waited. She heard Andy say, "Would you quit it?" followed by the sounds of scuffling.

"What's going on in there?" Brenda called. She didn't need to look up to find the proper tone of voice that indicated she may or may not have seen who the initial perpetrator was.

Jon answered first: "Nothing," he called. That meant he had thrown the first punch. Since the divorce—rather since the night Ed left in a manner not unlike the Colts slinking out of Baltimore—Jon had become a bit more aggressive and prone to tantrums than a nine-year-old should have been. Andy, at twelve, was generally a calm, almost indulgent older brother. Lately, however, his patience seemed to be wearing thin, and Brenda wasn't sure if this was because he was getting tired of Jon's trying ways or just hormones. She tried to pretend that Andy was still a little boy, but he'd be thirteen before the end of the summer.

With the boys quiet, she focused on making the perpetually tiny total in her checking account stretch in unnatural ways. She had moved on to unloading the dishwasher and cleaning the counters when she heard footsteps. She looked up to see Andy standing in the door to the kitchen, one ear bud hanging around his shoulder (his single concession to politeness, courtesy of Brenda), his pale blue eyes looking slightly red.

"Dad isn't here yet," he said.

The clock on the stove read 10:40. "I'll call him, Andy. He's probably just running late."

"Let me call his cell and see where he is," Andy said. "He's gotta be on his way here."

""I'll call him, honey. Don't worry about it." Ed answered on the fourth ring. All he had to do was say "Hello" and Brenda knew the boys wouldn't be seeing him that day. She could almost see him stretched out in bed, one hand making grabbing stabs at the telephone, the other running through his bristly brown hair, as though his brain needed to be massaged before it could begin functioning properly.

"Hi, Ed. The boys were wondering what time you think you'll be getting here." She chose her words carefully, because Andy and Jon were now standing in the kitchen.

"Wow, I didn't realize it was so late." Ed coughed, his voice sounded raspy and dry. She recognized it as Ed's hangover voice. "I'm definitely coming down with a cold. Would you believe I just woke up?"

"Yes, I would," Brenda replied, still trying to sound neutral.

"I don't know if it's a good idea for me to see the boys today. I don't want them to get sick or anything."

"I understand, but you should probably be the one to tell them that," Brenda handed the phone to Andy before Ed could protest.

"Dad?" Andy said. "Where are you? What time are you getting here?" Brenda watched Andy's face go from questioning to disappointed to concerned. He was actually concerned because Ed said he had a measly cold.

"Let me talk to Dad," Jon said, trying to grab the phone.

"Wait a minute," Andy snapped.

Before they resorted to a tug-of-war with the telephone, Brenda told Jon to wait a moment and asked Andy to finish up so his brother could talk.

Jon didn't take the news that his father wasn't coming that day as well as his brother had. After he hung up the phone with Ed, he stood by the kitchen just staring out into the backyard. Then he kicked the door and yelled, "It's not fair!" again and again. Brenda counted to ten (which was also ten kicks) then went over and enveloped Jon in a bear hug. He resisted for half a second, then melted into his mother, crying and repeating "It's not fair," over and over.

"I know, sweetie. I know," she whispered into the blond hair that was as thin and fine as he. After a few minutes, he calmed down and was pestering her for a snack. A few crackers and some string cheese later, Jon was placated but Andy was nowhere to be seen. She went down the short hallway to his room.

Andy was sitting on the edge of his bed, glove on, throwing a baseball into his mitt over and over. It made a certain satisfying *thwump* each time the ball hit the worn-out leather. He was moving up to the twelve-to-fourteen Little League division and would need a new mitt. He had used this one since he started in the nine-to-eleven group and it was too much of a little kid's glove for this division, where the older boys were practically men. By the time his birthday rolled around, it would be too late for a new glove. She could possibly get Andy a new mitt by calling it an early birthday present and giving Andy's old mitt to Jon. That might satisfy them both. She was so engrossed in momentarily planning how to keep both boys in decent sports equipment she didn't even hear Andy the first time he asked, "So now what?"

"What do you mean?" she asked.

"Now what? What are we supposed to do all day?" he said without looking up.

Brenda didn't have to think—she just gave the first answer she knew would make her kids happy. She could do the chores later and reschedule lunch with Robin. "We're going to play baseball," she said.

After a few days, where the weather had teased and hinted at spring, the day had unfolded to full-blown perfection. The sky was the brightest blue it had been in months, and the last remnants of snow from another Cleveland winter had finally melted. The infield at Quarry Park wasn't too bad, but the moment she stepped on the outfield, Brenda could feel her sneakers squishing into the soaked grass. Andy and Jon had their cleats and were kids besides, so it didn't seem to bother them, but Brenda knew she'd be walking around in wet shoes and socks until they got home.

Brenda had always hoped both boys would inherit their father's height. At this point, it wasn't clear whether either of them would reach Ed's six foot two. Andy was stocky, with a thick torso and hips and broad shoulders. His low center of gravity made him an ideal catcher, and that had been his position the past couple of seasons. Jon was slight and small for his age. He was getting ready for his first season with kid pitchers instead of parent pitchers, and the thought of some eleven-year-old throwing a baseball as hard as he could at her baby gave Brenda heart palpitations.

Jon wanted to hit and Andy wanted to get behind the plate, so Brenda was enlisted to pitch batting practice. When Andy said, "It's okay for you to pitch to Jon. The younger kids don't throw that hard either," she tried not to be insulted. She just took the mound, threw a couple of warm-up pitches, and then Jon stood in the batter's box.

Pitching to Andy without a batter wasn't much of a problem. It was like playing catch with someone who happened to be squatting. It was only when Jon stood in that she wavered. She didn't want to hit him. Of course, when she said this, Andy said, "It's not like you're gonna throw it hard enough to hurt him."

She tried to focus on the general vicinity of the strike zone, that tiny space between Jon's narrow chest and perpetually skinned knees. She could almost see the rectangle demarcating the strike zone, like they sometimes used on ESPN when analyzing a game. She tried to focus on it, but Jon's presence made the rectangle shrink to almost nothing. After throwing ten pitches, all of which the boys called balls, she heard Jon, her darling little Jon, mutter to his brother:

"I wish Dad wasn't sick. At least he knows how to pitch."

"I know," Andy replied.

Her sons' words lingered in the dead space between the plate and the pitcher's mound. The boys didn't know that there had been no custody battle, that Ed had never once said, "I want the boys to live with me," while Brenda had gotten an ulcer wondering if she could get full custody when she didn't have a job. They didn't know that Ed never checked their rooms in the middle of the night as she did, making sure that they were covered, that the rain wasn't coming in their open window, that they were still breathing. Andy and Jon knew nothing of this. They didn't even know that Ed wasn't really sick today. It wasn't fair that she got the arguments and the homework and the dirty dishes and the laundry and the chauffeuring and the tears and, frankly, all the crap and Ed got to sweep in every other weekend (or not) and play the good guy.

It pissed her off.

"Jon, stand in!" she yelled. "Andy, where's that target?"

Andy squatted down with a sigh and lazily held his mitt in the general vicinity of the strike zone. Jon stepped back into the batter's box with a half-hearted stance.

"Get the bat off your shoulder," Brenda said. "Here comes the heat."

She heard one of the boys mutter, "Oh please," but she ignored it, instead focusing on the catcher's mitt. She stared at it, transforming its brown leather pocket into Ed's face. All at once, she saw that rectangle demarcating the strike zone, and it was as though she could see thin golden lines running from her right hand straight to the mitt like a tunnel. All she had to do was throw the damn four-seamer as hard as she could down the tunnel and into the mitt.

She heard a *thwump* and an almost simultaneous, "Holy shit!" from one of the boys (when did they start swearing?) and saw Andy fall backwards. She ran to him as fast as she could and bent down over her first-born. "Are you okay, sweetie?" she asked. "What happened?"

"Holy shit, Mom," Andy said with a huge smile. "That was a great pitch."

"Really? Thank you."

"That was awesome, Mom," Jon said, a little breathless at what he had just witnessed.

"I finally found the strike zone," she laughed, surprised that she had actually done something her sons admired.

"That was a strike and it smoked," Andy said.

"Can you do it again?" Jon asked.

"I can try." She trotted back to the mound, wondering if she could indeed do it again. It had been a great pitch, that she knew. How to do it again seemed like a mystery. She stood on the mound, stamped her right heel on the muddy pitching rubber a few times, and tried to remember the invincible feeling that comes from being nine years old and making your father proud. She went into her windup, threw, and the ball hit the backstop far above Jon's head.

"Come on, Mom," Jon said. "Throw it like you did before."

"Right in here, Mom, "Andy said, slapping his hand in his mitt. "Right here."

Brenda tried to clear her mind, tried not to think about what she was doing. Thinking about her dad didn't mesh with the rush of power she had felt when she thought about Ed. Focus. She stared down Andy's mitt. Again she saw Ed's face in it, this time with the falsely innocent smile that had, in the past, accompanied many a lie. She could hear the lame excuse about why he had to disappoint the boys today. The fucker. This time she didn't think, just threw the ball down the tunnel. Again she heard a satisfying *thwump* and watched as Jon swung at the air.

"Wow. Nice one, Mom," Andy said as he threw it back. She noticed he gave his glove hand a little shake.

"Do it again. I'll hit it this time," Jon said.

The second good pitch was a surprise because it meant the first one wasn't a fluke. Brenda looked at the mitt, visualizing Ed's face again. "Asshole," she muttered, went into her wind-up, and threw. She threw about a dozen good, hard strikes in a row, none of which Jon touched, but he seemed too much in awe to care. Andy tried standing in, but Jon didn't want to catch, so instead she pounded the backstop with another series of hard fastballs. Andy whiffed on all but one, and that one was a foul tip. At one point, Andy swung and missed so hard that he fell on his rear end. Jon burst out laughing. Andy sat in the mud and looked from his brother to his mother. Brenda ran over to the plate to see if he was all right. Jon was still giggling as Andy stood up. She tried to ask if he was okay but one look at her mud-covered son made her snort back a laugh.

"I'm fine," Andy said then added, "Snorty McSnorty."

"Snorty McSnorty!" Jon yelled, as though it was the funniest thing he had ever heard.

Brenda looked at Jon and said, "Giggles McDonald," which made him laugh even harder.

Andy's expression went from annoyed to a smile. "Muddy McDufus," he said. This made Jon scream even harder with laughter, and he made an overly exaggerated fall in the mud. In a heartbeat, the three of them were chasing each other through the muddy infield. For a few minutes, the world consisted only of her and two dirty, laughing boys.

When they got home, she made the boys leave their shoes by the back door and herded them into the downstairs bathroom to get cleaned up. She brought their muddy clothes down to the basement laundry room and threw them in the wash. While she was down there, she saw that one of the boys had left the computer on in the adjacent rec room. It was a small room, but the glass block windows let in plenty of natural light. It was supposed to have been her studio, back when she still felt she had something to say as an artist. Now she couldn't even remember the last time she had picked up a pencil.

Brenda went upstairs to her bedroom, which was the only place in the house where she could find a modicum of privacy. When Ed first left, the room had seemed cavernous, but now it felt cozy. The bed was still by the front window, but the dormer where Ed's dresser had been now held a small bookcase, an old easy chair, and a lamp. After seven months, it was finally feeling like her space, not space that had once been occupied by Ed.

She was cleaning up in the miniscule half-bath attached to her bedroom when the phone rang. A few minutes later, she heard Andy yelling that grandma was on the phone.

Brenda grabbed the cordless phone from the bedside and plopped down on the easy chair in the dormer. It was only when she sat down that she realized how tired she was. "Hi, Mom," she said.

"Weren't the boys supposed to be with Ed today?" her mother said.

"He said he was sick."

Brenda heard something that sounded like "Pfffft," which clearly indicated what her mother thought of Ed's excuse. "What did you and the boys end up doing?" Adele asked.

"We went up to Quarry Park and played baseball."

"Your father always said you had a great arm. I remember him taking you over to Wildwood Park to play catch almost every weekend in the summer."

"That's because he wanted a boy."

"No," her mother said gently. "That's because it was the only thing he knew how to do that you both liked."

"I guess that's a nicer way of looking at it." Brenda wasn't sure what else to say to this. Her father had been a silent man who worked as a draftsman for an engineering firm. He had rarely talked about his work or his life, just got up every morning and did what needed to be done. On Saturdays he would take his only child out to the park to play baseball. Brenda liked to think this was one of the few tasks that Janusz Puchall had not done out of duty.

Brenda and the boys went to the ball field as often as possible, even after Little League practices began. Through some strange natural law, it seemed as though Andy and Jon's obsession with baseball and the

Cleveland Indians grew in inverse proportion to the Indians' prospects. From a disappointing spring training, Opening Day started with a loss and just got worse.

The third week of the regular season, Andy's Little League team got discount tickets to see the Indians play the Tigers. Brenda went as a parent chaperone, and Jon went because he was the younger brother and would raise holy hell if he couldn't come along. Even with the discount, tickets for all three of them, plus factoring in a hot dog and a drink each, put a serious dent in the entertainment budget. Brenda had made a "no souvenirs" rule for the outing, but when the boys saw the Test Your Speed pitching cage, they begged to be allowed to try. It didn't help matters that every other boy on Andy's team tried it, as did all five chaperoning parents and two other accompanying siblings. She hated caving in to peer pressure, but she didn't want Andy and Jon to be the only ones not to have a go. She took some of the money she had budgeted for snacks (she didn't really need a hot dog or a drink) so Andy and Jon could each take a turn. Andy was pleased with his top speed of 48 mph. Jon's best try was 33 mph, which disappointed him. Carl, Andy's coach, kept trying to tell him that 33 mph was great for a kid his age, but it didn't help. Brenda saw the familiar pink blush spreading up Jon's face. Jon's tantrums hadn't eased up, and Brenda walked the fine line between trying to be understanding and not wanting to spoil him.

"Let me try again," Jon whined. "I know I can throw harder than that."

Brenda put an arm on Jon's shoulder and walked him a little bit away from the rest of the group. "If I give you the money for another turn, then I can't buy you a hot dog."

"Why not? I want a hot dog!" Jon said loudly, the tears in his eyes threatening to start falling any second. Brenda felt herself blushing as red as Jon's face. "Why can't I do both?"

"Sweetie, I'm sorry," she lowered her voice. "You had one turn already and you did great, but I don't have enough money with me."

Carl wandered over and put a hand on Jon's tiny shoulder. "Come on, sport. I'll spot you another try." He looked up at Brenda with a smile. "You don't mind, do you?"

"You don't have to do that," she said.

"I want to," Carl replied as he walked with Jon back over to the pitching cage.

"Thank you," Brenda said. "I'll pay you back," she called after him, but Carl just gave a little wave that said, "No need to." Carl coached his son's Little League team and was always patient with the kids, even the benchwarmers. He was one of those men who seemed kind enough and decent enough that you couldn't believe some other woman had gotten rid of him. Brenda wondered if Carl's ex-wife ever called him a jerk under her breath or wished he'd be stricken with a bad case of crabs.

Jon was all smiles as he took the first of the three baseballs offered to him by the man running the pitching cage. He threw another 33 mph and then a 35-mph pitch. Jon was reaching for his third and last ball when he stopped and turned to Brenda.

"Mom, you haven't had a chance to pitch yet," he said.

Brenda tried not to get misty at her son's gesture. "That's very sweet of you to think of me, Jon, but it's okay," she said.

He turned and handed the ball to her. "It's your turn, Mom." Brenda heard a little "awww" from the other chaperoning parents as Jon moved aside. She was touched by his generosity and figured she'd just throw the ball and get the boys to their seats.

Ball in hand, Brenda approached the faux pitcher's mound in the middle of the stadium concourse. A quick glance showed her that every kid on the team, as well as the adults and tagalong siblings (did she really just now notice that they were all male?), was watching her. A few people on the concourse had even stopped to watch, as if a forty-year-old woman with saddlebag hips couldn't pick up a baseball without embarrassing herself. She stopped for a moment and focused on the image of a catcher painted on the electronic backstop.

The guy running the pitching cage said, "Anytime you're ready, sweetheart." Out of the corner of her eye, she saw him flash a condescending smile.

"I'm not your sweetheart," she muttered. Without thinking, she threw.

She heard the familiar *thwump* and a small murmur of approval from the men standing around her. She looked up at the digital clock that displayed the pitch speed. It read 72 mph, which just seemed unbelievable. The guy running the game looked more than surprised, but just said "Not bad."

"That was more than not bad," Carl said. "That was great. Here." He shoved a few dollars at the guy and handed Brenda three more baseballs. "Would you do that again? Please?"

This time, Brenda didn't protest. She took one of the baseballs and faced the painted catcher again. She didn't look around but could hear some of the guys talking about her last pitch. She would swear a few more people had stopped to watch. Fine. Let them watch.

Brenda's next three throws were 79, 77, and 82 mph. She stared at the display for a moment, trying to figure out where that 82 came from. All the people standing around congratulated her. Some mumbled that the radar must be broken, that there was no way a woman could throw that hard. She saw a couple of flashes of light, like someone taking a picture. The game was about to start, and the boys started running to their seats. As she and the other parents tried to get all the kids situated without losing anyone, Carl mentioned that he played baseball in the local Roy Hobbs league and maybe Brenda would be interested in playing.

"Roy Hobbs, like Bernard Malamud's Roy Hobbs?" she asked.

"Yeah, *The Natural*. Great movie."

"Great book."

"Never read the book. I'm not much of a fiction reader," Carl said, as he gave a quick look around to see that they hadn't lost anyone. "Josh! Ben! Stay with the group," he called to his son and another boy who were dawdling behind. "I'm more into history and biography. So anyway, it's the veterans league—thirty-eight and over, so you have a few guys who think they're hot stuff and a couple of them still are—but mainly it's just guys who love to play baseball. You'd be great."

"I don't know. I haven't played hardball since I was a kid. And I can't hit."

"Don't worry about it—we use a DH. Josh! Ben! Get away from the beer stand!"

Their conversation was permanently interrupted by the process of getting all the boys into their seats without losing anyone. Brenda ended up in the row in front of Carl, with Jon on her right and a stranger on her left. Andy was next to Jon, talking only to the boys on his right or behind him and trying to pretend that he wasn't with his mom and little brother.

Once the boys had gotten their hot dogs and drinks, they settled down and were quiet for the first couple of innings, giving Brenda a little time to think. She considered the fact that she had thrown a baseball an improbable eighty-two miles an hour. She might have cellulite, a sagging rear end, and a stretch-marked stomach, but she had an arm. It was a satisfying thought.

"What are you smiling about, Mom?" Jon asked in between innings.

"Nothing much," she said with a little smile. "Just happy to be here with you and Andy."

"Mr. Fleishman asked you to play baseball with him, didn't he?"

Brenda hadn't realized that Jon had overheard their conversation. "Yes, he did. What do you think? Should I join a baseball team too?"

"Yeah, you should. You'll need a new mitt," Jon said sagely. "Your old softball mitt stinks. But I think it's a good idea. Then everybody in the family will be on a team. Andy's on the Bears. I'm on the Twins. Dad's on the Beeraholics. And you'll be on a team."

Brenda actually snorted. "Dad's on the what? The Beeraholics?"

"Yeah. It's his softball team. Is a beeraholic somebody who likes beer a lot?"

"Yes."

"Like how sometimes you say you're a chocoholic because you like chocolate?"

"Yes."

"The Beeraholics play on Monday nights, so we haven't seen any of their games, but Dad and Darlene told us about it."

Andy had evidently heard at least part of the conversation, because he turned to Jon and punched him in the arm.

"Ow! Mom, Andy hit me," Jon wailed.

"I can't believe you told mom about Darlene," Andy snapped in what was obviously meant to be a whisper but was loud enough to be heard three rows away.

Jon started slapping at Andy, who waved him off with a laugh that only infuriated Jon more. As embarrassed as she had been in recent memory, Brenda managed to cease the escalation of hostilities by moving Jon to her other side.

Jon was silent until just after the seventh inning stretch, when he looked up at her and said, "I'm sorry I told you about Dad's girlfriend." He looked like he was about to cry, as though even uttering the name "Darlene" had been treason of the highest order.

Brenda put her arm around him. "It's okay, sweetie. I didn't know her name, but I figured Dad might have a girlfriend. He's allowed to. We're not married anymore—you know that. He's allowed to date."

"But you don't have a boyfriend," Jon whispered in a voice so plaintive that Brenda had to lean in very close to hear him over the noise of the ballpark.

"I live with the two greatest guys on earth," she whispered back. "I don't need anybody else."

•◊•

Excerpt from the transcript for *Today in Sports* with Charlie Bannister, ESPN, April 24:

> Charlie: I'm here with former major leaguer Howie Wojinski for our weekly look at how the season is shaping up. Howie, we're three weeks into the major league season. What kind of crazy predictions are you going to make about how it'll all end up?
>
> Howie: I've stopped making predictions because you always throw them back in my face at the end of the season when it turns out I'm wrong.
>
> Charlie: Who me? I'd never do that. Come on— one prediction, oh wise and venerable baseball sage.
>
> Howie: Since you put it that way, okay. In the

National League, it's going to be the Braves and the Dodgers in the NLCS.

Charlie: Excuse me, I think I just spit coffee all over my notes. Well, there's one I'll be able to throw back in your face come September. What about the American League?

Howie: ALCS—Yankees-White Sox.

Charlie: The White Sox? Are you kidding me?

Howie: If Jorge Racino can stay healthy for Chicago, he'll drive in 110 runs.

Charlie: Is that another prediction?

Howie: That's not a prediction, that's a fact.

Charlie: As much as I hate to admit it, you're probably right. Gimme another fact.

Howie: The Indians are going to end the season the way they've started it.

Charlie: In the basement with the Christmas decorations?

Howie: Was that one too easy?

Chapter Two

•◇•

BRENDA HAD WORKED AS A GRAPHIC DESIGNER BEFORE THE BOYS WERE BORN, BUT WITH AN OUTDATED SKILL SET AFTER TWELVE YEARS OUT OF THE WORKFORCE, SHE HAD TAKEN THE FIRST JOB SHE COULD FIND, AS A DATA ENTRY OPERATOR FOR AN INSURANCE COMPANY. Most of the people she worked with were kids just out of college or women like her who had recently re-entered the workforce. The next day at work, she got a cryptic email from Robin. It merely read: "OMG, now you're famous" and had a link to Cleveland.com. When she clicked on the link, she was surprised to see her photo—going into her windup in the pitching cage—as the photo of the day.

"You've got to be kidding me," she said.

Her coworker, Derek, from the next cubicle poked his head around the wall and asked what was up. Derek was in his mid-thirties and still dressed like a hipster, with skinny pants and square black glasses. They sometimes chatted and commiserated about divorce over lunch.

"Nothing," she replied, clicking the window closed.

"Nice picture in the paper today, by the way. I put up a copy of it in the kitchen," Derek said.

"Excuse me," Brenda said. "I'm going to get lunch." She grabbed her cell phone and went outside to one of the two picnic tables set up on the grassy strip between the parking lot and their two-story industrial park building.

Robin was number four on speed dial. "My ass looks positively huge," was the first thing Brenda said when Robin answered.

"Aren't you glad we aren't on speaker phone?" Robin replied. "And no, it doesn't. You look fine. Did you see it says you had the highest speed recorded so far this season?" She paused for dramatic effect. "Or last season. That's impressive."

"I guess so," Brenda said. She had been sitting on the picnic table but now got up and starting pacing back and forth between the two tables. "It's just weird to be singled out for throwing a ball. It's fun and all, but it's still just a game. Oh, and did I tell you that Andy's Little League coach plays baseball in a Roy Hobbs league and wants me to pitch?"

"Cool. When's your first game?"

"I'm not sure I'm going to do it. They play on Thursday nights, way over in Westlake. So it'd be forty minutes each way on a work night, plus I'd have to find someone to keep an eye on the boys . . ."

"Are you making excuses because you really don't want to or are you just looking for someone to tell you it's okay to do it?" Ever since college, Robin had had a knack for honing in on the heart of someone's true feelings. Brenda figured that's probably why she had gone into art therapy.

"I'll admit, I kind of do want to play. When we all played softball together, back before we had kids, I had fun. Granted, I couldn't hit . . ."

"But you had that rocket arm out in left center. And it *was* fun. Why not do it again?"

"You and Dan and Ed and I were all on the same team and we played against people we knew. That's what made it fun. I don't know anyone in this league."

"You'll get to know them."

"And it's all men."

"You say that like it's a bad thing. Remember, you're a single woman now."

"I'm not ready to date anyone. And I certainly wouldn't start dating anyone I played ball with."

"More excuses?"

"What's that line about not peeing where you sleep?"

Robin laughed. "You know you're going to do this, right?"

"Yeah, I just needed you to talk me into it." After she hung up with Robin, Brenda called Carl to tell him she wanted to play ball.

A few nights later, Brenda played her first game with the Lake Erie Lightning. Jon was happy about it. He was very big on things being even and fair, and Brenda's joining the Lightning balanced out the family member-to-team ratio. Andy wasn't as supportive. When Brenda told the boys at dinner where she'd be every Thursday night, he was aghast.

"Why do you want to do that?" he asked. "You'll be the only girl."

"So what?" Jon said before Brenda could even open her mouth.

"I mean, it's okay for you to play with us, but in a league? Come on. Why can't you just play softball or something like a normal mom?" Andy asked, absentmindedly flopping the tines of his fork up and down in his mashed potatoes.

"Andy, it's something I want to do. It isn't going to affect your life too much."

"Fine," he replied, still slapping the mashed potatoes with his fork.

"If I stink, I'll quit. How's that?" she added with a grin.

"Fine."

"You won't stink, Mom," Jon said. "You're really good. I heard Mr. Fleishman talking to Mr. Barrett at the Indians game. He said he never saw anything like it."

"Thank you, Jon."

"What are we supposed to do while you're playing baseball?" Andy asked. "I'm not babysitting *him*."

"I don't need you to babysit me," Jon snapped.

"After summer vacation starts, you can come to the games if you want. Until then, you'll have dinner with Grandma. She said she's looking forward to having you two all to herself on Thursday nights."

"The Roy Hobbs League plays way over on the west side. I'm not going there."

"Great. Then you'll have more time to hang out with your grandma this summer."

On Thursday morning, Brenda reminded the boys that she was going straight to the game after work and that their grandmother was coming over to make dinner. She was so preoccupied getting her own gear together for the game that she didn't even notice what time it was when Jon asked if she was going to walk down to the bus with them.

"Of course," she replied, and made a mental note to remember to put a ponytail holder and an extra pair of socks in her bag before she left. As she walked down the driveway with Andy and Jon, she asked, "Do you two have everything you need for the day? Homework? Lunch?"

"Yep, got everything," Jon said. Andy just nodded with a bored "Uh-huh."

"Grandma will be coming over around 5:00. Try not to set the house on fire between the time you get home from school and the time she gets here."

"We won't," Jon said.

"And you'll be playing baseball," Andy said. He said "playing baseball" in a sarcastic, sing-songy voice. Brenda pretended not to notice.

"You'll do good," Jon said. "I know it. Don't be scared, okay? Coach always says 'It's just a game.'"

"If it's just a game, why do you cry every time you strike out?" Andy said.

"Shut up. I do not!"

"Come on, guys. Don't start the day fighting," Brenda said, keeping herself solidly in between the two boys in case Jon started throwing punches. They reached the end of the driveway and turned to walk to the corner. The school bus was due any minute.

"Did you send in the registration form for the sports camp this summer?" Andy asked.

Brenda paused, trying to keep the first words to pop into her mind—'Oh crap'—from being the first words to pop out of her mouth. "I'm mailing it today," she said, as though the form was completed, an unbounceable check written, and both sitting in an already addressed and stamped envelope.

"The deadline's tomorrow."

"It'll get there."

"What happens if it doesn't get there in time?" Jon asked. "I want to go to the camp."

"It'll be fine. You're both doing the sports camp." Inwardly, she knew they had to do the sports camp because there was no way they were staying home alone all day every day all summer long. Last summer, Ed had still been in the house and she had been home. Now here it was, a year later, and life was completely different.

Brenda gave Jon a big hug good-bye as the school bus came down the street. She reached for Andy but he pulled away, so she just patted him on the back. It was as though he had turned into a teenager overnight. When the boys got on the bus, Jon waved. Andy didn't.

Brenda went back to the house and grabbed the sports camp registration form, an envelope, and a stamp. She'd fill it out and mail it at lunch. She was going to have to write a rubber check for the registration and hope Ed's child support payment wouldn't be late. Writing bad checks didn't seem like the most auspicious way to start the day.

She didn't tell anyone at work that she was playing baseball that night. Robin had said she wanted to go and watch, but Brenda asked her to wait a week or two, "Just until I establish myself a bit."

"Establish schmablish. I'll be there for moral support, but I'll act like I don't know you."

Feeling like one raw, dangling nerve with a baseball glove attached, she arrived at the field after work. It was in a municipal park in a far west exurb that was seemingly able to spend more lavishly on one park than Brenda's inner-ring suburb was able to spend on one of its schools. The park had four softball and two baseball fields, plus a picnic area, a playground, and a rubber-paved jogging track around the entire perimeter. It was a far cry from soggy old Quarry Park.

She saw half a dozen guys in full baseball regalia—black baseball pants, socks pulled up, real spikes, and gray jerseys with gold lettering—standing by the cars at the end of the parking lot closest to the fields. A couple of the guys glanced over at her car when she pulled in. She didn't see Carl, but she had parked clear at the other end of the lot. She moved the front seat back as far as it would go and put on her black sweatpants (she wondered if she'd have to invest in baseball pants as well as cleats or if she could get away with the sweats) and put her jersey on over her long-sleeved T-shirt. April night games could get very cold. She put on her sneakers and that was it. She was dressed. It was time to get out of the car.

As she walked across the parking lot to the group of men in Lightning jerseys, she felt their eyes watching her. She glanced down at her billowing jersey. Carl had laughed when she asked if he had any small jerseys—they were all large or extra-large. She didn't tuck it in—the elastic on the sweatpants was kind of old and it always made her look chunky if she tucked her shirt in. After two kids, she knew her stomach would never be flat again, but she still looked pretty good from the waist up. It was just her hips and thighs that made her feel like a parade balloon.

When she reached her new teammates, she introduced herself, adding, "Carl Fleishman recruited me." She tried to sound casual but confident, like she was an established baseball entity instead of a green rookie who hadn't played ball with anyone over the age of twelve in more than a decade.

"Right," one of the guys said. "I saw your picture in the paper. Can you really throw eighty-two miles an hour?" He looked a bit older than most of the players. Maybe in his very early fifties with one of those goatees guys his age often grow to mask a double chin. Somewhere in her memory banks, Brenda remembered that was called a Vandyke and not a goatee because there was no separation between the moustache and the beard. That didn't seem like an appropriate contribution to the conversation.

"That's what the speed clock said," she replied, hoping she didn't sound coy or like a jerk.

The guy smiled and nodded. "I'm Gary. Nice to meet you." Brenda shook hands all around. All of the guys said hello and mumbled some niceties, but she could tell most of them were skeptical. She tried to focus on learning her teammates' names and not thinking about the fact that very soon she was going to have to pitch to real adult men who would be far less forgiving of bad pitches than Andy and Jon were.

Gary asked her if she wanted to throw, so she warmed up with him, just playing an easy game of catch. It felt good. The baseball seemed to fit the size and shape of her hand better than a big, ungainly softball ever did.

She heard someone yell "Hey Carl! Are we home or away today?" and recognized Carl's compact, squareish form stretching over by the dugout as he called back, "Away." Brenda gave a little half wave but focused on Gary's throws. He kept chucking the ball hard, head-high, as though daring her to throw it back with equal force. After a few more throws, she told Gary her arm felt good and that she needed to talk to Carl. As she walked behind the line of other players playing catch, she heard a voice say in a stage whisper: "Well?" and heard Gary's reply: "She's got nothing," and felt a tingle in her stomach, not from nerves, but from anger. She had something. She wasn't sure yet what it was, but she knew it was *something*.

She walked the last few steps to the dugout with a new focus, and when Carl introduced her to Bob, a hulking guy with a mocha brown complexion and a kind smile, she made sure to give a firmer grip to her handshake.

"Bob's the catcher because he has the youngest knees on the team," Carl joked.

"Just aged out of the open division this winter. Now I gotta play with the old guys. Looks like you and me are the babies on this team, Brenda," Bob said.

Brenda tried not to let his good nature ruin her newfound bad mood. They quickly went over the signs, then she trotted out to the mound and turned to face Bob, whose body dwarfed his catcher's mitt, making her target look very small indeed.

There were eleven other players on the team, and all of them now stopped to watch Brenda throw her first pitch as a member of the Lightning. They were standing along the first and third baselines or in the dugout, and they were all watching her. She tried not to look around, tried to focus only on the catcher's mitt, looking for Ed's face in its deep pocket. Bob held down one finger. Her right hand felt numb as she ran her fingers over the ball, as though the seams were a bastardized form of Braille that she was trying desperately to read. She knew what she had to do, knew she had to focus, but somehow her body wasn't cooperating.

Bob punched his hand into his glove once and shouted an encouraging, "Right in here, B!" She nodded, thought too much about what she was doing, and threw. After what seemed like five minutes, the ball hit the catcher's mitt. She heard a couple of snorts from the other players.

"What's with the Peggy Lee fastball?" Carl called. He looked a little worried. She was there on his word and didn't want to make him look bad. Hell, she didn't want to make herself look bad.

Someone off to her left sang a snippet from "Is That All There Is?"

"No, that's not all there is," she mumbled to herself. She could feel the anger starting to bubble a little more wildly inside her. She focused on it, feeling the anger rush through her body until she swore her toes were tingling with adrenaline.

Bob held down two fingers and then three, both of which Brenda shook off. Then he held down all four fingers and wiggled them, which wasn't even a sign they had talked about. Brenda shook her head. There were grumbles from the peanut gallery, as those watching started telling her to throw something.

"Come on, Brenda. We don't have much practice time," Carl called.

"Keep your jersey on, Carl," Brenda mumbled. She looked down and kicked around some dirt on the mound. When she looked up, it was as though someone had suddenly flicked on the Christmas lights: the imaginary golden lines running from her hand to the catcher's mitt were illuminated, and Ed's smirking face now seemed to be floating in Bob's mitt. He held down one finger. Brenda nodded. This time, she didn't think, she just threw a screaming four-seamer. The *thwump* the ball made as it hit the catcher's mitt was loud and sure. Brenda heard someone say, "HEL-lo!"

"That's what I'm talkin' about," Bob said as he threw the ball back. Brenda threw a dozen or so more pitches. Her curve was on, and the sinker appeared to drop about half a foot just before it hit the plate. She was feeling good, but not too good. Carl hustled her off the mound the minute some members of the opposing team showed up, saying that he wanted to keep his "secret weapon" secret as long as possible.

Sometime during the first inning, Brenda noticed Robin and her husband, Dan, in the bleachers behind the dugout. She caught Robin's eye and gave a quick wave. Robin nudged Dan, and they both waved but didn't call her name, thankfully. It was weird enough being the only woman on the field side of the fence. The other team and those watching the game kept stealing glances at her. Carl might as well have put a big target on the back of her jersey.

"What do you care what other people think?" she murmured quietly. She kept that silent mantra going until the seventh inning. With the Lightning down by three, Carl told her to go in. She wondered if Carl thought it was safest to send her in when they were down so she couldn't blow a lead. "Be cool, Brenda," Bob said to her as they rose to take the field. "We know what you have. Just get in there and throw strikes."

"I'll try," Brenda replied. When she took the mound, Robin and Dan cheered loudly. A couple of warm-up pitches took the edge off her embarrassment. Then the manager of the opposing team walked over and started talking to the home plate umpire. The infield umpire joined in, and then Carl. She couldn't hear the discussion, but instinctively knew it was about her. Sure enough, after a couple of minutes, Carl waved her in to join the conversation.

As she got closer, she could hear the opposing team's manager, a squat, round-shouldered sixty-something with a red knobby nose, saying, "It's unprecedented."

"There isn't anything against it in the rules, Hank," the home plate umpire said. "How old are you dear?" he asked Brenda. If he hadn't had the look of a once-tall now-stoop-shouldered, kindly grandfather, she would have taken offense at being called "dear."

"I turned forty in January," she replied.

"She's over thirty-eight, Hank," Carl said, "and that's all the rules say. They don't mention sex."

Brenda had to stop herself from saying, "Gender." The issue here was gender. Sex was something she vaguely remembered as having brought about her two children.

"When did you put her on the roster?" the opposing manager asked.

"I added her to the online roster last Sunday night. Right before the deadline."

Brenda briefly caught Carl's eye. He had added her name to the roster before she had said she wanted to play. That was an unexpected vote of confidence. The manager tried every argument possible to prevent Brenda from playing. His nose went from red to a deep purple, and the way his jowls were flapping, she half-expected them to stir up a dust storm in the infield. There wasn't any rule against women playing in the Roy Hobbs league—Brenda had checked the rules online herself—there was just the assumption that only men would play.

Finally, Hank talked himself out, and the ump called "Play ball." Brenda trotted back out to the mound. Robin and Dan cheered again, and this time, some of the girlfriends and wives who were watching clapped a little too. The extra support from an unexpected quarter was kind of nice. The infielders had gathered at second base to chat during the interlude, while the outfielders just plopped down in the grass to wait it out. Brenda waited for her fielders to go back to their positions, then turned to face her first batter.

He was interchangeable with most athletic guys in their early forties—long arms, long legs, and a chest broad enough so you could read the full team name, "Loco Leprechauns," in white letters on his Kelly green jersey. Brenda gave a quick glance down at her too-big jersey. She'd have to stuff her sports bra in order for the word "Lightning" to be fully legible across her chest. The fact that Mother Nature had given her wide hips and no chest helped the anger to start growing again. So did the cocky way the batter came up to the plate, glancing at Brenda and shaking his head with an "I-can't-believe-this-crap" grin before taking his stance.

Bob extended one finger, signaling it to be low and inside. She saw the lines leading from her hand to her target, and then, as easily and on the mark as throwing a balled-up pair of socks down the laundry chute, she threw.

She would not soon forget the expression on the batter's face after he had swung and missed the ball by a mile, but she still had to get the guy out. It only took three more pitches. The Loco Leprechauns' dugout was eerily silent as the batter skulked back to the bench, as though they weren't sure they had witnessed one of their own striking out to some woman none of them had ever seen before. It was only after she got the second guy to ground out and the third one to pop up that Brenda allowed herself to smile. This time, when Robin and Dan cheered, it wasn't so embarrassing.

•◇•

Excerpt from the transcript for *Today in Sports* with Charlie Bannister, ESPN, May 4:

> Charlie: Before I sign off today, I feel compelled to share one of the most impressive things I've seen in a long time. Our great intern, Ziggy—actually his name is Al but he's got a round head—Ziggy came across this amazing video on YouTube. This was supposedly taken on the concourse before an Indians game and is reported to be undoctored and genuine. I'm not going to say anything else except that, if this is real, it's nice to know there's at least one decent pitcher in Cleveland.

Chapter Three

•◇•

A WEEK LATER, BRENDA WAS SITTING AT HER DESK THINKING ABOUT THE PREVIOUS EVENING'S GAME—HER SECOND FOR THE LIGHTNING. She had come in at the top of the eighth, fanned two, allowed only one hit, and no runs. Her arm was a little sore and her stomach was still a bit upset, but she chalked that up to residual nerves.

She was trying to work when an email popped up from her coworker, Derek. The subject line read: "You need to take a look at this," and had a link to a YouTube video. When Brenda clicked on it, she was shocked to see video of herself in the pitching cage on the day she threw 82 mph. It had clearly been taken with a cellphone and only got the last two pitches, but it showed her going into the full windup, throwing, and the pitch speed. Sadly, it was titled "Chubby Mom Throws Heat." The comments (184 of them) ranged from "You go, sister!" to "Impossible" to "Who rigged the radar?" It had been viewed 112,806 times.

Brenda stared at the computer monitor, scrolling through the comments, unable to comprehend that 184 people had actually felt compelled to share their thoughts about her pitching. She tried to visualize 112,806 people sitting in front of 112,806 computers watching the video. That would fill up two and a half average-sized baseball stadiums. "Who are all these people . . . ?" she murmured.

At least a few of them were Andy's friends. They'd sent him the link, which set him off.

"I can't believe it's on YouTube. Make them take it off," he said that night after dinner. It was a Friday, and since Brenda hadn't been with the boys the previous night, she suggested they all stay in and have a family movie night. Andy nixed the movie Jon wanted as being for "little kids," then laid into his mother about the video.

"I didn't put it on there. I can't make them take it off." Brenda said. "Trust me—I'm not crazy about having it up there either."

"Have you tried? Have you contacted the site administrator and asked him to remove the offending video?"

"No, I haven't. And why are you speaking like a cease and desist email?"

Her joke fell flat. "How many more people are going to see it before they take it down?"

"I don't know, Andy."

"I bet a million," Jon said. "Nobody else's mom can pitch like that. It's cool."

"It's ridiculous," Andy said and went into his room. He stayed there the rest of the night while Brenda and Jon watched some Pixar computer-animated movie. Brenda found it hard to concentrate on the movie; her thoughts kept creeping back to the YouTube video. How was it possible that 112,806 people had watched that thirty-two-second clip? Who were these people and didn't they have anything better to do than watch videos of strangers on the Internet? Maybe 112 obsessives had just watched it a thousand times each. By the end of the weekend, Jon had probably contributed a hundred views on his own. Brenda surreptitiously checked the video's progress over the week and on Monday at work and watched as the number of views slowly increased.

Ed called on Monday night at 11:28. The boys had long ago gone to bed, and Brenda was reading in her room. "Did you know you're on ESPN?" he said, without even saying hello.

"Ed? What are you talking about?" she asked. Ed never called except about the boys, and even then he didn't always call when he was supposed to.

"Well, you're off now. It was a short video."

Brenda almost dropped the phone. "Wait . . . the video's on ESPN?"

"So that really was you? It looked like you from behind."

"Yes, it was me."

"How'd you manage to break the radar gun?"

"I didn't break the radar gun. I threw a baseball eighty-two miles an hour. Now tell me why the video was on ESPN."

"It was just on *Today in Sports* with Charlie Bannister. I guess it's his oddity of the day."

"Thanks a lot, Ed." Brenda sighed, trying not to let his little digs hit their mark. "What time should I tell the boys you'll be picking them up on Saturday?"

"It's only Monday. I haven't thought about Saturday yet."

"It's just like you to not plan ahead." She hadn't wanted to get into it with him, and the moment she said it, she felt like a shrew, but there it was.

"Why do you feel this need to control everything?" he said.

"I'm not trying to control everything. I just want to know what time you'll be coming to get them."

"I don't know. Um . . . ten o'clock, like I always do."

"Thank you. I need to go now, Ed. Thanks for letting me know about the video."

"Anytime, sweetheart," Ed said, as though she still was his sweetheart and nothing had changed.

Brenda replayed the phone call in her head as she tried to fall asleep. It never ceased to amaze her how Ed seemed completely unfazed by the divorce. He didn't seem to have spent any time grieving the end of their marriage or worrying about what effect it was having on the boys or wondering if he was still a worthwhile person. But in the phone call, he had sounded a little peeved. And he had kept taking little jabs at her. She realized that after sixteen years, she had finally succeeded in making Ed jealous.

•◊•

Thanks to Charlie Bannister, within two weeks the video had a total of 562,483 views. People at work started calling her an Internet celebrity (which Brenda had always thought was the worst kind of celebrity to be). Jon was in awe of his mother's fame and would share it with anyone who'd listen, much to Brenda's embarrassment. Even Andy seemed a little impressed. He didn't say anything, but one evening she was downstairs doing laundry and poked her head into the rec room where he was surfing the Internet. He was watching the video of Brenda pitching.

The whole thing might have been fun to someone else, but to Brenda, it felt precarious. Lightning games had started to attract spectators—not many, maybe a dozen people in addition to the regular motley assortment of wives, girlfriends, children, and buddies with bad knees who couldn't play anymore. But these new people were there to see her, to watch this oddity of physiology play baseball.

After the games, the team always went out for a beer or two. The first few games, Brenda declined, because she was either going out with Robin and Dan or because she just wanted to get home. After playing with the Lightning for a month, Gary and Bob finally convinced her to go out with the team. She went, figuring that Andy and Jon would be done with school in another week, and Jon had said he wanted to come and watch his mom play. Since she wasn't going to be bringing her children to a bar, this might be her last chance to go out with the team.

A place called Players seemed to be the hangout for all the teams in the Roy Hobbs league. It was located in the kind of sprawling strip mall off a six-lane road that can only be found in a newer suburb. Tiny inner-ring South Euclid on the other side of town where Brenda lived seemed crowded and aged in comparison to this behemoth avenue.

She found a parking spot and, with a small sense of trepidation, went into Players. It featured a square bar in the center of a cavern-like room, with booths and tables on all sides. The number of televisions mounted on the walls and above the bar seemed roughly equivalent to the number of channels available on Brenda's basic cable. The entire place was decorated with old photos, hats, framed jerseys, and other sports memorabilia that everyone thinks should be worth something but would never actually buy.

The Lightning had taken over one side of the bar, and the thicket of gray jerseys was a welcoming sight. Bob, Carl, and Gary were sitting in one of the booths and called for her to join them. She noticed that they seemed to be the only unattached guys on the team. Everyone else seemed to have a girlfriend or a wife with him.

She knew Bob was married with an infant daughter—they had shared that much conversation sitting in the dugout. That left Carl, Gary, and her as the single ones on the team. *Yippee*, she thought. Robin and her mom would occasionally suggest she start dating again, but there never seemed enough time for it. You had to go out and meet people, which was itself a challenge, and learn their life history and see if you clicked. It just seemed like a huge investment of time for something that probably wouldn't work out. Derek at work used a fair amount of company time emailing women he met through online dating services. He even had a small notebook in which he wrote down the vital statistics and basic biography of each woman as he got to know her, so he wouldn't screw up any burgeoning relationship by asking, for instance, if she had spent Easter with her parents when the woman in question had previously informed him that her father was dead and her estranged mother lived in Alaska. Thus far, Brenda hadn't observed that Derek had had much luck in getting a girlfriend.

So no, she wasn't interested in dating at the moment. Not that this was a date. It was just the team going out for a beer. And it was probably just coincidence that Bob and Gary were on one side of the booth and it was the spot next to Carl that happened to be free.

"Hey B," Bob said. "Glad you finally made it out with us."

"Thanks. Glad I made it too," she replied. "Although I can't stay late. The kids are waiting at home."

"I hear you," Bob said. "This is my one night out a week. Charisse goes out with her girlfriends on Mondays and I get baseball night."

"Who's with your kids when you're playing ball, Brenda?" Gary asked.

"My mother comes over to make them dinner and see they get their homework done and don't stay up all night watching TV or beating the crap out of each other."

"What did they think about you being on ESPN?" Carl asked. "Andy didn't say anything about it at practice."

"Jon thinks it's cool. Andy is embarrassed," she replied. "Honestly, it's not that big a deal."

"Yes, it is," Carl said. "Charlie Bannister is the number one sportscaster in the country."

"Charlie's the man," Bob said. "Probably the only sports anchor who isn't a moron."

Brenda used to watch *Today in Sports* once in a while when Ed was still in the house, but typically only during baseball season. Bannister was a slightly chubby, boyish-faced African-American guy in his mid-forties. He had always struck Brenda as being wittier and more entertaining than the average sportscaster, but she hadn't realized that he was such a big deal or had such high ratings. Carl, Gary, and Bob spent most of the evening letting her know exactly how big a deal he was, what his approximate ratings were, and estimating how many people had seen the video of Brenda pitching on his show.

The thought of several million people watching the video was unnerving. It was one thing for it to get 562,483 views online (not that she was counting). That didn't necessarily equate to 562,483 different people. Brenda tried not to worry too much about what other people thought, but this wasn't just some random person in the grocery store or a couple of skinny kids in the car next to hers. This was 4.9 million people, predominantly male, sitting there watching their favorite sports show and then suddenly being confronted with her—the high showgirl-like kick in her windup, the minimal makeup—doing something most of the world couldn't do. What did they think?

She had a lot to ponder on the long drive home: several million strangers watching her pitch and the mythical ten pounds added by the camera, plus Carl had flirted with her. There had been some moments during the evening when he had held her gaze a bit too long or rested his knee against hers for a moment under the table or gently nudged her shoulder with his while making a joke. Then there was the whole business of walking her to her car and suggesting that they carpool out to games, since they both lived in South Euclid and the games were played way the heck over in Westlake on the other side of town. She shrugged off the suggestion with some lame excuse about work schedules and office locations.

It would be convenient to date someone she already saw three times a week at Little League and Lightning games. "Convenient or overkill," Brenda muttered. Carl was a good guy, but there was no spark when she was with him. Why even start going down that road with someone who didn't make you feel more alive? Carl, she decided, was destined to be some other woman's good guy. When she finally pulled into her own garage and looked at the ever-growing mileage on her eight-year-old Honda minivan, she patted it on the dashboard. "I need you to hang in there, Molly," she said. "I don't think you and I are going to be carpooling with Carl anytime soon."

•◇•

Excerpt from the transcript for *Today in Sports* with Charlie Bannister, ESPN, May 26:

> Charlie: It used to be that locker rooms had an underground black market for PEDS. This season, you could make a tidy profit selling ulnar collateral ligaments. Last week, the Brewers sent pitcher Frank Barnes to the DL, and now relief pitcher Roberto Pena of the Indians is down for the count. Both pitchers are having the ubiquitous Tommy John surgery and will almost certainly miss the rest of the season. Barnes' loss won't hurt the Brewers too much, since they still have one of the deepest bullpens in either league, but for Cleveland . . . well, we'll see you next year, guys. With the loss of their only reliable stopper, the Indians have a hole at short relief that's bigger than an elephant's outhouse.

Chapter Four

•◇•

Brenda took vacation time for the week between the end of school and the beginning of summer camp. The check to the camp did not bounce. Jon went off the high diving board at Bexley Park for the first time; Andy actually seemed to have slightly lessened in his resistance to having a mother who could throw harder than his Little league coach; and said coach hadn't flirted with her in two weeks. Plus, her fastball was getting guys out on a regular basis. It seemed like the summer might go well.

They had a cookout late in the week. In addition to Adele, Robin came over with Dan and their fifteen-year-old daughter Lindsey. Andy declared he was going to man the grill. Brenda noticed he puffed himself up a bit when Lindsey was around. She and Robin tried not to giggle too much about it.

At one point, Andy was having trouble flipping all the burgers and dogs and dropped a hot dog on the ground. Brenda and Robin were relaxing together, chatting and watching Lindsey show Adele how to play *Fruit Ninjas* on her smartphone, and listening to the grandmother and teenager talk about books and boys. Dan and Jon were noodling around with the basketball. When Jon yelled, "Andy, you dropped my hot dog!" Brenda stood up, but Dan intervened.

"I've got it," he said. Dan went over to the grill and managed to stop an argument between the boys before it happened. Then he showed Andy and Jon a couple of what he called "Master Griller" tricks. "For male ears only!" Dan said with a flourish.

Lindsey watched her father with the two boys. "Oh yeah, he doesn't wish he had a son," she said.

"He loves you," Brenda, Robin, and Adele said simultaneously. Even Lindsey laughed.

"I used to think the same thing about my Dad," Brenda said. "I was an only child too. He didn't say much, but he took me out to play baseball every weekend. We'd see all these fathers and sons out there, and sometimes it felt kind of weird. I didn't like baseball at first."

"Then why did you go?" Lindsey asked.

"Because I wanted to be with my Dad."

"I always thought you liked playing baseball," Adele said.

"Once I learned what I was doing, I did. And as I got older, I realized that Dad teaching me baseball was no different than you teaching me how to bake or giving me your favorite books to read."

"You *were* the only one in high school whose mother encouraged you to read dirty books," Robin quipped.

"*The Unbearable Lightness of Being* is not a dirty book," Adele said. "It is great literature." Adele Puchall made a point of reading Eastern European authors in an effort to support the varied ancestral homelands that made up the family heritage.

"Just kidding, Adele."

"Robin, you have always been my favorite troublemaker," Adele said with a smile.

They were interrupted by Jon announcing that the burgers were ready. Eating outside on an early summer evening seemed to make everyone's jokes funnier and the food taste better. They had just finished eating when Brenda felt the first raindrops. There was a mad rush to grab plates, bowls, and cups and get everything and everyone inside. In the midst of putting away leftovers and cleaning plates, the phone rang.

Adele was closer to the phone. "Do you want me to get it?" she asked.

"That's okay. The machine can get it," Brenda replied as she wrapped up the leftover hamburgers.

After one more ring, the answering machine clicked on. Brenda's outgoing "We can't come to the phone right now . . ." message was audible, then a beep. Then even the kids, who had retreated into the living room, heard a relentlessly perky voice leave a message:

"Hi, this is Kathi O'Leary from Action News Channel 3 calling for Brenda Haversham. I'm told that you're the same remarkable woman who was featured in a video on *Today in Sports* with Charlie Bannister, pitching eighty-two miles an hour!" (Brenda could almost hear the exclamation point.) "We'd like to come out this Thursday and get some better footage of you in action." This was followed by Kathi's copious contact information, which Brenda didn't hear the first time because the kids walked into the kitchen and Andy asked who the hell that was.

"Please don't say 'hell,' Andy," Brenda said. She noticed Lindsey gave a little smirk of teenage solidarity at this.

"Sorry. Who the *heck* was that? She sounds like a cheerleader or something."

"Close enough. It was Kathi O'Leary from Channel 3. She wants to do an interview with me."

"Why would she want to interview you?" Andy asked with a look of disdain that only one on the cusp of adolescence could master.

"Because your mother is an unusually talented ballplayer, that's why," Dan said.

"She really is, Andy," Robin added.

With all the adults staring at him, Andy glanced at Lindsey, who kind of shrugged in reply. "Whatever," he said, and the two older kids went back into the living room.

"Does this mean you're going to be on TV?" Jon asked.

Brenda was about to say she wasn't sure, but Adele interrupted her with a loud "Yes. And you can be very proud of your mother for that."

"I am. Can I go to the game when you're going to be on TV?"

"I haven't actually said I'm going to do it," Brenda protested. "I don't want to be on the news. I'm just playing baseball in a rec league. I'm pretty sure other women have done the same thing."

"None of them have pitched the way you can," Dan said. "Trust me. When Robin and I went to your game a few weeks ago, I was talking to a couple of older guys who used to play in the league. They said once in a while they've had female players, but none of them had your talent."

Robin hastened to add: "Actually, they said they had never seen anybody in that league with your talent. Anybody."

"Mr. Fleishman said the same thing," Jon said.

"Do the interview," Robin said. "You might inspire someone."

"Oh, you would pull out the inspiration card. Fine, I'll do it."

Her mother seemed to think that the interview was important enough that the whole family should go to the game. Brenda was content to let Andy spend the evening at home on his own, but Adele was convinced her grandson would spend the evening looking at pornography on the Internet and claimed he'd be better off at the baseball field. Brenda wasn't sure, but she suspected money had changed hands, because Andy was perfectly amendable to going after talking to his grandmother.

Brenda left work half an hour early so she could stop home to get her mom and the boys. The entire day, the thought of the interview nagged at her. Although she felt that she could never let down her guard entirely, Brenda enjoyed being part of a winning team and being very good at something. It was only an amateur recreational team, but the Roy Hobbs league did have a sprinkling of guys who had played minor league ball or even an undistinguished season or two in the majors once upon a time. None of these guys had ever done anything wrong to her personally, but it was a sure bet that somewhere along the line just about all of them had trampled on some woman's heart or made a sexist joke or cheated on a wife or girlfriend. There was an indescribable feeling of satisfaction in striking them out.

They were late getting to the game because Brenda had to stop at a Taco Bell and get the boys something to eat or she knew she'd spend the entire game listening to Jon's plaintive voice from the bleachers whining that he was hungry. Food also seemed to be one of the few things that placated Andy, who was growing so fast Brenda sometimes thought he must be taking human growth hormone on the side.

When they got to the field, Brenda left Adele and the boys to their own devices and ran to the dugout as fast as she could. She got a "Where the hell have you been?" from Carl, who had been stalling turning in the roster to the scorekeeper, then she said hi to the rest of the team and sat down on the bench.

Bob plopped down next to her as he pulled on his batting gloves. "Hey B. How's it going?"

"Okay. Running a little late. My boys and my mom came to watch the game tonight," she added, as though that was the reason for her tardiness. She wouldn't confess to anyone that in the ten minutes she was home to change her clothes and pick up the boys, she had also thrown on a bit of makeup.

"Your kids are here?" Bob asked, turning around. "Where are they?"

Brenda turned to look. "My mom and Jon are over there behind the backstop—Jon likes to stand behind the umpire so he can watch the pitches—and Andy is sitting in the top row of the bleachers."

"Sandy blond hair?"

"Yes, with the mp3 player permanently attached."

"You have a nice-looking family."

"Thanks. So when is Charisse coming to a game? I want to meet her and Brittany."

"Soon. Charisse wants to wait until it's a little warmer before we have the baby out at night . . ."

Bob was interrupted by a petite blond standing at the end of the dugout who looked as though she was ready for her close-up. In a stage whisper she said, "Hi, Brenda? I'm Kathi O'Leary. I'm so happy to meet you."

"Oh Lord, the interview," Brenda mumbled.

"Is that Kathi O'Leary from Channel 3?" Bob said. "Wow. You get around, B."

Brenda burned with embarrassment as the rest of the dugout and the opposing team's infield glanced over at O'Leary and her entourage of two cameramen. Brenda didn't realize that the second guy wasn't holding a camera but a radar gun until she had extricated herself from the dugout and led Kathi O'Leary about forty feet away.

"Hi," Brenda said. She knew she should add a nicety, but felt disingenuous saying, "Nice to meet you." "Glad you're here" would also be a lie. She opted for politely stating the obvious: "Well, you made it." She could feel the eyes of everyone who wasn't actively involved in the game watching her and O'Leary.

"We sure are," Kathi O'Leary said with a huge smile. "I'm so glad to finally meet you. I must have watched that YouTube video of you a thousand times. It's just so impressive."

"Thank you," Brenda replied.

"Let me introduce my cameraman, Rick," Kathi said, motioning to the broad-shouldered, dark-haired guy who was holding the camera. Rick nodded to her. He looked as though he was expending an awful lot of energy holding his stomach in and his chest out. "And this is Alan," she said, motioning to a reedy, nerdy African American guy who was wearing a short-sleeved shirt buttoned all the way to the top. "He's going to be running the radar gun."

"You brought a radar gun?"

"Well of course. How else are we going to measure your pitch speed?" Kathi replied in a bubbly tone that made Brenda feel like a kindergartner.

Of course it made sense for them to bring a radar gun, Brenda just hadn't thought about it. She had alternately been trying not to think about the interview at all or praying for a rainout or a raging warehouse fire that would draw O'Leary and her crew away. But Kathi O'Leary was there, in the flesh. And so was the TV camera and the radar gun.

Drawn by the sight of Kathi O'Leary and the camera, Adele and Jon came over. Andy stayed firmly perched on the top bleacher. Brenda turned at the sound of her mother's and Jon's voices. "I can't believe you got me into this," she muttered to her mother.

"Oh, don't be such a spoilsport. Be proud," her mother whispered back and then moved in to shake Kathi O'Leary's well-manicured hand. Brenda noticed that she had scarlet, almost slutty red nail polish. It figured somebody like O'Leary would think that shade made her look like a bad girl. Brenda glanced down at her nails and realized they hadn't seen nail polish since her cousin's wedding two years ago. What's more, she had dried Taco Bell salsa under the nail of her left index finger. She put her glove on.

The good thing about having her mother and Jon there was that she was able to sneak back to the dugout. If Brenda had felt isolated from the rest of the team before, having a TV crew there to interview her didn't help matters. The guys hardly said a word to her. Maybe Andy was right—maybe she should have just joined a women's softball team.

The news crew taped the first two innings of the game from the bleachers, then Kathi O'Leary came to the edge of the dugout at the top of the third inning and asked of no one in particular if Brenda was going to be playing that day.

Every person in the dugout stopped—whether they were rooting around for their batting gloves or grabbing a drink of Gatorade or tying a cleat or talking about the last out, they all stopped. As one person, they looked at Kathi O'Leary and then turned to Carl. Since physically melting into the ground and disappearing was not an option, Brenda just said, "That's our manager's decision."

Carl took a few steps toward the end of the dugout where O'Leary was standing and planted himself in the middle of his players. "Brenda's short relief," he said. "If we need her, she'll go in. I can't tell you what will happen during the rest of the game."

"Okay," Kathi O'Leary said. "I understand. It's just that we're on kind of a tight schedule here."

"If we need her, she'll go in," Carl repeated.

The rest of the team was still watching this exchange, as were the opposing team's first baseman and the infield umpire. The home plate ump called "Batter up," but Gary, who was supposed to be leading off that inning, was standing just behind Carl's left shoulder. From the look on his face, it was quite possible that Kathi O'Leary's choice of nail polish was more effective than Brenda had first thought. He looked positively mesmerized.

"Batter up!" the home plate ump yelled again.

Brenda could almost see the little lightbulb go off over Kathi O'Leary's head. "Why don't I interview you and Brenda now, while your team is batting? Then we won't be disturbing anyone."

To her surprise, Carl said, "Sure. Come on, Brenda. Let's go get interviewed."

"If you want to sort of round things out by talking to a couple of Brenda's teammates, I'll be happy to do it," Gary said to Kathi.

"Strike one!" the home plate ump yelled.

"Gary, you're up, man," somebody said.

Gary looked around as though he had momentarily forgotten they were in the middle of a game. "Was that strike one for me?" he asked. "Can he do that?"

"Yes," Brenda said. The Roy Hobbs league played by Major League Baseball rules and she had read everything pertaining to pitchers, batters, and base runners before her first game. "He can do that. Go bat."

In the ensuring movement of bodies in the narrow dugout, Gary went to bat and Brenda and Carl went to the open area behind the bleachers so Kathi O'Leary could interview them. Adele and Jon came around again, but O'Leary made them stand off to the side. "This is Brenda's turn to shine," she said with that big, unnerving smile. "You have a lovely family," she said to Brenda. "Little Jon is so sweet, and your mom is just a riot. But I couldn't get Andy to talk to me," she added in a faux scolding voice that was deliberately loud enough for Andy to hear (and which he might have heard had he not had his ear buds firmly in place and his mp3 player blasting).

"Yeah, well, Andy's his own man," Brenda said with a smile. "I'm not going to force him to do anything he doesn't want to do." She heard Carl give a faux little cough but refused to acknowledge it.

"Oh, you're such a good mom," Kathi said. Then without even taking a breath, she said, "Let's get straight into the interview. Rick, roll it and keep it rolling. We'll cut it later."

Rick hoisted the camera to his shoulder. The infamous little red light went on, and butterflies simultaneously seemed to erupt in Brenda's stomach. "Anytime you're ready, Kath," Rick said.

Kathi O'Leary turned to face the camera and started to speak in a voice that was about an octave bouncier than Brenda had ever felt in her life. "Sports fans all over the country have seen a cell phone video of a woman in a pitching cage throwing at near-major-league speed, and they all wondered the same thing: Who is the woman in the video and can she really throw a baseball eighty-two miles an hour? Well, I can tell you that the answer to the first question is standing here with me. As for the second question, we'll soon find out." Brenda noticed that O'Leary said "we'll soon find out" as though she was an actor in an old B-movie. It sounded very much like O'Leary didn't think Brenda could throw that hard.

Kathi O'Leary took a step back so she was standing next to Brenda. "It turns out that the mystery pitcher is from right here in Cleveland. America, meet Brenda Haversham of South Euclid. She's the woman in the video. She's also a relief pitcher for the Lake Erie Lightning, a recreational team that plays here in Westlake's Roman Park. Brenda, how long have you been pitching?"

Brenda had been watching Kathi O'Leary do her spiel and almost forgotten that the whole point of O'Leary's presence was to talk to her. Now, with O'Leary's sparkling brown eyes and the business end of the camera trained upon her, she remembered. "Not very long," she replied. She paused, even though it was clear O'Leary was expecting her to say more, so she added, "A few months."

"Did you play in college?"

"No. I played a lot when I was a kid, with my dad, but that's about it."

There was a long pause, during which Brenda felt conspicuously on display. Kathi O'Leary quickly changed gears and asked Carl how he felt about coaching a woman.

"It's no different than coaching anybody else," Carl said. "I just try to give her the same advice and treat her the same as I would any other player."

"Brenda," Kathi O'Leary said, "when did you first realize what a talented ballplayer you are?"

"Right now, maybe?" Brenda said with a weak laugh. "Sorry, I'm not that good at talking about myself."

"Well if you'd rather let your pitching do the talking, you're in luck," Kathi O'Leary said, looking overly happy that Brenda had just given her a segue. "We have Alan here, a volunteer from the Society for American Baseball Research, and he and his radar gun will be tracking every pitch. We'll be right back with more from Roman Park after these messages." Kathi O'Leary's face froze in a huge smile that showed every tooth. Brenda decided it would be impossible for O'Leary's teeth to get any whiter.

Rick put down the camera and Kathi O'Leary put down her microphone. Brenda breathed a sigh of relief. "Sorry. I'm a little nervous," she said.

"You did fine," Carl said.

"You just need to relax and open up a bit," Kathi O'Leary said. "Let people see the real you."

"I'll try," Brenda said, adding that she and Carl had better get back to the dugout. As they were walking away, she heard O'Leary say, "Geez, I hope she pitches better than she interviews," and Rick (or maybe it was Alan) respond with, "That'd be too much to hope for."

Carl obviously hadn't heard this exchange because he just hurried into the dugout and grabbed his glove. Brenda sat on the bench and felt stupid. *A ham sandwich would have been more eloquent*, she thought in disgust.

As she watched the game, Brenda thought about life before children, before marriage, before Ed. She had been a talented designer with a clean, bold style that even won a couple of local awards, but that was years ago now. The last time she'd picked up a pencil to sketch an idea, the pencil had felt awkward in her hand and her mind's eye saw nothing. It seemed her muse had skipped town.

She'd stopped working when Andy was born, then later Ed kept saying having her home with the boys was more important to him than a second income. She never regretted being a stay-at-home mom, but when Ed left and she needed to find a job, a small part of her wished that she had been able to keep up with all the changes in the industry. Her portfolio was outdated and she didn't know any of the new design software; she couldn't find a design job without knowing the software, but she couldn't afford the time or the cost of any classes to learn it.

"It always comes back to Ed," Brenda mumbled, kicking at the ground in front of her.

"What'd you say, Brenda?" Gary asked.

Brenda looked up. She had lost track of what was happening in the game and had to sneak a peek at the scoreboard to find out what inning it was (thank God the city of Westlake could afford a good scoreboard). "Nothing," she replied. "Just talking to myself."

"Getting in the zone, huh?"

"Yeah," she said in a voice that sounded more confident than she felt. She wondered if other players' zones were fueled by large doses of adrenaline and anger.

Brenda watched and waited until the bottom of the sixth. The home team, the Medina County Monsters, were down by two. The Lightning had had a comfortable lead, but their starting pitcher, a lanky forty-five-year-old named Scott who always seemed to want to talk pitching with Brenda, gave up four runs and two walks in the fifth and Carl pulled him. As Brenda trotted out to the mound, she passed by the Monsters' first base coach, who muttered, "Hey, movie star" as they crossed paths. He was about the same height at Ed, and when he briefly took off his cap to adjust it, she saw that his hair was the same brown as Ed's. It really did seem to always come back to Ed in one way or another.

She threw one warm-up pitch, trying to ignore Kathi O'Leary and Rick the cameraman, who had commandeered the field end of the dugout to get a better shot, and the audible smart-aleck comments from the opposite bench, and especially trying to ignore scrawny, milquetoasty Alan and his radar gun. When Bob threw the ball back and set himself up for the next warm-up pitch, she waved him off. She didn't need any more warming up.

The first batter stood in—the Monsters' right fielder, who didn't even look to be as tall as she was. What he lacked in height he made up for in width. When Brenda first saw him earlier in the game, he struck her as resembling an overgrown dwarf, with stubby legs and arms and a slight waddle to his walk. It was clear that he was on the team because of his bat, not his speed.

He gave her a cocky, dwarfy grin, and she hated him for it.

She looked at the catcher's mitt and saw Ed's face in the pocket, saw the lines leading from her hand to the mitt. She muttered "Motherfucker" and threw the ball ninety-three miles an hour.

•◇•

Excerpt from the transcript for *Today in Sports* with Charlie Bannister, ESPN, June 19:

> Charlie: Welcome back to *Today in Sports*. I'm Charlie Bannister. With me, as every Friday, is former major leaguer Howie Wojinski for our weekly look at the world of baseball. Howie, this week, I don't want to talk about the MLB.
>
> Howie: You don't?
>
> Charlie: Nope, because the big news this week isn't from the major leagues, it's from somewhere beyond the Bush Leagues. I'm talking about the woman who was clocked pitching a fastball ninety-three miles an hour. Go to YouTube and search for "fast-pitching mom." The video is from an NBC affiliate in Cleveland that clocked her throwing ninety-three miles an hour. Something like half a million people have already watched it.
>
> Howie: Oh that . . .
>
> Charlie: Ninety-three miles an hour, Howie. Do you know the percentage of human beings who can throw a baseball ninety-three miles an hour?
>
> Howie: No, what is it?
>
> Charlie: Very, very small. Miniscule.
>
> Howie: There are women college softball players who throw that hard. This isn't such a big deal.

Charlie: NCAA softball pitchers throw somewhere around seventy to seventy-five miles per hour—it's the short alley between the mound and the plate that makes it appear faster to the batter. But this woman from Cleveland is throwing major-league-speed pitches. And they're good pitches—she has control, she has movement, she has nuance. This is astounding.

Howie: So what do you want me to do about it, Charlie?

Charlie: I want you to join me in a campaign to urge the Cleveland Indians to sign her as a relief pitcher.

Howie: [laughs hysterically]

Charlie: I'm serious.

Howie: [Makes noise that sounds like "creaaak-kkk"] Hey Charlie, you hear that sound? Know what that is? That's the sound of Ford Frick rolling over in his grave. [laughs again]

Charlie: Come on, Howie. Come on into the twenty-first century. It's nice here, we won't bite. Look, if she can do the job, why not sign her? If it were some unknown young guy throwing ninety-three miles an hour, you'd be all over this. You can't assume that the only talented, unknown ballplayers in the country are playing in the minor leagues or in college. And you can't assume they're all male. Talent shows up anywhere it wants. And right now it's decided to show up in the form of a woman named Brenda Haversham from Cleveland,

Ohio. So what I'm asking you to do—you, Howie, and you, the person sitting there watching this at home—I'm asking you to go to the website that Ziggy the intern set up for me called SignBrenda. com and sign the petition urging the Indians—or another team—to sign her.

Howie: You really are serious.

Charlie: Heck yeah, I'm serious. Why not give her a chance? Somebody somewhere once gave you a chance, didn't they? The Twins gave you a chance back in '78 when no one else would sign you.

Howie: Thanks for reminding me.

Charlie: The point is, they took a gamble on you. The old WDHO in Toledo gave me a chance when I got out of college with nothing but a bachelor's degree and an attitude to my name. Let's share the wealth and give this woman a chance. All I'm asking you to do is visit SignBrenda.com and add your name to the petition, okay? Thank you, America, and thank you, Howie.

Howie: Can we talk about MLB now, Charlie? Because the Braves are on a hot streak that is not to be believed.

Charlie: Anything for you, buddy.

Chapter Five

•◇•

S O MANY PEOPLE WERE CALLING ABOUT CHARLIE BANNISTER AND THE
VIDEO AND THE WEBSITE THAT IT SEEMED LIKE THE PHONE HADN'T
STOPPED RINGING FOR A WEEK. Andy refused to answer the telephone and had taken to giving one-word answers to anything Brenda
asked. Every morning he would greet her with a sullen "Hi," eat a
silent breakfast with his brother and her, and ride his bike with Jon
to the sports camp. The boys got home a couple hours before Brenda
got back from work. That time was always fraught with worry for her
but she figured it probably felt like freedom to them.

A few days after the second video aired on Charlie Bannister's
show, Brenda came home to find Jon in the living room playing his
DS. She could tell right away something was wrong by Jon's face.
She was already exhausted. She hadn't expected to start out Monday morning with the president of the company calling her into his
office to ask if she was quitting (the answer was "no") and then to try
and recruit her onto the company softball team (the answer was also
"no"). And she hadn't expected virtually every male and half of the
females in the office to come by her cubicle and ask if she had seen
SignBrenda.com (she had and found it lacked basic design principles
but was shocked to see it already had seventy-five thousand signatures), whether she knew Charlie Bannister personally (two people
asked if she was sleeping with him), if it was true that she was going
to sign with the Indians (which made her snort back a laugh), why
she hadn't told them she played baseball, could they go and watch,

how she learned to throw, was the video real, and if she wanted to go out to dinner (the latter was asked by Frank, a vice president who wore enough cologne that his scent preceded his physical presence by a good ten seconds; Brenda said no). On top of all this, she came home to have Jon tell her that Andy had gotten into a fight at camp.

"Don't tell him I told you," Jon whispered. "He'll kill me. Andy's really mad."

"It's okay, sweetie," Brenda said, sitting down next to him on the sofa. "I know Andy's angry, but he's angry with me, not you."

"He acts like he's mad at everybody. Some kids were teasing him about you, and then Madison Gallagher said she thought it was great that you played baseball and had your video on ESPN and stuff, and that's when he hit her."

"He started a fight with a girl?" Brenda's stomach dropped to somewhere in the vicinity of her ankles, but she tried not to sound as concerned as she was. Andy was getting big enough and strong enough that he could inflict real damage on someone smaller.

"Well, she's not really a girl. She's a lot older—she's like sixteen or something."

"Sweetie, the camp is only for kids twelve and under. A girl that old wouldn't be enrolled."

"Madison's a CIT."

"Oh Jesus Christ."

"You said we aren't supposed to use the Lord's name in vain," Jon said as she stood up.

"You're right, Jon. I'm sorry," Brenda replied. Inwardly, she swore a blue streak. Andy had gotten into a fight with a counselor in training. There was no way they'd let him back into the sports camp, which meant she was going to have to find something for him to do all day for the rest of the summer. She didn't even want to think about the potential legal implications.

"Jon, did Madison get hurt?"

"No, I don't think so. She's really big—she plays basketball for Brush High School. Dante Jackson's sister goes to school with her and he said Madison's six feet tall."

While this fact didn't excuse Andy's actions, it made the situation appear a tiny bit less dire. Knowing she'd have no time to make dinner that night, she ordered a pizza (vowing to make an extra-healthy dinner the next night) and knocked on Andy's door.

Clearly, he was expecting the knock, because he said, "Hi, Mom" through the closed door. Sullen though it was, Brenda took that as an all-clear to enter. Andy had a bruise on his right cheek that threatened to turn into a genuine shiner, a scraped elbow, and some miscellaneous tiny scrapes and bruises here and there. Although he claimed to have iced it when he got home, Brenda put an ice pack on his eye and hydrogen peroxide on his elbow, but wasn't sure what would heal his pride. Once she had played medic, it was time to talk. The pizza hadn't arrived yet—Jon was stationed by the front door to wait for it—and she sat Andy down at the kitchen table.

"Do you want to tell me what happened?" she asked.

"Not really," Andy replied, avoiding her gaze.

"I'd like to get your side of the story."

"Madison wouldn't leave me alone." Brenda nodded to keep him talking. "All day long she kept going on about you and that stupid video on the news and ESPN and the petition and she wouldn't shut up. Then she asked if she could come over and meet you. I mean, that's like an invasion of privacy, right?"

"I don't know." She paused. All she wanted to do was cuddle her son (even though he would refuse to be cuddled) and tell him that she was sorry for doing anything to hurt him and sorry that his father wasn't here and that she felt horrible seeing him in pain. But all she could say was: "Did you hit her first?"

Andy took a deep breath, and Brenda could see the beginning of a tear welling up in his unbruised eye. "Yeah. I know you're not supposed to hit a girl . . ."

"I'd be just as angry if you had gotten into a fight with another boy. You *hit* another human being, Andy. Fighting is . . . it's not the way people should treat each other. No matter how angry someone is making you, violence isn't the answer." She tried not to feel hypocritical when she said this. After all, she took out her anger on baseballs.

"I know," he replied with a sigh that was hard to decipher. Her older son had become such a mystery to her, it was mind boggling.

"Do you want to talk to your dad about this?"

"Not right now."

"Okay. I won't tell him either. You and I will figure out your punishment later." Brenda got up to get some plates and glasses out of the cupboard for dinner. "Is there anything else you'd like to talk about?"

For a moment there was only the sound of Brenda placing three plates on the table. Then Andy asked: "Why are you playing baseball?"

"Because it's . . . fun," Brenda said.

"You don't act like you're having fun."

"I just came home to find out that my son got in a fight with a counselor in training—I'm allowed to be a little peeved."

"I'm sorry," Andy said.

"I am too, sweetie. I never thought that my playing baseball would affect you. I just thought it would be something interesting to do. If it really bothers you, I won't play anymore."

"That's okay. If you like it, you should do it," Andy said, and for a moment he looked like a little adult sitting in the kitchen, reversing the parent and child roles just as she sometimes did with Adele. Then came Jon's voice ringing in from the living room, shouting that the pizza had arrived.

Later that night, Brenda sat down to get the messages off the answering machine. Since the news report and SignBrenda.com, she occasionally got irate messages from strangers (almost always male) telling her that she had no business trying to play major league baseball, as though she was campaigning to play.

Of the eleven messages on the machine, one was, predictably, from the sports camp asking her to meet with the director in the morning when Andy arrived (she prayed they'd let him return with promises of good behavior). One was from Robin. One was from Adele. One was from Carl asking if they could drive together on Thursday because he was having car problems. Five were from strangers telling her they had signed the online petition, which was kind but made her feel at a loss for how to respond. Two had actually left their phone numbers, as though expecting Brenda to call them back. She erased them all. One was from an irate man who said that she had terrible delivery, had obviously rigged the radar gun, should stay away from the pitcher's mound, and that he would cancel his season tickets to the Indians if they signed her. His voice was high pitched and slightly wheezy, as though he were speaking through a leaky bellows instead of a telephone, and it sounded as if he'd had a few drinks before calling.

She thought both boys were in bed, but when she had had enough and hit the "delete" button on the machine to erase the message, she heard Andy's voice behind her. "That guy sounds like a real asshole," he said.

"Andy, what are you still doing up?"

"I couldn't sleep. Who was that guy?"

"Just somebody who found our number and decided that he had nothing better to do than call up a stranger and insult her," Brenda said.

"So he really is an asshole."

"Andy, please try to watch your language."

"Just calling them like I see them," he said with a self-consciously casual sigh and plopped down on the sofa.

"Back in bed, please. And tomorrow morning, I'm driving you and Jon to camp. You and I have a meeting with the director first thing."

Andy's determinedly impassive face suddenly looked worried. "We do? Is that because of the fight?"

"Yes." She was tempted to say more—to tell him to please stay out of fights, to learn to control his temper, to not let his anger get the best of him, to look appropriately penitent and apologetic when they met with the camp director—in short, to give him another mom lecture, but she restrained herself. Instead, she hit the play button to listen to the last message.

She heard a voice so smooth it sounded as though it could pick the lock to your front door with nothing but its pleasant timber saying that the speaker was a sports agent named David Samuels who wanted to discuss possible representation.

"Representation for what?" Andy asked.

"Me," Brenda replied, more than slightly amazed. "It sounds like he wants to be my agent."

Andy snorted a laugh. "You don't need an agent. That's only for people who play baseball professionally, right?"

"Yes."

"So, not you."

"No, not me," Brenda said. And she left it at that, ignoring the little voice in the back of her head that whispered on and on about possibilities and potential and why not her.

She and Andy managed to get through the meeting with the director of the sports camp relatively unscathed. Madison's parents agreed not to file any charges as long as Andy was switched out of her group. Andy was allowed to remain at the camp for the remainder of the summer on a probationary basis—if he was involved in any other altercation, he'd be out. The director also reminded Brenda that the next installment for the boys' tuition at the camp was two days over-due. She had no choice but to write a check on the spot, feeling as she did so that the minute she tore it out of the checkbook, it would bounce out of her hands and out the window, never to be seen again

"Would it be too much to ask for you to wait until Friday before bringing this to the bank?" she asked cautiously. "I hate to ask after how kind you've been in letting Andy stay. It's just that payday isn't until Friday and . . ." she let her voice trail off, embarrassed to have to admit to this man that she didn't have enough money to pay what was owed and to have to say this in front of her son.

The director gave her a begrudging "I'll see what I can do," and that was it. Andy was still in the camp for the summer, and Brenda felt like she had just bought her son another six months of therapy once he was an adult. At least her childcare issue was settled. As she said good-bye to Andy and watched him jog off to join his group, the word "childcare" seemed highly inappropriate. She knew he wasn't a child anymore. But the thought of a burgeoning adolescent on his own all day every day for the rest of the summer was as worrisome as hoping the check wouldn't bounce.

That night was Little League night for both boys. Brenda was for-tunate that their games fell on the same night and were close by. Jon played at Quarry Park in their city, while Andy's team played across the street at Denison Park in neighboring Cleveland Heights. It was just a question of going back and forth between the two. She generally dropped Jon off first, then Andy, and walked across the street and through the park to watch Jon's game, since the younger kids played shorter games. Afterward, she and Jon walked back through the park and across the street to watch the last innings of Andy's game.

Jon wasn't exactly struggling in his new league, but Brenda could see that he was still a little intimidated by the older, bigger kids and by the opposing pitchers. He was facing kids who could afford to be meaner and throw harder than any parent. The nine-to-eleven league still had some female players—a handful of sturdy little souls who never caught soccer madness like their friends and hadn't yet lost the confidence to go after a bouncing grounder on the run or face a boy pitcher who still thought girls had cooties. There was actually a girl on Jon's team and two on the team he was playing. Just about every team had its token girl. In Andy's entire twelve-to-fourteen league, there were only two girls. That was all.

Brenda had never really wondered if those girls would have a chance to keep playing baseball when they got older. For now, they were just other children playing a game with her children. Then one of the girls came up to her near the end of Andy's game. She was about thirteen, with long, dark brown hair in a single braid going straight down her back. Andy's team had played hers the week before, and the girl had jumped like a pixie at second base, stopping everything that came her way. She was tanned and angular with a bright smile. If Brenda had had a daughter, she would have wanted her to have this confidence and strength.

"Excuse me," the girl said as she walked up to where Brenda was waiting for Andy just beyond the bleachers. The girl was in her uniform—their game must have just ended over on the other diamond. "You're Brenda Haversham, right?"

Brenda tried not to look too apprehensive or surprised. "Yes, I am."

"My name's Emma. I play baseball too. I just wanted to tell you that I signed your petition and watched your video on YouTube about a gazillion times. And my mom watched it too, and now she doesn't ask me if I want to switch to softball anymore." The girl smiled. "Softball is boring."

"Thank you. And I'm glad to hear your mom is supporting your baseball career." It was one thing to have her mom or friends say 'You'll be a role model,' it was overwhelming to realize that she actually *was* one.

The girl nodded, still smiling broadly. "I hope the Indians sign you."

Brenda wasn't sure what to say to this. It would be rude to say that she didn't really want to be signed by the Indians and that the petition wasn't her idea and that it wouldn't do any good anyway because no major league baseball team was going to sign a woman. "Well," she said, "it won't be the end of the world if they don't. We play because we like it, right?"

"Yep! Baseball's the best game ever."

Brenda thanked the girl again, then Andy and Jon came over and she made a graceful exit. She tried to ignore the extra attention people had started to pay her, just as she tried to ignore the curious bystanders who continued to come to Lightning games to see her pitch. She also tried to ignore the phone calls from David Samuels, the smooth-voiced agent who had called her every day at varying times, obviously trying to catch her in person. Brenda listened to the messages and promptly erased them. She didn't think about him again until Thursday night after the Lightning game.

Brenda went in for the last two innings, struck out three, and allowed no runs, no hits, and no walks. She had a great game and kind of wished the boys or Adele and Robin and Dan had been there to see it. The number of curious and incredulous people in the bleachers had been growing throughout the summer. There were even more this week, no doubt thanks to Charlie Bannister's show. In addition to friends and family of the team, tonight there were three couples—two who looked retired and one in their twenties—a trio of men who looked like young retirees and who refused to be impressed by anything Brenda did, a group of six older women who made sure to cheer after nearly every pitch Brenda threw, and a lone man who looked to be in his early fifties. Brenda thought he might be a friend of someone on the opposing team, so she was surprised when, at the end of the game, he started strolling alongside her as she headed toward the parking lot.

"At last I get to speak with the elusive Brenda Haversham," the man said. There was no mistaking the silky voice, which sounded as though it was going to pick you up and tuck you into bed.

"Mr. Samuels?" she asked.

"In person."

She briefly appraised him. He had closely cropped curly hair that was so dark it looked almost blue in the fading light. His creased jeans (who still had creased jeans?) and linen shirt made it clear that his casual outfit cost more than Brenda's best suit. "I'm not that elusive," Brenda said. "You didn't seem to have any trouble finding my telephone number or finding me."

"It's one thing to get the answering machine, it's another to get the woman herself."

She wasn't entirely fond of the familiar way he addressed her, and yet she found herself doing the same thing, speaking to him as though he were a long-lost friend instead of a stranger. He was too charming by half. Without thinking about it, she shifted the gym bag with her glove, hat, and cleats in it from her right hand to her left so it wouldn't bump into him, but kept walking. "Look, I apologize for not returning your calls," she said. "But honestly, I'm not interested in representation. I thought if I didn't call you back you'd realize that."

"I figured as much," David replied, sounding completely unfazed. "But when an athlete has as much earning potential as you do, I don't let a few unreturned phone calls get me down."

Brenda snorted back a laugh. "I think my earning potential peaked a few years back. Unless you have an opening for a graphic designer with outdated skills, I think I've plateaued." They were at her car. Good old Molly, who was overdue for an oil change and tire rotation, was waiting right where Brenda had left her. "Look, it's flattering that you came all the way to Cleveland from wherever . . ."

"From Cleveland. I'm with Stratagem Management—we're based here."

"Oh. Well, it's still flattering that you took the time to come down here and watch my game, but I'm not interested in representation."

"Why not?" David asked. "You don't feel like making some serious money in endorsements or playing in the big leagues?"

"Playing in the big leagues? Are you out of your mind?"

"No, I'm not. I want you to think about something, Brenda. Your video on YouTube . . ."

"It's not my video—I didn't post it."

"Fair enough. The latest video of you pitching has now been viewed 1.5 million times on YouTube in three weeks. The petition on SignBrenda.com has received over two hundred thousand signatures in one week. You have been clocked throwing a baseball ninety-three miles per hour and have clearly captured the public's attention, and yet you say your earning potential has plateaued and that you aren't interested in representation. So Brenda, I need to ask you something." In a move reminiscent of a lover lying back on a bed covered in rose petals, David leaned against the dusty blue minivan and asked: "Are *you* out of *your* mind?"

•◇•

Excerpt from the transcript for *Today in Sports* with Charlie Bannister, ESPN, June 25:

> Charlie: The Tigers are still sitting pretty atop the American League Central division, but it's too early to rule out the White Sox, who've been tearing it up in divisional play. The Indians made a rare show of strength today, with a solid 9-3 trouncing of the Boston Red Sox. The team has showed signs of life lately, and they might be able to salvage the season if they can fill in some of the holes in the bullpen. [Holds up sign reading "SignBrenda.com."] I've been told by the powers that be that I, quote, "am not permitted to use this show as a platform to lobby for women in baseball," end quote. So I'm not going to mention any names. And I'm not lobbying for women in baseball—I'm just lobbying to give an unknown pitcher a chance.

Chapter Six

•◇•

THE IDEA OF A WOMAN—ANY WOMAN—PLAYING FOR A MAJOR LEAGUE BASEBALL TEAM WAS SO IMPROBABLE THAT HAVING THE FIRST WOMAN IN THE MLB BE AN OVERWEIGHT FORTY-YEAR-OLD WITH NO TRACK RECORD WOULD SIMPLY ADD TO THE ALLURE. And the allure could sell a whole lot of tickets and merchandise. At least this was the rationale given to Brenda by David Samuels. She didn't appreciate him stating out loud that she was overweight when it was really just her hips.

"That's part of your charm," he said. "You're accessible—you're an everywoman with a killer fastball." They were sitting in Samuels's lush office in a reflective glass building on East Ninth Street in downtown Cleveland. From his window, Brenda could see Lake Erie, looking cool and alluring just a few blocks away. She wondered if David ever took a moment just to sit and gaze at what a gorgeous view he had.

Brenda had asked Adele to come with her. The thought of bringing a lawyer felt too much like she was actually planning on signing, and that thought still seemed a little ridiculous. The whole thing felt a bit like a game. Adele kept telling her that it wasn't a game, that this was serious business.

"If he's right," Adele said, as though they weren't sitting on David's oversized leather chairs in his corner office flanked by two walls of windows with him sitting right in front of them, "then you could make some big money doing endorsements. You could pay off the house and give the boys their college funds and make sure you have something for retirement. You'd have some security."

"Your mother is both right and wrong," David said. He leaned on the edge of his massive oak desk. "You could make some serious money doing endorsements, but this really is all a game. And I know how to play it so that you and I both win."

"How?"

"If you agree to representation, you won't just be represented by me, you'll have all the resources of Stratagem behind you. We will help you maximize your earning potential and establish you, Brenda Haversham, as a unique brand. Which won't be hard, because there aren't any other women playing baseball at your level."

"My level? I play in a rec league."

"But she's very good, isn't she?" Adele said.

"Mom, please."

Adele turned her shocking red hair to her daughter and raised her right index finger for the infamous Adele Puchall finger wag, which was legendary at the Slovak National House on East 185th Street. "I watch baseball too, Brenda. And you're very, very good."

"Your mother is right again," David said. "I've watched you play. I've watched all the available footage of you pitching—including the footage that didn't air on the news. Whether you know it or not, you've been scouted by several teams and their reports were all favorable. You're the real deal. I wouldn't have wasted my time tracking you down if you weren't. I'll be honest with you, Brenda . . ."

"Have you been dishonest up until now?"

She got the finger wag again for this. "Be nice."

"It's okay, Adele," David soothed. Brenda marveled at how quickly he was able to turn her mother into an ally. "Brenda's right to be skeptical. Look, my job is to help my clients. As your agent, Stratagem takes fifteen percent—I get seven percent of that. So it's in my best interest for you to succeed. I know we can get you some good endorsements, but we have to act fast. Your popularity is going to peak by the end of the year. Now if we somehow manage to break the Major League gender barrier, all bets are off. They'd most likely start you off with a low base salary and a ton of incentives, but your endorsement potential would skyrocket. Is this making sense to you?"

"Perfect sense. You want me to do my dancing bear act as a pseudo-celebrity and make as much cash as possible before I become yesterday's news."

"Unless we get you a contract with a team."

"Yes, you'll get me a contract with the Indians, and tomorrow I'll wake up and suddenly be five foot ten and built like a supermodel." Suddenly, it all felt like too much—too sleazy, too much like prostitution. She turned to Adele. "Mom, let's get out of here while I still have some principles."

"If that's how you really feel," Adele said, "then let's go. But please tell me which of your principles is being compromised here. Will your dignity somehow be compromised by being the first woman to play major league baseball? Or is it being a good role model for young women that compromises your principles? I'm just checking."

Brenda hated it when her mother made a good point. She had always called herself a feminist. Wouldn't a feminist say it was high time a woman played major league baseball? If she were honest with herself, it was easier to say she was acting on principle than to say that she was scared. But what would be worse—staying in a job she didn't like or doing something big, something different? So what if she had to put up with unwanted attention from strangers and rude comments from the small minded and the feeling of being on display. It would be worth it to take care of Andy and Jon on her own, to not live paycheck to paycheck or worry whether she could afford small extras for the boys. Ed only had to pay alimony for four more years. And the boys seemed to get more expensive as they got older. Then there was the house, which was going to need a new roof soon and had a leaky basement and a sinking foundation. It would take more than an entire year's salary to fix everything wrong with the house. She could put up with a lot to give Andy and Jon big, juicy college funds, a paid-off mortgage on a sturdy house, and a sense of security. And playing baseball beat the hell out of data entry.

She took a deep breath and said, "Okay. I'll sign."

"You won't regret this," David said.

"I sure hope not."

•◊•

David called Brenda at work two days later.

"I really can't talk now," Brenda said. "I'm kind of behind on some work and they rate us on our number of keystrokes." All around her, she could hear the gentle click-click-click of dozens of fingers doing the same frantic dance hers did every day. "Can I call you back?"

"This won't take long," David purred. "I just wanted to tell you that I've finalized your first endorsement deal. You're going to do some print ads for this new line of moisturizer with sunblock. It's called Fountain. They said you already had nice skin, by the way. It's not a huge contract, but they think your image will go over big with sporty, active moms. They're going to run the ads in a few women's magazines and online. You need to fly out to New York on Monday morning for an afternoon photo shoot. You fly back on Tuesday."

Brenda felt like someone had just taken her desk chair and spun her around a dozen times. She could barely say, "Wow, that's great news." And once she had spoken, she could swear she heard three or four fewer hands typing. The cubicle walls were supposed to deaden sound, but that didn't stop everyone in the cube farm from listening in on any conversation that might be juicy.

"This is only the beginning," David said.

Talking to David about not having enough vacation time accrued to take Monday and Tuesday off was futile. She managed to beg two days off, got Adele to stay with the boys for the night, and found herself on a plane on Monday at 6:00 a.m.

Whenever she and Ed and the boys had gone on vacation, they had always driven because it was cheaper than buying four airline tickets. Brenda almost couldn't remember the last time she had flown, and she had never flown first class. It seemed like a first class ticket for an hour and a half trip would be a waste of money, but as she settled back in a seat that was easily as comfortable as the living room recliner, she reconsidered that theory.

She was met by a driver at the airport and taken directly to the photo shoot. There was a hair person, a makeup person, a lighting person, an art director, a photographer, and a few assorted assistants who kept asking her if they could get her some lunch or something to drink. Having so many people ask what they could do for her was a far cry from single parenting. Then she sat down in the makeup chair. The hairdresser was an impossibly thin woman in her late thirties with a jet black pageboy haircut who looked as though the world would end if a hair were ever out of place. She gingerly held up the end of the ponytail holding back Brenda's shoulder-length, dark blonde hair and said to the art director, "What am I supposed to do with *this*?"

"Should I have left it down?" Brenda said. "I wasn't sure."

"I don't think leaving it down would have helped much," the hairdresser said. She removed the ponytail holder and fiddled with Brenda's hair for a moment. "You swim, don't you?" she said accusingly.

"I've been going to the pool with my kids," Brenda replied. "You know, summertime fun . . ."

"Right . . ." After another minute of fiddling with Brenda's hair, she announced: "You have a *lot* of split ends. We're going to need to trim this."

Brenda tried to think of the day as being paid to get a free makeover and haircut, although there were moments when she felt more objectified than pampered as her hair and skin and clothing were fussed over through three different clothing, set, and lighting changes. The haircut turned out to be less drastic than she thought—most of the length was still there, but her hair framed her face better. She hated to admit someone as rude as the hairdresser could be right.

A car drove her to a midtown hotel called the Bedford, and the driver told her he'd pick her up in the morning to take her to the airport. Once she had checked in and gone up to her room, which turned out to be charming, it was after 5:00. Too early to call home. Just for kicks, she called Robin.

"I'm in a swanky hotel room that someone else paid for, and I have a fabulous new haircut and more makeup on than I wore to my own wedding," she said when Robin answered.

"Sure you aren't doing a remake of *Pretty Woman?*" Robin said.

"While there are some similarities, no."

"How did the photo shoot go? I want to hear about it. It's so crazy cool that you're there."

"I think it went okay. I got a great haircut from a mean hairdresser. It was like a free makeover, except they were paying me to be there, which still kind of blows my mind."

"Think of it as getting paid to be your awesome self."

"Thank you," Brenda said. Sometimes her friends said things that were so kind it took away her ability to say much more than "thank you."

"So what are you going to do tonight? Go out on the town and show off your fabulous new haircut from the cranky hairdresser?"

"I'm thinking about it."

"I would say 'Don't do anything I wouldn't do . . .'" Robin began.

"But that still would leave the door wide open for trouble."

"Exactly."

"I'll either go out and have a torrid one-night stand with a guy half my age or stay in and enjoy the novelty of having the remote all to myself. And some uninterrupted reading time."

"Tough choice. I'm sure you'll make the right decision."

Brenda ended up taking a walk down Lexington Avenue and getting takeout from an Indian restaurant called Nirvana on the way back. The restaurant was sleek and modern and stylish—the type of place that could make a woman on her own feel self-conscious about everything. But it smelled heavenly, so she sat down at the bar, ordered a Kingfisher and some samosas and dal makhani to go. Sitting at a bar alone felt odd; Brenda could still hear Adele admonishing her and Robin as college students to "Stay out of the bars. No nice man wants a girl who sits in a bar all night." She smiled and shook her head at the memory.

"You have a nice smile," said a voice to her left. She looked over and saw a late thirtyish guy in a gray suit and a buzz cut on the barstool next to her.

"Thank you," she said, wondering if he would think she was flirting if she smiled again. He wasn't all that cute, but the fact he had noted her smile suddenly made her feel self-conscious.

"Waiting for your husband?" the guy asked. Nothing like being direct.

"No, just some take out. What about you?"

"I'm meeting some friends, but I have a habit of being terminally prompt," he said with a smile. He extended a hand. "I'm George."

"Brenda."

"Nice to meet you, Brenda. Look, this is going to sound like a lame pick-up line, but haven't I seen you somewhere before?"

"Probably not. I don't live here." It had been so long since she had had a conversation with a stranger that she felt unsure what information to reveal and what not. What would it matter if she told the guy she lived in Cleveland or that she was in town to do a photo shoot? She and George talked for a few minutes and she could sense his growing interest. How easy would it be to invite him back to the hotel, to give into temptation and be a hedonist for a night? Easy. Really easy.

The bartender brought over a bag with Brenda's take out order. She paid him and turned to George. It was now or never. As she looked into this stranger's eyes, she thought "Not this time." While there might have been a small sexual spark, she knew it was just as likely to have come from a beer on an empty stomach than a guy she had just met.

"Well, it was nice meeting you," she said. "Hope you and your friends have a good night."

"Would you care to join us? They're good people." George cocked his head slightly and gave her a grin that probably got him a lot of dates.

"Thank you, but no. I have an early flight." And that was it. No torrid one-night stand, no night on the town. And Brenda was okay with that. She went back to the hotel, ate a fabulous dinner, read for a while, then watched TV. The quiet, the latitude to watch whatever she wanted, to sit around in the over-sized T-shirt she wore as a night-gown without feeling she had to cover up (or undress) for anyone, the ability to just be on her own without any interruptions felt more decadent than anything she might have done with another person.

She channel surfed until later than she normally stayed up then switched over to ESPN to check out the score of the Indians game. Ever since the conversation with the guys from the Lightning about Charlie Bannister, she had taken to watching *Today in Sports* once in a while. She told herself she wasn't waiting to see if Bannister mentioned her again and that she just liked the show.

The *Today in Sports* theme played and Brenda felt an odd sort of lift when Charlie Bannister's round face appeared on the television screen and he started talking. "Good evening, America, I'm Charlie Bannister and you're watching *Today in Sports*," he began. "And tonight I'm here to tell you why baseball is superior to all other sports. Why? Because every baseball game is the opportunity to see something you've never seen before, and tonight was no exception. Now basketball has a triple double, and hockey has a hat trick, and horse racing has the Triple Crown, and football has, well, field goals. And touchbacks. Baseball has the triple play, which you might see once or twice a season. Baseball also has the double play. If one team turns three double plays in one game, you might call that a triple double. And if both teams turn three double plays, you might call that a sextuple double. And if you throw a triple play into the mix, well then you might just call it historic, and that is exactly what happened in today's meeting of the St. Louis Cardinals and the Pittsburgh Pirates."

"He does have a way with words," she said to the TV. Charlie didn't mention SignBrenda.com or women in baseball, but he still had some good turns of phrase. As Brenda sipped a room service glass of red wine, she reflected that her evening had still turned out okay. "Sorry, George," she murmured, "maybe next time."

The New York trip was a welcome twenty-four-hour vacation, then it was back to the usual churn of kids, work, laundry, cooking, cleaning, repeat, with occasional pauses to sleep. The Thursday night games had become the highlight of the week if only because the novelty had worn off for Jon and Adele and most of her friends, so they didn't attend games too often, and Andy didn't want to go in the first place. The long drive out to the west side and back was one of the few times Brenda could just drive along listening to some of her old favorite bands—The Smiths, The Clash—without having the boys complain.

Just after the Fourth of July weekend, David called her at work. Brenda hadn't talked to him for about a week and a half and was, frankly, not sure how often one did speak to one's agent.

"How's your arm?" David asked.

"It's fine," Brenda replied, hunching over the phone in a feeble attempt to prevent the rest of the cube farm from overhearing her side of the conversation. Ever since the ensuing publicity from the Fountain contract, people at work had been speculating as to when she would quit. They laughed when she told them that she needed the health care benefits for her family and that after taxes and the agent's cut, the endorsement contract would pay off her mortgage and that was pretty much it. Derek had confessed that there was actually a Brenda Quit Pool, in which most of the office had placed bets as to the date and time she would resign.

"Fine?" David asked. "It should be spectacular."

"Why?" Brenda noticed that the omnipresent sound of fingers hitting keyboards that normally permeated the office had stopped. She was being listened to. "Listen, I need to get back to work."

"Brenda, I want you to do something for me," David said in that voice that involuntarily made Brenda think of silk sheets, even though she didn't find him the least bit attractive. "I want you to go into your boss's office, and I want you to tell him that you quit."

"I don't think that would be wise," Brenda said, feeling painfully aware of the dozen or so co-workers who were listening to her end of the conversation. She could hear several voices in Derek's cube, which was right next to hers, whispering to each other to be quiet and that they couldn't hear. It looked like the cubicle wall was moving, as though several people were pressed up against it in order to hear better and not be seen. "Hold on a minute, please," she said.

Brenda put the receiver on her desk and quickly pushed her office chair back. The chair stopped rolling just beyond the thin metal and carpet wall separating her and Derek's cubicles. She saw Derek and her friend Rachel sitting hunched over on the desk (it was apparently Derek's shoulder that had been hitting the wall), one person in Derek's chair, and two others sitting on the floor.

"Could I just have a private conversation, please?" Brenda asked.

"Sorry, Brenda," Derek said and climbed down from the desk. "Come on, guys."

"Thank you." Brenda rolled her chair back into her cubicle and picked up the phone. "Sorry for the interruption," she said.

"I don't mind. Now, are you there?"

"Yes. Could we get to the point, please?"

"You have a tryout with the Indians next Monday."

Brenda gave a little gasp and dropped the receiver. She had fantasized once or twice about such a thing happening, less because she wanted to be the first woman to play major league baseball and more because she liked the idea of a woman—not necessarily her, just any woman—breaking a few conventions and rubbing sexism in the noses of the old boys' network. But those were just fantasies—daydreams of a woman who would be content to vote for female candidates and raise two sons who respected women. Being the groundbreaker herself wasn't an integral part of the fantasy, yet here was David putting it on a plate for her to take.

She picked up the receiver and asked: "Are you serious?"

"As serious as a heart attack in a prostitute's bed."

The allusion to infidelity and sleaze made her suddenly think of Ed and his cavalier attitude toward monogamy and commitment and made her fingers involuntarily grip a non-existent baseball.

"What time on Monday?" she asked.

•◇•

Excerpt from the transcript for *Today in Sports* with Charlie Bannister, ESPN, July 12:

> Charlie: It's hard to believe we're heading into the All-Star break—I'm still trying to figure what happened to April. At the halfway mark, in the American League West, it's all Mariners, all the time. The A's are so far back, they may have already been mathematically eliminated. It seems like the Red Sox and the Yankees have alternating custody of the AL East. Despite what everybody else says about this year being Boston's turn, believe me when I

tell you the Yanks will end up on top, but the Sox will get the first wildcard spot in the playoffs. The American League divisional races only get interesting in the AL Central, where the White Sox and the Tigers have been doing a do-si-do between first and second place like a couple of square dancers. Unless some sort of miracle happens in the AL Central basement, my mid-season prediction is the Tigers take the divisional title and the White Sox take second wildcard spot.

Chapter Seven

•◇•

THE WEEKEND BEFORE THE TRYOUT WAS ROUGH. Ed had been scheduled to pick the boys up at ten on Saturday and was late. Brenda was out in the front yard weeding the flower bed and hoping that the boys wouldn't wander from the back yard to the front while she was muttering under her breath about Ed. Their bungalow didn't have much of a yard in terms of space—the front was maybe forty by forty—but Brenda considered it her personal mission to make sure as much of it as possible was covered in flowers. Back before Ed moved out, she had had a small vegetable patch in the back and occasionally slipped in a few tomato and squash plants here and there in the front. She loved feeding her children vegetables she had grown. When the boys were smaller, they had enjoyed helping in the garden, getting just as big a kick out of growing and eating their own food as Brenda did. Now, between working and solo parenting, even this little pleasure had fallen by the wayside.

There wasn't any noise coming from the back yard, but Brenda left the boys alone. Andy and Jon hadn't said anything all morning. They hadn't fought or argued either, just drifted from the living room to the front porch to the backyard, as though they needed to be in the right place at the right time in order to make their father appear.

The boys were still in the backyard when Ed pulled into the driveway. Brenda was on her hands and knees, pulling weeds with her back to the street, but she heard Ed's car. It was a sporty little retro number made to resemble one of the muscle cars of the 1950s. When their old Civic died a few years back with over 250,000 miles on it, Ed had said he thought he deserved to drive a decent car for once in his life. They had decided on another Civic, but then Ed changed his mind. It was shortly after he had turned forty, and Brenda always attributed the car to a midlife crisis. It was a black coupe with a back seat barely large enough to accommodate two small children, much less two growing boys, groceries, or anything a father might need. It was about five grand more than they had decided to spend, but that hadn't seemed to matter, either then or now. She remembered the first time he pulled that car into the drive. He'd gotten out with a wide grin and said, "Check it out." The boys had originally gone crazy for the car. Although she'd been concerned about the cost, she hadn't really thought about it until Ed said he couldn't take the boys to baseball practice or to friends' houses or doctor's appointments or anywhere else because the car was too small. Brenda always marked the purchase of Ed's car as their marriage's point of no return—the moment when he seemingly decided that it'd be a lot more fun to be single again than to live with the family he had started.

"Just like Ed to start something and not finish it," Brenda muttered every time she saw the half-tiled bathroom upstairs, the shoddily repaired garage door, and every other partially completed project around the house. When she heard Ed's car purr into the driveway, she felt her hand grip the trowel a little harder.

She stood up and faced Ed's car. Its metallic paint job reflected the mid-July sun back into her eyes. Ed unfolded his tall frame from the stupidly small car and stood looking at her, keeping the vehicle between them.

"Hi, Brenda," he said cheerily, as though there weren't thirty feet, fifteen years of marriage, and ten months of separation between them.

"You're awfully late."

"I had some errands to run and lost track of time." He still sounded too happy, his voice trailing up and down like the bouncing ball in an old sing-along cartoon. It was the same lilting cadence that he had always greeted her with after a night of particularly vigorous love making.

"You didn't even call the boys to tell them you'd be late."

Ed rested his arms on the roof of the car. "They're boys. They don't care."

"They're your sons, and they do care." Brenda was now squeezing the trowel so tightly that she felt as though she could crush the solid wood handle and turn it to sawdust.

A slight motion out of the corner of her right eye caught her attention, and she turned to see Andy and Jon standing by the chain-link gate that separated the fenced-in backyard from the driveway and the front yard. The gate was open but they didn't cross its invisible line, just stood standing in the backyard, a Frisbee in Andy's hand and wary looks on both their faces.

"Hey guys," she called. "Your dad's here." She tried to make her voice sound as light and cheery as Ed's, but she was too nervous, tired, frustrated, and disappointed to sound like anything but a frazzled single mom who hadn't had sex in over a year.

"Sorry I'm a little late," Ed said. "What do you two feel like doing today?"

Andy shrugged his shoulders, while Jon simply said, "I don't know."

"Well, we'll think of something. Wanna go play baseball in the park?"

"I'm sick of baseball," Andy said. Brenda could see in his face that he'd made an on-the-spot decision. "I don't want to go today."

"I want to go," Jon said. "Andy, we have to go."

"Come on, Andy," Ed said, walking over to the gate. "Let's go play ball."

"Yeah, let's go. I want to play baseball," Jon said.

"Well, I don't, and I'm not going today."

"Mom, tell Andy he has to go."

"We don't have to play baseball. We'll do something else, right?" Ed glanced over at Brenda for backup, the way they had sometimes done when the boys were younger and being obstinate.

"This is between you and the boys." As much as she looked forward to having a day to herself every other Saturday, there was no way she was going to force one of the boys to spend time with Ed if he didn't want to. Brenda tried to convince herself that she was backing Andy's decision because she wanted to support him, not because she wanted to hurt Ed.

"That's not fair!" Jon snapped. "It's our day with Dad. Andy has to go. Mom!" He practically screamed the last word, as though it were a command to Brenda to fix everything that was wrong. Brenda knew she couldn't fix a damn thing, that day or any day.

"Jon, even if Andy doesn't go, you can still spend the day with your father."

"If Andy doesn't go, I'm not going."

"Wait a minute . . ." Ed said. "Brenda!" He looked at her as though it was her fault that the boys didn't want to spend the day with him.

"Jon, if you want to go, then you should go. Andy doesn't want to go. It's okay that you want different things today."

Andy looked down at his younger brother with the closest thing to a smile she had seen on his face in weeks and mumbled something to his brother that Brenda couldn't hear. Jon nodded and went to get his baseball glove, bat, and ball. And that was it. Ed and Jon went off for the day, leaving Andy and Brenda standing in the front yard. The entire time Ed was at the house, Brenda could feel every nerve standing on end. It was all she could do to not launch the trowel into the unblemished side of his car.

After Ed and Jon and pulled out of the driveway, Andy muttered, "He didn't even call to say he'd be late."

"He probably just lost track of time," Brenda said. She had vowed to herself long ago not to be one of those women who badmouthed their exes to their children, no matter how difficult this was.

Andy turned to face her. "Are you blind? He does this all the time. I know three different kids whose parents are divorced and they spend the entire weekend at their dads' houses. They have their own rooms and stuff there and everything. Dad never does that. He doesn't even have a room for us. We've never slept over. He doesn't want us there."

"I'm sorry, sweetie." She reached out to touch his shoulder, but he pulled away.

"I'm going to go ride my bike," he said and headed for the back yard.

Brenda resisted the urge to follow him and waited until he re-emerged in the front yard with his mountain bike before asking what time he'd be home. She was happy he had at least thought to grab his bike helmet. Somehow that seemed like a small parenting victory.

"I don't know," he muttered, kicking at one of the pedals and watching it spin.

"Do you want any lunch before you leave?"

"No. Can I go now?"

"I have to go to the grocery store today, but that's it. If you come home when I'm out, I'll leave the extra key under the big rock by the back door. If you go to a friend's house, just give me a call so I know where you are."

"Okaaay . . ." he sighed without looking at her. "Can I go now?"

"Yes. Please be home or call by four, okay?" she said to his back as he headed down the driveway.

She thought she heard him said something like "All right" in response. She figured this was about the most she was going to get from him. It was actually the longest conversation they had had since the first video aired on Charlie Bannister's show.

This thought brought with it a reminder that she had a tryout with the Cleveland Indians in less than forty-eight hours. She had been so consumed with the boys and Ed that she hadn't even thought about it. She wondered if she should spend the entire day gardening or if it might make her arm sore.

David had said just to do whatever she normally did but not to do anything too strenuous. Sometimes it seemed like everything was strenuous. Being both father and mother to the boys and lugging around groceries and piles of laundry and cleaning gutters and fixing faucets and taking out garbage and mowing the lawn and doing all the other piles of work that she and Ed had formerly split seemed strenuous, not so much on her body as on her spirit. It seemed like the only time she found time to herself was on Thursday nights. Even more than the peace and quiet of the drive out, she liked being on the pitcher's mound, where she was in charge of the clock and could be completely alone with her thoughts. The mound meant solitude.

Brenda spent a couple hours doing yard work, washing the kitchen floor, cleaning the bathrooms, running a few loads of laundry, and generally trying to catch up on all the tasks that seemed to elude her during the week. Adele and David had both suggested she use some of the money from the endorsement contract to hire a cleaning service and a landscaper to take care of these things, but that seemed like a waste. There was no guarantee that she'd get any other endorsements or that she would get a contract.

Around two o'clock, she was having Nervous Breakdown Number 142 about the impending tryout when the phone rang. It was the manager of the CVS drugstore at the corner of Mayfield and Richmond Roads saying that her son had been caught shoplifting baseball cards.

In a fog of shock and fear, she drove the mile and a half to the drugstore, sat with the manager, an undercover security guard, and Andy in a small office at the back of the store while they showed her video of Andy snaking along the candy aisle and furtively shoving a few packs of baseball cards into the pocket of his cargo shorts.

Andy didn't say a word in the store—he didn't protest his innocence, didn't claim that he was planning to pay for the baseball cards, didn't apologize, in fact, didn't show any emotion at all. The store manager was kind enough not to file charges with the police. Andy was released into his mother's custody with a lifetime ban on entering that particular drugstore. Brenda thanked the manager profusely, managed to get a robotic "thank you" out of Andy, and got out of the store as fast as possible.

Andy didn't say anything in the parking lot, just put his bike in the back of the minivan when Brenda told him to and sullenly climbed into the passenger seat.

Brenda tried to think what Andy Griffith might do in a situation like this. She remembered watching *The Andy Griffith Show* as a child and thinking that he was the best father she had ever seen, far kinder and more understanding than her first-generation Slovak father, who rarely spoke and died before she was an adult. Andy Griffith would probably have taken Opie out for ice cream and had a long talk about right and wrong and all would have been well. But Mayberry was a long way away from South Euclid, Ohio. In the end, she brought Andy home and tried to talk to him about why he had stolen the baseball cards.

Andy sat on the sofa, sinking in among the pillows. His dark blond hair was almost the same hue as the sage green of the sofa, and there was something about this pairing of colors and the distractedly melancholy way Andy looked half at her and half at the ceiling that reminded Brenda of an Edward Hopper painting. She sat down on the other end of the sofa and didn't say anything for a moment, wondering if perhaps Andy would offer some explanation. Her silence clearly got to him, because he blurted out, "Look, I know you're not supposed to steal. I just wanted to see if I could do it. I won't do it again."

"Well, I'm glad to hear you won't do it again, but that doesn't explain why you did it this time."

"I told you, I just wanted to see if I could do it."

Brenda took a deep breath, trying to stay centered and not lose her temper. "And now you know—you're not a thief."

Andy rolled his eyes. "No, I'm not a thief. Can I go now?"

"Not yet. I'm willing to look at this as a one-time mistake, but it doesn't excuse what you did. And we still haven't talked about your punishment for shoplifting." It took everything she had to speak the word "shoplifting." It sounded too much like what one would charge a juvenile delinquent with—not her son.

"I have my punishment. I can't go back to the CVS," Andy said indignantly, as though that was enough.

"That's the store's punishment," Brenda said. "This is mine." Truly, she had no idea what type of punishment could possibly convey to Andy how severe this was. She didn't believe in corporal punishment and had never spanked the boys. But shoplifting . . . "Give me your mp3 player," Brenda said.

"What? No!" Andy said. "No way."

"Way. Hand it over. One week."

Andy glared at her outstretched hand. "Mom, this isn't fair," he said.

"What isn't fair? That I'm taking away the most precious item in your life as punishment for stealing? I think that's perfectly fair."

Andy reached into his pocket and pulled out the mp3 player. The ear buds were, as always, around his neck. He took them off and grudgingly placed the mp3 player into Brenda's hand.

"I've told you not to listen to music while you're riding your bicycle," she said. "It's incredibly dangerous."

"One week starting now?"

"Yes, now." She glanced at the clock on the DVD player. "You can have it back at 3:34 p.m. next Saturday."

Andy slinked off to his room, still muttering that this whole thing was totally unfair. Brenda tried to convince herself that it was just a one-time mistake, that he was angry and confused and acting out. She didn't know if it was easier to worry about Andy and not think about the tryout or to think about the tryout and not worry about Andy. She ended up doing both.

Jon came home from his day with Ed tired and cranky but full of the news that his father had taken him to see the Lake County Captains, a minor league team that played a short drive away. Despite having said that he was sick of baseball, Andy was furious that he had missed the game, a fact that Jon lorded over him for the rest of the weekend.

Keeping with the old adage of not saying anything if you can't say anything nice, Brenda said "Hello" to Ed when he brought Jon home and "Good-bye" when he left and that was about it. She didn't have the energy to tell Ed about the shoplifting. It happened, Andy had his punishment, time to move on.

She also didn't tell Andy and Jon about the tryout. On Monday morning, she sent them off to camp and acted as though it was any other day. She didn't have any personal days left at work and wasn't about to tell her boss that she needed the day off in order to try out with the Cleveland Indians, so she called in sick. Then she was so nervous that she threw up in the downstairs bathroom, so it wasn't as though she had been completely dishonest about being sick

She met David at the Stratagem offices at ten, and he drove them to Progressive Field. Brenda kept wanting to call it by its former name, Jacob's Field. "New sponsor, new name," she reminded herself, and wondered if the front office was progressive enough to sign her. Driving south on East Ninth Street, Brenda watched the white steel-beamed lights of the ballpark grow larger as they drew closer. Even though she had grown up going to the cavernous old Cleveland

Stadium, it was hard to feel nostalgic for that behemoth when the graceful lines of the new ballpark were so visually appealing. It felt like an old-time ballpark, although Brenda was sure that the stadium lights' resemblance to huge white toothbrushes standing at attention around the perimeter of the ballpark was a case of unintended whimsy. Even from a block away, she could see the huge banners featuring black and white photographs of the players displayed along the top edge of the stadium.

David caught her staring. "In a few weeks, there's going to be a banner up there with your picture on it."

"We'll see," she replied.

"Brenda, they wouldn't be giving you a tryout if they weren't ready to sign you."

"Do you think so?" She was genuinely surprised. A large part of her—the cynical, jaded part—figured this tryout was just to satiate the public. Then the Indians could say: "See? We gave her a tryout and she wasn't good enough. Now take down that stupid website."

"You do know that no woman has ever played in the majors or even for an affiliated minor league team."

"Of course," she replied, trying to sound as though this was something she had known for a long time instead of something she had only researched online the day before.

"They wouldn't jump through the huge number of hoops they're being forced through if they didn't want you." Gary's voice moved out of its familiar seductive purr into a tone that seemed almost businesslike. "I'll be honest—I'm fairly certain their motivation is almost entirely financial. Yes, they want to win ballgames, but they also need to sell tickets. Ford Frick banned women from baseball in 1952 because he didn't want teams signing women as a publicity stunt. You can see all the hype around you already, and you haven't even had a tryout. If they sign you—and unless you completely choke, I'm pretty sure they will or they wouldn't be wading through all the crap Major League Baseball is throwing at them—I have no idea if they'll ever put you in a major league game. I'm fairly confident we'll get you into a few minor league games, then you'll either sink or swim.

Either way, you'll get a contract and endorsements and they'll sell a boatload of tickets and merchandise, and that's their bottom line."

"Tell me again why I'm doing this?"

Gary smoothly turned his BMW onto Carnegie Avenue and made a quick right into a curved driveway that led to a fenced-in parking lot. "Brenda," he murmured gently. "You're doing this to make a buck, just like everybody else in the world."

In all the times Brenda had driven past the field, she hadn't really noticed this little parking lot perched almost directly on the corner but hidden from the street by trees and landscaping. David told her it was the players' lot and to get used to parking there. When he said this, her stomach jumped. The beams of the stadium were almost directly overhead, and Brenda found herself momentarily woozy when she stopped and craned her neck to look all the way to the top.

"Quit gawking. You're on," David murmured and motioned to the steel door where a security guard was waiting. Standing next to the guard was a trim, athletic-looking woman perhaps a few years younger than Brenda who appeared as though she could toss back a few drinks with the guys, bench press her own body weight, and still find the energy to steal your boyfriend.

She smiled at them as they crossed the parking lot to her. "Hi, I'm Sheri Donohue, Director of Baseball Administration for the Indians," she said when they reached her, giving Brenda a firm handshake. "I'm really pleased to meet you."

Brenda wasn't sure what the job description for Director of Baseball Administration entailed, but having memorized the names of the Indians' front office from the team website, she knew that Donohue was the highest-ranking female in the front office. It figured that they'd send the only woman out to meet her.

David and Brenda introduced themselves and allowed Sheri to lead them down a narrow, cinder-block stairway and into a wide, well-lit tunnel in the bowels of the building. The pipes and ducts that fed the ballpark were visible high above them. The cavernous hallway was wide enough to accommodate eight or ten people walking in a row. Brenda carried her small duffel bag with a pair of baseball pants (a splurge that she found on sale at the sporting goods store), a

T-shirt, cleats, and her glove. She had gone back and forth that morning about what to wear. David had told her to look professional and
respectable, so she wore the navy pantsuit that she had worn to job
interviews the previous fall. It seemed neutral.

"We're all very excited to have you try out," Sheri said as she
led Brenda and David down the tunnel. Brenda murmured a polite
"thank you" and let David make his smooth brand of small talk as they
walked. "We're going to do quick introductions, then have you throw.
After that, we'll go upstairs for some lunch, and you can talk more
at length with some of the front office brass," Sheri said. "You can
use the visiting manager's locker room to change. With the All-Star
break, it's pretty quiet around here right now."

"Great," Brenda said. "Thank you." The reality of what she was
about to do was growing exponentially. She was actually walking
through Progressive Field about to have a tryout with the Cleveland
Indians. She had always thought it was lack of strength or training or
experience that kept women out of the major leagues—not an out-
and-out ban. This changed things. It was one thing to be kept out of
the club because you weren't good enough. It was entirely another
thing to be forbidden even to try simply because you were female.
This thought helped to counter the nervous energy that was making
her limbs tremble.

As they walked, she saw a couple of forklifts loaded with palettes
of stadium food parked near a set of double doors marked "Media
Room." A bit farther on, they stopped in front of a set of double
doors marked "Visitors' Clubhouse." Brenda couldn't help but notice
the large white sign on the deep blue door stating that only male family members and credentialed journalists were permitted.

Sheri didn't mention anything about the sign. She just passed her
keycard in front of the sensor mounted to the left of the door and
then unlocked it. Sheri opened one of the double doors and led them
into a wide hallway that ended in a concrete stairway. It was clean
but utilitarian, painted white with a lone beige stripe along the top
portion of the wall standing in for design. Brenda figured it probably
didn't do much for the visiting team's psyche to have such a boring
color scheme.

Sherri showed Brenda to a door immediately to their right. A small outer office held a sofa, desk, and chair. A secondary room held a sink, toilet, shower, and a cubbyhole-like locker with a couple shelves, a rod with a few empty hangers, and a small cupboard at the top. Brenda had to admit that it was kind of cozy. Sheri made sure she was settled and then left her alone. David waited in the hallway, no doubt charming Shari to see if she would give any information regarding the front office's preliminary thoughts.

Brenda stood in the locker room, just breathing, trying to steady her nerves. She realized she was perhaps the first female ever to remove her clothes in that room (unless some visiting manager had ever hired a stripper or snuck in a groupie). Brenda tried not to waste time, but quickly changed her clothes and made a last emergency pee break. As she washed her hands, she got a good look at herself in the mirror above the sink.

While the new black baseball pants were better than the old sweatpants she had been wearing, she didn't cut a very imposing fig-ure. She had actually lost a few pounds that summer—probably due to her inability to eat much of anything on game days—but she was still just a housewife with a size six top, a size twelve bottom, and a lousy attitude.

"This is it," she murmured to her reflection. She thought that the moment should give her a lift of some sort, some kind of Rocky-like momentum that would carry her out to the field, but all she got was the same reflection she saw every day. There was nothing to do but go outside.

Sheri led her and David down two short flights of stairs. Brenda wondered how many stars, everyday players, and cups of coffee had clomped down the same steps. "We'll go out through the visitors' dugout," Shari said as they entered a dark, somewhat dank concrete room that clearly functioned only as an unimportant place between two important places. Brenda saw the door to a bathroom off to the left. In front of her were three concrete steps, painted dark green. Sheri led the way up the steps. Brenda hesitated, so David followed.

"Let's not keep them waiting, Brenda," he said over his shoulder.

She climbed the steps, took a sharp left at the top, and found herself in the visitors' dugout. It looked smaller and shorter than it did on television. There was the long bench and small cubbyholes set into the wall and a rack for bats. She turned to the right and saw the field and her heart skipped about six beats.

This was the lift she had been seeking. She couldn't help it. After years of seeing Progressive Field—when it was under construction, watching the occasional ballgame on TV with Ed, and going there with the boys—she had wondered what it would be like to walk on the field. She had a flash of memory back to when she had helped paint sets for a play when she was in college. During a rehearsal, the set designer had asked her to walk out on stage to look at a set piece. The idea of walking on someone else's stage seemed intrusive, like walking into the bathroom when someone is in the shower. She thought she'd have the same feeling when she walked out onto the red dirt of the infield and then onto the grass, but she didn't. It felt natural, as though the baseball field had been waiting for her to arrive.

Sheri introduced her to the big brass. Mark Munson, the manager, was familiar. He had played for the Indians when Brenda was in college—he was probably only a few years older than she was. Munson had always reminded Brenda of a huge walking rectangle— big head, big shoulders, no discernible waist, and thick legs. He had been a first baseman and always provided a sizable target for the rest of the infield.

"Good to meet you," he said as they shook hands. He seemed as straightforward and decent in person as he did in interviews.

The General Manager, Louis Adams, was familiar from the news. He was only a few inches taller than Brenda, and his barrel chest and broad shoulders actually made him seem smaller rather than bigger. He had an impish, mischievous quality that wasn't apparent in photos or on television. When he shook Brenda's hand, she felt like the most popular boy in fifth grade had just convinced her to play a prank on the teacher.

Jerry Chimelewski, the Director of Player Development, gave her an enthusiastic handshake, as though he was testing her grip. "It's great to meet you," he said. "I'm eager to see what you've got."

Brenda almost said, "Me too," but stopped herself. "Glad to be here," she murmured. It was starting to feel like a mash-up of a job interview and a cocktail party. She was introduced to Earl Donald, the pitching coach, and Roy Bridges, the bullpen catcher, who would be catching for her. Once they had made a few minutes of small talk, primarily around Brenda's arm, how she was feeling, and whether she needed to stretch, there was nothing to do but get started.

Walking out to the pitcher's mound was the longest sixty feet, six inches she had ever trod. She knew David was standing somewhere along the baseline with the front office brass, schmoozing them into a signatory mood, but she didn't look at them. She tried not to look at the overwhelming size of the stadium, at forty-two thousand empty seats that seemed to be staring back at her in anticipation. It occurred to her that she really had to do this, that she really had to throw good, hard pitches on demand. Playing in the Roy Hobbs league was fun, but it never felt serious. Those games didn't *matter*. Yes, it was fun if they won, but all they got were bragging rights over the other team. No one else cared if the Lightning won or lost. This . . . this was another planet.

For a moment, the thought of how much depended on this moment was overwhelming.

"Breathe . . . breathe . . ." she murmured to herself, trying to counter the pounding in her heart and the sudden feeling of numbness in her limbs. She allowed herself one quick glance at David and the front office brass. They were still chatting quietly, but all eyes were on her. What did they want from her? Was she a ballplayer or a way to sell tickets?

"I'm not a token," she mumbled to herself as she kicked at the pitching rubber. "I'm not their publicity stunt."

She stood on the mound and looked over her left shoulder to home plate. She knew it was Roy behind the plate holding her target, but she didn't look at him. And she didn't look at David or the front office brass, or Sheri—the token front office female. She just looked at the target, waiting for Ed's face to appear in its pocket, just like it always did. It occurred to her that this was the only time she could ever count on Ed.

•◊•

Excerpt from the transcript for *Today in Sports* with Charlie Bannister, ESPN, July 16:

> Charlie: There's nothing like the other side of the All-Star break to make teams start taking things seriously. In the AL Central, Detroit is still holding on to first place, but Chicago is knocking on the door. The Tigers were sitting pretty at the top of the division until they dropped two of three to the White Sox before the break, and now the White Sox are only a game and a half behind. At the other end of the division, the Royals continue their never-ending pursuit of mediocrity, losing two of three to the Orioles and then losing two of three to the Mariners. The only thing between them and last place is Cleveland.

Chapter Eight

•◊•

ONCE SHE SAW ED'S FACE IN THE CATCHER'S MITT AND THE TUNNEL OF GOLDEN LINES THAT LED FROM HER HAND TO THE MITT, ALL BRENDA HAD TO DO WAS FOCUS ON THROWING THE BALL AS HARD AND TRUE AS SHE COULD. There was no batter and no umpire, nothing to make her stop, nothing to pause the rhythm of focus, wind-up, throw, watch, catch, repeat. She had lost count of how many pitches she had thrown when she heard Munson's voice as though coming from off in the distance, telling her that was great, they had seen enough.

She stopped, then stood on the mound for a moment, wondering what she ought to do next. She felt like she had just woken up from a deep sleep in the middle of a crowded airplane. David called her over to the baseline. She saw David look to the coach and manager on his right, who were exchanging a few quiet words, and to the front office brass on his left, who were having a slightly more animated conversation, and then back to her. The look on his face brought the phrase "shit-eating grin" to mind, and she knew they liked what they had seen.

Her hand was trembling and her arm felt weightless as she again shook hands with the front office guys and then with her new manager and coach. It seemed that there had to be a catch, a punchline somewhere, but there wasn't. David and the team from Stratagem needed to iron out the details, but the major hurdle had been passed. Somehow, improbably, she was a professional baseball player.

It wasn't until after she had left the ballpark, left David, and started on her way home that the magnitude of what had just happened really hit her. She was driving along the Shoreway, with Lake Erie in all its summer glory on her left, when her heart began to pound all over again. Even though she had tried to be mindful and remember every moment, it was already blurring in her memory—who said what to her, what pitch she had thrown first. She pulled off the Shoreway and onto the marginal road. Gordon Park was just coming up on the right. It was an older city park that was now too close to a "bad" neighborhood to be popular. Nonetheless, Brenda pulled into the parking lot and got out of the car. There was a short grassy incline that led to a small playground, softball and baseball diamonds, and an open flag football/soccer field. She started to walk toward the grass then sprinted, just because she could. Out of breath, she reached her arms up and out and spun around a few times, looking at the perfect blue sky above. And then she screamed "Yeeeeeesss!" as loudly as she could.

Finally, whatever internal fire inside that made her want to shout and spin and burst seemed to ease. She slowed down, stopped screaming, and just stood there in the middle of the park, trying to catch her breath.

"What the hell have I gotten myself into?" she said.

•◇•

Telling the boys that their mother had signed a professional baseball contract was more difficult than she might have imagined. Although she was generally a rip-off-the-Band-Aid-fast kind of person, she felt it might be better to ease into this conversation. She had already invited Adele over for dinner that night as a thank-you for taking care of the boys every Thursday evening and waited until all four of them were seated and eating before she casually said, "I got a new job today."

"You did?" Jon asked.

"I didn't even know you were looking," Adele said.

"Did you get fired from your old job?" Andy asked.

"No, I didn't get fired," she replied. "I just found a much better job—one that pays tons more than what I'm making now." David had told her that the Indians would probably offer her a low salary (although low in his mind was exorbitant in hers), with hefty performance incentives. "You're an inexpensive risk," he said, as if Brenda needed a reminder that most people expected her to crash and burn.

"How much more?" Andy asked.

"About fifteen times what I'm making now."

Adele gasped and dropped her fork.

"Where are you going to work?" Andy asked. It was clear he knew something big was going on. It was equally clear from Jon's expression that he had no clue how much she earned.

Brenda took a deep breath. This was as nerve-wracking as the tryout. "I'm going to play baseball."

Jon jumped up and started screaming "Oh my gosh! That is so cool!" over and over.

"I knew it. I knew it!" Adele exclaimed, standing up and coming over to Brenda's side of the table. "That's wonderful." Brenda found herself in a group hug with Adele and Jon, who was still trying to jump up and down. Andy sat at his place.

"You're kidding, right?" he said.

"No, I'm not kidding. I had the tryout today. They signed me to a one-year contract. I'm going to start out in the minor leagues. I need to strengthen my arm and learn the ropes."

"And then what?" Andy asked.

"It depends on how I do."

"You will do beautifully," Adele said.

"Then are you going to play for the Indians?" Jon asked. He was nearly leaping out of his skin with excitement.

"I don't know."

"You can't. It's illegal," Andy said. "Women don't play professional baseball."

Adele gave him The Look, which was one step above The Finger Wag. "Your mother does."

"Can I be excused, please?" Andy asked. He stood up, pushing his chair so hard that it fell over.

"Yes. Just pick up your chair, please, and you can be excused," Brenda replied. Without a word, Andy righted the chair and left the room. Jon was still jumping up and down and pumping his fists, yelling, "That is so cool!" Adele gave her a questioning look but Brenda only shrugged. She was in no mood to try and deal with Andy's anger at that moment. With that, Adele turned and started jumping up and down with Jon. Brenda began clearing the table. She told herself she'd talk to Andy later, after he had cooled off.

Her contract was contingent upon the results of a physical, which was scheduled for Wednesday. A major press conference was scheduled for Friday, and she was due to report to the Class A Lake County Captains on Saturday. Everything had seemed theoretical before, but now she had to find someone to take care of the boys during road trips and answer questions from anyone who cared to ask, and actually go out and play baseball. And before she could do any of that, she had to quit her job.

Brenda considered calling in sick again or quitting over the phone or just not showing up and mailing in a resignation letter, but she didn't want to take the coward's way out. She resolved to go into work, speak with Tony, the president of the company, and highly scented Frank, the vice president, first thing in the morning. She'd just tell them she was quitting and taking another job. That was all she owed them—they'd find out the truth soon enough anyway.

She tried to slip into work early the next day, but she had barely turned on her computer when Derek popped into her cubicle and asked her how she was feeling.

"Great," Brenda replied without looking up. She was sitting at her desk, debating whether it was worth it to bring home a cheap silver Christmas ornament that Rachel two cubes over had hung in her cubicle last December. Brenda had inadvertently mentioned that it would be the first Christmas without Ed in the house, and Rachel had left the ornament with a little note reading, "This is a new and improved Christmas ornament to decorate your new and improved life." The note had been lost in the black hole that seemed to exist in the back corner of the cubicle where the power cords lurked, but the Christmas ornament remained. It was amazing how cluttered her cube had become in less than a year of working there.

"So you're feeling better?" Derek asked.

"What? Oh, yes, yes, I am," Brenda said.

"Oh, I was just wondering . . ." He let his voice trail off provocatively.

Brenda turned to face him. "What's up?"

"Do you ever read MajorLeagueRumors.com?

"No."

"Oh, well you should," and here Derek could no longer mask a smile. "So when are you quitting?"

"What?" She spun around and quickly opened her web browser. "What's the name of the site again?"

"MajorLeagueRumors.com," Derek said calmly. "Do a team search if it's not on the front page anymore." It was. Just a small item in a list of related baseball rumors: "The Cleveland Indians have reportedly offered a minor league contract to unsigned amateur pitcher Brenda Haversham, tweets Charlie Bannister of ESPN."

Brenda was incredulous. "How the hell did he find that out?" she said.

"So it's true? Oh my God!" Derek lowered his voice, "That's amazing."

Brenda glanced at her watch. It was ten after nine. Tony and Frank would both be in their offices by 9:30. She could talk to them, pack up her things, say her good-byes, and be out of there in an hour if she played her cards right. Even sooner if she didn't have to go around and give the whole spiel twenty different times to twenty different people. And why do that when she had Paul Revere crouched down in her cubicle? "Yes, it's true, but please don't tell anyone until I talk to Tony and Frank. I have to give them my notice."

"Wow, congratulations. Dreams really do come true," Derek said.

"I guess so, but I never really dreamt of playing professional baseball before this summer."

"Never?"

For a second, Brenda had an image of her father standing in front of her, holding a beat-up catcher's mitt, an ancient catcher's mask on the top of his head. "If you can just make the four-seam fastball fly as it wants to fly, you could be . . . anything," he'd said to her.

Brenda had been about ten at the time and answered, "Anything? Even a baseball player?"

"Yes, a baseball player," her father had replied. "If you want. Or an artist or an engineer or a circus clown or something else. But first you must loosen your grip. If you hold on too hard, it won't do what you want it to do. Gentle."

Brenda blinked and suddenly remembered that Derek was standing in her cubicle. "Well, yeah there was a brief time when I was a kid that I thought I wanted to be the first woman in the major leagues. But that only lasted about ten minutes."

"You're going to do it. I know you are," Derek said. His words were echoed by all of her co-workers as she gave her notice and said her good-byes. Former co-workers, she had to remind herself. The encouragement was humbling. How strange to have so many people rooting for her. Leave for any other new job and you'll get a slew of clichéd wishes for good luck. But play baseball, and it's as though you've taken a job walking on water. It was all she could do to say "thank you" to people, trade phone numbers, and get out of the building.

When she got home, Brenda carried the copy-paper box that contained all of the photos, drawings, knick-knacks, coffee mugs, and other detritus of her short-lived stint at the insurance company downstairs to the rec room. Most of it was office-related, so it seemed better suited down there, near the computer, than in her bedroom. And she wanted to investigate Twitter. While the page was loading, she called Robin.

"Hi, can you talk?" she asked.

"I have to leave for a client meeting in about twenty minutes, but I always have time for you," Robin replied.

"New client? Old client?"

"Newish—one of the big law firms downtown. They want to do a one-day art therapy workshop to help their new associates find meaningful, productive ways to deal with the demands of the job."

"They want them to replace booze with art?"

"Something like that. Anyhow, what's up?"

"Um, are you on Twitter?"

"Yeah, although I don't tweet too often."

"Well, you're one up on me."

"A Luddite is one up on you."

"I'm not a Luddite," Brenda protested.

"You refuse to even text."

"It's a phone. I use it to call people."

"Someday we'll bring you over to the dark side. So what's up?"

Brenda told her about the Charlie Bannister tweet and resulting rumor. "Can I send him a message about this?"

"Yeah, Twitter has a direct message function, but you can only message someone who's following you. But how the hell did he find out about your tryout and the contract? There weren't any media there, were there?"

"No, just people from the Indians."

"What about your agent? He sounds like the kind of guy to leak information. You know, to create a buzz?"

Brenda paused. She hadn't thought about David. He was her agent, so presumably he was on her side. But he was also in the business of selling. "You may be right. I'll talk to him, but I'm still going to email Charlie Bannister." Somehow she had the feeling that Charlie Bannister would give her a straight answer. She hung up with Robin and set up a Twitter account (@BrendaHav). The first person she followed was Charlie Bannister (@CABannister). Out of curiosity, she Googled her name and was surprised to see a ton of hits, mainly linking to baseball blogs and other sports sites. Some referenced the YouTube videos, while most merely quoted MajorLeagueRumors. Brenda chose one of the links at random, which took her to an Indians fan blog called Wahoo Warriors. Someone calling himself "Jason" had written a long diatribe on why no team should offer a contract to a woman. It relied on the most simplistic of logic, saying: "It's traditional not to have female ballplayers, and baseball is all about tradition." There were fifteen comments—twelve supporting the author and three saying, "Why not give her a chance?"

Even though the original post was poorly written, seeing herself being written about by random strangers made her stomach lurch. She went back to Twitter and was surprised to see a notification that @CABannister was now following her. She sent him a direct message. It took a few tries, because she kept using too many characters. Instead of being polite, she was forced to be blunt: "Not to be rude, but who told you I had a contract with the Indians?"

His reply was quick and to the point: "Being direct is never rude. Was the info wrong? If so, I'll redact."

"Way to throw the ball back in my court, Charlie," Brenda muttered. She wasn't sure how to respond. It was weird to be sitting there in her basement, sending messages to a guy she had seen on television dozens of times. Somehow that made him seem like less of a stranger. She replied: "Thanks, but still wondering about your source."

She received an immediate reply back: "Don't you know a journalist never reveals his sources?" Followed by: "What would have happened if Bernstein & Woodward had revealed their sources?"

Brenda couldn't help but smile a bit at that. "We wouldn't have had to wait thirty years to find out who Deep Throat was," she wrote back.

"Your agent leaked it. They do stuff like that all the time. Comes w/ the territory," Charlie wrote back.

"Thank you," she wrote and logged off.

•◊•

Excerpt from the transcript for Today in Sports with Charlie Bannister, ESPN, July 17:

> Charlie: Ladies and gentlemen of the viewing audience, history was made this week. Real life textbook history, not just some funky statistical anomaly. For the first time ever, a major league baseball team has signed a contract with a female player. For those of you who've spent the last few

days under a rock and don't know—the Cleveland Indians held a secret tryout with amateur pitching phenom Brenda Haversham during the All-Star break. She has been signed to a one-year contract and is scheduled to join the Class A Lake County Captains this weekend. A handful of women—and I'm talking a baby-sized hand, here—a *handful* of women have played at the minor league level for unaffiliated minor league teams. This is the first time a major league team has signed a woman. I don't know about you, but I think that's pretty cool.

Chapter Nine

•◊•

"ARE THEY GOING TO GIVE YOU A SHOT AT YOUR PHYSICAL?" JON ASKED.

"I don't think so, no," Brenda replied as she got two cereal bowls out of the cupboard.

"How come you have to get a physical in the first place?"

"They want to make sure Mom's not going to fall apart or tear a ligament or something," Andy said. Brenda heard the silent "idiot" at the end of this statement, but didn't say anything. It was so rare for Andy to give anything more than a one-word response that she was just happy to have him join the conversation.

"What's a ligament?" Jon asked.

"They're like rubber bands that hold your bones together. And sometimes if you move the wrong way they SNAP!" Andy's delivery had the desired effect; Jon was startled enough to spill the milk he was pouring on his cereal all over the table. Brenda grabbed a dishrag.

"Thank you for that enlightening explanation, Andy," Brenda said as she wiped up the milk. "Now both of you need to eat and get out of here or you'll be late."

Once lunches were made and the boys were on their way to camp, Brenda drove to the ballpark for what she was told would be an extensive physical exam. She pulled up to the gate of the Players' Lot and rolled down the window to speak to the security guard at the gate.

Brenda took a breath. "My name is Brenda Haversham. I'm here for my physical with Dr. Parker."

"*You're* Brenda Haversham?" the guard said. "Well, I'll be. You know, I saw that video of you on Charlie Bannister's show but it was hard to see your face in that. Welcome to the Cleveland Indians."

"Thank you," Brenda said, awkwardly reaching through the car window to shake his outstretched hand. "What is your name?"

"My name is James," he said. "They told me to be on the lookout for you." He was surprisingly soft-spoken, considering he was built like one of those burly, homerun-machine hitters that everybody loves. He pointed to the same door she had used when she came for the tryout. "Go through the main door and down the stairs. Mr. Chimelewski is waiting for you."

Brenda thanked him, parked, and went in the door and down the steep concrete stairs to that led to the interior of the ballpark. A cheery Jerry Chimelewski was indeed waiting for her.

"Hey, Brenda. Good to see you," he said. "Let me take you down to the exam room so Dr. Parker can see you, then Mark and I would like to meet with you to talk a bit about the organization's hopes for you and your development."

"That sounds great," Brenda replied. Jerry led her past the media room, the visitors' clubhouse, and various storage and stadium employee rooms until they reached the Indians' clubhouse. The outside was non-descript—just a double set of blue-painted steel doors much like the ones leading to the visitors' clubhouse. The same sign forbidding entry to any female who wasn't credentialed media was on the door.

They walked into a more dynamic version of the hallway she had seen in the visitors' clubhouse. The hall turned and curved off to the left and had the look of something long and labyrinthine. Doors marked "Equipment" and "Laundry" were on her immediate right (after years of schlepping around Andy and Jon's equipment and washing their uniforms, these two rooms were a welcome sight). An exam room and a door marked "Training" were on the left. Jerry introduced her to the team physician, Dr. Parker, who was tall, thin, and reminded Brenda of David Byrne from the band Talking Heads.

He seemed nice enough as he took a medical history, sent her into the restroom with a plastic cup for a urine sample, and then conducted the physical. It was far more extensive than any physical Brenda had had before. He had her walk and run on a treadmill ("We aren't going to do a stress test but I do want to get a basic fitness assessment," he said), the entire time checking her heart rate and blood pressure. He checked her grip and her range of motion. The entire time, Dr. Parker didn't say much, just "Great, now I need you to . . ." When it was all over, Brenda couldn't help but ask how she did.

"You're in reasonably good shape," he replied. "I'm going to recommend that they start you on a strength and conditioning program. But I've seen plenty of veterans show up for spring training in worse shape than you are," he added with a smile.

Brenda wasn't sure if this was supposed to make her feel better or not. Jerry had been hovering just inside the door to the exam room, and now he and Brenda walked down to the manager's office. Munson's office bore the mark of a man for whom the verb "decorating" meant hanging the obligatory poster bearing the Indians' mission statement (something about "relentlessly pursuing excellence"), one wedding photo, and one photo of his three children. No frills, no waste.

"Hi, Brenda. Good to see you. How'd the exam go?" Mark asked.

"I think it went okay," she replied and looked to Jerry for confirmation.

"Richard didn't see anything troubling. He's sending the results upstairs."

This got a big smile and an enthusiastic "Great!" from Mark. He couldn't always be this enthusiastic with every new signee. But Brenda already knew she was different.

Jerry started things off. "My job is to help each player in the organization develop into the best player he—or she—can be. I evaluate player performance and offer recommendations to Mark and the front office about players moving up through the system, and I also help guide players through some of the challenges that come along with a professional playing career, such as financial management and dealing with the media." He glanced at Mark.

"I'm not gonna sugarcoat it," Mark said. "You're going to get a lot of crap thrown your way." He seemed to hesitate just a nanosecond before saying "crap," as though he thought it wasn't okay to say "shit " in front of her. "You can't let it get to you. At least not publicly."

"I ought to play some of the messages on my answering machine for you," Brenda replied. "I'm getting used to it."

"I hate to say it, but it's just going to get worse. A lot of people don't think you belong here, and they will be very vocal about saying so. I don't care if it's a fan or a member of the media or a member of the opposing team, you cannot answer back. You can't get angry. That's non-negotiable. If you ever need to let off some steam, talk to me. Talk to your best friend, talk to your dog."

"You get the idea," Jerry added.

Mark nodded and continued. "Look, I don't know if any female players are going to come after you. But there might be a couple someday, which means you need to be the ideal player and ideal citizen on and off the field. Personally, I don't care what you say or do as long as you deliver on the mound. And I think you have the potential to do so. But the ball club looks at you as an ambassador. If you want any woman to ever have the chance follow in your footsteps, you're going to have to be perfect."

"So no pressure or anything," Brenda deadpanned.

Mark gave her a half smile. "No pressure." He leaned back in his leather desk chair and paused. "You have kids, right?"

"Two boys. The older one will be thirteen in August, and the younger one is nine."

Mark smiled. "Ah, a teenager. What joy. My daughter is twenty, and my boys are twenty-three and twenty-five." Brenda glanced at the photo of his children on his desk. It had to be at least ten years old. "At the risk of repeating myself, it'll get worse before it gets better," he added.

"Which? The surly teenage attitude or the media storm that's about to hit?"

He laughed. "Both. How are your boys handling all this?"

"The younger one thinks it's the greatest thing since the Wii, and the older one is . . . embarrassed."

"My son Aaron was twelve in my last year as a player. I'll be honest, I had a lousy year—I should have retired the season before. Aaron was so embarrassed by my batting average that he actually refused to go to a game that year."

"That's terrible," Brenda said, even as she could easily see Andy doing the same thing. Jerry just laughed, although Brenda couldn't imagine that he hadn't heard that story before.

"If you do well—and I believe you can—he'll come around. So will most of the hecklers and the media and bloggers and your team-mates. The only way to shut them up is by throwing like you did in your tryout." He paused, just to let this sink in. He leaned forward in his chair and for the first time looked like a regular, concerned guy instead the baseball manager. "Look, this is kind of an experiment. I think you can do the job, so does Jerry here, so does Earl, and so does the front office. I have no idea if the fans or the rest of the world are ready for a woman in the major leagues, but there's only one way to find out."

"Thanks for giving me a try," Brenda said. She wasn't sure what else to say. Her manager didn't need to hear how nervous she was. The nerves and the anger she could keep to herself.

"We're really pleased you're here," Jerry said. "Now I want to talk to you a little bit about Friday's press conference. Mark and Louis will both be on the dais with you. They'll talk first and formally intro-duce you to the media, and you'll take questions for maybe twenty minutes. These kinds of press conferences are pretty standard when-ever the team signs a major free agent or otherwise acquires a big name player or prospect. However, I think this one might be a bit dif-ferent. We've received inquiries from all over the place—not just the metro area. You're making national news, heck, international news. Have you ever done any public speaking before? Theater? Anything?"

"Well, when I worked as a graphic designer, I had to present drafts of ideas to the clients."

"Great, use that experience when you're talking to the media."

"Except instead of presenting an idea, I'm presenting myself," Brenda said.

Jerry laughed. "Kind of. Normally I'm having this conversation with a nineteen-year-old kid with no life experience except maybe some college. It's kind of refreshing to work with an adult. Just remember that having cameras and microphones stuck in your face can be unsettling. We do our best to keep it low-key and casual. Just be yourself."

Mark added, "If there's a question you don't feel comfortable answering, pass it off to me or Lou. We've got your back."

"Thanks," Brenda replied.

"I didn't know you used to be a graphic designer. Do you still draw?" he asked.

Brenda had to answer honestly: "No, no, I don't."

Despite all the prepping, when Brenda walked into the Indians' media room on Friday morning, she felt like Dorothy spinning around in her little farmhouse in the middle of a twister. Adele, Andy, and Jon were sitting front and center, David was just off to the side, and she knew Robin was hiding somewhere in the back. Her family and friend were surrounded by a standing-room-only crowd of reporters wielding a larger selection of recording devices than you might see at an electronics store—television cameras, flip cameras, cell phones, iPads, and voice recorders. She even noticed one or two old-fashioned types who appeared to have nothing more than a notebook and a pencil. They were charming oases of calm in the midst of their digital brethren.

She walked onto the small dais at one end of the media room, flanked by Mark and Louis Adams, who started things off by welcoming Brenda and her family and all of the media representatives. "It's fitting that the Cleveland Indians, who integrated the American League by signing Larry Doby in 1947, are once again taking the lead toward equality by being the first major league team to sign a female player," Louis said. There was some applause at this statement, which seemed out of place at a press conference. At first Brenda wasn't sure where it was coming from, because the front rows of seats were packed to the gills with serious-looking male sportswriters and a tiny smattering of female writers. Farther in the back, she could just make out half a dozen young women and two younger men as the source of the applause. They clearly weren't part of the traditional media.

Brenda was so focused on scanning the crowd, in shock at the huge number of people who had come out to see her, that she almost didn't hear Louis when he said, "On behalf of the Cleveland Indians organization, I'd like to introduce you to our newest signee, Brenda Haversham."

Her heart seemed to be pounding in time to the applause from the audience as she stood up and turned sideways so Mark could put an Indians jersey on her. When she turned to face front, she was blinded by the flashes from fifty cameras, but she remembered to shake Louis's hand, then Mark's. Then she just stood there for a moment and smiled, wondering how many unflattering photos would find their way into the papers or online. Jerry had said to "give it a second for the applause to die down," and it did, but the cameras kept flashing, so finally she just sat down. Honestly, how many pictures of her—of any one ballplayer—did they need?

She glanced over at Mark, who nodded to her. She leaned forward toward the microphone—not too close—and said, "Thank you for the warm welcome." She knew she had to say more. These people were here to see her, to hear what she had to say. Jerry and Mark had told her to just be herself, but herself—her real self—had nothing to do with baseball. "I'm really happy and honored to be a part of the Indians organization because I've been a Tribe fan all my life," she said. That seemed safe enough. She looked around the room and saw Jon give her a little wave. "So . . . what would you like to know?"

Two dozen hands immediately went up in front of her. Louis had said he would call on the reporters for her because he knew just about all of them. "Chuck," he said, pointing to a guy with a bushy salt-and-pepper moustache.

"Hi. Chuck Farley, *The Plain Dealer*. Brenda, welcome to the Indians. You're breaking some sacred ground here. Do you think more female players will follow in your footsteps?"

Brenda didn't want to be known as the dumb blonde jock who vacuously said: "I don't know" to every question, but who the hell could answer this accurately? "Gee, I don't . . . know if I'm the right person to answer that question. I'm sure there are plenty of other female players out there, but whether or not they get a chance to play isn't up to me. You should ask the front offices of the other twenty-nine teams."

This actually got a little chuckle out of the room. Mark called on someone else. "Hi, T.J. Hoffman, MLB.com. Brenda, you didn't play high school or college ball. In fact, the only organized baseball you've played is in a recreational league. Do you honestly think you have what it takes to make it in professional baseball? Isn't this really just a publicity stunt to sell tickets?"

Brenda stared at T.J. Hoffman from MLB.com for a moment. He looked like he might be kind of tall when he stood up and had pretty broad shoulders and long arms. A failed ballplayer himself? She didn't know. She also wasn't sure how honestly to answer the question. Hell, she wasn't sure she *should* honestly answer it.

She heard Mark clear his throat and glanced over at him. "Yes. No," he said simply. Poker-faced, he briefly caught Brenda's eye. She figured she now owed him one. He called on another person. "Hi, Daryl Goodman, Fox Sports. This question is for Mr. Adams. Will you be releasing the results of Ms. Haversham's physical, including the results of testing for banned substances?"

Great, people thought she was doping. Louis deftly handled the question, promising that the organization would release what results it could, although he made a point of adding that Brenda had tested negative for any banned substances and would be subject to the same testing as any other player.

Mark called on a woman next. She looked like a reasonable person. "Hi, Brenda. I'm Connie Covington from ABC. What type of accommodations are being made as far as changing areas for you? Will you be in the locker room with the other players? If not, how do you think that might affect your ability to function as an effective part of the team?"

"I'm told that with the Captains, I will be changing in the manager's office. As far as the second question, I'm not here to make friends. I'm here to throw strikes." Maybe that sounded harsh, but it was true.

Then she heard Mark say, "Charlie, how about you?" Charlie? She looked around and saw a face she had seen on television a hundred times on the left-hand side of the room. If it had felt odd messaging him, having him stand and ask her a question as though he knew her felt even stranger.

"Hi, Brenda," he said, sounding more conversational than any of the other reporters had thus far. "Can you tell us a little bit about your baseball history? Who taught you to pitch?"

As she said the words, "My Dad," Brenda suddenly felt her father's absence more acutely than she had in years. "He would take me out to the park just about every weekend, and we'd play baseball. When I was pretty young, he noticed I had a good arm and started teaching me how to pitch. I grew up watching the Indians with him, which makes signing with the team now such a treat. If he were here, I think he, more than anyone I know, would appreciate this moment." The way Charlie smiled and nodded at her answer, as though they had a shared understanding, made her want to talk to him more. She had to stop herself from asking, "Do you have a follow-up?"

Mark called on someone else, a tall, thin guy from Sports Illustrated.com who asked: "You're at the age when most athletes are thinking about retirement, not jumping into professional sports. Are you worried about your age and your ability to compete?"

Even as she was saying, "Sure I'm a little worried, who wouldn't be?" Brenda knew it was probably the wrong answer. Not wrong factually—she *was* worried—but she shouldn't be showing any sign of weakness, no lack of confidence. "But I suppose that's natural. A little fear is a good motivator, right?" she added with a bit more gusto than was probably necessary.

Other questions followed. The kids in the back (who, it turned out, ran a couple of Indians blogs), wanted to know what she thought her best pitches were and if the coaching staff had her adding any pitches. A woman from National Public Radio asked if Brenda thought female players would add a new element to the game. The beat writer for *The Lake County Herald* asked what she thought of the Chief Wahoo logo. Brenda tried to answer the questions as best she could, but after a while every person seemed to be asking variations of the same question: Why are you here? She was grateful when Louis said, "Last question" and called on another blogger, who wanted to know what she thought fan reaction would be to having a female player on the field.

As the reporters and cameramen began shuffling out of the media room, Brenda followed Louis and Mark off the dais and into the back hallway. Somehow, David met her there—she hadn't even seen him moving through the crowd. "Not a bad first press conference," he said. He said hello to Mark and Louis and asked to "borrow" Brenda for a while, adding, "Media Day, Part Two."

"What part two? I thought this was it," Brenda said.

"You're doing a one-on-one interview. This just came up last night. I sent you a text about it."

"I keep telling you, my phone is just a phone. I don't text."

David put one hand lightly on her shoulder and led her farther down the hall. "Go out and buy yourself a new phone and a big, juicy data package," he said in a quiet bedroom voice. "I just closed a deal with Bam! Sportswear for you. Sports bras—print, TV, and online. Huge deal."

"I have to model bras?" Brenda doubted whether there was a sum of money large enough to make her feel comfortable being photographed in a bra, sport or otherwise.

"It'll be fine. I'll give you the details later. Right now you need to talk with Charlie Bannister. It's only fitting that you do your first interview with him."

They went back into the now-nearly empty media room. Adele and Robin were waiting by the front row of chairs. "There she is!" her mother said proudly.

"Hi, Mom. Hey, Robin. Thanks for being here." She was about to introduce David to Robin when she realized the boys weren't there. "Where are Andy and Jon?"

Robin pointed a thumb to the back of the room. "Jon wanted to make a new friend, and he made Andy go with him."

"I think Andy might even be a little bit impressed with you now," Adele added.

Brenda scanned the back of the room. Two camera crew guys were setting up some lights around a couple of chairs and checking light and sound levels. Andy and Jon were standing by someone seated in one of the chairs and they were both laughing. "Excuse me," she said.

As she walked closer, she saw that the boys were talking to Charlie Bannister. She heard Jon say, "Do you know Francisco Jimenez?" Everybody in Cleveland knew Jimenez, even the ones who didn't follow baseball. He had saved the game that won the division series three seasons ago by striking out the side in the bottom of the ninth on a mere thirteen pitches. Since that time, it seemed that every time you turned around he was on a billboard or in a commercial or a public service announcement for everything from National City Bank ("Francisco knows how to save") to Hough Bakery (for a baker's dozen of Dugout Dippers, which were long, skinny donuts that Andy thought looked like monkey tails) to the Cleveland Public Schools ("Save your future—stay in school").

"Yep. Interviewed him his rookie year. Nice guy. He's really quiet, but he does a mean karaoke version of 'Born to Be Wild.'"

"I don't know that song," Jon said.

"It's like this old hippie song," Andy said to him.

Now it was Charlie's turn to laugh. As Brenda walked up and put a hand on Andy's shoulder, Charlie stood up and said in mock horror, "Old hippie song? What are you teaching these children?"

If it had been someone else, another almost-stranger, Brenda might have been taken aback by how familiar Charlie was. He acted as though they already knew each other. Somehow, he didn't come off as presumptuous or too forward. Just friendly. Maybe it was just a journalistic trick to get her guard down and make her spill her guts, but she did feel as though she already knew him. "We haven't done the chapter on classic rock yet. We're still working on punk and Brit pop"

"Hmm, a chronologically unsound approach, but I like it." Charlie had a roundish face that seemed perpetually on the verge of breaking into a smile. While he was typically seated behind a desk on his show, in person, she saw that his hips were easily as wide as hers. Even though men could carry extra pounds more easily than women, it was still comforting to see that he was as physically imperfect as she. "Hi Brenda," he said, giving her a warm, two-handed handshake. "It's great to meet you in person."

"Thanks, you too," she replied.

David, Adele, and Robin had joined them by now. "We genuinely appreciate all the support you've given Brenda," David interjected. "You helped to show that the public is ready for women in major league ball."

"I just think people ought to be given a chance," Charlie said. "If the talent is there, it should be used."

"Hear, hear," Adele put in. Brenda made some quick introductions then gratefully allowed David to shoo her family out of the room so they could do the interview.

"Now don't be nervous," Charlie said as they got settled. "We're just going to have a conversation. Think of the camera as that one friend who hangs out but doesn't say much."

"Okay, only I'm usually that one friend."

Charlie gave her an amused look. "Thanks for giving me fair warning."

•◇•

Excerpt from the transcript for *Today in Sports* with Charlie Bannister, ESPN, July 17:

> Charlie: Good evening, sports fans. Tonight I'm pleased to bring you the first major interview with pitching phenom Brenda Haversham. She's set to join the Cleveland Indians Class A Lake County Captains tomorrow, making her the first woman ever to play for a major league affiliate. Hi Brenda, it's great to finally meet you.

> Brenda: Thank you. It's nice to meet you too.

> Charlie: Well, here you are, officially the first woman to be a member of a major league organization. How does it feel?

Brenda: Kind of surreal, actually, but it feels great. It really does.

Charlie: Now our viewers know I've been a fan of yours since the beginning, but in case there are a couple of people out there who still don't know your background, can you take us through the series of events that brought you to this point?

Brenda: Well, I'd been throwing batting practice for my sons during the spring. In April, we went to an Indians game and my younger son, Jon, said I should try the test-your-speed pitching game. I did, and just for kicks, really gave it everything I had, and the pitch was clocked at eighty-two miles an hour . . .

Charlie: That's pretty darn good for an amateur.

Brenda: Someone took a video of it and posted it on the Internet—and that's where you stepped in. Thank you for your support, by the way.

Charlie: You're more than welcome.

Brenda: I started playing in a local Roy Hobbs League, just for fun. Then a local news station did a story on me and clocked me at ninety-three, and that video made it to the Internet. Things just sort of snowballed from there.

Charlie: I'll say. I think it's safe to say that you are the best-known female athlete in the country at this moment. Now the first thing I have to ask you is: How do you do it? Ninety-three miles an hour is impressive for a pitcher half your age. I don't know that any woman has ever been clocked throwing that hard. How do you summon that kind of heat? Do you lift weights? Eat nothing but protein shakes and raw eggs? Inquiring minds want to know.

Brenda: No, nothing like that. It's just a lot of concentration and good genetics, I guess.

Charlie: One of the elements that makes your story so charming but also troubling to some people is that you've essentially come out of nowhere. You didn't play high school or college ball, correct?

Brenda: No, I didn't.

Charlie: You're about to join a minor league team, but conventional wisdom says you're on the fast track to The Show. It's like a big fairy tale. But there are guys in the minor leagues who've been working at their game and dreaming about the big leagues for years. Is it fair for you to go from amateur to the majors when you haven't paid your dues?

Brenda: I don't know that it's fair that women have been banned from professional baseball for nearly sixty years. It seems like all the talented girls get sent off to play softball. How are they supposed to pay their dues when the door has been closed to them?

Charlie: Good point, but I think you're side-stepping my question. Is it fair for you to jump over the heads of all the guys who've been sweating in the trenches in the minors?

Brenda: Honestly? Of course not. But I'm on my way to the minors too. I don't know how long I'll be there, but I'd be foolish to give up this chance. If I get the chance to move up, I will. And it's not as if another player would step aside for me.

Charlie: Jackie Robinson, Larry Doby, Billie Jean King, Arthur Ashe, Brenda Haversham. How does it feel to be part of a long line of barrier breakers?

Brenda: Wow, I'm honored to be mentioned in the same sentence with those athletes. But the Indians' ball club is the one taking the chance and breaking barriers. I just feel very lucky, and I'm very happy to be given the chance to play.

Charlie: When you signed that contract, a hundred thousand little girls all across America decided they could grow up and become baseball players . . .

Brenda: They did?

Charlie: Oh, they did all right. Now that you've blazed the trail, do you think more women will follow you into the major leagues?

Brenda: That would be wonderful, but I don't feel qualified to make any predictions.

Charlie: Well I do. Brenda Haversham, I predict you are going to have a fantastic career.

Chapter Ten

•◇•

WHEN MEDIA DAY WAS FINALLY OVER, BRENDA RETREATED BACK HOME WITH THE BOYS. She was due to report to the Captains early the next day and was expected to suit up for that evening's game. There was a game Sunday afternoon, then the team left on a road trip Sunday night. All afternoon and into the evening, as she puttered around the house doing laundry and cleaning and figuring out what to pack, her mind was racing. Before dinner it was: "twenty-six hours from now I'll be at the ballpark, getting ready." When she was cleaning up from dinner, it was: "twenty-four hours from now, the game will be starting."

Jon was, in theory, helping her load the dishwasher, although he was doing more dancing around and asking questions than helping. "What number are you going to wear?" he asked.

"Number twenty-nine," Brenda replied.

"Num . . . berrrr twen . . . ty . . . nine . . ." Jon sang, plopping a piece of silverware into the dishwasher with each syllable. "Why Are You Num . . . berrrr Twen . . . ty Nine . . . ?"

"Because I like that number. And it was Satchel Paige's number." Brenda replied.

"Who . . . Is . . . That . . . ?"

"He played for the Indians and he was old too. Jon, could you please not *throw* the knives?"

"I'm a Knife Thrower!" Jon said. "Like in the circus or something. Whomp! Whomp! Whomp!"

"Gentle. Please."

"I am." Jon threw a fork, missed the silverware rack, and hit the glass that Brenda was putting into the dishwasher. It shattered.

"Jon! Why——?!" Then she saw blood on her left hand and said, "Shit!" and felt guilty both for getting mad and for swearing.

"I'm sorry. I'll help you clean it up," Jon said, reaching for a piece of broken glass.

"Honey, not with your bare hand."

She heard Andy's voice from the kitchen doorway. "What happened?"

"We had a little accident with a glass. Could you please grab a plastic bag?" Brenda shooed Jon out of the way and grabbed a paper towel for her hand.

"Are you okay?" Andy asked.

"Yeah, I'll be fine. It's not my throwing hand."

She heard a little gasp from Jon. "I'm sorry," he said again, much quieter than he said it the first time.

Having spent the last almost thirteen years worrying about her children and the many ways they could hurt themselves, Brenda had almost forgotten that she herself could be hurt. *It's not my throwing hand . . .* she repeated to herself. The fragility of her own body, the reality that so much depended on her and the well-being of her body hit her with the same shock as the glass breaking.

"Do you want me to help clean up?" Andy asked.

"I'll help too!" Jon piped in.

Brenda took a deep breath. There was no reason to be angry with them. It was an accident, and she was all right. "That's okay. It's really a one-person job," she replied.

After cleaning up all the broken glass (and running a wet mop over the kitchen floor just in case), Brenda took a better look at her hand. She had a small cut on the ring finger of her left hand. The Band-Aid was in almost the same spot formerly occupied by her wedding ring, but she didn't have the energy to ponder any ironic analogies.

Early the next afternoon, Brenda drove half an hour out to Classic Park, a snug little ballpark that had been plopped down into the middle of a commercial district on Route 91. Somehow it fit into the landscape. Brenda could only hope that the homey, good feeling would continue once she was inside.

She pulled into the parking lot and walked past the broad white concrete steps and open plaza where the box office and administrative offices were. She had been to the ballpark once before, when she and Ed went to a game a few years back. Walking past the main entrance and around to the players' entrance made her stomach start jumping. It felt equal parts first day of school, first day at a new job, and jumping out of an airplane without a parachute. This wasn't some rec league; this was professional baseball.

There was the door. Just a non-descript steel door painted a dull red. There was nothing to do but open it.

Inside it looked like a Lilliputian version of Progressive Field, with a tunnel-like hall that ran half the length of the ballpark. Palettes stacked with boxes, presumably of ballpark food, lined the walls. A wiry guy who looked to be in his late forties or early fifties was walking toward her.

"Hey, you must be Brenda," he said as he approached. "I'm Stuart Radcliffe, the Pitching Coach. I'm here to help you get settled in, and then we'll do a bullpen session before tonight's game."

"Great. It's nice to meet you," Brenda said, and extended her hand. She touched his hand first as they shook hands. As they began walking down the tunnel to the clubhouse, Stuart put his hand on her shoulder, just for a second, then removed it. He pointed out the door to the Visitors' Clubhouse, which was at the far end of the tunnel, and they entered the Captains' Clubhouse through another steel door, this one painted the same deep blue as the Captains' uniforms.

He held the door open for her, and Brenda's shoulder accidentally brushed against his elbow as she walked through the doorway. Stuart again quickly but gently touched her shoulder. It seemed that every time she accidentally touched him, he touched her back. It happened a few more times as they walked by the training room, the locker room and showers, and the manager's office ("You'll be changing in there," he said). Everything was clean and serviceable. The facility didn't have the swagger and size of a major league clubhouse, still, it was going to be home.

The door to the manager's office was open, and Brenda saw a man who was roughly Stu's age in a room that was just large enough to hold a desk and two chairs. An attached bathroom held a toilet and shower.

"Scotty? Haversham's here," Stuart said.

Scott Hudek, her new manager, stood up to greet her. She vaguely remembered his name as having played a season or two in the majors. He still had an athlete's build but sported a pot belly that seemed to be developing a mind of its own. "Hi, Brenda. Well you made it," he said.

She wasn't sure how to respond to this, so she just said, "Yep. And I'm happy to be here." Happy wasn't the most accurate description of how she was feeling, but it was, at least, polite.

"I'd like to talk with you for a few minutes. Why don't we do that now? When we're done, you can get a bullpen session in with Stu before the rest of the guys show up."

Stuart left them alone, saying that he'd see her in the bullpen. She sat down in the one other chair in the room, a simple wooden captain's chair that had a subtle slope to the back that kept the design from being boring. As she pulled the chair out to sit down, Scott glanced at her hand. "Your finger okay?" he asked, nodding toward the Band-Aid on her hand.

"Yes, I accidentally cut it last night. It's not my throwing hand. Nothing to worry about."

"Great." He leaned back and smiled. Brenda did the same. Mirroring someone's body language was supposed to build rapport. Anyway, it couldn't hurt. She waited for him to start the conversation, although she had a pretty good idea of what he wanted to talk about. "Well, glad you met Stuart—you'll be working with him a lot."

"He seems like a great guy," Brenda said. Actually, "quirky" would seem to be a more accurate word. "I'm eager to work with him. I have a lot to learn."

Scott nodded. "I know you do." He paused for a moment that made Brenda feel a little uneasy. Maybe this wasn't going to be the same talk she had had with Mark and Jerry. "Brenda, I'm a traditionalist. I don't like designated hitters. I don't like inter-league play. I don't like instant replays. And frankly, I don't like the idea of having a female player on the roster. That being said, the folks downtown tell me you have talent. And you're here, so we'll do our best to get you some playing time and see what you can do."

A grudging welcome seemed better than a false one. Nonetheless, Brenda had to swallow her ego a bit as she replied, "That's all I can ask for."

"We're kind of limited on space here, so for home games, you can change in my office."

"Thank you. When we're on the road, I can just as easily change at the hotel," she added.

"And wear your uniform to the ballpark spring training-style? Not a bad idea." He added, clearly appreciative of her suggestion. This seemed like a good sign. She didn't need him to like her. She didn't need any of them to like her, but they didn't need to think of her as a prima donna either. "Look, the guys on the team know that you'll be joining them. I know some of them don't like it, and some couldn't care less. But you're part of my team. If any of them give you a problem, you just let me know."

Even as he said this, even as she said, "Thank you, I'll do that," Brenda was certain that she would never, ever let Scott Hudek—or anyone—know if she had problems.

There was a locker with her name on it in the locker room. A white and blue uniform was hanging in it. After her talk with Scott, he had directed her out there and then let her use his office so she could change. When she had put on the Indians jersey and hat at the press conference, it had felt like a prop for a play. As she put on her uniform, the idea became more and more real that she was now a legitimate member of a professional baseball team and she was suiting up for a game that was only hours away.

Jersey, pants, belt, socks, her own cleats, hat. This was it. She was in uniform. Her own clothes she folded and stacked neatly on the extra chair in Scott's office with her shoes underneath. It was like being at the doctor's office.

Stuart had said the other players usually showed up at the ballpark around 2:30 or 3:00, and it was almost 1:30 already. Scott pointed her in the right direction before he returned to his office.

She tried not to notice his little sigh of resignation when he saw her clothes folded on the extra chair, but just went straight down the dark tunnel to the field.

Classic Park felt cozy, like the cuddly little brother of a big-league stadium. She spied Stuart sitting in one of maybe half a dozen chairs along the wall out in foul territory by right field. He had said he'd meet her in the bullpen, and it took a moment to realize that Classic Park was so small that the bullpen *was* the foul territory in right field. He was waiting, so she jogged across the field to him. The grass felt springy under her feet, like it was ready to play with her.

"Hi," Stu said as she neared him. He didn't seem put out at all by having to wait for her. Quite the opposite—it was almost as if she had interrupted his quiet moment. He stood up. "You ready?"

"I guess so."

"I asked Archie, our reserve catcher, to come and catch your bullpen session. He should be here any minute. Let's throw a little to get you warmed up."

"Okay," Brenda replied and trotted a few yards out to right field. She wasn't sure how close she should start. Too close, and he might question her ability to throw farther or harder. Too far, and it might look like she was overcompensating or didn't know what she was doing. "Except I don't know what I'm doing," she mumbled to herself and the right field grass. "Not really."

Stu threw the ball, and she caught it. The familiar sound of a baseball landing in the pocket of a glove, the hard, compact feel of the ball in her hand, those were things she did know about. She threw the ball back, perhaps a bit harder than necessary.

"Easy," Stu said as he caught it. "Give your muscles a minute to warm up." They played catch for a few silent minutes. Stu was a lefty, and before each throw he would almost imperceptibly pump his throwing hand back twice before releasing the ball. It wasn't enough of a motion to add any velocity to the throw—it was just a quirk. "What sports did you play in high school?" he asked.

"Um, I didn't," Brenda said, feeling somehow ashamed that she had spent most of her free time in high school in the art room.

"Okay." Stu was a little odd, but he seemed pretty non-judgmental. She thought she could get along with him. "I understand your dad taught you to pitch."

"Yes. How did you know that?"

"I watch Charlie Bannister too," he said.

Archie, the reserve catcher, showed up. The first thing that struck Brenda was how like Andy he was—they had the same type of stocky build, the same blondish hair, the same look of reserved introspection. But Archie was huge, and he didn't look a day over twenty. It seemed impossible to think that her own son could grow that much in eight years. Seven years—Andy was going to be thirteen in just a few weeks.

Archie was polite but seemed a little nervous as Stu introduced them. "Hi, welcome to the team," he said, with a hint of an accent that she later learned had its roots in southern Kentucky. Stu wanted her to throw from the mound, just to give her a feel for the park. As she walked toward the pitcher's mound, she heard Archie say to Stu, "I've never caught a woman before."

"She's not going to get estrogen on the ball, Archie. It'll be okay."

As the rest of the team arrived at the ballpark, it appeared some of them did seem worried about stray estrogen or the unholy effects of double X chromosomes, because most of them gave her a wide berth. A few said a quick "Hi," and that was about it. With most of the clubhouse filled with young men in varying stages of undress, Brenda realized her options were limited to Scott's office or the dugout. She chose the latter. Each of the other players had his own ritual. Some were doing warm-ups—light calisthenics, stretches, or a couple of slow-jog laps around the outfield—while others played catch or just seemed to hang out shooting the breeze. The one thing that kept going through Brenda's mind was how young all these guys were. They were professional ballplayers, but they were just boys.

She heard someone walking up the dugout steps, and another player walked past her to the field. He smiled and murmured a polite "Hola" then trotted out to run a couple of laps. The back of his jersey read "Diaz," and she realized he was Eduardo Diaz, the teenage phenom shortstop the Indians had signed at the ripe old of age of sixteen.

So he had to be, what, *seventeen* now? A baby, just a few years older than Andy.

Stu had worked with her for almost an hour, going over her mechanics and motion. Now, sitting in the dugout having had a long workout and feeling pretty darn warmed up, she felt conspicuous, as though the rest of the team would think she was a slacker because she wasn't doing anything. A few more stretches wouldn't hurt her, but the closer it got to game time the more nervous she became. The only place she could think of for a pit stop was Scott's office.

His door was open, but she knocked anyway. "Excuse me, may I just use the restroom in here?"

Her new manager's expression told her he was being disturbed, even though he said, "Sure." Scott stood up, stretched, and walked to the door. "Take as long as you need. How'd the bullpen session go with Stu?" he added.

"Great, thanks. He's a good coach."

Scott took a step as though he was about to leave, then stopped. "One thing to know about Stu, he's very superstitious," he said.

"A lot of ballplayers are," Brenda replied.

Scott lowered his voice just a bit. "He has the usual superstitions about not stepping on the foul line, not messing with a hot streak. He likes ritual. But he has this other superstition where if you touch him then he has to touch you back."

"*Has* to? That sounds more like a compulsion."

"It's a superstition," Scott said in a voice that made it very clear she was to refer to it as nothing else. "Every once in a while, some joker decides to mess with Stu and they touch him and run away or jump into their car so he can't touch them back. It drives him nuts. I trust you aren't that kind of person."

"No, I'm not," Brenda said.

"Good. Oh, and your phone was ringing earlier," he added as he shut the office door a bit harder than necessary.

She wasn't sure if she entirely liked her new manager or if he liked her, but his protectiveness of Stuart was at least a point in his favor. Anybody who sticks up for the oddball can't be all bad. Of course, *she* was the new oddball in the organization, and Scott didn't seem all that interested in sticking up for her.

Was she wrong for wanting to be part of this or was the system wrong for not making room for her? "I don't even know if I want to be here," she mumbled as she checked her voicemail. She had two messages. The first was from Jon, asking if he could run the bases or go into the clubhouse after the game. She had no idea. How many of the other players had kids old enough to run the bases? It was questionable whether most of them were even allowed to drink legally. The second message was from David saying that she had a photo shoot for the Bam! sports bra scheduled for Monday—the team's travel day. While the rest of her team would be getting on a bus and driving to Iowa after the Sunday afternoon game, she'd be getting on an airplane, flying to New York, doing the photo shoot Monday morning, then flying to Iowa to meet up with the team for the game on Monday night.

David's message said it was "all cleared" with the Captains' front office. Even so, she couldn't imagine Scott would be too happy about the idea of her not traveling with the team on her first road trip. But the Bam! endorsement was part of the ticket to security. "Whatever it takes," she murmured as she picked up her glove and headed for the dugout.

Adele and the boys, and Robin, Dan, and Lindsey were all at the game that night. Actually, judging from the phone calls and emails she had gotten in the previous two days, just about everybody she had ever met was in attendance, except perhaps for Ed. She heard a couple players mention the big crowd and didn't think it was her imagination when most of them glanced at her when they said it, as though she was responsible for putting more butts in more seats.

She was the first woman to play for a major league organization. Okay, she understood that. But was that reason to buy a ticket to a game you wouldn't have bothered going to otherwise? Was she that much of a freak show or were people just waiting to see if she'd screw up? In the moments before the team took the field, she felt like she might treat the crowd to the sight of a rookie throwing up.

Just before the National Anthem and the start of the game, the entire team gathered in the dugout, waiting as the PA announcer first called out the starters for the opposing team, the Lansing Lugnuts, then the Captains' starting lineup. Brenda was standing behind Archie, staring into the navy blue "9" on the back of his huge jersey. He glanced over his shoulder at her. "Nervous?" he asked.

"A little," she replied.

"You look green."

"Okay, a lot."

"You threw a good bullpen session. You'll be okay."

Brenda's "thank you" was drowned out by the beginning of the National Anthem, when every other player was at least making a polite show of staring at the American flag waving at the far end of the ballpark. Brenda found herself staring at the bodies in the stands or sitting on the grassy little hill out in right field. Now that she was here, the enormity of the situation, the sight of a packed stadium staring at her, judging her, was almost immobilizing. They were expecting—what were they expecting? A flamethrower of an arm? A miracle? At the moment, she was so overcome with nerves she wasn't even sure she could move her right arm.

The National Anthem ended, the home plate umpire yelled "Play ball!" and the starting players jogged out to their positions. Brenda sat down between Archie and one of the bench players, a skinny kid with curly brown hair sticking out from under his cap. He had an Adam's apple the size of a goiter. Brenda had to stop herself from staring at it, even though the guy was tall enough that his neck was practically at her eye level. No doubt he was used to comments about it because he muttered, "My mother says I'll grow into it."

Brenda felt herself blushing as bright as a ripe tomato. "It's Lincolnesque," she replied and got up and moved to the far end of the bench. Stuart had introduced her to another relief pitcher, a dark-haired guy with ridiculously broad shoulders. Cody Farnhurst. There he was. She reasoned that if she stayed with another relief pitcher and followed his lead, she'd end up in the right place at the right time. Brenda took a seat next to Farnhurst, who didn't say anything but promptly scooted a few inches away from her. Lovely. Apparently she had managed to offend two teammates in less than five minutes.

Once the game started, Brenda just tried to watch and stay out of the way. The Captains' starting pitcher was having a good game, and the score was tied 1-1 at the end of three innings. That's when Brenda noticed a few—but not all—of the relief pitchers heading out to the bullpen. Scott was at the end of the bench, seemingly looking at everything and everyone but her. Brenda stood up. Stu was closer and, quite frankly, friendlier, so she went over to him and tapped him lightly on the shoulder. "Should I go out to the bullpen or stay here?" she asked, trying to keep her voice low in case the question was as dumb as she feared it was.

"Yeah," Stu replied, giving her arm a light touch back, "this would be a good time to go out there."

She followed him out to the bullpen. They had to run the last few yards to get seated and out of the way before the next inning started. The sight of Brenda's jersey, emblazoned with her last name on the back, caused an audible wave of chatter among the crowd, as well as a few cheers (although she figured that was probably Robin, Dan, and Jon) and a scattering of boos. Both the cheers and boos gave her another round of stomach-churning nerves.

The bullpen was open on two sides, with just a row of chairs and a stand with a cooler of water tucked into the L-shaped alcove made by the right field wall. Brenda quickly sat down in the closest open chair without even looking at who she was sitting next to.

"Getting a little close there, aren't you, cougar?" Farnhurst sneered. A couple of the other players snickered.

Brenda's heart was pounding. What do you say to the bully on the first day of school? She had to remind herself that these were just young men. Boys, practically. Compared to her, they were babies. "It was an empty chair," she said without looking at him. She couldn't think of anything else to say.

The sounds of the ball game were going on around them, but everyone in the bullpen seemed more interested in watching the growing animosity between Brenda and Farnhurst. No one said a word or even seemed to notice what was happening in the game.

Then Stu broke the tension by saying: "Hell Whipper, if Haversham was a cougar, she'd be playing for Kane County," which made everyone except Brenda and Cody laugh.

She did her best to ignore Farnhurst, although the nickname "Whipper" kept running through her head. *Stupid nickname for a stupid jerk*, she thought. If he wanted to dislike her simply because she was female, fine. She didn't need him. At this point, the only people whose opinion mattered were her coach and her manager. And while she needed to stay on speaking terms with the catchers, the rest of the team could go pound salt.

Farnhurst was going on about "this chick I always hook up with in Davenport," and how big her tits were and the other guys in the bullpen were asking if she had any friends, etc. etc. It was locker room bragging moved out to the bullpen. How much of it was normal bullpen conversation and how much of it was to get a rise out of her, Brenda didn't know. At a certain point, she stopped listening, instead trying to focus entirely on the tight, angry little ball of anger bubbling inside. That was the only thing that made sense.

Neither Scott nor Stuart had indicated whether or not they would put her in that night. Still, Brenda had a feeling. With all the hype surrounding the press conference the day before and a packed ballpark to watch a team that wasn't even playing .500 ball, there really was no way they *wouldn't* put her in.

She already knew she wasn't like any other player on the team, but the root of her presence on the roster had become clear. Other players were here to win ballgames. She was here to sell tickets and hopefully not embarrass the team while doing so. That really was it. When she looked at her situation in this light, she wasn't the least bit surprised when, in the bottom of the sixth inning, with the Captains down by two, Stuart told her to start warming up.

There was the buzz rumbling through the stands again, louder than before. Seeing her up and throwing seemed to make every fan in the place want to start talking and pointing at the Captains' bullpen. And when Stu sent her out to the mound at the top of the eighth inning and the PA announcer said: "Now pitching for the Lake County Captains, number twenty-nine, Brrrrenda Haaaaversham," the crowd noise swelled. It was no longer possible to distinguish cheers from jeers, it was all just sound. Somehow that made it easier to shut out. It was like being back in college and trying to cram for a test while a party was going on down the hall.

Somewhere along the first base line, in the family section, Brenda knew that Jon and Andy and her mom were watching. At least two of them surely hoped she did well. It seemed like Andy would be happier if she failed and went back to the insurance company, back to being his mom and nothing else. But there was no turning back now. The only problem was, as she walked to the mound, it felt like her brain was moving farther away from her body with every step. Every limb was numb with fear.

The starting catcher, a guy named Diego who looked too young to shave, tossed the game ball out to her. She had a sudden wave of new terror—what if she didn't catch the ball when he threw it? Just catch the ball, catch the ball . . . With an arm that no longer felt attached to her body, Brenda raised her glove hand and managed a respectable catch. There, there was the ball in her hand. It was brand new, with smooth, unscuffed white leather and perfect seams. Normally, the feel of a baseball in her hand was comforting, its compact solidity reassuring. This one felt like a walnut. She looked up at the umpire, almost ready to say that there was something wrong with this ball and she needed another one. The instant she took her eyes off the ball in her glove, the sound of the crowd came sweeping back.

Diego was in his crouch, waiting for her to throw a few warm-up pitches from the mound. The umpire was waiting. Her team was waiting, the other team was waiting. Apparently seven thousand people in the stands were waiting. Throw the ball.

She took a warm-up pitch. It wasn't a hard throw, but it made it across the plate. As soon as Diego tossed it back, she went into her windup and threw another one. Then another. There, this was something for people to watch. A woman pitching a baseball. That's what they all came to see, wasn't it?

After about five pitches, the first batter of the inning stepped into the batter's box. He was another baby, all of these guys looked like children. This was professional baseball? Brenda knew she had to focus, tried to muster up the anger that had been bubbling up inside her only minutes ago, but couldn't. She was too wired, too nervous. Then the umpire yelled "Play ball!" She had to pitch to him.

Later that evening, over a very large margarita, Robin would say something about inauspicious beginnings being the best kind of beginning because there is nowhere to go but up. Brenda would have liked to agree, but giving up a home run on her very first pitch as a professional baseball player was not how she wanted to start her career.

•◊•

18 July Direct message from @CABannister:

> @BrendaHav Sorry your first night out was rough.
> It'll get better.

Chapter Eleven

•◇•

AFTER THE HOME RUN, BRENDA GAVE UP A WALK. Thankfully, the next batter grounded into a double play and she then recorded her first strikeout to get out of the inning, but she knew all anyone would remember was that first pitch home run. As she walked into the dugout at the end of the inning, Scott said, "Well, you got out of it" as she walked by him.

"Yeah," Brenda replied blankly. She took a seat on the dugout as far away from Scott as possible.

Huge Adam's Apple Guy sat down next to her. Brenda recalled that his name was Jason. She was pretty sure he was a reserve infielder. "Coming from Scotty, that's actually high praise," he said.

"Thanks."

He didn't say anything else, and neither did she. She just stayed out of the way and watched the game. As soon as it was over, she fled to Scott's office, changed her clothes, and got out of the clubhouse as fast as she could. Her family was waiting for her outside the players' entrance. Jon came running up and gave her a huge hug that almost knocked her over. He was definitely going through a growth spurt. "That was so cool how you struck that guy out. That was a great pitch. SWING and a miss! You're out!" he babbled.

Brenda tried to smile, accepted the hugs and the congratulations from the people she loved best, but wanted nothing more than to run away. The sight of that first pitch sailing over the left field fence kept running through her mind.

"Are you up for a celebration?" Adele asked.

Brenda looked at her dear, sweet, understanding mother. "Honestly?"

Adele nodded. "Understood." She turned to the boys. "Jon and Andy, let's get you home."

"I want to stay with Mom!" Jon protested.

"It's past your bedtime, sweetie," Brenda said, giving him a hug. She glanced over at Andy, who had been hanging back with Lindsey, away from everyone else. "And getting close to yours." Andy just shrugged.

Robin put an arm around Brenda. "Jon, Andy. I'm sorry to say that I'm stealing your mother for the rest of the evening." Even though it was clear that Andy, at least, was ambivalent about what time she came home, being stolen away by her best friend still sounded really good at that moment. She and Robin managed to extricate themselves from their families and ended up at Don Tequila, a little hole-in-the-wall Mexican restaurant near Brenda's house that had great food and cheap drinks. Brenda loved it for the chairs, tables, and booths, which were decorated front and back with brightly colored paintings of flowers, shining suns, burros, and other iconic scenes of Mexican rural life.

Brenda had been too nervous to eat anything before the game, but now she was ravenous and ordered a couple of spinach and cheese enchiladas. "The spinach helps to assuage the guilt of eating a big meal at 11:00 p.m.," she rationalized.

"Absolutely. The spinach balances out the cheese. And the chips. And the alcohol," Robin added.

"Be nice to me. I have to go back and play this stupid game again tomorrow, and then I have to get my picture taken wearing a sports bra."

Robin leaned her elbows on the booth table and rested her chin in her hands, her pale blue eyes focused entirely on Brenda. "If it's a stupid game, why are you playing it?" she asked.

"What else am I going to do? There's no other job I could do that would pay me as much as I'm getting in endorsements."

"I understand the financial incentive. But if you truly believe it's a stupid game and you don't want to play it, then don't. You've shown that a woman can get signed by a major league club, you've helped open a new door for other women. That's huge. If you don't want to continue, don't. Go back to graphic design. Go back to drawing."

Brenda sighed. "I haven't drawn in so long . . . I don't think like that anymore. You know what I mean? I don't think in *pictures* anymore. I'm so, so proud of you for doing your art and bringing art to other people. I'm glad one of us stayed with it." She picked up a tortilla chip from the bowl and held it out in the palm of her hand. "The last couple times I picked up a drawing pencil, my hand felt like this," and she crushed the chip in her hand. "Clumsy. No nuance, no subtlety. There's nothing there anymore."

"I'm sorry you feel that way," Robin said. "So I guess now you're stuck with being a ground-breaking female icon."

"Who gave up a home run on her very first professional pitch."

Robin shrugged. "It happens."

"It happened to me."

"But then you did fine. Double play ball, you struck out the last batter . . . You did more than fine. Let it go."

"I'll try," Brenda replied. But as she took a hefty sip of her margarita, she knew she wouldn't be able to.

She and Robin hadn't stayed out too late, but Brenda still showed up for Sunday's game feeling hungover and worn out. Saying good-bye to the boys hadn't helped. She was about to embark on an eight-day road trip and had never been away from the boys for that long. Andy feigned nonchalance, but Jon suddenly didn't like the idea of his mother going out of town and made a stink. Talking him out of his tantrum took an extra fifteen minutes and almost made her late for her bullpen session with Stu.

Working with a coach while other players were around had a different dynamic. No one was overtly watching them, but still, as other players were on the field either doing laps or throwing or stretching, she noticed more heads turning her way and staying turned a little longer than necessary.

She didn't go into the game that night, just hung out in the bullpen with the other relief pitchers and tried to stay out of the way. Farnhurst gave her the silent treatment, which was fine; Brenda preferred to ignore him right back. The other players had varying degrees of coolness toward her—a few said hello, but that was about it. It was like being invisible.

Invisible or not, Brenda knew she didn't want the rest of the team to see her get in a car when they were looking at a nine-hour bus ride. How could she become part of the team when she wasn't even traveling with them? True, she'd join them tomorrow night, but she was flying and would spend the night in a comfortable hotel room in Manhattan, not pulling into a budget motel in the wee hours of the morning.

The one advantage to changing apart from the rest of the team was her proximity to the exit. The manager's office was just outside the locker room. When the game was over, she changed quickly and found Scott waiting outside his office as she was getting ready to leave.

"So you're out of here," he said not as a question but not quite as an accepted fact either.

"Yes, I'm sorry. I'll fly into Davenport tomorrow evening and rejoin the team there before the game." He didn't say anything. "My agent arranged this," she added feebly.

"A lot of these boys would kill to have an agent like yours," Scott replied.

"I understand that. I know that I'm lucky." Really, what was else there to say? They both knew why she had the endorsement, why she was disappearing for twenty-four hours. She was an attraction who sold tickets. When he said, "Okay, get out of here," it didn't even sound that mean. *Maybe I'm growing on him*, she thought.

Robin was waiting to drive her to the airport, and Brenda just threw her duffel bag into the car, hopped in, and said, "Hit it."

"In a hurry much?" Robin asked as she put the car in gear.

"No. I don't want anybody to see me."

"I think they might notice that you aren't there."

"But it feels weird not getting on the bus with everybody else." Brenda leaned back and closed her eyes. If she let herself, she might almost relax for a minute. "I hardly feel like part of the team as it is. This just looks like preferential treatment."

"You have another gig. It's just bad timing," Robin replied. "Idiot" She glanced quickly at Brenda. "Not you. The car in front of us."

"I know." Having been friends for more than twenty years, Brenda was so used to Robin's car-chase style of driving that she no longer needed to spend half the ride with her eyes shut.

"Chances are you won't be with the team that long anyway. The going odds are that you'll be called up before the end of the season."

It took Brenda a second to realize that Robin wasn't joking. "What the hell are you talking about?"

Robin sighed. "Sweetie, do you ever . . . I don't know, look at the Internet? Read the Sports section of the paper? You are a recurring topic of conversation."

Inwardly, Brenda had suspected as much, but she had made a point of not reading about herself since she signed the contract. "My self-esteem is precarious enough. Why would I want to read what some troll has to say about me?"

"It's not all bad. There are plenty of people out there who support women in baseball. When you get into your hotel tonight, do some 'net surfing."

"I don't have a computer with me."

"And you're a sweet old-fashioned girl who refuses to get a smart phone . . . Well rest assured you're getting kind of famous." She gave Brenda a pointed glance. "Whether you like it or not."

"I like it not," Brenda replied.

The flight into New York felt like a replay of her trip two weeks earlier—a car and driver and a nice hotel in mid-town. She called the boys when she got in and tried not to worry too much about the photo shoot the next day or what the rest of the team thought of her or whether Jon and Andy missed her. She didn't get much sleep and had to be up far earlier than she would have liked. There wasn't even time to enjoy the hotel room—she was packed, out the door, and in a cab by 7:00 the next morning.

The photo shoot was much like the first one. There were any number of people scurrying around setting up lights and a green screen. Brenda felt like one more prop as she was dressed (almost dressed), coifed, and made up. They put her in baseball pants and cleats and the sports bra. No jersey. She had to admit, it was a comfortable bra. The photographer, Ken, handed her a brand-new baseball mitt and a baseball. He was one of those guys who are so impossibly thin that Brenda thought he could probably wear Jon's pants.

"Now I want you to just pretend that you're on the mound and forget that we're all here."

"I'll do my best," Brenda said.

"You're going to have to stop covering your chest with your arms," he said.

"Right. You know, I don't think I've had my picture taken in my underwear since I was about two . . ." Brenda said feebly. Ken didn't laugh.

Once she was standing under the lights, she realized she really did have to stop covering her chest with her arms and actually pose for the pictures. With a deep breath, she put the mitt on. "Am I in the right spot?"

"Move two inches to your right," Ken said. With the camera held directly in front of his face, it was like listening to a disembodied voice giving her direction. "Good, good. And go into the wind-up . . . Great . . ."

Brenda overheard someone say, "We'll have to do some airbrushing to fill out the cleavage for the final product" and someone else respond, "Of course." The comment made her grip the ball a little tighter, and she had to remind herself not to release it. She knew she should let the comment go, that they weren't meaning to be insulting, that her body, to them, was merely an image for an advertisement. The thought didn't make her feel much better.

With a lot of teeth-gritting, she made it through the photo shoot, but they finished later than expected. She didn't have time to change—just threw on her shirt, grabbed her duffel bag, and ran out the door. Up till now, having a car and driver had felt pretentious, but now Brenda was incredibly grateful to be able to step into a car and hightail it to LaGuardia. It wasn't until they were on the road to the airport that Brenda realized she was still wearing the baseball pants from the photo shoot. And the bra. The latter could stay, but the former needed to go.

"Excuse me," she said to the driver. "Is there a screen or something you can put up?"

"No, ma'am," he replied. "Only the limos have those. Sorry."

"Okay. Well, you might not want to look in the back seat for a minute." A summer's worth of Lightning games had given her plenty of practice in changing her clothes in a car, and she managed to ditch the baseball pants and put on her jeans before the driver even seemed aware he had a half-naked passenger.

She got to the airport and through security with just enough time to kill to make it seem like all that hurrying hadn't even been necessary. She had to look at her ticket twice to make sure she was at the right gate. The flight was to Moline, Illinois, and she had a moment where she thought maybe she *should* get a smartphone so she could do things like figure out how to get from Moline to Davenport. When the flight finally landed in Moline in the late afternoon, Brenda realized that the hour time difference was perhaps the only thing that would keep her from being late to the ballpark.

A fifty-five dollar cab ride got her from the airport to Modern Woodmen Park in Davenport, home of the Quad Cities River Bandits. The charming U-shaped brick front of the park looked to be from the 1930s, and Brenda wondered how much was original and how much was new. There wasn't enough time to ask about the name or to admire the view of the Mississippi River, on whose banks the ballpark was built. Duffel bag in hand, she paid the cab driver and ran into the players' entrance. First pitch was at 7:05 and it was now 6:15. She should have been at the ballpark more than an hour ago.

Once inside, she found herself in a long, somewhat dank hall that seemed to run the length of the main stadium structure. She went to the right and had only jogged a hundred feet or so down the hall when she saw a sign on a brown steel door that read "Visitors' Clubhouse." Bracing herself for Scott's anger, she opened the door and walked in.

The clubhouse had a similar layout to Classic Park. To her right was the visiting manager's office, to her left were double doors leading to the locker room. Stuart was standing in the doorway to the office, and Brenda heard her name.

"I'm here. I'm so sorry I'm late," she said quickly.

"Hey, Brenda," Stu said with a slight smile. "Glad you got here in one piece."

Scott came to the door of his office and glared at her.

"I'm sorry, I didn't have time to change. I came straight from the airport."

"Then get changed and get warmed. The bus broke down and nobody got any sleep last night, so unless Brody pitches a complete game—"

"Which he won't," Stu interjected.

"I'll probably need to send you in tonight."

Brenda tried not to look scared or worried. "Great," she said with far more enthusiasm than necessary. She scurried into the office, changed as fast as possible, and did some stretching before going out to the field. Most of the other players were already off the field by this time, and the ballpark was filling up fast. It was an old-style park, with a wide U-shaped main concourse and bleachers and grass for the outfield seating. Far out in left field, something tall and green caught her eye. It looked like a garden, although what a garden would be doing in the left field bleachers of a minor league ballpark was anyone's guess.

It wasn't until Brenda was hanging out in the visitors' dugout with the rest of the Captains, waiting for the home team River Bandits to be introduced, that she realized it was cornfield, a little tiny cornfield growing just beyond the left field wall. As each member of the River Bandits' starting lineup was introduced, he walked out of the cornfield and trotted across the field, accompanied by the cheers of the crowd.

Brenda couldn't help herself. "Oh my God, that's so cool," she exclaimed. "Very *Field of Dreams*." It was loud enough in the ballpark that the only person who heard her was Jason and his Adam's apple.

"I find it rather over the top," he murmured and half-turned his head to look at her. "Then again, just about everything in the minors is kind of over the top," he added.

It was hard to tell if that last comment was a dig at her or not. Jason was one of the few players on the Captains to have spoken more than two words to her, but that didn't necessarily mean he liked having her around. She had six innings to ponder whether Jason was being rude and whether any of these guys would ever cut her a break. It was a high-scoring game—by the top of the seventh, the Captains were up 9-8, but every time they scored, the River Bandits answered.

Brenda was sitting in the bullpen along the first base line with the rest of the Captains' relievers. Everybody looked worn out, and Farnhurst kept complaining about how tired he was and how that bus ride the night before had "just sucked."

"I know. We were all there," Stu said. Brenda was grateful that he didn't look at her when he said this. "Lucky for you, Scott wants to put in Haversham this inning."

Brenda felt seven pairs of eyes flick from the game and over to her. She shrugged with shoulders that felt like rubber. She wasn't even sure she could feel her right arm. All she could think about was the home run she had given up in her first game and the look the rest of the team had given her as she walked back to the dugout afterward. Like she was an idiot and a failure.

"Great," Farnhurst said. That asshole. As she thought the word "asshole," Brenda felt a surge of power zip through her arm. Ed wasn't the only jerk in town. There was also Cody "Whipper" Farnhurst. *Whipper*. You could almost see the quotation marks in the air when you called him that.

As she started her warm-up throws, Brenda could feel the fear and doubt start melting away, replaced by pure, beautiful, reliable rage. When it was time to take the mound, she strode out of the bullpen without the pounding fear she had had in the first game. This time, she felt invincible. This time, as she looked at the first batter, the sight of a player who was only a handful of years removed from her oldest son seemed almost ludicrous. How could she have ever been afraid of *him*?

As she went into the wind-up, Brenda could see the tunnel of invisible light reaching from her hand to the catcher's mitt as clearly as the graceful curves of the Centennial Bridge that rose up just beyond the right field wall. And when she threw, she knew that ball wasn't going anywhere but into Diego's catcher's mitt. And it didn't.

Brenda struck out the first batter, got the second batter to pop up, and struck out the third batter. Three up, three down. When she walked down the three shallow steps into the dugout at the end of the inning, Scott looked at her and nodded. "Nice work, Haversham," he switched the chaw in his mouth from one side to the other. "I'd keep you in for the ninth, but I don't wanna push our luck."

Brenda just said, "Okay," and took a seat on the bench next to Brody, that night's starting pitcher. He nodded politely to her. "Thanks for keeping the lead. I need a W," he said quietly.

The guys on the team didn't seem to do a whole lot of extraneous talking. So she just said, "No problem," and spent the rest of the game in silence. Silence was starting to be her standard operating procedure. The Captains closer, a burly kid named Antoine who was likely to be called up to Class AA any day, shut down the River Bandits to close out the ninth inning and save the game. While the rest of the team was high-fiving and congratulating each other, Brenda went to wait on the team bus.

The team was staying at the Quad Cities Inn a few miles from the park. It was a low, gray two-story motel that looked short on frills but appeared reasonably clean. As the team got off the bus and got their room keys, Brenda hung in the background. All of the other players had a roommate. As manager, Scott roomed alone, but even the coaches, Stu and Brian, the hitting coach, roomed together. When Scott handed Brenda her key, he said, "Haversham, no wild parties, okay?" to a chorus of snickers.

It seemed best not to respond. Instead, she went up to her room, which featured two double beds about twelve inches apart, a dresser, a chair, and a window. The bathroom seemed to be an afterthought, as it was about the size of a closet. It was tiny, but for two nights it would be just fine.

It was close to 11:00 p.m., and Brenda found the conflicting pangs of hunger and fatigue setting in. She ought to just go to bed, but she *had* just pitched a great inning. A laminated, two-page "Get to Know Davenport" brochure on top of the dresser listed a pizza and pasta place about a block down from the motel, and suddenly the idea of a glass of wine and maybe a salad sounded magnificent. She quickly changed her clothes, grabbed a book and her room key, and headed for the door.

As she walked down the concrete steps of the stairs at the end of the hallway, she could hear talking and laughing from the parking lot. Just about all of her teammates appeared to be in the parking lot or already walking down the street. Brenda had always thought of professional baseball as men playing a boys' game, but sometimes she'd look at her teammates and think they were boys playing a men's game. Out of uniform, in their own clothes, they looked . . . normal. They were just a bunch of guys, no longer teenagers but not really adults, out to have a good time. Brenda fell into line behind Jason, Farnhurst, and Diego, the catcher. They didn't say "hello" and neither did she. In fact, she wondered if they even noticed her walking behind them. The pizza and pasta place was called Shenanigans, and it was located in a beautiful building that looked to be from the late 1800s. But while the outside featured gorgeous masonry detailing around the windows and door, the only sign of that beautiful design inside was a scuffed maple floor that looked as though it could be original.

It was less a restaurant than a café, with small tables in the front by the door, booths along one wall, and a deli-style counter and kitchen along the other wall. They were open late and the menu board behind the counter listed inexpensive pizza slices, pasta, and sandwiches, plus beer and wine. No wonder the team ended up there.

The place wasn't too crowded this late on a Monday night. A lingering couple was in one of the front tables and a small group of older guys was in one of the back booths. Brenda had to laugh at herself as she sat down at one of the tables. Those "older guys" were probably her age.

Jason, Farnhurst, and Diego took over the booth closest to her and ordered two beers and a glass of wine. It didn't surprise her that Jason was the wine drinker. Other Captains players were slowly coming in. Brenda ordered a salad and a glass of Chianti before things got too busy and settled in with her book. She found that she could bear the solitude pretty well. It was the feeling of being treated as invisible, as nothing, that was disturbing.

Her teammates were a little loud. Archie, baby-faced Eduardo Diaz (wasn't there a curfew for seventeen-year-olds?) and a few of the outfielders who hadn't yet deigned even to say hello to her were in the booth behind Jason and Co. They were horsing around, joking about the evening's game. Diaz had turned a stupendous dive-summersault-and-throw double play in the ninth inning that had stopped a couple River Bandit runs and certainly saved the game. At one point, Farnhurst practically stood up in the booth and reached over to the other booth so he could give Diaz a noogie on the head. Brenda had to wonder why boys felt the need to give congratulations by physically abusing each other.

Farnhurst sat down awkwardly and knocked over Jason's glass, spilling red wine all over the table and the front of Jason's blue and white striped shirt. "What the hell, Cody?" Jason snapped. "This was my only good shirt, man."

"Oh, sorry bro. Here," Farnhurst said as he started grabbing napkins to wipe up the mess.

Brenda couldn't help but watch as Jason began scrubbing away at the red wine on his shirt with a handful of napkins. Advice was pouring in from the other players in both booths: "You gotta soak it in hot water," "We need to find an all-night Laundromat," and "Call your mom." She knew his scrubbing away with a dry napkin was only going to make the stain worse. She went over to the counter and asked the server for a glass of soda water with no ice and a dry service towel.

"You gonna rescue them?" the server asked as she handed over the soda water and towel.

"I kind of have to," Brenda replied. "They're my teammates."

Brenda went back to her table and laid the towel on it. "Jason," she said, then repeated his name a bit louder to be heard over the sound of half a dozen young men chattering about how to clean a shirt. The sudden silence was a little unnerving. "Give me your shirt," she said.

"Damn, cougar. You don't waste any time, do you?" Farnhurst said.

Brenda sighed back her annoyance. "Give me the shirt and we'll get the stain out."

Now it was Jason's turn to squirm under everyone else's gaze. It was only when Brenda said, "Oh for crying out loud, I'm a *mom*" that he stood up and walked over to her table. He unbuttoned his shirt and handed it over. She had to admit he and his Adam's apple still managed to look dignified in just a wine-stained white T-shirt and jeans.

Brenda spread the shirt on top of the towel and doused the spill with soda water. Then she grabbed the salt shaker from her table, unscrewed the lid, and began sprinkling a layer of salt on top of the stain. "Could you get another salt shaker, please?" she said, looking up from the shirt for the first time. All of the other players, even Farnhurst, were crowded around her table, watching. For once, they actually seemed glad to have her around. "Okay, let this dry and then wipe the salt off of it. That should take the wine with it. And . . . yeah, tomorrow I'll teach you how to get bubble gum out of your hair."

•◊•

Excerpt from the transcript for *Today in Sports* with Charlie Bannister, ESPN, August 4:

> Charlie: Good evening baseball fans. The trade deadline passed us by four days ago, and we're starting to see what the new additions bring their new clubs. Second baseman Ray Kowalski has already made a big impact on the White Sox's defense, including turning a spectacular double play against the Blue Jays last night. With Bob Chambers on third and Marty Walsh on second, and Toronto down by two, the Francisco Ruiz line drive looks like it could tie the ballgame. But check out Kowalski's beautiful dive. One nonchalant behind-the-back toss to Harry Tagiashi and Walsh is out at second. In a much quieter move yesterday, the Cleveland Indians sent reliever Ed Robinson down to the AAA Columbus Clippers. Who they're making room for, I can't say.

Chapter Twelve

•◊•

THE NEXT DAY, WHEN SHE GOT ON THE TEAM BUS TO GO TO THE BALLPARK, JASON SAID, "HI, MOM" AND IT DIDN'T SOUND IRONIC. A few other players said "Hey, B" or gave her a little upward nod the way they did to each other.

They had two more games in Davenport, played a three-game series in Peoria, and then headed back to Cleveland. It was too early to call it morning but too late to call it the middle of the night when they finally arrived in the parking lot at Classic Park. A few of the other players had their own cars, which they had left in the lot, and a smattering had girlfriends or roommates waiting to pick them up. Because she hadn't started the trip with the rest of the team, Brenda's car wasn't waiting for her. Instead, she had Robin, who was leaning against the hood of her car with an amused grin on her face.

"I feel like that girl in *Bull Durham*," she said as Brenda walked over to the car. "The one who ends up getting married."

"You're the most chipper groupie I've ever seen," Brenda replied and threw her duffel bag into the back seat. "But I thank you for picking me up at this ungodly hour."

This was the only day off for another ten days, and Brenda wanted to make the most of it. She had envisioned getting a few hours of sleep then spending the day with the boys, maybe puttering around the house and doing some laundry and cleaning and just being home. Instead, she dropped her duffel bag on the kitchen floor, laid down on the sofa, and slept until noon. She woke up expecting to see her family but instead found a note from Adele:

> Welcome home! We decided you needed your sleep. The boys are at camp. I'll be over later to make dinner. How does halusky sound?
>
> Love, Mom

Her mother's halusky—potato dumplings that were the ultimate Slovak comfort food—always sounded wonderful, but Brenda had been gone a week and was looking forward to doing something normal, like making dinner. When the boys were younger and it seemed like the laundry and chores and chauffeuring would never end, there had been many days when she wished someone would sweep in and do everything for her. Now all she had to do was go to work and come home. Was this how fathers and husbands sometimes felt? Extraneous?

Extraneous or not, the few hours of solitude before the boys came home from camp were more enjoyable than she wanted to admit. It had only been a week, but somehow the house looked different. All of the things wrong with it—from the garage that needed painting to the sagging front porch to the gutters hanging on by a thread—seemed to stand out. If she was careful, the endorsement money would fix all of that with enough left over for a nest egg. She just had to stay focused on playing.

Once the boys got home from camp, it was impossible to be focused on anything but them. Jon talked a mile a minute, wanting to hear all about what life was like in the minor leagues. Even Andy seemed interested in hearing about some of the games and the players. And when her mother arrived, Brenda let her make dinner and tried not to feel too left out.

The Captains had a ten-day home stand, and Brenda and the boys settled into a routine. She got them out the door to the sports camp in the morning then typically went back to sleep for an hour (she couldn't always go to sleep right away after a night game). Then

Adele came over and stayed with the boys in the evening. Some nights Brenda pitched an inning. Some nights she didn't. But she threw every day and was spending some time in the weight room at the park and knew she was getting stronger. And better. When she did play, she was consistently getting swings and misses. Between Ed, Farnhurst's insistence on calling her "cougar," and the pain in her lower back after long rides on the team bus, she had plenty to keep her angry.

It seemed like the summer could go on like this indefinitely when she got a call from David on a Wednesday afternoon. She was on her way to the ballpark for warm-ups and a bullpen session before the game. Although she never wanted to be one of those people who chatted on their phone while driving, she had already learned that when her agent called, it was a good idea to answer.

David's voice sounded silkier than usual as he said, "Are you sitting down, Brenda?"

"Yes, I'm sitting. I'm driving to the ballpark." She didn't mean to sound snotty but it came out sounding that way all the same.

"This is the last time you'll need to go to Classic Park," he cooed in a voice so gentle that Brenda thought perhaps she had been fired or demoted.

"What do you mean?"

"You're going to the AAA affiliate in Columbus for a couple of games, and then The Show."

"Holy crap balls . . . Are you serious?" She meant to pull over but instead accidentally accelerated and almost ran a red light. She jerked the car to a stop and took a deep breath. "Okay. Tell me."

"They're moving you up. This is your last game with the Captains. Tomorrow you report to the Columbus Clippers. If you do there what you've been doing for the Captains, next stop is Progressive Field," David purred. "Chimelewski will be calling you in a little while but I wanted to give you a heads up."

"Thank you . . ." There was so much to say and nothing to say. She was moving up. Brenda drove the rest of the way to the ballpark with the steering wheel clenched so tightly that her knuckles ached when she finally parked and took her hands off the wheel. She had to sit for a moment, just sit and think. This was the goal, wasn't it? If she wanted security for her and the boys, this was the next step. This would do it. Major league salary incentives and more endorsement deals, she thought, making a conscious effort to silence the part of her that hated advertisements and selling things, the part that felt like a mercenary and a sellout.

"I'm not selling my soul," she said out loud, and this thought was enough to propel her out of the car and into the players' entrance. Once inside, she found Scott in his office/her locker room.

"Congratulations," he said when she knocked.

"Thanks."

Scott stood up to leave so she could change. "Suit up, but I'm not going to put you in tonight. They want you to have a fresh arm tomorrow."

"Okay," she replied. Brenda went through what had become her pre-game routine—suit up, stretch, and do a slow jog around the field once or twice, throw fifteen or twenty pitches to Archie, then wait in the dugout for the team to be introduced. Things went along as they had at the other home games. She ended up standing in dugout next to Jason again during the National Anthem.

"Good to be back home, huh?" he said.

"Yes, yes it is," she replied.

"Hey, congrats. Go up there and kick some ass."

Well, word got around quickly. "I'll do my best."

"You'd better," Jason said, then added with a slight grin that made his Adam's apple shrink away to almost nothing. "I have a little sister with a sweet swing. She oughta get a chance too."

Once the game was underway, she took her standard spot in the middle of the bench, out of the way. Archie came over and plopped his six-foot-two-inch self down on the bench next to her.

"How come you aren't like, dancing around or something?" he asked.

"There's a baseball game on," Brenda replied.

"I can't believe you didn't tell me while you were warming up," he said incredulously.

Telling anyone on the team seemed like bragging, even Archie, with whom she had developed something of a friendship, or at least a positive working relationship. "Sorry, thanks for all your help. You're a good catcher."

"Thank you. I hope we play together again someday." Archie sounded like he really meant it, and when Brenda said, "I hope so," she meant it too.

She watched from the dugout as the Captains lost to the visiting Fort Wayne Tin Caps 3-2. During the game, most of the other players sat down next to her at one point or another to say congratulations and chat for a moment. It was a different kind of being apart from the rest of the team. A couple weeks earlier, none of these guys wanted to have a thing to do with her, and now any of them would trade places with her. She couldn't fault them.

Knowing that she wouldn't go in that night made the game easier to watch. She didn't have to worry, didn't have to conjure up an adrenaline-inducing surge of rage, all she had to do was sit and enjoy the game. After the final out, as the other players were grabbing their mitts and batting gloves, Brenda stayed in the dugout, just leaning against the railing. The empty ballpark, with its orderly rows of seats all focused center into a wide green bowl, held a certain intangible allure. She was moving up to much larger ballparks and doubted they would be so inviting.

Scott's voice broke the calm. "Haversham!" She turned around and saw Scott and Stuart waiting to talk to her. Scott reached out his hand. "Good luck to you. You have the stuff to do well." For a guy as reserved as Scott, that was as personal as he was going to get.

Brenda shook his hand. "Thank you. I know you weren't crazy about having me around, but I appreciate that you were always fair to me. You're a good manager."

"Thanks."

Stuart, who had been genuinely kind to her since day one, reached out his hand and said, "Good luck, Brenda. Knock 'em dead."

"I'll do my best," she said. Figuring Stu would go all to pieces if somebody hugged him, she shook his hand with both her hands, touching him twice. He gave her shoulder a gentle tap to even things up. Somehow she doubted she'd find anyone as quietly quirky as Stuart anywhere else in baseball. Then she went to the manager's office, changed, and gathered up her things. That was it. She was expected to report to Columbus the next day at noon.

Brenda spent less than a week with the Clippers—barely long enough to learn her teammates' names. She knew some of them. The Clippers had a handful of players who had been bouncing back and forth between AAA and the majors due to injury or because they couldn't quite hack the level of play in the majors. Brenda kept her head down and threw strikes. Enough for her to go hitless in 3.1 innings of work over three games. Enough for the Indians to make the call to bring her to The Show.

Brenda almost expected it. Whenever she was at the ballpark, attendance soared. It didn't matter if people were cheering or boo-ing, the club sold tickets. The Clippers had just lost a game to the Toledo Mud Hens. Brenda hadn't gone on in, which was her first clue. At the end of the game, the manager said "good luck" and shook her hand. The two-hour drive up I-71 to Cleveland gave her plenty of time to think. Part of her didn't want to have to tell the boys and her mom and her friends that she had been called up. It just made things too complicated. She was too scared to want to be congratulated. When she got home, it was nearly two in the morning and the only thing awake in the house was the Internet.

Tired but not sleepy, Brenda went downstairs to the rec room to check her email and saw a notification that she had 321 new followers on Twitter. "Three hundred twenty-one?" she said. "What the hell?" She had posted exactly one thing on Twitter, and that been in the business center of the motel in Davenport two weeks earlier when she couldn't fall asleep after a game. She had written: "Just saw a bunch of ballplayers come out of a cornfield in Iowa. Not heaven, just the minor leagues." That was all, yet people were following her.

Clearly the news of her call-up was out because her name was trending on Twitter and had provoked some heated discussions. Charlie Bannister (or @CABannister) seemed to be in the thick it. She counted replies to seventeen different people, and in each one Charlie advocated for her right to play. Or at least, the right for a woman to play. He obviously wasn't defending *her* specifically, just the principle of giving someone a chance.

She had a direct message from Charlie that she had never replied to, and here he was fighting the good fight in her name. She sent him a quick message: "Thanks for all the support. It's much appreciated."

A minute later she was surprised to get a direct message back. "No problem," his reply read. "Glad to see you liked the River Bandits cornfield. It's pretty cute."

She was tempted to write "So are you" but why would she start flirting with Charlie Bannister? She hardly knew the guy. Plus there had to be an unspoken rule about athletes not mixing with journalists. There was just something about him that sometimes made her want to flirt with him. Which was silly.

Instead she wrote back: "Yes, it is." And then: "I feel like my call-up just broke the Internet. It isn't the freaking apocalypse. I'm just playing baseball."

Charlie replied: "For some trogs, a female on the ball field is more frightening than a horde of rampaging zombies."

Brenda hated the use of "LOL," but she actually did laugh out loud. She wrote: "Trog?"

Charlie replied: "I'm too tired to remember how to spell 'troglodyte.' Time to sleep. Good night."

"Good night," she wrote back. Brenda went up to the living room and collapsed on the sofa in her clothes. She slept for a few hours, but the sound of Jon screaming her name immediately kicked on the Mommy Instinct. In an instant, she was awake and asked, "What's wrong? What happened?"

Jon was dancing around the living room in front of her. "You got called up!" he squealed. "You got called up!" Andy had the television tuned to ESPN, and he and Adele were riveted to a panel discussion about the ramifications of a woman playing at the major league level. Brenda took the obligatory bear hugs from Jon and Adele and even a half-hearted, one-armed hug from Andy. She knew she should be happy, but her heart started pounding and her limbs started tingling just thinking about it.

After a quiet day that was mostly spent catching up on her sleep, Brenda reported to Progressive Field at 3:30, right when the clubhouse opened. Pulling into the Players' Parking Lot, she noticed that Molly was the only minivan there. Every other car was smaller, newer, and cleaner. Brenda parked and grabbed her duffel bag. She was embarrassed to see that Jon had written "Now who needs a bath?" in the dust on the passenger side. She wondered how many players had wives or ex-wives who were stuck driving boring mom cars while their husbands or ex-husbands drove the expensive, fun cars.

Jerry Chimelewski was once again waiting for her in the small reception area at the bottom of the long concrete stairway. "Brenda, welcome to the Indians," he said, shaking her hand. "We're really pleased with how you've handled yourself the last couple weeks with the Captains and the Clippers, and we think you may be ready for the big leagues."

"Thanks. I think I'm ready too," Brenda replied with more confidence than she felt. She didn't bother adding, "And you're selling a lot of tickets and merchandise, right?"

She and Jerry started walking down the wide tunnel that circled the ballpark. "Follow me. The front office thinks it's more appropriate if you have a separate locker room. And I think most of the players' wives do too," he added with a chuckle.

He led Brenda into the familiar blue door to the Indians' clubhouse, past the locker room and manager's office, and down the hall. They stopped in front of a single steel door painted the same deep blue as the locker room door and marked with a small sign reading "Private." Brenda wondered what other signs had been rejected. "Women?" "Women's Locker Room?" "Locker Room Annex?" "Token Female?"

"Here," Jerry said as he opened the door. "It used to be an extra storage room, but we've converted it into a locker room." Brenda walked into the room, which was about ten by twelve feet. A single cubbyhole-type locker shared one wall with a built-in shower stall. A chair, a sink, and a toilet completed the room. It wasn't fancy and it wasn't big, but it was worlds better than sharing the manager's office.

"This is great," Brenda said. For a minute she felt like she was being shown an apartment by a realtor. There was a small box on the chair with Brenda's name written on it in marker. Jerry picked it up and handed it to her.

"This came by messenger from your agent. I believe it's a new phone."

"Thank you," she said as she took the box. She glanced inside and saw a note that read, "Brenda, Stay in touch. David" and a razor-thin smart phone that she was sure she'd never figure out how to use.

"I'll leave you alone so you can get into uniform, and then I'll show you the shortcut to the bullpen," Jerry said and left the room.

Uniform? The white and red uniform hanging in the locker cubby made the reality of where she was and what she was about to do come screaming back. Brenda felt her heart skip a beat. It was just a uniform made out of a cotton-polyester blend, but when she picked it up, the fabric felt substantial in her hands, as though the uniform held secrets that it would share the moment she put it on.

Brenda changed as quickly as her trembling hands would let her. She tried to muster up some angry frustration when she tried to button her jersey, or to get ticked that they had shunted her off to an unused storage room. And she couldn't. The team had made a locker room for her. They made that investment just for her. It was all a little too amazing.

She finally managed to get suited up, and as she buttoned the last button on the jersey and tucked it into her pants, she felt transformed. She looked down at herself. "It's just another outfit," she muttered. Then she looked up and saw her reflection in the mirror above the sink. "No, it's a uniform," she said.

•◊•

Excerpt from the transcript for *Today in Sports* with Charlie Bannister, ESPN, August 5:

> Charlie: Welcome back to *Today in Sports*. I'm Charlie Bannister. And the big news today, the Cleveland Indians have called up right-hander Brenda Haversham, making her the first woman ever on a major league roster and the second-oldest rookie ever. The oldest, of course, was Satchel Paige. Not bad company to be in.

Chapter Thirteen

•◇•

JERRY DIRECTED HER DOWN THE TUNNEL TO THE BULLPEN WHERE EARL DONALD, THE BULLPEN COACH, AND ROY BRIDGES, THE BULLPEN CATCHER, WERE WAITING FOR HER. She had met them both at her tryout. With his long face and droopy gray moustache to match a shock of salt and pepper hair, Earl reminded Brenda of one of the figures in the background of Rembrandt's *Night Watch*, only without the lace collar. She got a "Hello" from Earl and a quiet nod from Roy.

"Okay," Earl said. "Let's see what we need to work on."

The transition from "Hello" to throwing was abrupt. Usually she had half an inning or so to find the anger and let it start festering. Now she needed to turn it on like a faucet. Brenda took a few easy warm-up throws. Roy caught the fourth pitch with his bare hand and threw the ball back to her. He didn't say anything, but she noticed the tiniest shake of his head, as though he couldn't believe the team had made the colossal mistake of signing her.

"Let's stop right there," Earl said. "What's going on? Where's the flamethrower I saw at your tryout?"

"Sorry. I just need to focus," Brenda said.

"Yes, you do," Earl said calmly. "We want you in short relief. Which means you're going to be sitting for a couple hours before you throw and there may be games when you have as little as two or three minutes to get ready to go in." He wasn't yelling or insulting. She couldn't muster up any anger at him. She wanted to. Dear God, she wanted to get mad at Earl and throw the hell out of the ball, but he was engaging her intellect, not her emotions. It would have been easier if he had just acted like a jerk and told her she threw like a girl and made a few other disparaging remarks.

"Okay," she said, and tried to sound focused but agreeable. She turned back to face Roy, focusing, as always, on the center of the catcher's mitt.

"Ed . . ." she muttered.

"What'd you say?" Earl asked.

She didn't respond, just grunted her favorite expletive as she launched the ball as hard as she could at Roy's mitt. From the way his body reacted to the ball, she could see that the pitch had woken him up.

"Now that's more like it. Let's run through your pitches." She went through the identical routine. It had worked before, why mess with it? Pair Ed's name with a swear word and throw. Although it was difficult to see his expression through the catcher's mask, she was grimly pleased to see that Roy no longer looked bored. Earl stopped her again after about half a dozen pitches.

"Okay, I don't want to mess with you too much because whatever you're doing, it seems to be working. But we need to work on your lead shoulder. You're throwing it out too early and it makes you drag."

"Um, I'm not sure what you mean," Brenda admitted. "Can you show me? I mean, I'm kind of a visual learner." She handed him the ball and took a few steps back. Maybe asking was a breach of protocol, but she knew that she learned best when she could watch something done.

Earl took the ball from her a little awkwardly, almost as though he didn't want to touch her hand accidentally. Once the ball was firmly in his hand and he had mounted himself next to the bullpen's pitching rubber, he looked as comfortable as though he were sitting on the sofa in his bathrobe reading the Sunday paper. Moving in slow motion, he demonstrated how Brenda was throwing her left shoulder back before her ball hand had completed its movement.

"When did you play?" Brenda asked. Again, she wasn't sure if she was breaking protocol by asking personal questions (or if she was supposed to know Earl's bio).

Earl looked surprised that she had asked but replied that he had played in the minors thirty years ago. "But I realized pretty early on that I was a better coach than player," he added with a small smile. "Now you try it," Earl said. "Go through your windup very slowly and focus on your left shoulder. You should notice a shift in your balance."

Brenda tried not to feel self-conscious as she went through her windup in slow motion. There was something vaguely ridiculous feeling about the exercise—as though she was playing at being a big league pitcher instead of actually being one. Then again, focusing on her own body had never been a favorite pastime.

She had always wanted to be graceful and lithe. For about two weeks when she was seven, she wanted to be a ballerina. At her first ballet class, she saw all the other little girls moving their bodies gently while pretending to be leaves dancing in the breeze and then caught sight of her own sturdy but clunky little body jerking around like a plastic bag in a cyclone. At that moment, Brenda knew graceful and lithe were probably not in her future. In her mind's eye, she could see how her body should move, could watch it imitate Earl's easy lean-back-lean-forward motion but found it difficult to make her limbs move the way she knew they should.

"Try it again," Earl said. "I know you're eager to get the ball across the plate, but if you stop leading with that shoulder, you'll get the ball across more effectively."

After a few more minutes of slow motion windups, Brenda felt as though she had the movement down. She had never thought so much about what her body was doing when she pitched, but simply imitated the same motions she had seen dozens of major league pitchers perform and let the anger bubble and boil. Intellectualizing the movement doused the anger so much that when Earl told her to throw at full speed, she was barely able get the ball the full distance to Roy's catcher's mitt.

"Sorry about that," she mumbled as she took the throw back from Roy.

"Why are you holding back?" Earl asked. "I expect all of my players to work at one hundred percent during workouts and during games. None of this half-assed stuff. This is not the minor leagues. Put it all together and let's see what you've got."

"Okay," Brenda said. It was embarrassing to be called out as though she wasn't trying when she was. Finding the anger when she wasn't angry had seemed artificial, but now she realized it was survival.

Turning on the anger was getting easier, or maybe it was just starting to bubble closer to the surface. She mumbled Ed's name in vain and threw. The pitches weren't her fastest, but they were on target, and Earl said they had good movement. She didn't allow herself to smile when he said this, just nodded. She had too much work to do to be happy about it.

After the bullpen session, Jerry gave Brenda scouting reports and an iPad that was preloaded with a proprietary app called On the Ball that allowed her to access video of all MLB batters when the team was on the road. He also showed her the film room so she could study even more batter video. She had so much to learn in such a short time that she focused only on the lineups of the next few teams they'd be facing. She had the scouting report in front of her, but reading, for instance, "Has a tendency to chase outside pitches" was one thing. Seeing the placement of the pitch and the twitch of an arm and the split-second expression on the batter's face as he went for a ball that broke just below the line of his swing was quite another. Brenda had never given that much thought to how a pitcher throws to a particular hitter; she just always assumed it was some combination of fastballs, curveballs, and sinkers or sliders (she noticed there seemed to be an endless supply of names for pitches that moved in one direction or another). As she watched the film, she focused sometimes on the hitter, but found herself looking more and more at the catcher and his signals and where he placed his mitt. No wonder Andy liked catching so much. All this time, she had thought the pitcher controlled the game, but it was the catcher who was the anchor around which everything else revolved.

By the time she finished in the film room, the visiting Yankees were already taking batting practice and other Indians players were in the clubhouse, going through their pre-game rituals. There was more than an hour to game time. Hanging out in her locker room and reading through scouting reports seemed like the best use of her time.

The Indians' clubhouse felt like a rabbit's warren of hallways, and Brenda got turned around coming back from the film room. There was the manager's office to her left, and in front of her was the door to the Indians' locker room, which was probably not a place she needed to be while the guys were changing. She heard voices coming down the corridor behind her and turned around. She recognized Fred Pasquela, the second baseman, and Phil Cipriani, another relief pitcher. Most of the guys on the Lightning seemed to gripe about Pasquela being a lazy ballplayer. Cipriani seemed to be all legs and arms—his windup resembled a windmill moving at high speed—but he walked gracefully, with the smooth gait of a big cat.

"Hey, pecker checker," Pasquela said. They were in uniform, and so was she. They were on the same team, but it was clear that was in name only. "I believe *your* locker room is around the corner."

The hallway to the right, with its big print of the Indians' 1920 World Series team, looked familiar. They weren't steering her wrong, at least. "Thanks," she murmured and tried to walk away with some measure of dignity, although they had done their best to make her feel like an idiot. She felt like more of an idiot when she opened the door to her little locker room. At least one hundred tampons were hanging from the ceiling on extra-long strings. Her Fountain ad was taped to the mirror above the sink. The text was doctored to read, "Make a fountain on my face!" About the only positive thing she could say was that the tampons were clean.

The jokers (although she used that term lightly) had taped the tampons to the concrete ceiling. It should have been an easy enough task simply to stand on the one chair in the room and pull them down. She managed to get most of them, but there were a few hanging just inches from the ceiling that she was too short to reach.

"Ingrates," she muttered. There wasn't anything in the locker room suitable for breaking, and kicking a cinderblock wall was just asking for trouble. Brenda let fly a few curses, then tried to figure out an appropriate response.

This had to be the work of Pasquela and Cipriani. Getting mad or saying anything about it would just feed their stupid little fire. She couldn't let them see any reaction. *Besides, everyone plays jokes on the rookies, right?* she thought. By the time she was done picking them off the ceiling, it was almost game time.

With the Captains and Clippers, she had only ventured into the locker room in the few minutes right before game time because the manager always had a quick pep talk for the team. Figuring the routine was similar, Brenda braced herself to enter the Indians' locker room for the first time. She walked back down the corridor, past the print of the 1920 World Series team, and stopped in front of the beige double doors that led to the locker room. She could hear conversation and some laughter—the sound of a bunch of guys staying loose before a game. The Yankees were in town for a four-game series, which always meant sellout crowds and a lot of energy in the park. With twenty minutes to first pitch, every player in there had to be dressed.

She waited by the doors for a minute, hoping someone would come in or out and give her some indication as to whether it was all right for her to enter. Finally, she just said, "Oh what the hell" and walked in.

The Indians' locker room was huge and comfortable—like a surprisingly clean frat house. A few round tables with chairs were near the doors; a circular leather couch and a couple of leather-upholstered easy chairs sat in front of a wide-screen TV in the middle of the room. Around all four walls were multiple clones of her locker. Each one had a player's name on the top and was filled with clothes, shoes, maybe an extra glove. Some players had pictures or other personal items hanging in their lockers. She could hear the voices of other players on the other side of the two wide pillars connected by a low counter that cut the room in half.

Brenda took a seat at one of the round tables just inside the double doors. A few players glanced over at her. Doug Stone, the veteran left fielder, had the locker just opposite her table. He was sitting in the chair in front of his locker, fixing the laces on his cleats just so. Stone had always struck her as a decent guy—one of those non-marquee players who just comes in and does his job and doesn't get involved in off-field drama. He looked up and his large brown eyes regarded her. It wasn't just his eyes—everything about him seemed large. These were the grown-up, filled-out versions of the kids she'd spent the last couple weeks playing with. Finally he said, "Hey, rookie."

"Hi," she said, trying not to sound weak or intimidated. Stone went back to what he was doing, not rudely but simply in a manner that said this was his ritual and he was going to follow it. A couple other players nodded when she made eye contact with them, but no one else seemed to acknowledge her. She didn't count Cipriani and Pasquela, who glanced over at her a couple times and didn't bother to hide their snickering.

The buzz of conversation in the room settled down when Mark Munson came in to give his pre-game manager pep talk. Brenda had been correct in her initial assessment of him as a no-nonsense straight shooter—he walked in, said "Hey guys," and stood in front of the wide-screen TV where a few players were playing *Grand Theft Auto* to loosen up before game time. His presence was such that his players just naturally paid attention to him. "Just a couple of things before we start this series. This is the last time we'll see the Yankees this season." (He was interrupted by a couple of subdued "Yays.") "They are always contenders, and they will capitalize on your mistakes. I need you to focus on attention to detail, to doing the little things that win ball games. We've got a sellout crowd tonight, so this should be a lot of fun. Oh, and if you haven't met our newest rookie, Brenda Haversham was just called up from the Clippers." As Munson said her name, he sort of pointed in her general direction. It seemed kind of funny for him to point her out when she was the only female in the room—how hard could it be to spot her? "Have a great game tonight. We need the W. Let's go."

Munson walked purposefully to the red double doors at the far end of the room, pushed them open, and headed to what Brenda presumed was the dugout, followed by the rest of the team. Brenda instinctively held back before following Ryan Teeset, the huge rookie first baseman, out the doors. She was pretty sure her feet were touching the ground, but she was so nervous she wasn't even sure if her limbs were still attached.

She wanted to be mindful of everything that was happening but was so overwhelmed by the noise of the sold-out crowd screaming at the top of their lungs as the Indians were introduced and the hyper-stimulation of being at the center of all the action, that the first few minutes went by in a blur. Before she knew it, she was in the dugout watching Jimmy Panidopolous throw the first pitch.

Panidopolous starting meant that the ballpark had more than the usual share of Panidopo-Nuts—members of the Jimmy Panidopolous fan club. They were mostly young, always female, and typically wore T-shirts reading, "Mrs. Panidopolous" or "Marry me, Jimmy." Having been treated to the sight of Panidopolous jumping in front of the TV playing *Grand Theft Auto* and yelping for joy like a kid every time he gained points, she found the hoopla over his most-eligible-bachelor status more than a little amusing.

As she had in the minors, Brenda tried to take her cues from the rest of the relief pitchers. Francisco Jimenez, the closer, seemed friendly but quiet. He spent the first inning in the dugout and then retreated to the bullpen at the top of the second inning. Brenda followed.

The home bullpen at Progressive Field looked as though someone had taken a cake knife and cut a large slice out of the green left field wall. The screened-in dugout was at field level and sat in front of the little rectangular area where pitchers warmed up. Jimenez sat down on the dugout bench about three-quarters of the way down from the single entrance. Earl was already out there. Before Brenda sat down, Earl said quietly to her, "Don't sit too close to Jimenez's left side. That's where Roberto Pena always sat. Francisco says he's keeping the spot open until Pena is off the DL."

Brenda nodded her understanding. She remembered reading that Pena had had Tommy John surgery and would be out for the season. Having Jimenez save his friend's spot on the bullpen bench was poignant and seemed almost feminine in its thoughtfulness. He nodded to Brenda and said, "Hola," as she sat down in the middle of the bench.

The rest of the relief pitchers came out to the bullpen around the fourth inning. They all seemed to have their own favorite spot. Cipriani sat as close to the end of the bench as possible while still leaving room for Earl to do his sit-stand-pace-sit-stand-pace routine. The far end of the bench was empty and Brenda moved down and claimed it as hers, using Jimenez and Anderson Sparks as a buffer between her and Cipriani, who was sprawled over the middle of the bench. Sparks was a little shorter and more compact. He was a left-handed long reliever, and his broad chest and arms made him look as though he could go in and give you ten good innings if you needed it. They didn't look like bad guys. With his close-cut, curly black hair, blue eyes, and square jaw, Sparks was actually a good-looking guy. If he weren't a ball player, he might even have been able to make it as a model.

She liked the view from the bullpen. It was expansive and immediate. And she liked being close enough to the field that she could smell the grass. Brenda held a baseball in her hand during most of the game; just holding it, feeling the slightly rough bump of stitches that curved over its surface like a never-ending Möbius strip. Even from her spot at the end of the bench, she could hear Cipriani spouting his mouth off to Anderson Sparks. It was very obvious he was talking about her. Cipriani wasn't the team captain—that honor went to Art "Pepper" Groggins, the veteran centerfielder—but the others in the bullpen seemed to listen to him anyway. Brenda figured it was only because he did a lot of talking.

"You gotta have three things to succeed in this game," Cipriani said. "Heart, brains, and balls. From what I can see, she doesn't have any of those."

"I knew we were in bad shape this year, but this is ridiculous . . ." Anderson Sparks' voice trailed off into half a laugh.

"I just can't believe they sent Robinson down to make room for her."

Brenda had never met Ed Robinson, but this was the third time she had heard his name mentioned. It hadn't occurred to her before that someone had lost his job so that she might have one. She felt for Robinson. No one wants to get demoted. At the same time, she couldn't imagine Robinson feeling all that bad if she lost her job. She wondered what the other players' lives were like outside of baseball, if they even had lives outside of baseball. It was likely that she was the only one on the team who had actually had a non-baseball career.

Design and drawing had always been her great love. Why was it that art seemed to have stalled, while this newly discovered talent had already brought her so far and so fast?

In the top of the seventh, with one out and the Yankees up by two, Panidopolous walked two in a row. The call to the bullpen came after the first walk. Earl told Brenda to start warming up. Brenda never really warmed up so much as started seething—it wasn't her body that needed to get hot, it was her emotions. She sat on the bull-pen bench for a moment, willing the anger to begin to rise.

"Move it, meat," Earl said.

Brenda's heart dropped somewhere into the vicinity of her stomach, and she took a few deep breaths, trying to conjure the flood of angry adrenaline she needed in order to pitch.

"I am warming up," Brenda said.

"Warm up off your ass. Start throwing, princess."

She picked up her glove and quickly walked through the bullpen dugout, past the other relievers (making sure to avoid Cipriani's evil eye, which she could practically feel boring a hole in her back), and went out behind the dugout where Roy was waiting for her to take her warm-up throws. For the first time, instead of Ed's face in the catcher's mitt, she saw Earl's leathery old mug as it spit out the word "princess."

"Shove it, Earl," she muttered as she threw her first warm-up pitch. Roy looked a little surprised.

"Save something for the field," he said as he threw it back.

She threw a few more pitches and began to be aware that the fans whose seats were nearest the bullpen were watching her warm up. She tried to focus on the catcher's mitt, but then she heard a male voice yell, "Hey, they're gonna let the fat chick pitch" and the sound of other men laughing. Earl had been walking back and forth behind her as she warmed up, and he muttered "Look at them, and you're running thirty laps a day for the next month," just loudly enough for her and no one else to hear.

Brenda stopped but didn't move her focus from the catcher's mitt in front of her. She nodded slowly, just once, and threw another pitch. It went wild, and she could hear more laughter from the fans sitting nearby.

Stupid armchair quarterbacking, fantasy baseball playing yahoos, she thought. It occurred to her that there were more things in life to be angry with than just Ed. There were sexist, loudmouth idiots like the ones heckling her right now. There were obnoxious jerks like Pasquela and Cipriani. There were troglodyte sports radio hosts and their callers who thought no woman should even be given the chance to play pro ball. There was the piece she saw on the news last week about women and girls—little girls nine years old—being sold to brothels in Thailand. What kind of sick bastard would have sex with a nine-year-old? There were child pornography rings. There were AIDS orphans and genocide and mass rapes in Darfur and those young women factory workers in Juarez who kept getting murdered and violence in the Middle East and serial killers and just a hell of a lot to be angry about. The thought of so many horrible, horrible things, of so much suffering—and so often women and children suffering at the hands of men—infuriated her.

She was a reasonably well-informed adult. She knew the ways of the world and, like most people, had always shaken her head at the news of the world's latest atrocities, said "what a shame," maybe whispered a small prayer, and went about her daily life. But suddenly these things angered her in a way they never had before. She felt the anger more palpably than ever before, as though every other time she had ever thrown a ball was just practice for this moment. She let the anger fill her up. It prickled—she could almost feel it coursing through her body. She heard the sold-out crowd roar.

Earl patted her on the back and said, "Haversham. Get out there."

She expected to feel nervous, but she didn't. The anger had her now. She finally understood what people meant when they said they were in the zone. She looked Earl in the face and was tempted to tell him to go fuck himself. He just gave her a little smile and said, "Go get 'em." Brenda nodded.

As she left the bullpen and started the long, solitary walk across left-center field to the pitcher's mound, she heard the stadium sound system start playing Tom Jones' "She's A Lady." She hated that song. She had been asked for a couple of songs that she might want played when she went into a game, but couldn't decide and so she chose nothing. It hadn't seemed that important. Now, walking across the seemingly endless expanse of outfield grass, she wished she had picked something. Anything. The idea of perfectly sensible women throwing their underwear and hotel room keys onstage to some smarmy guy in pants that were purposely two sizes too small just irked her. She broke into a trot. The sooner she got to the mound, the sooner they'd shut off that insipid song.

After Panidopolous walked two, he had given up a double, which scored two, and then another walk. The Indians were now down by four with men on the corners and only one out. She just had to get out of the inning without giving up any more runs. *Two outs,* she thought. *Six strikes. That's all.*

"She's a Lady" was still playing as she took the mound. Johnny Gonzalez, the catcher, nodded to her as he squatted down for her warm-up pitches. She threw, aware that this might be the first time in history everyone in the stands actually watched a relief pitcher take warm-up throws. She knew she was being watched, had known she was being watched since the first time she picked up a baseball in front of anyone besides her kids. She wasn't supposed to be playing baseball; her presence, her arm, her power threw all sorts of masculine certainties into doubt and made her an object of derision, even hatred. She could most definitely hear boos and jeers as she took her pitches. The only thing that would silence those boos were strikes and outs.

She didn't even look at the first batter or the mob of cameras that ringed the infield. She just focused on Gonzalez's glove. He signaled for a sinker. She resisted the urge to shake him off—she wanted to throw the heat. She could feel the anger churning away inside her—anger at Ed, at injustice and racism and sexism and cellulite that wouldn't budge despite eight weeks on a low-carb diet and stupid jokes at her expense and people who booed before she even had the chance to prove herself. "Fucking assholes," she muttered and threw. The sinker sank. Indeed, it hit the ground and only Gonzalez' quick reflexes kept it from being a passed ball. If the runner on first had taken a bigger lead, he could have stolen second.

More jeers. More boos.

"You know, if I were a guy, you'd all be rooting for the rookie, wouldn't you?" Brenda muttered. She remembered watching Mark Fidrych pitch when she was a little kid and how he was famous for talking to the ball. She didn't want to be known as the chick pitcher who talked to herself. She just wanted to earn her paycheck so Andy and Jon would continue to have a roof over their heads and a secure future.

Gonzalez signaled for the fastball, bless his heart. She focused on his mitt. Without looking, her fingers found the grip for the four-seamer—index and middle finger perpendicular to the widest part of the seams, thumb underneath. "Like you are holding the wings of the bird," her father always said. "Look at the shape of the cover. When they make a baseball, they sew the bird's wings down. Hold it gently, like an egg. Then let it fly."

Brenda let it fly and swore she could feel the breeze as the batter swung and missed. She was told later that the speed clock tracked the pitch at 96 mph. Brenda didn't look. All she knew was that she needed five more strikes to get out of the inning.

The batter took the next pitch, a curve, for a ball, then grounded into a double play on the fourth pitch. And that was it. That was Brenda's major league debut. They sent Sparks in for the eighth and Jimenez for the ninth. The Indians didn't manage to come back with enough runs to win, but that wasn't Brenda's fault. She had done what they paid her to do.

•◊•

Excerpt from the transcript for *Today in Sports* with Charlie Bannister, ESPN, August 6:

> Charlie: Good evening, America, and welcome to *Today in Sports*. I'm joined tonight, as I am every Friday, by the great Howie Wojinski. Howie, let's talk baseball.
>
> Howie: [pause] Okay, let's talk baseball.
>
> Charlie: Okay. You start.
>
> Howie: Why are you waiting for me? Everybody knows you're dying to talk about Haversham's major league debut.

Charlie: I want you to start. I want to hear you talk about how history was made this week and how the nice lady from Cleveland did not disappoint.

Howie: [sighs] Okay, fine. Haversham pitched a good inning last night.

Charlie: And tonight . . .

Howie: And tonight.

Charlie: Like it or not, this woman has changed the face of the game forever. Just like Jackie Robinson and Larry Doby added a bit of melanin to the lineup, Haversham adds the X factor.

Howie: X factor?

Charlie: X chromosome, buddy.

Howie: I still don't see how a woman can throw that hard. And a lot of other people don't either. There are already allegations floating around the blogosphere that she's doping.

Charlie: All reports say that she's passed every drug test they've given her. She has been watched more closely in both the minors and the majors than any pitcher in recent memory.

Howie: Then how does she do it? How does this short housewife from Cleveland, Ohio, who didn't play college ball, who didn't even play in high school and isn't particularly muscular throw a baseball ninety-six miles an hour?

Charlie: Well correct me if I'm wrong, but a lot of pitching power comes from the lower body, right?

Howie: I was an outfielder, but yeah, that's what I've always heard.

Charlie: So Haversham's got those big, powerful thighs and hips . . .

Howie: Are you allowed to say that?

Charlie: I said the same thing about Carlos Velasquez last year, and you didn't say anything.

Howie: True.

Charlie: Some of those sabermetric guys have looked at the overall statistics of tall and short pitchers and big and little pitchers and found that it's the smaller, heavier ones who seem to have slightly better numbers overall and who seem to have longer, better careers.

Howie: Is that true?

Charlie: You could look it up.

Howie: I still don't know what to think about this. I find it hard to believe that this is anything more than a misguided effort to sell tickets. I mean, the Indians have already gone from thirtieth in major league attendance to fifteenth just since they signed Haversham.

Charlie: You just wait, Howie. The times, they are a changing. In other American League news, White

Sox outfielder Jorge Racino has started the second half on a hot streak, getting seventeen hits in his last twenty at bats and . . .

Howie: Diomedes Olivo.

Charlie: What was that, Howie?

Howie: Diomedes Olivo. Yesterday you said Haversham is the second-oldest rookie ever. But she's not. Olivo was forty-one years and eight months when he made his debut.

Charlie: I stand corrected. This makes Haversham the third-oldest rookie ever and still the first woman to play at the major league level. Say Howie, you're looking a little pale over there. Are you okay?

Howie: I still can't believe she's doing this.

Charlie: That's okay. Denial is but the first step on the road to acceptance. We'll got to a commercial while you get used to the idea.

Chapter Fourteen

•◊•

THE HALLWAY OUTSIDE BRENDA'S LOCKER ROOM WAS DELUGED WITH REPORTERS BECAUSE THERE WASN'T ROOM INSIDE THE LOCKER ROOM FOR MORE THAN THREE PEOPLE. It was as though the entire press box had emptied directly outside her door. Brenda's stomach was in knots and she felt like she was going to throw up, but she forced herself to stand and talk to reporters for nearly twenty minutes. She was only rescued by the arrival of her mother, Andy, and Jon, the former cutting her way through the crowd with the intensity of a snowplow in a blizzard and the latter scurrying in her wake.

The shot of Brenda hugging Jon and Adele appeared in just about every paper in the country the next morning, with accompanying editorials on the nature of her accomplishment, the women's movement, the nature of feminism, the future of baseball, the history of baseball, and whether a thoroughly respectable performance by a woman in the major leagues was a sign of the impending apocalypse.

She tried to keep an air of normalcy around the house, but it was almost impossible. She had changed their phone number twice already that summer, but somebody was sharing it, because the phone still rang constantly the next morning with old friends and neighbors and people she hadn't talked to in twenty years calling to congratulate her or, in some cases, ask for tickets.

Jon was enjoying all of the attention. He was only too happy to answer the phone and talk the ear off of anyone. Brenda gave him a note pad and a pen and appointed him her new secretary. He could take messages from anyone who called provided he didn't give them any vital information or make any promises.

"While I'm at it," she said. "Here. Set this up for me," and handed him the box with the new phone.

"Cool! Sweet phone, Mom!" Jon said as he ripped the plastic wrapping off the phone. "Can I do the ring tone? And your voice mail?"

"Sure. And speed dial the house and Grandma and Robin."

"What about Dad?" Jon asked.

Ed. The boys still had their weekends with their father, but being out of town had kept Brenda from seeing her ex since the week-end before the tryout with the Indians. Even so, Ed's presence in the house, in her life, still hung around.

"Um . . . sure, you can put Dad into speed dial too."

"Excellent!" Jon said and happily went to work on her new phone.

Jon was persistently cheerful. He remained her sweet little Jon who would still allow himself to be hugged and occasionally cuddled and who wanted to talk all the time, while Andy kept to his room and to one-word answers.

The entire family's life now revolved around the ballpark and Brenda's schedule. There were night games Friday and Saturday and an afternoon game on Sunday (in which Brenda faced two batters, struck out one, and got the other to fly out). Then the team would leave for a road trip as soon as Sunday's game was over. There wasn't a lot of time to think or plan. Brenda packed her suitcase, kissed the boys and her mom good-bye, and that was it. Directly after the end of the afternoon game, she went to the airport and got on an airplane with twenty-four other players, five coaches, three trainers, and one equipment manager. She was the only female.

The team was shuttled through security in a private line and walked down to a little-used, cordoned-off gate at Cleveland Hop-kins Airport. Brenda had never traveled like a VIP before, and it felt a little odd to have the rest of the world treat her as something spe-cial just because she could throw a baseball very fast. It was a far cry from the crowded, dirty bus in the minor leagues. As the team walked through the airport, she noticed heads turning and murmurs of recognition. She didn't say anything beyond "Hello" and "Fine, thanks, and you?" to anyone until they were hanging out by the gate, waiting for their plane. Earl came over to where Brenda was sitting with a book.

"How're you doing, Brenda?" he asked.

"I'm fine, thanks," she replied. "And you?"

"Good, good. You looked good in your first couple games. Mark's not going to use you every game, so make sure you throw a little bit every day or every other day—Roy or Eric or Johnny will be happy to catch you. Just watch that lead shoulder."

She wanted to tell him that she would keep watching her lead shoulder but pitching was too new, the movements too involuntary for her to start breaking down what she was doing. The biggest help would probably be having him change his name to "Ed" and start lying to her, but that wasn't a realistic option. So she just said, "Will do."

"What are you reading?" he asked.

"*Northanger Abbey*," she said, holding the paperback up for him to see. "It's always nice to come back to Jane Austen once in a while," she added.

"Haven't read it," he said. "Keep reading your scouting reports and watching video."

"Will do," Brenda said. Shorter answers seemed to be the norm among her teammates and coaches. The last thing she needed was to be looked at as the gabby female. She put *Northanger Abbey* away in her carry-on bag, a cotton monstrosity designed to look like a carpetbag, and pulled out the iPad the team had given her.

On The Ball showed the starting lineup for every major league team. Each player had a page that listed career and current stats and brief comments like, "Good against right handers; almost always hits in fair territory, can be gotten out with breaking balls." Each report included diagrams showing the frequency of that particular player hitting to a particular area and where in the strike zone a player got most of his hits. All of this information and more was also available through the On the Ball app. The amount of data was staggering.

As the team was boarding the plane, Brenda held back a bit, noticing that the other rookies on the team gave deference to the veteran players. She did the same and ended up being the last player on the plane. Mark Munson was just behind her in line.

"Hi Brenda," he said with a wide grin. "Welcome to your first road trip."

"Thanks," she replied, and tried to look like the relaxed, well-adjusted player he needed her to be.

When she got on the plane, just about every seat was taken. The coaches all seemed to congregate near the front of the plane, and the first row on the left was empty. Brenda figured that must be reserved for Mark and edged her way down the aisle. The veteran-rookie dichotomy played out in the seating arrangements too, as it seemed that most of the veterans were near the front of the plane—typically sitting two to a row with an empty seat in between them—and most of the rookies and younger players were farther back. Just about everyone was already seated or stowing his bags in the overhead compartment. Brenda felt a quick pang of panic, wondering if there was a seat left for her. That would figure—on her way to her first game with the team and she had no place to sit.

Most of the other players avoided her eyes as she walked down the airplane aisle. A few, like Francisco Jimenez and Josh Bandkins, the right fielder who had been traded from Texas at the beginning of the season, gave her a polite nod, but they were already sitting down. It seemed they all wanted an empty seat next to them. She honestly didn't see any place to sit. She took a deep breath and willed herself to stay cool and not read too much into the moment.

Don't let it upset you, she thought to herself. *Let it make you mad, but don't let it upset you.*

Through the chatter of other voices, she heard someone say, "Hey, Haversham!" She looked around and saw Doug Stone half-standing up in his seat. "Come and have a seat, rookie," he said. As a veteran, Doug was sitting near the front, and Brenda had to walk back past several rows of seats to get to him. She tried to ignore the fact that half the plane went silent when Doug called her name.

Doug was sitting in the window seat and miraculously had two empty seats next to him. The middle seat held his jacket and a book—she noticed he was reading a graphic novel. She sat down in the aisle seat.

"Thank you," she said.

"Not a problem," he said with a smile that showed he heard more than she said. "It takes everybody a while to figure out the, uh, social hierarchy," he added in a quieter voice.

Brenda grinned and tried not to look as lost as she felt. "It feels a little like the high school cafeteria," she said quietly.

When Doug laughed, he smiled so broadly that his eyes seemed to disappear. It seemed like the mark of a good guy. "That's exactly what I thought my rookie season. Don't worry—you'll get used to it." He paused just long enough to take a breath or possibly to decide if he should keep talking. "And they'll get used to you."

"Thanks," Brenda replied.

She and Doug didn't talk again until after the plane was in the air and on its way to Kansas City.

"What are you reading?" she asked.

Doug gave a little laugh. "*The Umbrella Academy*. Superheroes and stuff. It's really good. I wanted to read it before my kids did, just to make sure there isn't anything in there they shouldn't be reading."

They talked about children for a while—Doug's older daughter was Jon's age. She asked if he had ever read Art Speigelman's work (he hadn't yet). He asked if she had read Harvey Pekar's *American Splendor* ("I'm a native Clevelander. It's required reading," she replied). As they talked, the flight attendant came by to ask if they wanted anything to drink.

"Just some juice, please," Doug said.

"Ice water, please," Brenda said. She had never been on a charter flight before and was pleased to see that there were more flight attendants than on a commercial flight. And the service was better.

As the flight attendant handed Brenda her water, she asked, "Who do you know that you're on this flight?"

"I beg your pardon?" Brenda asked.

"Who do you know that you're on this flight?" the attendant asked, her blue eye-shadowed eyes growing wider as she asked the question. "Do you work for the team? Or are you married to one of the players?"

Brenda took a deep breath and remembered the conversation she had had with Mark. She had to play nice. "No, I'm not a player's wife. I'm one of the players," Brenda replied with what she hoped was a friendly rather than an annoyed tone.

The flight attendant laughed as though Brenda had just told the punchline to a great joke. "No, seriously, who are you?" she asked.

"I'm one of the players," Brenda said, a bit more earnestly but still trying not to sound snippy.

"She's our newest relief pitcher," Doug said. "And a damn good one."

"Wow. Really?" The flight attendant asked. "I thought women didn't play in the majors."

"They do now," Doug said.

•◊•

The team played a three-game series in Kansas City and then took a red-eye flight to Dallas for another three games. Brenda pitched in two of the Kansas City games, facing a total of six batters and giving up a couple of hits but no runs. She managed to sleep for an hour or two before the plane landed. In a daze, she filed along with the other players through the airport, to the bus, through the hotel lobby where she got her room key, and finally collapsed on her bed for a few hours until it was time to meet the team bus in front of the hotel and do it all over again.

This was something she wasn't prepared for. Growing up and watching games on TV or occasionally going to the ballpark, the players looked like they had a pretty easy life. And in many ways, they did. After all, when the rest of the world was getting up and going to work, Brenda and her teammates were playing a game and making far more money at it than most people would ever earn. And traveling long distances by plane sure beat the minor league team bus. But she had already discovered the monotony to the whole routine of living out of a suitcase and being away from her family. Doing all this in the public eye just made it worse. Brenda kept telling herself that losing her privacy and time with Andy and Jon in exchange for loneliness, financial stability, and a secure future for the boys was a fair trade.

The other guys on the team clearly felt the same pressure she did. She noticed this on the bus and in the clubhouse. Someone was always pulling a prank or telling jokes or engaging in an insult contest, but most of it seemed good natured. The number of pranks played on her during her first week in the majors went far beyond what she had seen. The tampons in her locker room and the graffitied Fountain ads had just been the tip of the iceberg. She routinely found hardcore pornography in whatever room was designated as her locker room, and before the last game in Kansas City, she found a used condom and a case of douches in her locker room.

Still, she didn't say anything to Earl or Mark. She didn't retaliate. Then in Arlington, she was the last one on the bus to the ballpark. Just like on the airplane, the veterans had first pick of seats, then the rookies. As she walked down the aisle, searching for a place to sit, Cipriani looked up at her and said, "Hey, Pork."

Brenda glared at him but kept moving down the aisle. The online comments that referred to her as "Pork" were one of the reasons she had stopped reading the news online. It was a variation on calling rookies meat—she was "the other white meat." She could avoid the Internet idiots, she could try and tune out hecklers, but having a teammate say it to her face put her over the edge.

Brenda could feel the adrenaline start coursing through her veins, could feel the anger ignite as she found a seat next to Ryan Teeset. She didn't even bother to say anything to him as she sat down. She was tired of this crap. *Change the dynamic*, she thought.

The trip to the ballpark was only a few miles through downtown. As the bus merged onto the freeway, she heard Cipriani talking about how he had grown up in a suburb of nearby Fort Worth and how they were now on "his" turf. "You take 30 out to 820 and that loops right down to Echo Heights," he said to no one in particular. "I love the 820!"

Brenda hadn't planned on saying anything. She never said anything on the bus or on the plane or in the clubhouse, but she heard herself loudly say back, "Why? Because it matches your ERA?"

Cipriani half stood in his seat and turned to where Brenda was sitting four rows back. The laughter of everyone else on the bus felt like a flak jacket, protecting her from anything Cipriani might say or do. She glanced out the window and saw they were approaching Exit 115.

"Hey Pasquela," she yelled. "Look, they named an exit after your batting average." A dozen heads on her side of the bus looked left. There was more laughter, which drowned out Pasquela's weak reply.

Next to her, Teeset was leaning against the window, laughing into his huge, oven-mitt-like hand. She knew he had grown up on a ranch, and sitting next to him, the term "corn-fed" invariably came to mind. He was a big kid. "You're brave," he said quietly. "I don't know that I'd have the nerve to say that to one of the veterans."

"Just because they've been here a few seasons doesn't mean they have the right to treat the rookies like dirt. Or anyone else."

"I don't mind it too much," Teeset said sheepishly. "It's baseball tradition to give the rookies a hard time." He stared out the window for a moment, looking uncomfortable. Brenda couldn't remember how old he was. Twenty-three? Half the guys on the team looked like they should be in high school. "But I don't blame you for getting mad," he said, still keeping his voice low. "They've already been a lot harder on you than they have on me, and I've been here all season."

"Do you think so?" Brenda asked.

"Well, I seen them with the magazine ads you did, and Cipriani had about ten boxes of tampons in his locker that one day, so I knew it probably had something to do with you."

"What have they done to you?"

"The usual. Making me carry their bags and or putting Vaseline in my shoes, dumb insults. The first road trip I had to use this pink Hello Kitty backpack. Stuff like that. There was one thing they did that was just plain mean though." He paused, as though waiting to see if Brenda wanted to hear what he had to say. She nodded for him to go on. Frankly, Teeset had the slightest twang to his voice that made it a delight to listen to him talk. "My mom's a really good seamstress. She does side work making prom dresses and stuff for people. It's extra money, and there isn't much else to do on the ranch in the winter."

"Where is your family's ranch?"

"Just outside of Mitchell, South Dakota. My dad's a cattle rancher. Anyhow, she made me a suit that was the most beautiful piece of clothing I've ever had. She sent it with me to spring training for luck, and it worked, because I made the Opening Day roster. It was a really nice summer suit, and I decided to wear it on our first road trip of the season—you know, they have the dress code when we're traveling as a team, so I thought I'd do it up right. It was in my locker and at the end of the game, I go to my locker and somebody had cut the sleeves off the jacket and cut the pants into shorts. And Cipriani and Pasquela and Hodges were all laughing like hyenas and saying, 'Oh, why are you so upset? You can just go buy another one,' like I had blown my first big league paycheck on the suit. They didn't know that my mom had spent hours making it for me."

"Those fucking assholes," Brenda said, the words sliding quietly out of her mouth like a snake about to strike.

Teeset looked shocked. "I don't think I've ever heard a woman swear like that."

"Get used to it, son," she replied.

•◇•

Whatever push of adrenaline Brenda was riding when she arrived at the ballpark had dissipated by the time she got the call in the bullpen. Julio Ochoa, the Indians' starter, had been lit up almost from the get-go, giving up six runs in four innings. Brenda came in for the fifth and sixth innings and gave up two more runs on five hits and two walks. Meanwhile, the Indians' bats were largely silent, and they were down 8-2 when Brenda left the game. To make matters worse, things seemed to get better when Cipriani came in. He gave up a couple of hits but no runs (the only bright spot for Brenda was that she had managed two strikeouts during her two innings and Cipriani had only one). Cipriani pitched scoreless seventh and eighth innings, the Indians had two big innings and pulled ahead 9-8, then Jimenez shut down the Rangers in the ninth. Brenda was glad that Teeset ended up being the hero with a game-winning three-run homer but was embarrassed that she had done nothing to contribute to the win.

After the game, she figured the media would want to talk to Tee-set and hoped for some relative calm in her locker room (a little-used handicapped bathroom down the hall from the visitors' locker room). Instead, she found a mangle of media people, all asking her thoughts on the protest outside Ranger Stadium.

"What protest?" Brenda asked.

"The anti-Haversham protest out front," said the reporter closest to her, a man with vaguely Asian features and short, spikey black hair. He was backed up by a cameraman; Brenda had already spent enough time dealing with the media to know that they would keep the cameras rolling indefinitely and edit at their whim. She had quickly learned to be polite while saying as little as possible.

"I didn't see the protest, so it would be impossible for me to comment," Brenda replied and squeezed into her locker room. She was pretty sure the door closed on the guy's foot.

It wasn't until she was back in her room at the hotel that she saw footage of the protest. She had the television tuned to one of the local channels while she got ready for bed and suddenly, there it was: a group of thirty or so people (primarily men) standing around holding signs that read, "Go back to softball" or "Pitch me some dinner" or simply her last name with a line through it.

"Are you kidding me?" she said to the television.

The news reporter on the scene was the same guy she had spoken to outside her locker room. He had managed to corner one of the leaders of the protest, a pasty-looking man in his early sixties who was standing by something that at first looked like a giant rotisserie. As the camera panned out, she saw that the pasty man was turning a handle attached to a homemade coffin, in which lay a dummy dressed in a gray suit and wearing eyeglasses. When the man turned a crank sticking out of the end of the coffin, the dummy somewhat clumsily flipped over.

The reporter asked the protester a couple of basic questions, but Brenda didn't pay attention to the answers. She was too riveted by the almost grotesque contraption that was at the heart of the protest. But then the camera zoomed in on the man's hand holding the crank and the protest leader said, "This here represents Ford Frick, baseball commissioner from 1951 to 1965. He banned women from professional baseball in 1952 to prevent teams from using them as publicity stunts. We're pretty sure if Ford Frick could see the hijinks the Cleveland team has gotten into with this Haversham woman, he'd be turning over in his grave."

The reporter did an admirable job of swallowing a laugh. "So this is Ford Frick rolling over in his grave. Very clever."

Brenda couldn't tell if the protestors meant for the Ford Frick contraption to be serious or ironic, but it was definitely an attention getter. The news station showed a few seconds of the protesters shouting, "No women in baseball!" and a hastily assembled group of counter-protesters shouting, "Let her play!" Then the segment was over and the station cut back to the studio, where a female and male anchor, both of whom seemed to use the same hair coloring and styling products, commented that "It looks like it was a crazy night down there at Rangers Stadium."

"You can say that again," Brenda said as she turned off the television. She went to sleep and was awakened late the next morning by the ringing of her cell phone. The phone showed a Manhattan area code and a number she didn't recognize, so she ignored it. Instead, she called home, hoping it was still early enough to catch the boys before they went off on some Saturday activity. Adele answered on the first ring. "*Ahoj*," her mother said.

"Do you always answer my phone in Slovak?" Brenda asked.

"I only answered in Slovak because I knew it would be you, but that isn't a bad idea. It would be an easy way to cut out all the junk calls."

"I just wanted to check in. How are Andy and Jon?" Brenda settled down on one of the double beds. Having a hotel room to herself was one of the few perks to being the only female on the team.

"They're wonderful."

"Really?"

"They're my grandsons. Of course they're wonderful."

"Are they around? I'd love to talk to them."

"They're with Ed," her mother replied. "This is his weekend, remember?"

"Oh, right. Of course," Brenda said. Of course the boys would still have their weekend days with Ed while she was gone. It wasn't as though the world stopped just because she had a road trip. But it felt strange to know that Andy and Jon were out at some unknown place and she was fifteen hundred miles away. "How late was Ed today?" she asked.

"Ten minutes early. And he picked them up at 9:00."

"Really?"

"I couldn't believe it either," Adele replied. "Eh, maybe he's trying to be a good father. Stranger things have happened."

She and her mother talked for a bit longer. There was so much Brenda wanted to say about her worries and feeling out of place and wondering if she had made a mistake in pursuing baseball, but somehow the words didn't come out. She had dumped enough responsibility on her mom—she didn't think it was fair to dump her worries and fears on Adele too.

Almost as soon as she hung up with her mother, the cell phone rang again. It was the same Manhattan number as before. Curious, she answered it.

"Hi, Brenda," a friendly voice said. "It's Charlie."

It took her a second to realize that Charlie was Charlie Bannister. They had talked online here and there, but this was the first actual conversation she'd had with him since the interview. "Hi," she said, trying to sound neutral. She kind of liked talking on Twitter with him but wasn't sure she needed more than one hundred forty characters of him at a time. What the hell did he want? Another interview? "What can I do for you? Is there something wrong?" she asked.

"No, no emergencies or anything like that," Charlie replied, and she thought she detected a momentary hint of embarrassment in his voice. "I just heard about the protest and wanted to check in with you and make sure that you were all right."

"I'm fine," Brenda replied.

"I figured you were, but you know, crowds can get ugly and ugly people can get even uglier when they're in a crowd, and I wouldn't want anything to happen to you. Anything bad, I mean."

Every time Brenda had heard Charlie speak prior to this, the words just seemed to spin out of his mouth, uncoiling like a silk ribbon. But now he was stammering and sounded so earnest and sincere that when Brenda said, "Thank you," she tried to sound a little friendlier.

"You're welcome. Hey, um, I noticed that the Indians are going to be playing in Baltimore in a couple weeks. I'm actually going to be in the area around that time. Would you maybe want to get together for lunch when we're both in town?"

This was different. She almost said something about him having just interviewed her, but she knew he wasn't asking for another interview. This sounded like a date.

She briefly considered Charlie Bannister. He was not conventionally attractive—his features and his body had a certain roundness to them, giving him a boyish look. But his eyes twinkled and he had a great smile. And while she estimated his height at around five ten, he carried himself with the self-assurance of a six-foot-four home-run hitter. He didn't swagger. His confidence didn't stem from his physicality; it clearly bubbled forth from a deeper well. Having lunch with a man who was obviously comfortable in his own skin might not be a bad way to kill a couple hours before a ballgame.

"That would be nice," Brenda said. "Nice" sounded like the proper adjective. "Great" might give him the impression that she was seriously interested, while "fine" sounded as though his company would be merely adequate. "Nice" seemed about right.

They settled on a Wednesday, which was in the middle of the Baltimore series, giving Brenda nearly two weeks to question whether she actually wanted to go out with him. Living in the midst of a bunch of men, there was no one to talk with about this. Adele and Robin would just say it was high time she showed an interest in someone other than Ed.

The protesters were out again for the remaining two games in Texas. Brenda didn't go in during the second game, which the Indians lost, but she struck out two batters in the bottom of the eighth and helped the Indians get a win during the rubber match on Sunday. Watching the Rangers bat two days in a row helped Brenda key into their batters' strengths and weaknesses. Studying video on the iPad helped, but it was no substitute for the real thing.

As expected, her comments to Cipriani and Pasquela on the bus didn't go unanswered. After the second game in Texas, she found a sweat-stained jock cup in her locker room. It was a wonder how anyone managed to get in there to leave it. Outside of game time, when she was in the dugout or the bullpen, she was in her locker room (or whatever space was designated as her locker room), only venturing into the team locker room when necessary for team meetings.

The cup was right in the middle of her locker cubby. She grabbed some paper towels to pick it up and noticed that there was something thickly wet sitting in the cup part.

"I'm going to pretend it's spit . . . I'm going to pretend it's mucus . . ." Brenda muttered to herself as she quickly wrapped the cup in the paper towels and threw it in the trash can. She threw a few more bunched-up paper towels into the trash can to hide the cup then scrubbed her hands twice.

She tried to put the jock cup out of her mind, but as she boarded the team bus back to the hotel, she couldn't help but scan each of her fellow players, wondering who had left it. He would have had to slip out of the dugout, go to the locker room, get the cup (or take it off), and then leave it in her locker room. The thought of one of these guys also taking the time to add his calling card to the cup added a layer of disgust that she didn't want to contemplate. She figured it was a good thing she never shook hands with any of them.

•◊•

Excerpt from the transcript for *Today in Sports* with Charlie Bannister, ESPN, August 17:

> Charlie: In the American League, the Rangers hosted the Indians over the weekend. The Indians were not polite houseguests, winning two of the three-game series, including a truly beautiful come-from-behind win on Friday on a three-run

homer by first baseman Ryan Teeset in the top of the ninth. Outside of Rangers Ballpark, however, it wasn't as pretty, as fans of ground-breaking rookie pitcher Brenda Haversham clashed with anti-Haversham protesters, who believe she is breaking some sort of ancient code by being allowed to play professional baseball with men. The protesters hung around for the entire series, after which they reportedly went back to their treehouse and held another meeting of the He-Man Women Haters Club.

Chapter Fifteen

·◊·

BRENDA READ THE SCOUTING REPORTS RELIGIOUSLY, BUT SHE ALREADY KNEW SHE NEEDED TO SEE A PLAYER IN ACTION TO GET AN IDEA OF HOW TO PITCH TO HIM. Her outings in Texas were polar opposites. While she had gotten shelled on Friday, she had been in charge on the mound on Sunday. Seeing the Rangers lineup for the previous two days definitely helped.

Through the road trip, Brenda missed Andy and Jon. She found herself waking up in her hotel room, happily expecting to hear the boys talking or laughing or arguing, but instead being greeted by the lonely hum of the room's air conditioner clicking on. That was it. She called the house every day while she was gone. Jon or Adele always answered and offered animated conversation about what was going on. She was able to get Andy on the phone about half the time, but he still stuck to one-word answers.

The team came home from the road trip late Sunday night after a quick charter flight from Dallas. Brenda had never been so happy to see beat-up old Molly the Minivan as when the team bus pulled into the players' parking lot. It was well after midnight by the time she pulled into her own drive. The boys and Adele were waiting for her. Jon and Adele had even made a little banner that read "Welcome Home" and pasted it along the top row of kitchen cupboards.

"We're not going to do it every time you come home," Jon said with a pointed look at Andy. Clearly the banner had been a point of contention. "But we thought it would be nice after your first road trip."

"Thank you so, so much," Brenda said. She was standing by the kitchen table with one arm around Jon and the other around Adele. Andy was standing in the doorway to the hall, doing his best to look bored. "Thanks for waiting up for me, Andy," she said.

"It's not that late," he replied.

She ignored his sarcastic tone and tried to sound positive. "You're right. I'm just so tired, it feels like it must be later. It was a tough road trip."

"You had a bad outing on Friday," Andy said. She didn't bother trying to decipher whether he was being sarcastic or sympathetic— she was just happy that he was initiating a conversation.

"Don't say that," Adele said. "It isn't nice."

"It's okay, Mom. Andy's right. I've got a lot to learn about the opposing teams, and there's only so much time I can spend watching video of batters."

"Do you have to do that tomorrow?" Jon asked.

"No, tomorrow is for you and Andy. But I do have to go to the stadium early on Tuesday."

"Can we come to the game Tuesday night?

"Sure, but don't you have a game that night?" Brenda asked.

"Oh yeah. I forgot," Jon said. "Can you come and watch us?"

"I wish I could, sweetie, but I have a game too. I have to work."

"Jon left his mitt at Dad's," Andy said.

Brenda felt a familiar lurch in her stomach when she heard this and for half a heartbeat, the idea of them being with their father while she was out of town scared her. She had read that most child abductions are by non-custodial parents. If Ed suddenly decided he wanted the boys to himself, all he would have to do would be to take them when she was out of town.

"Maybe Dad can go to my game and bring me my mitt?" Jon said.

"I can get it for you," Adele said.

"I'll pick it up," Brenda said quickly. This was one instance where she could be the hero. "Don't worry about a thing." She gave Jon a little extra hug and then walked over to the sink and got a glass of water as she talked. She hadn't yet given Andy a hug hello and wasn't sure if he'd let her. Her oldest child seemed like a skittish stray dog, around whom she had to be very careful and calm so he wouldn't run away. Andy was within arm's reach. She put her glass down and gave him a one-armed hug. "Thanks for taking care of things while I was away," she whispered. Andy waited a moment before pulling away.

"No problem," he muttered.

"Can we go to the game with you on Wednesday?" Jon asked.

"Yes. You can go to any game you want."

"That is so cool. Andy, we can go to any Indians game we want. Isn't that cool?"

Andy hesitated for a moment, as though he didn't want to admit he was impressed or excited by the prospect of seeing any game he wanted to in person. "Yeah, that's pretty cool," he muttered.

Brenda spent the next day with the boys and Adele at Bexley Park swimming pool. Andy and Jon mainly played with their friends, coming over to Brenda here and there if they needed money to get something from the snack bar and occasionally yelling "Hey Mom, watch this!" It felt so good to be with her family that Brenda almost felt normal.

They came home around mid-afternoon to find a slew of messages on the machine. Two were from David, the first telling her to call him about an endorsement deal and the second chiding her for not using the wonderful phone he had sent her. (She had, in fact, checked the voicemail but chosen to ignore his call until she got home.) Four were from journalists wanting interviews. One was from Ed, telling Jon that he had left his mitt at the apartment on Saturday. One was from the neighbor down the street asking for tickets to Saturday's game.

Adele had been rooting around in the largest cupboard, looking for a pan to start cooking dinner, but now she paused and asked how the road trip had gone.

"It was fine."

"*Neklam mi*," Adele said, diving back into the cupboard.

"I'm not lying, Mom."

"I saw the news reports about the protests. They looked like a bunch of idiots." She triumphantly emerged with the pan she wanted and placed it on the counter, then began chopping peppers and onions.

"They never came anywhere near me."

"Good. I wouldn't want to have to go to Texas and straighten them out." Adele gave an onion a particularly hard chop with the French knife as she said this and looked up with a laugh that Brenda didn't return. "You don't laugh anymore," her mother commented.

"I'm waiting for you to say something funny," Brenda dead-panned back.

Adele gave a little sigh and went back to preparing dinner. "When you feel like talking about it, we'll talk," she said.

Her mother infuriated her when she spoke like this—as though she knew the innermost workings of Brenda's psyche and could read her thoughts at will. But why worry her mom with stories of obscene items left in her locker room or hecklers or rude teammates or the scary guy who had come up to her in the hotel lobby in Kansas City and called her a whore for playing with men? Instead, she just said, "You've done enough, Mom. I can make dinner."

"No. You relax a little bit. Return your phone calls, read a book . . ." Adele replied.

Calling Ed back was somewhere in between root canal surgery and washing Cipriani's jock strap on the list of things she wanted to do, but Jon needed his glove for his game the next night—a game she would have to miss and Ed could attend (if he really wanted to). Leaving her mother to make dinner, Brenda went up to her room to return her calls.

"Hey, Brenda. Nice of you to call back," Ed said when he answered.

"Sorry I didn't call you earlier today—the boys and I were out and about . . ." She wanted to sound happy and confident, as though she and the boys shared just as intimate a bond as they did with their dad, but she couldn't even convince herself of this.

"Yeah, I figured you were off doing something," Ed replied. "Anyhow, Jon needs his glove for tomorrow night. I was thinking of going to his game anyway. I can just drop it off beforehand."

It wasn't like Ed to be so helpful, and it made Brenda a little wary. "No, that's okay," she replied. "I can come and get it."

"Well, I have a softball game at Campbell Field tonight at 7:30. Do you want to swing by there? It's probably closer for you than my place."

"Where's Campbell Field?"

"Willoughby Hills. On Eddy Road off of 91. Just a local rec league, nothing like you're doing," he added, and again the statement left Brenda wondering if he was taking digs at her or just making an innocent remark.

She arranged to meet him at 7:00 to get the mitt. She wasn't sure why she felt compelled to get Jon's glove rather than making Ed drop it off. She gave herself and him the excuse that she had some errands to do, although all she really had to do was make a quick stop at a drug store.

Leaving the house right after dinner made her feel as though she was getting away with something. The boys didn't seem to mind. Andy was going to a friend's house down the street to play video games, and Jon and a couple friends wanted to play soccer in someone's backyard. She left.

Willoughby Hills was only a twenty-minute drive away, but it was in the next county and the area had a rural feel. She knew Ed had a new life now that didn't include her or the boys; this only solidified that realization.

"I guess I have a new life too," she murmured as she absentmindedly stole a peek at her face in the rearview mirror. It wasn't primping exactly—any feelings for Ed for were long gone. It was more the idea that looking horrid in front of her ex would have a sad air of defeat to it.

The parking lot for Campbell Field was right off the road, with a winding path about seventy-five yards long leading to a picnic pavilion and rest rooms. Farther beyond that she could see a couple of softball and baseball fields. The parking lot was starting to fill up with cars and people. She looked around and saw Ed's car but not Ed. Resisting the urge to key his car, she started walking up the path toward the pavilion. As she neared the end of the path, she saw Ed coming out of the men's room. He was tying the drawstring on his shorts as he walked out and for a moment looked as vulnerable as a skinny teenager.

After having spent the past few weeks around men who were broader and wider than the average man, the sight of Ed's tall but lean body seemed very welcome. She had to admit he still had sexy hips—narrow enough to make his shoulders look broad but substantial enough to want to grab and hold on to for dear life.

Ed looked up and saw Brenda. He was still holding the drawstrings of his shorts and kind of motioned with his hands as he said, "Wanna help me tie it?"

That sounded suspiciously like a come-on. "Why don't you have your girlfriend tie it?" she replied in a manner that was far more flirtatious than she intended.

"What girlfriend?" Ed asked. Brenda raised her eyebrows just enough that he added, "Well, I was seeing this woman named Darlene, but that's been over for a while now. So, no girlfriend. No gentle female hands to caress my uh . . . drawstring."

"Is that what you kids are calling it now?" Brenda said and was immediately annoyed with herself.

Ed just smiled at her and told her Jon's mitt was in his car. As they walked back to the parking lot, Ed's hand brushed against hers and an involuntary tingle went up Brenda's spine. She had to remind herself that this reaction was merely because the only time any grown man had touched her in the last twelve months was to give her a high five.

They reached Ed's car—the one that had seemed to mark the beginning of the end of their marriage. In the indirect early evening light, the paint job wasn't nearly as annoying as it was in bright sunlight. It almost looked cute. Ed got the glove off the passenger seat, closed the door, and turned to face her but didn't hand Jon's mitt over right away. Instead, he gave her a quick once-over.

"You look great," he said.

"Thanks," Brenda replied, reaching her hand out for Jon's mitt.

Ed ignored this. "Have you lost weight?" he asked.

"I don't know. A little, I guess."

"Playing hardball with the boys seems to suit you," he said and handed Brenda the mitt, letting the moment when they were both holding it last just a bit longer than necessary. "Come on, I'll walk you over to your car," he said, as though Brenda was the one who was lingering.

Brenda couldn't quite figure out what Ed was playing at. He had always been a flirt—it was one of his best and worst qualities. When she was standing next to the minivan, she said, "Well, you'd better get going. You have a game."

"I've got time," Ed replied, and he shifted his weight to one leg, moving his left hip closer toward Brenda.

"I should go," she said.

"You know, I still think about you."

Brenda wasn't ready for that statement. And she definitely wasn't ready to have Ed gently take her face in his hands and kiss her, but there he was doing just that. It had been so long since she had been kissed that she was frozen in surprise for half a second then started kissing back. Ed moved closer and pressed her up against the car and for a couple delicious heartbeats Brenda felt wanted and feminine and sexy, then she remembered that it was Ed she was kissing and pushed him away.

"That's not a good idea," she said.

"If that's really how you feel . . ." Ed said. Did he look peeved or amused?

"I'm not sure why you did that, but I . . . Please don't do it again," she stammered, feeling stupid that she had let things get this far.

"I just wanted to check and see if there was still anything there."

"There isn't," Brenda snapped. "I'm leaving. Thank you for bringing Jon's mitt."

Ed just stood in the parking lot as she got in the car and pulled away, as though he was waiting for her to turn around and come running back to him. The whole thing was just confusing. It didn't seem as though he wanted to get back together, and she didn't see the smallest trace of regret in his face. There was definitely no regret in his kiss. Maybe he really did just want to see if there was still anything there.

"The only thing left is anger, Ed," Brenda muttered. She took the turn out of the parking lot onto Eddy Road so fast that poor old Molly squealed in protest, but she didn't care.

•◇•

Excerpt from the transcript for *Today in Sports* with Charlie Bannister, ESPN, August 21:

Charlie: Good evening and welcome back to Today in Sports. I'm joined tonight, as I am every Friday, by former major league great Howie Wojinski. Before the commercial break we ran through the National League, now it's time to look at the American League. Howie, how do you think the second half of the season will shake out?

Howie: In the American League East, I think the Red Sox can hold on and take the division.

Charlie: Excuse me, did you say the Red Sox? Because I have this memory from, oh, April where you predicted the Yankees would go to the ALCS.

Howie: Since when is it far-fetched to predict the Yankees in the playoffs at the beginning of the season? I thought it'd be the Yankees, now I think it'll be the Red Sox. The Yankees will still get the first wildcard spot.

Charlie: Fair enough, but I think you were right the first time. And as far as the other half of your original prediction . . .

Howie: I'll stand by the other half of my original prediction. The White Sox will get the second wildcard spot and will make it to the ALCS. They'll still have to get through the Mariners, of course, but they don't have the pitching to be a threat, and with Racino playing the way he is and . . .

Charlie: I hate to interrupt you again, but I beg to differ. The AL Central is starting to get very interesting, but not because of the White Sox. Detroit is still in first place and beating up on Chicago Sox in just about every match up, but have you noticed that the Indians have also been having their way in divisional play since the break?

Howie: [laughs] The Indians? Are you serious?

Charlie: They just swept the Twins at home and they're just half a game behind the White Sox. Now that they have a reliable stopper, the rest of their game seems to be coming into place.

Howie: I wouldn't call Haversham "reliable." She seems to do well at home, but on the road she's inconsistent.

Charlie: Show me a rookie who isn't inconsistent.

Howie: So you're saying you think the Indians are going to take their division?

Charlie: I'm not saying that, but I did have Ziggy the intern calculate some potential outcomes, and the Indians have a legitimate shot at the wildcard spot in the playoffs.

Howie: Charlie, I never realized you were such a heavy drinker.

Charlie: You scoff now, my friend. But wait and see. In a month you'll be hailing me as the most prescient being this side of Nostradamus.

Chapter Sixteen

•◇•

ANDY AND JON HAD BEEN RIDING THEIR BIKES TO AND FROM CAMP ALL SUMMER WITHOUT INCIDENT. The camp was at the YMCA, which was just a one-mile straight shot down Mayfield Road from the house. The boys liked the extra freedom of riding to camp on their own, and it was close enough that Brenda felt comfortable letting them do it. Everything was fine until the last day of camp.

The Indians were opening a three-day series against the Mariners that night and then leaving on Sunday night for Baltimore. Brenda had seen the boys off that morning and spent the day doing laundry and some much needed cleaning, with occasional breaks to study scouting reports. She had the team iPad to watch video, but she preferred being in the film room at the ballpark. Somehow it felt more like going to the office rather than taking her work home with her. And when she was home, she was fair game for whatever the boys needed. At the ballpark, she could genuinely focus. Even though she needed more time to study the Mariners' starting lineup before the clubhouse opened, she wanted just one day where she was home when the boys got home. If she got out of the house by 3:30, she'd still have time to get down to the ballpark and warm up with the rest of the team. The relief pitchers were the last people the coaches and manager looked for.

Brenda had tried to convince the boys to do something with her that day, but Andy turned down the offer, giving the excuse that they were doing archery at camp that day and he didn't want to miss it.

Jon was in a mood to do whatever his brother did. She knew the real reason was more likely that she and her older son didn't have much to say to each other. She hated the thought that by playing baseball she was driving Andy away from his favorite sport.

The camp let out at 3:00, and she had made them promise to come right home so she could at least see them before she left. They had a tendency to dawdle. Brenda was sitting on the sofa in the living room, one eye on the scouting report on her lap and one eye on the front window, when she saw both boys come flying down the sidewalk on their bikes at 3:10. For a moment, Brenda's heart lifted. They knew she was going to the ballpark late in order have a little time with them, and they had reciprocated by hurrying home.

From where she was sitting, Brenda could just see the gate across the driveway. They hadn't closed the gate regularly since Jon was much younger, so Brenda was surprised to see Andy practically shove Jon inside the gate, then turn and slam it shut. Instinctively, her eyes went to the street, where she saw a dark colored, older sedan inching along the street. She was too far away to see the license plate, but her inner Mommy Meter went off the scale. She jumped up and ran to the back door, where the boys were just entering.

"Are you okay?" she asked. Jon's cheeks had the bright red blush that typically preceded a tantrum, but that was the only color in his face. Andy looked like he was trying to calm himself down. For a moment, Brenda wondered if she was overreacting. Maybe they had just had an argument. If they had raced home and Andy deliberately beat Jon and then rubbed his face in it, that would explain a lot. But why had Andy locked the gate?

Neither of the boys said anything for a second, then Jon ran into the living room, dove onto the couch, and poked his head up just enough so he could see out the front window. Andy hung back in the kitchen. She stood in the hall, looking from one son to another and one room to another.

"Andy, what happened?" she asked.

"This guy . . ." he stammered.

"That car I saw going really slowly?" she asked.

"He followed us home," Jon said. He sounded as though he was going to cry. Brenda took a quick glance out the window as she sat down next to Jon and gave him a hug. The car was gone.

Andy stood in the door to the living room. "He said some really nasty things about you," he said finally, as though saying it made him guilty of bad-mouthing his mother.

Brenda held out her free arm and said, "Come here." She knew Andy must have been pretty shaken up because he sat down next to her and allowed himself to be hugged. Brenda sat with an arm around each boy and listened. Apparently, the guy in the dark sedan had stopped his car and called to the boys shortly after they left the YMCA. First he asked directions to Oakmount—their street. Andy had gotten a bad feeling, told the guy that they didn't know where Oakmount was, and kept riding. The sedan had been going the opposite direction as the boys, but then made a U-turn and slowly paced the boys from the other side of the street as they rode.

"We rode as fast as we could, but he kept following us," Jon said, as though the power of his nine-year-old legs should have been enough to outrun a car.

"We turned down Sheffield instead of Oakmount," Andy said, naming a street one over. "And we thought maybe he went away, but when we turned onto Oakmount, he was there."

"He knew exactly where our street was," Jon whispered.

"And then he started yelling some really nasty things." Here Andy paused, and Brenda could feel her throat tighten and every nerve in her body tense.

"Did he threaten you?" she asked.

"No." Andy's voice grew slightly softer. "He threatened you."

"He said you shouldn't be playing baseball," Jon said, and she could see tears welling up in his eyes.

"He said worse than that." Andy's eyes looked a bit red and wet, even though he was almost obsessive about not crying and made fun of Jon whenever he cried. "He said he'd hurt you if you kept playing."

"You two are not to go out by yourselves. I want you each to have at least two friends with you at all times," Brenda said. "No biking by yourself, Andy." It was the first rational thing she could think of to say. No one, but no one was going to terrorize her kids. She knew "terrorize" was a strong word, perhaps too strong, but it was the only word she could think of that accurately conveyed how shaken both boys were. It was the word she used when she phoned Mark Munson and the police.

Brenda had almost forgotten that her mother was due to come over until Adele burst in the front door. She surveyed Brenda, Andy, Jon, and two police officers sitting in the living room and asked who had been arrested.

"Nobody's been arrested, Mom," Brenda said. "Some nutcase followed the boys home from camp."

Adele actually started swaying back and forth, and Brenda thought she might pass out. One of the policemen caught her and helped her sit down while Brenda got a cold compress for her mother's forehead. Taking momentary care of Adele took Brenda's mind off of worrying about the boys and transferred her concern to how late she would be getting to the ballpark.

The boys had a decent description of the car and its driver but hadn't gotten the license number. The police suggested an alarm system for the house, emergency cell phones for the boys, new locks, and promised they would patrol the neighborhood and watch the house. The sergeant who came to the house said he would personally call Progressive Field and ask for additional security, then he asked Brenda for her autograph.

The idea of leaving her family and being in a different place than the boys seemed untenable, so Andy, Jon, and Adele came with her to the ballpark. There were always seats available in the family section.

Brenda didn't tell anyone on the team about the incident, only Mark and only because he was her manager. Even so, it was obvious that she was incredibly late—she hadn't been around for warm-ups or batting practice. Showing up this late without a legitimate excuse would typically cost a player a fine. This was one of the times that having a locker room apart from the rest of the team was an advantage, and she hoped that her absence hadn't been generally noticed.

As a mother, Brenda knew that somewhere, sometime, someone would say something cruel to her child—a bully on the playground or an insult from a queen bee in the lunchroom would hurt her kid's feelings and there wasn't any way to prevent it. But this was more insidious than a schoolyard taunt. This was a stranger menacing her kids. The rude messages on the answering machine had been showing up all summer long, and by now she had learned to brush them off. But a stranger following the boys home was something else entirely. It didn't matter if some crackpot threatened her—she had heard worse. The only thing that mattered was that Andy and Jon were safe and protected.

She managed to get dressed and slipped into the locker room before the team took the field, taking her standard seat alone at one of the small round tables near the door. The other players were shooting the breeze, re-lacing their cleats one more time, and generally trying to stay loose in the few minutes left before the game started. She tried to pretend that she had been in her locker room, but Doug Stone asked her where she had been and if everything was okay. If it had been any other player besides Doug and if he hadn't asked after her wellbeing, she probably would have lied and claimed to have warmed up on her own and merely been in her locker room. But Doug had been the first player to befriend her and deserved at least a half-truth, if not the entire truth.

"We had some family-related issues," she replied.

"Is everybody okay?" Doug asked as he took a seat next to her. She could tell he was genuinely concerned.

"Yes. We're all a little shaken up, but we're going to be fine."

He looked puzzled, obviously expecting slightly more detail than that, but accepted her reticence by saying, "If you feel like talking or blowing off some steam, let me know. Hope everything is all right."

"It will be. Thanks."

Fortunately, Mark came in at that moment, and his quick pep talk gave her an excuse not to speak. Munson reminded them that they had moved themselves into contention and had a shot at the playoffs if they kept their focus and made each game matter. As she looked around the room, Brenda was reminded that, like it or not, she was part of a team and her fortunes were now intertwined with those of the men in the room with her.

She wished that the rest of the world recognized her role on the team. The Ford Frick protesters showed up outside Progressive Field that night and the next two games that weekend. Brenda didn't see them, just got an eyeful from the news. It wasn't clear to her if this was the same group that had shown up in Texas or a different group using the same idea. Regardless of who they were or where they got the idea, they ticked her off.

Just about every player on the team got heckled at one point or another, even at home. Most of the guys just let the comments roll right off their backs. Some, like Dave McGall, the shortstop, would yell back at the fans. Brenda remembered reading about a game a couple years back where he had actually gone into the stands after a group of guys who had been ragging on him mercilessly the entire game. The story went that McGall was actually winning the three-against-one fight when Art Groggins and Greg Landers pulled him off. At the time, Brenda never thought she'd end up working with McGall, whom she considered a head case with a Gold Glove. Now he changed his clothes right down the hall from her. She supposed it was better than playing against him.

She still found hardcore porn in her locker room, and the bastardized Fountain ads were still making an occasional appearance in the clubhouse; she didn't even want to see what they would do with the ad for the Bam! sports bra. The last game of the home stand, Cipriani and Pasquela outdid themselves, with a photo of (presumably) one of them, shot from the waist down, with his uniform pants down and a full-on erection. It looked like it had been printed off on somebody's home computer to a piece of regular copy paper and was taped to the mirror in Brenda's locker room. Brenda was more disgusted than anything else. Her first impulse was to grab the photo and rip it into a million little pieces, but as she reached for it, she stopped. She wasn't allowed to respond to hecklers or blog rants or newspaper columnists or radio call-in shows or television talking heads who said she shouldn't be playing. But the front office had never said that she couldn't respond to her teammates.

Very carefully, she pulled the photo off of the mirror, folded it in half (being careful to fold it picture-side in), and placed it in one of the zippered compartments of her duffel bag. She would find a good use for it.

•◊•

Excerpt from the transcript for *Today in Sports* with Charlie Bannister, ESPN, August 24:

> Charlie: Over the weekend, White Sox lost two out of three to the Royals, while the Tigers were swept by the Twins. Meanwhile, the Indians swept the Mariners. All of this means that the Indians are tied with the White Sox in the race for second place in the AL Central and Howie Wojinski owes me two beers and the title of Prognosticator in Residence.

Chapter Seventeen

•◇•

THE TEAM LEFT FOR BALTIMORE RIGHT AFTER THE SUNDAY AFTER-
NOON GAME. During the shuttling of the team from the bus to
the airport to the evening flight to Baltimore, Brenda pondered how ironic it was that some things didn't change. The previous November, she had missed Jon's class performing an afternoon
Thanksgiving play because she had only been at her job a month and
didn't have any vacation accrued. And now work was keeping her
from the boys at an even more crucial time.

The airplane was dark and comparatively quiet. It was just a
short flight—not even two hours—but most of the players used it
an excuse to catch a cat nap. The team was traveling on a commercial
flight, so there were non-baseball types on the plane. Brenda had
been too tired to notice if the other passengers stared when she came
slouching onto the plane in the middle of twenty-four big league ballplayers. She wondered how many of the people sitting around her
had children at home they were already missing.

Luck of the draw had seated her in between Julio Ochoa and
Josh Bandkins. Ochoa was asleep, his marionette-like legs sprawling
into the aisle. Bandkins had the window seat and was fidgety, fiddling
with his smart phone and then with his pillow then shifting in his seat.
Sitting in between the two men, Brenda was struck by how large they
were, how much more space they filled than other people.

Brenda was too hyped up to sleep, especially on such a short
flight. She had pitched a full inning that afternoon and given up a

walk, a stolen base, two hits, and two runs. It was one of the worst outings she had had. Earl had told her not to let it get to her, that she had had an off day because her sinker wasn't breaking properly and that they'd work on it. Brenda knew it was because the entire weekend her mind had been on her kids and not on the game. And the Mariners hitters had her number because she hadn't done her homework on them. It was a certainty that, by now, every hitter in the American League had studied film of her pitching and knew her limited repertoire of tricks and her many tells. She had hardly had time to look at film of the Orioles' starting lineup, much less the Rays, both of whom they were facing on the upcoming road trip.

Bandkins glanced over at her. "Not taking a nap either?" he asked.

"Nope. I've got a lot on my mind," she replied.

"Today's game is history. Shake it off. We won it, so worry about the next one."

She wasn't sure if she really wanted to talk, but it was so rare that anyone on the team talked to her that she felt obliged to. "Easier said than done," she replied with half a smile.

"I remember my rookie year, if I made a mistake, I would replay it in my head a hundred times, and that's useless because you have to focus on the next pitch and the next playable ball."

"So shake it off and don't make the same mistake twice?"

"Yep," he said, fiddling with his smart phone. "You know this is my eighth season in the majors. The average major league career is only something like four. I think the guys who don't make it are the ones who play head games with themselves. You can't worry about whether you struck out in your last at-bat—you have to worry about not striking out in this at-bat. It's that whole thing about staying in the present moment, like the Buddhists."

"Are you a Buddhist?" Brenda asked. Religion was one of those topics you weren't supposed to talk about, even though the ball club had a number of avowedly, sometimes even aggressively Christian players, like Anthony Fleetwood. But it was late and the dimly lit space of their two seats in the otherwise quiet airplane somehow made it seem all right to ask a personal question.

"Dabbled in it. I was raised Presbyterian but haven't gone in years, even though Anthony seems to think it's his personal mission to have me born again."

"Oh good, I thought it was just me."

Bandkins grinned. "Are you another fallen away Presbyterian?"

"More like an ambivalent Catholic," she replied. "I love the beauty and ritual of the mass, but there's a lot in the dogma that doesn't sit well with me. And as a female, I always felt like a second-class citizen—observing but not actually participating."

Josh was silent for a moment, his face turned toward hers. Brenda was suddenly very aware of the proximity of their bodies. She could even see the prickly little black hairs coming in on his shaved scalp. "Is that why you're doing this?" he asked. "I mean, are you playing baseball to make some big feminist statement or something? Why *are* you here?" He emphasized the word "are" ever so slightly, as though this was a question he had been asking himself for a while.

It seemed like the best answer to another player would include something about loving the game and always wanting to play, but that felt disingenuous. "I need to support my kids," she said finally. Josh looked at her as though he was waiting for something more, as though that this one basic need wasn't enough of a reason to disrupt the baseball world. "And I'm too flat-chested to be a stripper," she added.

Josh snorted back a laugh that was loud enough to wake up Ochoa, who jerked straight up in his seat, saying "*Que? Que?*"

"Nothing, man," Josh whispered. "Sorry. Go back to sleep."

"Sorry, Julio. We'll be quiet," Brenda said.

Julio leaned back and shifted a bit in his chair, muttering something in Spanish that sounded drowsily annoyed.

"You're okay, Haversham," Josh said. "You just keep throwing the way you've been throwing—today excluded—and you'll be fine."

"Thanks," Brenda replied. They talked a bit more, mainly about music players and smart phones (Brenda was thinking of getting Andy a new one for his birthday), and Josh gave her a crash course on the best and worst ballparks.

Monday's workout was like every other team workout except that they were in a new stadium (to her) and both Bandkins and Teeset said "Hello" to her. That seemed like progress. She took a little walk through the neighborhood and brought Chinese takeout up to her hotel room for dinner, trying to ignore that the rest of her teammates were going out in small groups for dinner or drinks or fun while she holed up alone in her room.

She called home before bedtime. She just needed to hear the boys' voices. As usual, Jon answered. She could hear his nine-year-old energy through the phone and tried to remember what it was like to be that happy all the time.

"Hi sweetie. How are you?"

"Great! We went to the pool with Grandma today, and then later I went over to Cory's house and shot off bottle rockets."

"Bottle rockets?" Brenda bit her tongue.

"Cory's dad was there."

"Do you still have all your fingers?"

"Yeah," Jon laughed. "We're going shopping for school supplies tomorrow. I need notebooks and stuff and new sneakers and some jeans and a new hoodie."

"I know that. I left money for Grandma to take you and Andy shopping."

"She said I can't get an Ohio State shirt because it's too expensive and that I can get two plain hoodies for the price of one OSU hoodie."

"Well, she's right. You can."

"But I don't want a plain one. I want an OSU hoodie. We can afford it now, right?"

Brenda paused. "Whether we can afford it and whether we need it are two different things," she replied.

"Mo-ommm," Jon whined. "Come on. Please? It's just a hoodie."

"I'll tell you what. Why don't Grandma and I give you a set amount of money for school supplies, and you can choose what you need."

Jon started saying, "Yeah, I like that idea . . ."

"Let me finish," Brenda added. "You'll have to stay within your budget. So if you blow the whole thing on your new sneakers, that's it. You're getting a plain hoodie."

Jon considered this for a moment, then said, "Okay." He passed her off to Adele, who assured Brenda that everything was fine.

"You always say that," Brenda said.

"Andy and Jon are alive and kicking and so am I. Everything's fine. How are you?"

"I miss them."

"I know," her mother replied. "They're all right. But you knew that—a mother always knows if her child is in trouble."

Brenda didn't take the bait. She couldn't. The unwritten rules of the clubhouse dictated that what went on in the locker room or the team bus stayed there. For Brenda to go to Munson or anyone else and complain about being harassed would just set her up to be an even bigger target.

They spoke for a few moments about the boys, about nothing. Andy didn't feel like talking, "But he sends his love," Adele added. When they finally hung up, Brenda had never felt so alone.

On Tuesday morning, she went out and bought Andy something called a "Gismo" that Bandkins had recommended. It had loads of memory for music and video, was super-fast, super-hip, and could probably be used to perform open heart surgery in the proper hands. Andy hadn't actually asked for anything for his birthday. The new catcher's mitt he got at the beginning of the season was his early birthday gift from Brenda, but a new mp3 player was one of the few things he had actually talked about during the last home stand. At first it felt like a guilt gift, but as she thought about her first born, two things always came to mind: baseball and music. He listened to music constantly. Brenda remembered what it felt like to escape into music she loved. She had discovered The Smiths and The Clash when she was just a little older than Andy. With a father who rarely spoke more than two words at a time and a mother who didn't understand why her daughter wanted to wear all black when the other girls her age were wearing pastels, she had been sure that no one ever felt as lonely and isolated as she did. Even though she knew part of what Andy wanted to get away from was probably her, music was a safe escape and one she could give him.

Her cell rang about twenty minutes before the team bus left for Camden Yards. It was from Cleveland's 216 area code and looked familiar, but she couldn't place it. Thinking that it could have something to do with Andy or Jon, she answered.

"Hi, Brenda? This is Beverly Vanderfeld," an apologetic-sounding voice said. Vanderfeld was her divorce lawyer and had been so wishy-washy that if she weren't a friend of Adele's, Brenda would have thought she was secretly working for Ed. Brenda hadn't had occasion to speak to her since the divorce was finalized in December.

"Hi Beverly. Is everything okay?"

"Well, actually, no. Well, let's say, it's going to *be* okay, but there's a little problem now—just a little blip, really. I have to tell you that I've been contacted by Ed's lawyer because Mr. Haversham would like to make a change in the custody arrangement.

Vanderfeld's habit of saying in fifty words what could be said in ten was usually annoying, but now Brenda wished she'd just ramble on a while longer. It would delay her having to hear this.

"What kind of change in the custody arrangement?" Brenda took a deep breath. "I'm sure you'll remember from the divorce proceedings that Ed never expressed any desire to have the boys live with him—he only asked for visitation."

"He's filed for primary custody," Beverly said with a little sigh that made it sound as though she herself were to blame.

Brenda struggled to make a coherent sentence, but all she could say was, "Primary? Why?"

"Well, I think they said something about the recent incident in which the boys were nearly assaulted on their way home, and that Andy has been involved in some fights and was caught shoplifting. And they're also concerned that your current schedule has you out of town nearly fifty percent of every month, and the end result of all those things is that—and this only according to their statement, *I'm* not saying this—Ed, that is, Mr. Haversham is concerned that you are not providing the boys with a safe or stable environment."

"No," Brenda said. She wanted to scream and cry and kick something but she just repeated, "No," even as her heart started pounding. "The boys are fine, and Ed doesn't have space in his apartment for them. He doesn't even have a bedroom for them."

"His counsel stated that Mr. Haversham has plans to move to a larger home in order to properly accommodate the boys when he has primary custody."

"I would maybe—*maybe*—consider joint custody. But Ed will never have primary custody of my children," Brenda snapped, then caught herself. Vanderfeld was just the bearer of bad news; there was no reason to yell at her. "I'm sorry, Beverly, I didn't mean to snap at you, but Ed hasn't discussed this with me. This comes as a complete surprise."

"I'm sure it must be very shocking," Beverly said, sounding like her mother rather than her lawyer. That was Vanderfeld's problem throughout the divorce proceedings—she was too sympathetic to human beings in general to effectively represent one person against another. "They seem to think Andy especially would be better off with a strong male role model."

"Then they'd better find someone other than Ed for him to live with."

"Let's just hope he's trying to be a better father."

Brenda took a deep breath. Arguing with her own lawyer was not going to get her anywhere. "What do we do now?" she asked.

"Well—and this is assuming that you wish to retain me as counsel—we respond and then they'll schedule a hearing. Of course it might be easier if you and Ed could just sit down and talk this out . . ."

"At this point, I don't think that's a likely possibility. He could have done that before going to his lawyer."

"Agreed, agreed . . ."

Brenda suddenly found Vanderfeld's easy-going, solicitous personality grating. She didn't need amiable and understanding; she needed cunning and cut-throat. Without even realizing she had made a decision, she said, "Beverly, I think I'm going to seek other counsel for the custody hearing. You've been wonderful, but I think it would be best if we made this switch. I hope you understand." She only half-heard Vanderfeld's lengthy but polite response. All Brenda could think about was that she had thirteen minutes before the team bus left and wondered if that was enough time to find a barracuda from three hundred fifty miles away.

She knew getting rid of Vanderfeld was the right move. If Ed had expressed any desire for shared custody during the divorce proceedings, he would have gotten anything he wanted. As it was, Brenda ended up with five years' worth of alimony and child support payments that equaled minimum wage, circa 1982. All of her friends said that the boys had been robbed. Moreover, there were no provisions for health insurance or any type of college funds for the boys. Brenda wondered if Ed had a "My lawyer can beat up your lawyer" bumper sticker.

When she hung up the cell phone, she collapsed on the bed and almost let herself cry but knew there was no time for crying. As much as she worried about hurting Beverly's feelings (and Adele's), she had to find a new lawyer. Then she thought of David. His entire existence depended upon having a coterie of lawyers within arm's reach at all times.

By rights, her first phone call should have been to Adele, but that would have to wait. She couldn't be late for the team bus—especially not when she had had such a bad outing the night before. Feeling like a D-list actress portraying herself in a movie, she punched in David's number (putting him on speed dial just seemed too intimate). David's silky voice was a momentary balm on her anger.

"I know just the person," he purred after she told him the whole story. "Alex Clemowitz. He'll eat Ed's lawyer for lunch and then spit the gristle in Ed's face as the judge rules in your favor."

That was all it took. One call and she immediately had the most aggressive divorce lawyer on the southern shore of Lake Erie at her disposal. She didn't want to think about what Clemowitz's hourly rate might be, but with the Bam! endorsement, she would be able to afford the services of ten Alex Clemowitzes, if necessary. This was a sobering thought, and one that carried her in silence down to the lobby and onto the bus.

Inside, she was still seething with rage at Ed. How could he possibly think she'd agree to give up primary custody? And to top it off, he didn't even have the decency to call her first and talk about it like an adult. She didn't speak to anyone on the bus or in the locker room or in the bullpen. She didn't even notice the jock strap Cipriani left in her usual spot at the far end of the bullpen dugout. He had written "PORK" on it with a Sharpie, just to make clear for whom it was intended. She glanced at the jock strap, then calmly picked it up and threw it over her shoulder toward the other end of the bullpen dugout. The "What the hell?" she heard from Anderson Sparks made it clear that the jock had hit an innocent party.

None of the usual bullshit in the dugout or the bullpen mattered. Not when there was even the remotest possibility of losing the boys. Brenda just sat and simmered as the Indians made a valiant stand against the Orioles. Hodges started and pitched his usual five solid innings before falling apart in the sixth, giving up three runs on six hits and beaning one batter before being relieved by Anderson Sparks, who gave up another run. By the top of the seventh, the Indians were down 4-2. A solo home run by Doug Stone and a double by Pasquela that scored Dave McGall and Johnny Gonzalez gave the Indians a 5-4 lead, but they would need to stave off Baltimore's bats for three more innings. Sparks struck out one batter then gave up a couple hits and walked the bases loaded in the seventh. A double play got them out of the inning without allowing any runs, but it was clear Sparks was getting shaky. Then he started off the eighth inning by giving up a double and two walks in a row.

Both Cipriani and Brenda were up and throwing in the bullpen after the first walk. After the second walk, Munson went out to the mound. She and Cipriani only had about three minutes to prepare, but that was two minutes more than Brenda needed. She was throwing smoke from her first warm-up pitch. It was as though a geyser of rage was bubbling inside her as she pictured Ed's smug, spiteful face in the middle of the catcher's mitt. It didn't matter that she had almost no idea what the Orioles' starting lineup could do. She was right where she needed to be.

She saw Earl studying her and Cipriani, trying to decide which right-handed reliever to send in. Cipriani glanced over at her and threw one last warm-up pitch. Rather than take one more pitch, she looked at Earl. With her hands at her side, palm and glove open, she motioned ever-so-slightly toward herself, as if to say, "Pick me. Tonight I will not disappoint."

Earl gave a quick glance between Brenda and Cipriani, then barked her name. "Haversham! Get in there. Phil, stay warm."

Without a second look at Cipriani, Brenda trotted out to the mound, where Munson was waiting for her. The sold-out crowd in Camden Yards erupted into a conflicting chorus of boos and cheers when her name was announced. As it had been at every game since she signed, home or away, Brenda sold tickets. Fans were still mixed on her, but front offices uniformly loved her.

Munson met her at the pitcher's mound. As he handed her the ball, he asked, "How are you feeling? Think you can put them away tonight?" It was kind of a silly question, because it wasn't as though he was going to put in Cipriani if Brenda told him she wasn't feeling well.

Brenda took the ball from him. "I'm going to strike out the entire cock-sucking side," she said.

For half a second Munson looked surprised, then replied, "Do it."

Gonzalez signaled for a sinker. Although she was dying to throw as hard as humanly possible, Brenda decided to go with whatever Gonzalez suggested. She was on, and instinctively knew that the ball was going to go where she wanted it to go. It was as though her will had been added to Newton's laws of motion: Objects thrown by Brenda Haversham will sail unmolested to their intended target.

With every pitch, she thought of Ed and his attempt to take Andy and Jon away from her. There was no reason for her to be here, throwing this ball, if not for the boys. Strike. To think that Ed would just try and steal them away was beyond reprehensible. Strike. He didn't even have the decency or the guts to speak to her about it himself. Strike.

The first out came so quickly Brenda was almost disappointed. She rarely worked more than an inning, and Jimenez was almost always the go-to guy in the ninth. But she felt as though she could throw all night long, working off the infinite reserve of anger that was burning through her insides. After the second strikeout, it felt like the inning was going too fast, she wanted the chance to throw more. But she took one look at Carl Maladente, the Orioles' right fielder who had just come up to bat, and decided that a swift and cruel strikeout would be best. Maladente was built like a Redwood tree. Brenda had heard through the clubhouse grapevine that he had been arrested twice for spousal abuse. Brenda had never seen him before, never played against him before, but as he stood in the batter's box, she decided that Maladente looked like the kind of guy who'd hit his wife—overly developed chest and arms and an arrogant bearing that said he expected to be treated like a king wherever he went. Here was a man who deserved to strike out.

Brenda took her time, savoring the moment as Maladente stared right back at her from sixty and a half feet away. He raised his head—his chin, really—ever so slightly in a gesture of cocky defiance.

"You stinking wife beater," Brenda mumbled, and threw, wondering if the slapping of the ball in the glove was anywhere near as hard as the slapping of Maladente's hand across his wife's face. The look on Maladente's face after the called strike on the outside corner almost made Brenda feel better. She had to break him, make him realize that female force was something to be reckoned with and respected. Then she had a momentary twinge of panic—the Orioles were at home. What if Maladente struck out and went home and took out his outrage at striking out to a woman on his wife?

She stepped off the bag and made a "time out" signal with her hands. Gonzalez came trotting out to the mound, obviously thinking that she wanted to have a quick chat about how to pitch to Maladente. Brenda looked over at McGall at short and motioned for him to come to the mound too.

McGall and Gonzalez approached her with puzzled faces.

"What the hell do you need me here for?" McGall asked.

"I have to ask a question about Maladente," Brenda said to him. To Gonzalez she said, "Just keep calling the pitches like you have been. I trust you."

Gonzalez nodded and muttered "Thank you," in his quiet, accented English.

To McGall she said, "Are those stories about Maladente you told true? That he's been arrested for hitting his wife?"

"Yeah, they're true. Why would I lie?"

The normal response would have been, "Because you're crazy, McGall," but Brenda just said: "Nothing. I just . . . I don't want to strike somebody out if he's going to go home and smack his wife."

McGall threw back his head and laughed. He sounded like a donkey. "Haversham, you slay me," he stammered. "Worrying about shit like that."

"Why is this funny?" Gonzalez asked. "A man who hits a woman is a weak man," he added, taking a glance over his shoulder at the formidable Maladente, who was standing just outside the batter's box, leaning on his bat in an annoyed manner.

"He is," Brenda said.

"All Maladente is thinking right now is that there's another woman making him wait. Did you ever think that getting struck out by you might make him see the world a little different? Strike his ass out. Strike a blow for feminazis everywhere." McGall had this way of talking that made every conversation with him sound like the prelude to a revolution or a manic episode.

"Where do you get off calling me feminazi, McGall? Don't spout that crap on my pitcher's mound."

McGall snorted out another donkey-like laugh. "Now that I have you good and riled up, strike his fat ass out," he replied and trotted back to short.

"You are a very angry woman, no?" Gonzalez said.

"Yes," Brenda said, feeling a bit wary.

"Mi madre tells me always that I should . . . *Canaliza tu ira.* Um, use my anger to make good instead of bad." Brenda wasn't sure what to say to this. She just nodded. Gonzalez said, "Let's go," and trotted back to home plate.

That whack-job McGall had her number. And so did Gonzalez. Was she that transparent? Or maybe anger was part of the game face and the zone. Maybe all of these guys were quietly harboring inner cesspools of festering anger. Maybe some, like Maladente, were so angry they even took it out on the people they supposedly loved. She glanced over at the dugout and saw Munson standing with one foot on the top step, a sure sign he was debating going out to the mound. Brenda just nodded at him and then turned her attention to the sign from Gonzalez. Fastball, low and outside. Brenda saw Ed's face in the catcher's mitt, felt a new jolt of anger surge through her, and threw.

Striking out the side in bottom of the eighth with the bases loaded was not nearly as satisfying as it should have been. Brenda decided that was because she wasn't done yet.

Gonzalez and McGall and a couple others gave her high-fives or pats on the back as they left the field, but Brenda couldn't smile. Striking out the side didn't change the fact that Ed was trying to get full custody of the boys. She had nothing to smile about.

Munson gave her a pat on the back when she reached the dugout. "Nice work," he said. "Go hit the showers."

"No," Brenda replied, not even worrying about the fact that she was openly disagreeing with her manager. "I'm staying in."

Munson lowered his voice, as though he didn't want the rest of the dugout to hear a confrontation. He wasn't the type to dress someone down in front of the rest of the club, but he always did just enough to remind the team that he was in charge. "I think that's my decision."

"Please leave me in," Brenda said, enunciating each word slowly, as though Munson merely hadn't heard her properly the first time.

Munson considered her for a moment. "How does your arm feel?" he asked.

"Like I could do this all night long. Please leave me in," she repeated.

"You can start the ninth," he said finally. "Jimenez and Cipriani are both warmed up. If it even smells like you're running into trouble, I'm pulling you."

"I won't get behind on the count on anyone," Brenda said. The anger was like a drug, making her feel clear-headed and alert and focused. When she said she wouldn't get behind in the count, she knew it was true.

Munson sighed. "Okay."

Saying "thank you" felt too soft, as though the anger would dissipate if she let herself be the least bit polite. She nodded and sat down in the far corner of the dugout. No one bothered her; whether that was due to respecting a pitcher who was in the zone or the standard Avoidance of Haversham protocol wasn't clear.

An insurance run when the Indians were at bat would have been nice, but it didn't happen. As they walked out to the field in the bottom of the ninth, Doug Stone patted her on the back. "Keep on doing what you're doing, Brenda," he said as he jogged past her on his way to left field. The infield looked energized, and Brenda wondered if that had something to do with her and how she was pitching. When she glanced over at McGall, he gave her a thumbs up, although coming from him, you had to wonder if he was being ironic.

There was no question in her mind as to whether she'd be able to retire the side one-two-three. With every pitch, she could almost feel the ball being led to Gonzalez's mitt, like two magnets pulling toward each other and then connecting. No matter where he placed it, the ball would find his mitt.

Brenda ran the first batter to a 1-2 count before he grounded out to McGall on a breaking ball. She glanced over at the dugout as the next batter came to the plate. Munson was in his customary spot at one end of the dugout, both arms on the railing, watching. It looked as if he was going to leave her alone.

She delivered two quick strikes in a row to the next batter, Billy Carlos, the Orioles' shortstop. He wasn't much taller than Brenda—perhaps five eight. Brenda wondered if he had had a hard time on his way up or in the locker room because of his size. On another day, she might have felt some sort of kinship with him. "Today, Carlos, you're out of luck," she muttered as she threw the 0-2 pitch. Carlos hit it to deep right, but Bandkins was there to catch it.

There was no reason to bother glancing at Munson for the last batter. Brenda just faced him with the same poker face she had faced every other batter that night. The tidal wave of anger inside hadn't ceased, and this was her last chance to throw tonight. She knew she would get this guy out and that would be it for the night. It was tempting to play with him just so she could get in a few more pitches, but that might make someone think he was stronger than she was. Tonight, she wanted to dominate, to crush anything and everything in her way. She hoped Ed was watching the game from home, hoped his lawyer followed baseball so he could see that he had made the wrong person angry.

"You fuckers," she grunted as she threw the first pitch to the last batter. Two balls, one foul, and three strikes later, it was over. Everyone else on the team breathed a sigh of relief. Everyone else relaxed and goofed around in the clubhouse as they showered and changed. Everyone else had time to give a few smiling words to the media. Everyone else rode back to the hotel in a noisy, raucous mood. Everyone but Brenda.

•◊•

Excerpt from the transcript for *Today in Sports* with Charlie Bannister, ESPN, August 25:

> In the AL Central, the Tigers seem to be crumbling a bit more every day, dropping three in a row to the Yankees. In a bit of monkey-see-monkey-do, Chicago decided it didn't really want to be in first place and was swept by the Blue Jays. Meanwhile, the second-half turnaround by the Indians seems legit, as they smoked the Orioles tonight 4-5. The victory included a fantastic outing by rookie relief pitcher Brenda Haversham, who struck out the side in the eighth and then came back in for the ninth to close things out. Six batters, four strikeouts—not bad at all.

Chapter Eighteen

•◇•

Brenda managed to get through the standard journalistic hurdles and the frat house atmosphere on the bus on the way back to the hotel, but once she was back in her room, she felt the urge to move. She threw on shorts and a T-shirt and went to the hotel's fitness center where she found two sad treadmills, one elliptical, and a weight bench with a sparse set of weights. She hopped on the elliptical and turned the resistance as high as she could stand. Once she got going, momentum and rage carried her for half an hour. She went back to her room, showered for the second time that night, and mindlessly channel-surfed until she finally fell asleep around three a.m.

When Brenda awoke the next morning, she had one brief moment of hope in the new day, then remembered her conversation with Beverly Vanderfeld the day before. "Not even out of bed, and already the day stinks . . ." she muttered. She checked the clock and saw that it was 10:15. She called the house but Adele and the boys were obviously out enjoying the last week of summer vacation.

She wasn't hungry, so she just hung out in her room, reading and channel surfing. There was something else important going on today, but she couldn't remember what. At around 10:45, it dawned on her that she was supposed to meet Charlie Bannister for lunch at 11:30.

She hadn't given the date (was it really a date?) any thought or preparation. For a moment, she considered canceling but thought better of it. Maybe it would get her mind off the custody fiasco for a couple hours. She called down to the front desk and requested a cab, then turned her attention to what to wear, which was a mystery she would need to solve in the next twenty-five minutes. In a panic, she called Robin. "Hey, it's me," she said as soon as Robin answered.

"Hi," Robin said. "I have a client in like five minutes, but what's up? Is everything okay?"

"There's no time to talk about it, but I need your help. I have a date."

She heard a "WOOOO!" that was loud enough to be heard from Cleveland even without the phone. "I suppose I should ask with whom, but I'm just glad to see you're interested in *somebody*."

"Charlie Bannister."

There was dead silence for a second. "Isn't he that guy on ESPN? The one you did the interview with?"

"Yeah."

"Wow. I had no idea. How did this all come about?"

"We talked online some and then he called me. And we're going out to lunch."

"Honey, that's great. He seemed like a really funny, smart guy. And I have to admit, when I saw you two talking before the interview, it looked like there might be something there. So when is the date?"

"In half an hour."

"Oh my gosh . . . Why are you talking to me?"

"I don't know what to wear. I don't know what to do on a date. What do we talk about?"

"Wear a casual dress. You're going on a lunch, eat lunch. Talk about baseball. Or books. Or art. See if he knows anything about anything beyond sports."

"I don't want to get too dressed up. I don't want him to think I'm interested."

"You accepted a date with him," Robin said pointedly. "That in itself indicates a level of interest."

"I only have one dress with me—that light blue sundress with the jacket."

"Wear that. No jacket. Put your hair back in a clip because it shows off your eyes. And get the hell the out there."

"Thanks for talking me off the ledge," Brenda said. "Sometimes making decisions is just not what I want to do."

"I love making decisions as long as they aren't for me," Robin replied. "Now go enjoy yourself."

They hung up and Brenda headed for the elevator. When it got to the lobby, Brenda froze. Landers and Bandkins were standing just past the elevators. She'd have to walk by them to get outside. Head down, pretending to be engrossed in her own thoughts, she briskly walked past them.

"Hey, Brenda!" she heard Bandkins say. "How's it going?"

She slowed down but didn't stop, just turned and took a few steps backwards as she said, "Fine, thanks."

"Where you off to, Haversham?" Landers asked.

"Oh, I'm having lunch with my aunt. She lives out here. Well, Annapolis," Brenda said, surprised that the lie came as easily as it did.

"Have fun," Bandkins said.

"Don't miss the bus," Landers added. "By the way, what's his name?"

Brenda pretended not to hear, just turned and walked straight out of the lobby, praying they wouldn't follow her. Given Landers' last remark, maybe she didn't lie as well as she thought.

The restaurant was only a five-minute cab ride away in the Inner Harbor neighborhood. Had she realized how close it was, she would have walked. Charlie was waiting just inside the front door of the restaurant for her. Brenda wasn't quite ready for his broad smile when he saw her, even before she was close enough to say hello. She also wasn't ready for the little lift she felt when she saw him. On the air, he always wore a sport coat and tie, but now he just wore khakis and a deep blue shirt that made a nice contrast with his medium brown complexion. He looked good. Not having been on anything she would call a "date" in years, she chalked up the little pirouette her stomach did when she saw him to nerves.

"Hi," Charlie said. She said "Hello" back, and they stood looking nervously at each other until the hostess came and ushered them out to their table.

The restaurant was called Abundance and featured locally grown produce. She and Charlie sat outside in little courtyard behind the building. The outdoor dining area was divided into different sections by waist-high, narrow planters that contained trailing nasturtiums, herbs, and lettuce. She didn't know if Charlie had deliberately chosen a restaurant that would afford them a decent measure of privacy, but she appreciated it. It wasn't necessarily a conflict of interest for her to go to lunch with him, but she knew that people wouldn't think twice if it were a male player and a male journalist going out to lunch.

They were seated and made the usual small talk—commenting on the menu, the courtyard, how great it was to have some of the food growing alongside them. Then they ordered and the server took their menus and it was as though someone had taken away their cue cards.

Brenda wanted to say something, but she wasn't sure what. She didn't need to impress this guy, didn't feel the need to be witty or clever or flirtatious. For a moment, Brenda was content just being there with him. Charlie had a comfortable presence that made it seem as though they had known each for a long time. She reminded herself that it was his job as a journalist and an interviewer to make people comfortable so that they would open up to him. Her eyes momentarily scanned the courtyard, taking in the other tables—a younger couple holding hands at the table behind Charlie, a group of four laughing women and lots of white wine opposite them, two men and one woman having an incredibly earnest business meeting just over her left shoulder. When her gaze came back to Charlie, she noticed he was staring at her, a tiny, lopsided grin on his face.

"So have you figured out why you're here yet?" he asked.

That was certainly a different conversation starter. "First I need to figure out how I'm supposed to interpret that question," she replied.

"In case you were wondering, yes, this is a date, and yes, I'm interested in you. You intrigue me—not as a ballplayer or as a story, but as a person." Charlie said this matter-of-factly, as if he was noting that the restaurant grew all its own herbs.

Brenda was momentarily speechless. She wasn't sure if Charlie was being too forward, perfectly honest, or something else. She wasn't sure how she felt about him yet, but she had to admit that having him virtually hand all the leverage in the conversation over to her was incredibly brave on his part. It made her like him a little more. Charlie didn't look nervous as he sipped his glass of water and waited for a response. "I don't think I'm used to this level of candor," she said finally.

"Nobody is," Charlie replied, and he almost sounded apologetic. "But you should be. Everybody should be."

It only took Brenda half a second to remember any number of times someone had lied to her or told her a half-truth and she couldn't help but agree with him. "You're right," she said. "Thank you. In the interest of fair play and equal candor, I feel compelled to add that I have to question your judgment. I'm not intriguing as a person. As a ballplayer, I'm, at best, just an interesting footnote."

"That's where you're wrong. You've made history. I'm thinking you'll get at least two paragraphs in *The Baseball Encyclopedia* plus a couple footnotes." Brenda let herself smile ever so slightly at his bad joke. "That's the first time I've seen you smile," Charlie said. "Of course it's just a polite smile instead a real one, but it's a start."

"Has anyone ever told you that your bluntness can be a real conversation killer?"

"Yes. But I'm willing to muddle through if you are."

She couldn't figure Charlie Bannister out. He was funny, good-natured, honest, intelligent, and made her feel as though she knew exactly where she stood with him. It occurred to her that this was what it was like to be with a genuine adult. He made her want to be as honest and direct as he was. It was almost like being with Adele or Robin—there was an honesty that seemed to stem from sincere concern rather than an ulterior motive. But he was still a male and a journalist to boot, so by definition he had an ulterior motive. He had to. She retreated to safer topics.

"How did you get into journalism?" she asked. "Or rather, how did you end up hosting a major TV sports show?"

"I majored in journalism at the University of Toledo—did you know I'm a Buckeye too?"

"No, I didn't. Did you grow up in Toledo?"

"Yep. Anyway, I got into journalism because Jim Harkins, the station manager at WDHO, was broad-minded enough to give me a job and put me on the air. I graduated in 1984—we had *The Cosby Show* and Al Roker, but that was pretty much it for African Americans on TV then. He gave me a job as a sports reporter. I got all the scut work, mind you—I was the one standing on football fields in two-degree weather—but I was happy because it was *me* standing on that football field with a microphone. Then I got jobs in bigger and bigger markets and, I don't know, made a name for myself and got hired by ESPN." He paused for a moment, giving her space to speak. When she didn't, he asked: "Now what about you? I'm guessing you didn't start out wanting to be a ballplayer."

"And you would guess right. I used to be an artist and graphic designer. I took time off to have a family and then, well, you pretty much know what happened."

"Graphic design? Cool. So were you one of those paint-splattered art students I'd see walking around campus?"

"It wasn't always paint," Brenda said. "Sometimes it was oil pastels."

Their food arrived and they ate and talked. Charlie told her about growing up in Toledo with three younger siblings, an overworked mother, and no father ("none to speak of" was as much as he would say) and the book of essays on baseball he was trying to write and the woman he had almost married six years ago who decided at the last minute that she didn't want to be married after all ("at least not to me," Charlie added). Brenda told him about her sons and her divorce. She didn't tell him about her anger or how she pitched or the harassment from the other players, but still wondered if she had revealed too much.

After lunch, they walked a bit around the Inner Harbor area. It was a mecca for people—families, couples, big groups of friends. Walking alongside Charlie, for a brief instant Brenda felt like she was part of a couple and it was all she could do not to take his hand. There was a feeling of anticipation between them that was new and familiar at the same time. It wasn't the angry, adrenaline-fueled anticipation she had grown used to in the bullpen; this was quieter, subtle, and, in its way, more powerful than anything she had felt in a long time. She made a conscious decision not to touch his hand—that seemed like a can of worms that didn't need opening—and instead headed toward the water. Charlie followed.

It was a typically humid Chesapeake Bay summer day, but the slight breeze off the water was delicious. "Aaahh . . ." Charlie sighed into the breeze. "Makes me wonder why I ever decided to work indoors."

"I've definitely grown to enjoy spending my workday outside," Brenda said. She was going to tell Charlie about working in the cubicle farm at the insurance company when a big, hulking figure at the far end of the pier caught her eye. Charlie followed her gaze.

"What?" he asked.

"Nothing, it's just that the big bald guy over there looked familiar. Do you see? He's wearing a green T-shirt and is walking with a woman and a child."

"Oh, that's Carl," Charlie said. To Brenda's puzzled look he added, "Carl Maladente. I've interviewed him once or twice. And you struck him out last night."

Brenda almost missed the amused wink Charlie gave her as he said this. She was engrossed in staring at the little Maladente family. The wife was probably in her late twenties, slim, fairly tall, and from where Brenda stood, attractive although not model-glamorous like many players' wives. The child looked to be a bit younger than Jon—he still had a little kid's fidgety, excited way of moving in four directions at once. Looming over both of them was big, bad, bald Carl Maladente. His light-green shirt made him look like an atrophied Incredible Hulk. Brenda said as much and got a full taste of Charlie's rollicking, giggle-like laugh.

She watched as Maladente and his family came closer. The son had a huge cone of hot pink cotton candy, to which Maladente senior liberally helped himself. Brenda watched the interaction between the adults. At one point, they held hands briefly. Another time they stopped for a moment as their son pointed to something on the water, and Maladente picked off another piece of cotton candy and fed it to his wife.

"Do you know anything about him or his family?" Brenda asked.

"Not about his personal life," Charlie said, sitting down on a nearby bench. "He came up about eight or nine years ago. He's been with the Orioles the majority of his career, has a bit of a reputation as a badass. You know the type—the one who likes hazing the rookies, isn't above spiking somebody if he doesn't think he'll get caught."

Brenda stayed standing so she could keep Maladente and his family in her sights, but took a few steps closer to the bench where Charlie was sitting. "I heard rumors that he had been arrested for domestic abuse."

Charlie nodded. "That was quite a while ago from what I understand—he was still in the low minors. They made him go through some sort of anger management course when they brought him up. I haven't heard of anything since then." Charlie gently patted the spot on the bench next to him. "Why don't I introduce you? They're headed this direction anyway." Feeling like she had been caught cheating on an easy test, Brenda sat down next to him. "So are you worried that you might have embarrassed him in front of his son and scarred the little guy for life?" Charlie joked.

"No, I just . . ." The real reason she was interested in the Maladentes suddenly seemed very silly. "Okay, I didn't want to be the woman who strikes out a guy who's in the habit of beating his wife . . ."

"Because you were worried that he might take it out on her?" Charlie finished her thought. He smiled at her. "You're a good person, Brenda Haversham."

"Thanks."

Charlie raised one hand in greeting and Brenda turned to see that that Carl and his family were only about forty feet away.

"Hey Carl," Charlie called.

"Charlie Bannister! What up?" Carl replied.

Charlie stood up as the Maladente family got closer. Brenda did the same but hung in the background as Carl introduced Charlie to his family. When Charlie said: "Carl, I believe you know Brenda Haversham," Brenda saw an amused twinkle in his eye.

When she and Carl Maladente shook hands, he gave a harder grip than necessary and his eyes weren't nearly as friendly as his words.

His wife, on the other hand, seemed to hide a delighted giggle. And when she said, "I'm really glad to meet you," Brenda believed it. They made polite small talk for a few moments, then Sophie Maladente called their son, who had been wandering by the edge of the pier throwing cotton candy to the seagulls, and the Maladentes went on their way.

"I should probably get going too," Brenda said as she and Charlie watched them walk away. "Team bus leaves at 3:00."

"I love that they still put you on a bus to go two blocks," Charlie said.

"They want to make sure everybody shows up. I'd rather walk. Speaking of which, I could probably walk back to the hotel from here, right?"

"Sure, it's only about a fifteen-minute walk. Care for a guide?" As he said this, he held out one arm, elbow bent. Brenda wasn't sure if taking his arm was more intimate or less intimate than holding hands. Either way, it felt good.

•◊•

Excerpt from the transcript for *Today in Sports* with Charlie Bannister, ESPN, August 26:

> Charlie: Now I know most of the country thinks we New Yorkers don't get out of the city enough, so I'm here to tell you that some of us do. For instance, just today I had occasion to spend the day in Baltimore and had a wonderful time. And not only that, *Today in Sports* will be going on the road in two weeks. We'll be doing the show from Los Angeles the week of September fourteenth. So you see—some of us get around.

Chapter Nineteen

•◊•

PPARENTLY FEELING EVEN HALFWAY GOOD WAS A LIABILITY. Brenda wouldn't say that she was in a good mood after her lunch with Charlie—that was more optimism than she could allow herself. But the world appeared slightly brighter and less tarnished.

She went in for two-thirds of an inning that night and gave up two hits and a run. Earl said afterward that she was having trouble finding the strike zone, but Brenda knew she was having trouble finding her anger. Her mind kept going back to her lunch with Charlie and how comfortable she felt with him and the quiet moment two blocks from the hotel when he had kissed her cheek and the nearness of his body to hers. She spent the rest of the road trip trying to focus on anything but that moment.

She only went in for one of the three games in Tampa, facing one batter in the second game in the bottom of the eighth. She fell behind him in the count and when he hit the 2-0 pitch into deep right, the only thing that saved her from being charged with a home run was an outstanding leaping catch by Bandkins. All in all, the Tampa series was just one more batch of games and one more hotel room and set of buses and planes. And she had more important things at home to think about, like the custody case and Andy's birthday and the first day of school.

Andy's birthday was the Tuesday before school started, but they planned to celebrate it the Monday before, which was her only off day during the upcoming home stand. Brenda wanted to do something special, like take the boys and some friends to Cedar Point or a water park, but Andy had been non-committal on the phone. She could see he was torn between wanting to take her up on the offer and not wanting to take anything from her. He had been adamant that he didn't want to take a group of friends to the game on his actual birthday. To the best of her knowledge, Andy hadn't skipped any more visits with Ed, and she wondered if perhaps there was some anti-Mom influence from that quarter.

Andy finally decided he wanted to go to some big game center on the west side and play laser tag with a group of his friends. It was expensive, although they both knew the cost wasn't the factor it would have been even a couple months earlier.

It was nearly one a.m. by the time Brenda got home on Sunday night. Adele and Jon were asleep on the sofa. Brenda finally found Andy in the basement, surfing the Internet on the computer in the rec room. "Hi Andy," she said as she walked over and gave him a quick hug. Doing so also gave her a chance to peek at the website he was on. It looked like some sort of online game. Nothing pornographic. She breathed a silent sigh of relief. "Thanks for staying up to greet me. It looks like Jon and Grandma didn't quite make it."

"No. They fell asleep hours ago." He hadn't quite ducked out of her hug, but Brenda could tell he considered it an invasion of his space. Another week away had made him more like a man and less like a boy.

She took a step back and leaned on the edge of the built-in desk that ran the length of the narrow room. The desk was one of the things Brenda had loved about the house when they first bought it. She had set up the space to do her art work in her spare time, something that never materialized. Somewhere in one of the drawers was a stack of notebooks with sketches and ideas, drawing pencils, and other supplies that she hadn't touched in years. She tried to sound casual as she asked if he was ready for his birthday party the next day.

"Yeah."

"Who did you end up inviting?"

"Josh, Dante, Matt, and Aiden."

"Which Matt?" she asked. "Lee or Manning?"

"Lee." Brenda just gave a non-committal nod. She didn't dare tell Andy that she thought Matt Manning was a delinquent in training. "And you'd better tell Jon that he isn't playing every game with us," Andy added. "He's been all like, 'Oh, we're gonna have all these cool fights' and 'we're gonna do this' and 'we're gonna do that.' He's acting like it's *our* party instead of *my* party."

"I'll talk to him in the morning," Brenda said. "And I will keep him out of your hair *after* you let him play a couple rounds with you and your friends."

"He can do one fight with us, that's it."

"Two." Andy gave her an annoyed look. "Be happy you're going at all. Given that your mother is a pacifist, the idea that my son wants to fight on his birthday is something of a stretch."

"It's just a game."

"It's a war game."

Andy looked puzzled for a moment. "I don't get why you're so anti-fighting. Sometimes you have to fight—like if somebody is attacking you."

"I've said this to you before—I don't believe human beings were meant to hit other human beings," she said. "Hurting other people isn't entertainment."

"I know. But laser tag isn't really fighting. It's not like paint ball—nobody really gets hit with anything. And it's not as violent as football."

"I'm not interested in degrees of violence, Andy." Brenda realized that this was neither the time nor the place to have a reasoned debate on the necessity of violence. Andy wasn't in the mood for discussion, only concessions. "Look, if anyone ever attacks you, you have my permission to defend yourself."

"Gee, you're so generous."

"I try. Now go to bed."

The party went well. Brenda stuffed Jon and Andy and Andy's friends into the minivan and took them to the laser tag place, which was practically around the corner from where she had played with the Lightning earlier in the summer. Andy and his friends were nice about letting Jon tag along. Nobody argued, nobody got sick, and nobody threw food—in parenting terms, it was a big success.

When Brenda and the flock of boys got home, they were joined by Adele (who had picked up the ice cream cake, soda, and pizza), Dan, and Robin (who insisted on hearing all the details about the date with Charlie), and the parents of some of Andy's friends, including Carl, whom Brenda hadn't really talked to since her last Lightning game. They were all gathered in Brenda's postage-stamp-sized back-yard—kids on the driveway near the basketball hoop and the gate and adults in the back by what was once the vegetable patch. Brenda was slicing the ice cream cake when Carl arrived and didn't even see him until he came up to her and picked up one of the last two plates of cake.

"I think you deserve a treat after all your hard work," he said, handing one of the plates to her.

"Carl! Hi," Brenda said and looked around to see that everyone had cake before she took the plate from him. "Thanks. It's good to see you. And I've been meaning to call you. I'm sorry I just sort of ditched the team without much notice . . ."

"Don't worry about it," he said. "We're all really glad you're doing so well."

"Eh, I don't know about well. I've had some bad outings."

"And you've had some really great ones."

"Well, thanks . . ." Brenda replied, getting a little flustered with the unexpected praise. "Here, come and sit down. I want to hear about the Lightning."

Carl gave her the quick low-down on her fellow team members. Bob's wife and exceptionally cute baby had finally made an appear-ance. Gary had attempted to ask out Kathi O'Leary and been might-ily shot down. "And I'm doing okay, considering we don't have you to come in and save games for us anymore," Carl added.

"I'm so sorry . . ." Brenda began.

"Just kidding. Come on, you're living everybody's dream."

Brenda sighed and ate a bite of ice cream cake, but it tasted like whipped air. She put the plate down on the picnic table. "Playing baseball for a living was never my dream," she said after a moment.

"Sometimes it's like I've been plopped down into this life and I have no idea how I got here."

"I felt like that after Josh was born. Hell, I feel that way most of the time," Carl said. He gave her a small grin. "You're doing something good here. Too bad nobody can convince the Frickers of that."

"The who?"

"The Frickers. That's what we call the Ford Frick protesters."

Brenda felt a delicious little twist in her stomach. "I like it," she said.

Their conversation was interrupted by Jon, who came up to the picnic table and said that it was time for Andy to open his presents. Brenda rounded up the boys and the parents and the presents and watched as Andy opened a slew of gift cards, CDs, and computer games that she had never heard of. She trusted the other parents enough not to worry that there was anything egregiously misogynistic or violent in them, but still, she nonchalantly checked to see if anything had a parental advisory label.

The new Gismo she gave Andy was a huge hit. When Andy opened it, there was a chorus of "Cool!" from his friends. Andy stared at the Gismo for a moment and said simply, "Wow." Brenda had taped a note on the box that read, "For when you need to escape. Love, Mom." She saw him read the note and, for and instant, he stopped. Stopped moving and stopped talking to his friends and just sat and looked at her little note. A small smile crept onto his face. Andy looked up at Brenda and said, "Thank you, Mom." Across the crowded back yard, Brenda held her son's gaze for a moment and felt something shift between them. She hoped it was for the better.

Although she had no desire to see him, Brenda had invited Ed to the party—through Andy—because she knew it was the right thing to do. Since the call from his lawyer, she figured he wouldn't actually come. Much to Brenda's surprise, he showed up midway through the present opening, when the party was close to over.

Brenda was sitting with Robin, Adele, and Matt Lee's mother, Anna, when she saw Ed walk into the backyard. Jon immediately yelled "Dad!" and jumped up to give him a hug. Andy was sitting in the middle of his friends, all of them passing the gifts around and giving little exclamations of "Sweet!" or "Wicked!" over each item.

"Hey Dad!" Andy called. Brenda hadn't seen them together since the day Andy skipped his day with Ed. She kept trying to forget that was also the day Andy was caught shoplifting. Her eldest and his father seemed comfortable together—Andy holding up gifts and saying, "Check this out" and Ed smiling and offering some appropriate exclamation in return. Ed held his head slightly down, the only outward sign that he might be uncomfortable.

Brenda had given Adele and Robin a quick low-down on the custody issue that morning, and when her mother saw Ed, Brenda could have sworn she heard Adele growl.

"Are you okay?" Anna Lee asked.

"I'll be fine when he's gone," Adele muttered.

"What's going on?" Anna whispered to Brenda. "I thought your split was pretty amicable."

Brenda turned to Anna and her oh-so-high cheekbones. She didn't know Anna that well, only as the parent of one of Andy's friends, but they had talked at birthday parties or school events over the years. She supposed they were good acquaintances. The cheekbone thing had always bothered her. Ed used to say that the only thing higher than Anna Lee's hips were her cheekbones. Sometimes it was hard to like a mom who was built like a supermodel. Brenda took a deep breath and tried to remember that Anna wasn't the enemy.

"I thought it was too, but he's done some things lately that . . ." She shook her head and let her voice trail off just enough to allow Anna Lee's mind to ponder the possibilities.

Robin was sitting next to Anna and leaned over and whispered something to her. "Are you kidding me?" she exclaimed. As Anna's eyes narrowed, Brenda realized why Matt Lee was such a model student; with a mother who could throw evil looks like that, any kid would shape up.

After the present commotion had died down a bit and Jon was no longer hanging on his arm, talking a mile a minute, Ed walked over to Brenda and was confronted by four women, all sitting in lawn chairs with their arms crossed and glaring at him.

"Hi," Ed said. He looked sheepish.

"Good evening, Ed," Brenda said. She felt buoyed, being flanked by Adele, Robin, and Anna Lee and her cheekbones.

"Can I talk to you for a minute?" Ed asked.

"No, I'm sorry, but I have to start cleaning up. We're out of ice cream cake, but help yourself to pizza before I put things away." As Brenda said this, she could almost feel the ever-present anger spreading throughout her body. Usually a rush of angry adrenaline made her feel hot, but this was different. Instead of hot anger she had a cool rage and wondered how much her sinker would drop if she threw one at that moment.

"It'll just take a minute," Ed said. "This is important."

"Ed, anything you want to say to me you should say to my lawyer." With that, Brenda picked up an empty chip bowl and a couple dirty plates and went inside. She put the plates and bowl down and leaned on the counter for a moment, trying to calm herself but still remember this cool rush of anger for the pitcher's mound. She heard the screen door open and close behind her, and Robin walked in, carrying more dirty plates.

"It's none of my business," Robin said, "but maybe you should talk to Ed."

Brenda turned to face her best friend. "Why? Do you know how good it felt leaving him hanging for once? I've never wanted to hurt him before, but this whole custody thing . . . Forget it."

"Look, I know how poorly he treated you at the end, with that chick from his office and everything else. But Ed isn't a horrible person. You wouldn't have stayed with him for sixteen years if he was." Robin sighed, clearly choosing her words carefully. "Okay, did you tell him about Andy getting caught shoplifting or fighting with the camp counselor or the guy who followed the boys home?"

"No," Brenda replied, feeling defiant.

"If Dan and I ever broke up and Lindsey got into trouble, I'd sure as hell want to know about it. You haven't been exactly fair to him either. It's like you've decided what his role is going to be without even giving him the chance to be their dad."

"He had his chance, and he blew it," Brenda replied and went back outside to clean up from the party. Even if Robin *was* making a reasonable point, that didn't give Ed the right to file for primary custody. She wasn't going to be Ed Haversham's punching bag anymore—or anyone else's.

The next day, when she got to her locker room and found a *Hustler* centerfold with a photo of her face taped on the body, she decided that Pasquela and Cipriani should both pay. She knew her teammates' routines enough to know that Cipriani, Pasquela, and Greg Landers always played *Grand Theft Auto* in the clubhouse for about fifteen minutes after the media left the locker room but before the game. It seemed that pretending to shoot people and slap around prostitutes was their idea of mentally preparing. Brenda went into the locker room a bit earlier than usual and took a seat at one of the round tables near the door. Anthony Fleetwood saw her and said hello, but most everyone else ignored her. She hadn't realized how good she was at making herself invisible.

Her targets were sitting in the rounded leather sofa in the middle of the room, engrossed in the video game. Pasquela's locker was near the door on her side of the room. She stayed at the table for another thirty seconds or so, pretending to fuss with the lacing on her glove. Then she put her glove on a chair, silently stood up, and walked over to Pasquela's locker. She slipped her hand into her pocket and palmed a few of the handful of tampons she had grabbed from her duffel bag before she left her locker room. Pasquela's favored glove was sitting on the wide main shelf that ran the length of the locker. She picked it up and turned to face the rest of the room. She didn't need to look too closely to quickly shove one tampon into each of the finger openings on Pasquela's glove. If anyone noticed her, it would appear that she was fiddling with her own glove.

With one down and one to go, she walked over to the low half-wall that gave the illusion of dividing the larger locker room into two halves. She took a cookie from the jar that rested on top of the half wall and casually walked toward the back of the room and then to the other side. Cipriani's locker was right there. She noticed Anderson Sparks watching her from three lockers away.

"Hey Anderson," she said nonchalantly and took a bite of her cookie. Who cared if he ratted her out to Cipriani? As easily as picking up a stray magazine in a waiting room, she picked up Cipriani's baseball mitt and calmly inserted a tampon into each of the fingers. Sparks watched the entire thing. He stifled a giggle but didn't say a word. When she was done, Brenda gave him a polite nod and went back over to where she had been sitting.

The payoff came after the National Anthem, when the Indians took the field. Pasquela put on his glove as he ran out to his position at second base. Brenda had gotten into the habit of going out to the bullpen at the start of the game, but today she stayed in the dugout by the railing to get the best possible view. To her surprise, Anderson Sparks came and stood next to her, an amused look on his face.

It was obvious Pasquela had discovered there was something in his glove. Ryan Teeset was warming up the infield, throwing hard grounders to second, short, and third. Teeset threw to Landers at third and then to McGall at short. He went to throw to Pasquela, but the second baseman was searching with one finger inside his glove, trying to remove a foreign object. When he pulled out a tampon, his annoyance was visible from halfway across the field. Brenda had made sure not to shove them too far into the fingers. She didn't want to delay the game, just annoy him.

To her left, Sparks was laughing silently, his big square shoulders shaking helplessly as they watched Pasquela get the second of the tampons out.

From her other side, she heard Mark Munson say, "What the hell's the matter with Fred?" She hadn't even noticed Mark standing next to her.

"It looks like he has something in his glove, Skip," Sparks said, barely able to contain his laughter.

Landers and McGall had both noticed Pasquela's trouble, and McGall trotted over to help. She couldn't hear everything being said, but saw McGall approach Pasquela, saw Pasquela hold the glove out and say something to McGall, who threw back his head and laughed his hee-haw like laugh that carried all the way to the dugout. McGall was smaller and leaner than Pasquela, and he dug into the glove with one skinny finger and retrieved the last of the tampons just as the home plate umpire yelled, "Play ball!"

When the team came off the field later that inning, Brenda made sure to give Pasquela a wide berth. Even so, he came storming up to her in the dugout.

"What the fuck was that about?" he snapped, his sweaty, red-tinged face only inches from hers. All noise and action in the dugout suddenly stopped.

Brenda thought she should be scared or nervous by his anger, but she hadn't done anything that he hadn't done to her or Teeset or any other player. "What the fuck was what about?" she asked.

"Putting . . ." He quieted his voice. "Messing with my glove," he said, as though Brenda had defiled a sacred vessel.

Brenda was very aware that every man in the dugout was looking at her, even Dave McGall, who was in the on-deck circle. From the other side of the dugout, Munson watched, seemingly wondering if he needed to rescue her. "Is there anything wrong with your glove?" she asked.

"No."

"Then how did I mess with it?"

"You put . . . Stay the hell away from my locker."

"You do the same," she said, making sure everyone in the dugout heard her reply.

Art Groggins and Doug Stone chose that moment to intercede, Art putting a hand on Pasquela's shoulder and telling him that was enough, and Doug sidling up to Brenda and saying, "You've made your point."

This was enough to reset the mood in the dugout back to something manageable. Sparks' inability to keep a straight face made Cipriani suspicious, and he went digging in his glove before he even went out to the bullpen. Pasquela was still visibly seething, but he didn't say anything to Brenda, and neither did anyone else until Dave McGall scored on a Ryan Teeset double. He came back to the dugout and walked up to Brenda.

"I believe these belong to you," he said, and placed two dusty but still wrapped tampons into her hand.

Not knowing what else to do, Brenda just said, "Thanks" and put them in her pants pocket.

"And they call me crazy," McGall said with a wink.

•◇•

Excerpt from the transcript for *Today in Sports* with Charlie Bannister, ESPN, September 1:

> Charlie: In tonight's highlights, we start with Boston at Cleveland. Top of the eighth, score is tied at three with men in scoring position. Brenda Haversham on the mound in relief. She serves up a fastball high and tight to Boston's Barney Cornwell, who sends it up the middle. Fred Pasquela jumps and misses. It looks like Boston will take the lead, but wait, here comes Art Groggins charging in from centerfield, he dives, makes the catch, and stops the Red Sox rally dead in its tracks. Cleveland ends up winning 4-3 in extra innings. Great play by Groggins, who, incidentally, has announced that he'll be retiring at the end of the season. He's definitely going out at the top of his game.

Chapter Twenty

•◇•

THE GAME WENT INTO A DISAPPOINTING LOSS IN TEN INNINGS, AND BY THE TIME BRENDA GOT HOME, THE REST OF THE HOUSE WAS ASLEEP. School started in the morning, and she hoped Adele had been able to get the boys to bed at a reasonable time.

Adele was sleeping on the sofa, even though Brenda had repeatedly told her mother to just sleep in her bed upstairs. She had left on the light over the stove for Brenda, and it cast just enough light for Brenda to study her mother's face as she slept. Adele's too-red-to-be-natural-at-her-age hair was poofed out against an old pillow, her face relaxed, almost smiling.

She walked down the short hallway to the boys' rooms. She peeked in on Jon first, who was sleeping face down in the middle of a mass of blankets, one bare foot hanging off the edge of the bed, the other stuck in between the bed and the wall. His notebooks and folders and other school supplies were precariously stacked on top of the little desk next to his bed. Brenda gently moved both feet so they were on the bed and covered him up. His new Ohio State hoodie was draped over his desk chair and his new sneakers—though not the expensive ones he had wanted—on the floor next to the bed. She was glad Adele hadn't caved into his pleading and made him keep to the agreed-upon budget. As she stood there in the darkened room, looking at the new sneakers, she felt a jumble of emotions—gratitude that her mother could act *in loco parentis*, guilt that she wasn't doing the parenting job herself, and even a bit of envy at all the time Adele had had with the boys over the summer

She moved on to Andy's room. During the past year, he had slowly become less of a sloppy kid and more of a neat, organized young man. His backpack was sitting on his desk chair, and Brenda could see that he had already loaded his school supplies into it. The last book from his summer reading list was sitting on the edge of his desk, a bookmark on top of it. Apparently, Andy's growing tendency toward cleanliness and organization hadn't done anything to cure his procrastination, but he had his school supplies, he was under the covers, he had clean clothes. There wasn't anything for her to do. More and more, it seemed as though Andy had grown up while she was gone.

Within a week, Brenda knew she'd practically have to drag Jon out of bed in the mornings, but on the first day of school, he was up and noisy at 6:00 a.m. Brenda managed to drag herself downstairs to greet him. Jon was in the living room, his notebooks and other school supplies spread out on the coffee table in the living room. It looked like he was taking last-minute inventory.

"Good morning, sweetie. Are you ready for your first day of fourth grade?"

"Absolutely."

"Great. Where's your brother?"

"Probably in the bathroom. He's in there all the time now." Jon looked slightly disgusted at the thought of his older brother's foray into decent hygiene.

"Leave your brother alone. It's good that he wants to look nice for school." She sent Jon off to get dressed and wandered into the kitchen to make some coffee and start breakfast. As usual, Adele had beat her to the punch and was getting glasses and bowls out of the cupboard.

"I can do it," Brenda said. When Adele paused, the break in what had become her morning routine obvious, Brenda added: "I really want to."

"*Dobre rano* to you too," Adele said with a smile. "How was the game?"

"Long, and we lost."

"You'll get 'em next time." Adele gave her a kiss on the cheek and sat down at the kitchen table. "By the way, if you hadn't noticed, Jon is on a Lucky Charms kick. And it appears that eighth graders don't eat breakfast. At least not with their families."

Brenda had the big cast iron skillet in her hand, with the thought of making pancakes. What *had* the boys eaten for breakfast the last two days? She couldn't even remember. "What does he eat for breakfast?"

"I bought a bunch of protein bars. He can take one of those. And some fruit."

"That's it?"

Adele shrugged her shoulders as if to say, "Who am I to argue with what my grandson wants?"

"Then I'll pack their lunches."

Adele looked skeptical. "You might want to double check what they want. Rumor has it that bringing your lunch is passé in junior high and the cafeteria in the fourth grade building is actually good. They've both said they'd rather buy their lunch."

"I can't afford to have them buy their lunches every day," Brenda said. It was an automatic response, honed by months of watching every penny.

"Actually, you can," Adele said. She sounded almost apologetic. "I know that doesn't mean they should—it just means they know that you can afford it now."

Brenda slumped down in a kitchen chair across from her mother. "I don't want to have to deal with this," she said. It wasn't as bad as having to sit down with the boys and tell them that she and their father weren't going to live together anymore, but it was one more teaching discussion she had to have with them. One more instance where she had to stand up and say the right thing and teach the right thing and not be lazy and frankly, at this particular moment, lazy sounded wonderful. "Okay, I'll let them buy it today because it's the first day, then they start bringing their lunch. And once a week they can buy lunch. How does that sound?"

"They're your children. I'm just the enforcer," Adele said with a smile.

Brenda managed to convince the boys to eat a bowl of cereal before the school bus arrived, but Adele was right. They weren't interested in brown bagging it. "Everybody says the cafeteria at Greenview is really good," Jon kept saying. "And the first day they *always* have pizza." She gave them some lunch money and stuck an apple into each of their backpacks, trying to make herself believe they'd eat them.

Adele went back to her own house after the boys left, and Brenda went back to sleep. She spent the day doing laundry, returning phone calls from friends who wanted game tickets, and going to the grocery store. The house didn't need anything—Adele was taking good care of the boys. It was more the idea of doing something for the family that compelled Brenda to buy more fruit and vegetables.

She spent twenty minutes in the cereal and snack aisles reading labels, trying to find the healthiest take-along snacks she could for the boys. Then suddenly it was time to go to the ballpark and the boys weren't even home from school. She wanted time to sit and listen to Jon tell her stories about his new school building and how many kids there were compared to the elementary school and what he liked and what he didn't like. She wanted time to talk with Andy about how it felt to be an eighth grader at the top of the heap (the idea that he was going to high school in a year seemed impossible). Instead, she studied film of the Boston Red Sox's starting lineup, looked at scouting reports, and retired both of the batters she faced. And at the end of the long day, she found the windshield of her car littered with fliers from a local "gentleman's club."

When Brenda got home, she found Adele reading a book in the living room. Seeing her mother on her sofa always gave Brenda a tiny lift of feeling like a little girl again. She was too tired to smile but said hello and asked if the boys were in bed.

"Jon is asleep. Andy is a little too worked up to sleep. I know it's a school night, but I let him stay up a little late. He's downstairs, playing on the computer."

"Why is Andy too worked up to sleep?"

Adele made a production of picking up her bookmark and marking her place in her book and putting it on the coffee table. "Now I don't want you to get upset . . ."

"Oh God . . ." Brenda said as she plopped down in the easy chair opposite the sofa. She took a deep breath—better to rip the bandage off fast than to linger. "Hit me with it—how bad?"

"He got into a fight."

"On the first day of school! What the hell?"

"It's not as bad as you think," Adele said.

Brenda leaned back in the chair, wishing she could just disappear into the cushions for a month or so. Her head hurt and closing her eyes felt so good she could have fallen asleep on the spot if her mother hadn't said: "Go down and talk to him."

Brenda opened her eyes and looked over at her mother. At that immediate moment, the idea of having to be The Responsible Parent wasn't all that attractive.

"It's not as bad as you think," Adele repeated.

With a heavy sigh, Brenda got up and walked downstairs to the rec room. Andy was in his usual spot in front of the computer. As she walked in, she saw the computer monitor flash to a new image. In spite of herself, she asked, "Homework on the first day?"

Andy quickly spun around in the desk chair to look at her. "Yeah, but I did it already," he said. "Just downloading some music and stuff."

She noticed that his new Gismo was on the desk and plugged into the computer. "I'll take your word for it, Andy," Brenda said, leaning against the door. "But I do want to remind you that a lot of what's online is for adults, and even though you're thirteen, that doesn't make you an adult."

"I wasn't looking at porn," he said in a surprisingly patient voice. Now that Andy was facing her head-on, she could see that he had likely gotten the worst of the fight. There was a bruise on his cheek and a long scrape on his left forearm, as though he had fallen and slid across the pavement. The thought made her shudder.

Mother and son regarded each other for a moment, then Brenda asked, "How does the other guy look?"

Andy managed a small grin. "You mean other guys?"

Other guys? How could Adele say it wasn't as bad as she thought? Brenda went to him and gave him a hug. "Oh sweetie, what happened?"

Andy didn't pull away from the hug, but he wouldn't meet Brenda's eyes. "A couple of guys at school were saying stuff that was really nasty—you would have said it was sexist. And I told them to shut up and they didn't, and then we got in a fight."

"How many boys were there?"

"It started out with three, but then a couple other guys joined in." Brenda felt her heart skip a beat when he said this. "But my friends were there too."

"Is everyone else okay too?"

"Yeah. We're all fine. Did you know that Matt Manning is a really good fighter?"

"No, but somehow I'm not surprised," Brenda replied. "Andy, I'm just glad you're okay. I admire that you were standing up to somebody who was being a sexist jerk, but fighting . . ." She sighed, trying not to think of how much worse it could have been. "I'm just glad you're okay," she repeated.

"I watched the game tonight," Andy said. "You did really good, but why don't some of the other guys on your team talk to you? Like when you're all walking off the field at the end of an inning, most of the guys talk to each other or something. But hardly anyone talks to you, and Pasquela never says a word to you."

Brenda quickly considered what her response should be. "I don't think he likes me," she said simply.

"But he's on your team. You're supposed to back up the other people on your team." Brenda didn't say anything. "People give you a hard time, don't they? Like other players and people online and people in the stands." He didn't hesitate or think before he asked any questions, which made Brenda wonder how long he had been thinking about all this.

"Yes," Brenda answered. There was no reason not to tell the truth.

Andy was silent for a moment, as though he was sifting through what she hadn't said. "These guys at school kept saying that you didn't belong in the majors and they called . . . they said some really lousy things about you. And they said that the Fricker guys are right."

"Do you think they're right?" Brenda asked.

"No." This felt like a major accomplishment. "I mean, there's no point paying attention to those Fricker guys because they're idiots. You're . . . good," he added. He almost sounded surprised when he spoke the word "good," and Brenda knew how difficult this realization must have been for him.

"Thank you."

Although she hardly saw Andy the rest of the week, when she did, he actually talked to her. Sometimes it was about the previous night's game, other times it was about school or what one of his friends had done. He even asked her about what kind of music she liked. It was a joy just sitting or standing in the kitchen, chatting with her son. Jon dominated most of her free moments, keeping up a steady stream of banter about his friends and baseball and fourth grade and his new school building. It was joyous kid talk and Brenda loved it, but it could be tiring. Talking to Andy was starting to feel like a conversation with an adult. He was starting to think more and more for himself and not just repeating what he had heard his friends say or what he had read.

When Andy had taken his first steps and gone from baby to toddler, Brenda had almost wanted to cry. But now, watching him take his first steps from boy to thoughtful young man, Brenda found that watching the transformation made her happier than she thought it would. He was discovering the complexities and gray areas of life, but it didn't seem to trouble or perplex him, instead, he seemed to enjoy the intellectual challenge of figuring out why the world operated as it did.

Brenda had discovered that all the home stands flew by and all the road trips seemed to last two months. Tampa Bay came in after the Boston series, and Brenda did a bit better against them the second time, getting two strikeouts against the two batters she faced on Saturday night. And then it was Sunday morning again, and she had to pack for a two-week road trip that would take her to Chicago, Detroit, Los Angeles, and Oakland.

This would be the longest road trip yet. Adele brought the boys to the game on Sunday afternoon so they could say good-bye. Brenda didn't go in that game, which was fine with her. The stomach pains that had begun earlier in the season had only gotten worse, and she had fiery heartburn for hours after every outing, no matter what she ate. Most days it seemed easier not to eat, or to have just a glass of milk.

After the game, the players had a few minutes to say good-bye to their families in the players' parking lot before the bus left to take them to the airport. It was a ritual that Brenda had gone through a few times now, but it hadn't gotten easier. She looked around at her teammates and their families. How had they gotten used to not seeing their husbands and fathers for eight months of the year? This was an impossible lifestyle, yet here was Doug Stone and his wife and two daughters having a big family hug; there was old Art Groggins and his wife kissing good-bye; there was Pasquela and his wife and toddler son getting in one last hug, all of them seemingly unfazed by yet another departure. The guys who weren't married, like Teeset and Panidopolous and Cipriani, were already on the bus, waiting to go. Had they all become so inured to the continual rhythm of arrivals and departures that it no longer bothered them or were they just numb until the off-season?

Brenda looked at her family standing in front of her. Jon hadn't seemed too upset by the earlier road trips, but the prospect of having Brenda gone for two weeks right at the start of school was troubling him. Although his tantrums seemed to have eased off over the summer, she saw the familiar hint of red creeping across his face and knew that Adele was going to have to contend with some tears when they got home.

She pulled Jon close in a huge hug. "Good-bye, sweetie. I'll see you in two weeks. I promise I will call every day. And you have my cell number—you can call me anytime you need to."

Jon's face was buried in her shoulder, and he didn't look up as he whispered, "I know."

"And we'll have a picnic when I come back, okay?"

"Okay," came Jon's quiet answer.

"Andy, come here, sweetie," Brenda said, reaching to pull him into the hug. Andy held back a bit. Brenda didn't push him. This line between man and boy, macho and tender was difficult for both of them to maneuver. She saw the same thing in the locker room or on the bus with the guys whose eyes got slightly teary when they talked about their kids and the next minute were telling a dirty joke to off-set any display of emotion.

She took half a step back so she could see both boys' faces. "Look, I don't like leaving you, but this is my job now. I'm sorry I'll be gone for so long, but you're in great hands with your grandma."

"We'll be fine," Andy said. As he said this, he put an arm around Jon's skinny shoulder. Brenda had no idea that her older son could be that gentle with his brother.

"I know you will." She picked up the bag of books, scouting reports, and the team iPad that she always carried on buses and planes. "Now I have to go. I love you all so much, and I'll see you in a couple weeks."

"Mom, wait a second," Andy said. "I have something for you."

This stopped Brenda in mid-step. Andy wasn't the type to give gifts. She watched him pull his Gismo out of his jeans pocket and hand it to her. "Here," he said. "You need this more than I do."

Brenda was stunned. Why was he giving back his birthday gift? He had been in the basement half the week downloading music for it. "Andy, thank you, but I don't understand. I thought you really wanted a new mp3 player." she said.

"Yeah, I do, but I think you need it more. You'll understand once you see what I put on it for you." He turned to Adele and asked if she had the charger. As she handed it to Brenda, Andy added, "You'll definitely need this too."

Her sadness at leaving the boys was tempered by puzzlement and curiosity around the Gismo. She gave everyone one last hug and got on the bus. Andy refused to take the Gismo back, saying she'd under-stand once she started looking at what was on it. Brenda gripped it tightly in her hands as she got on the bus and found a seat near the back in Rookie Exile.

Through the bus window, she could see her family standing and talking. Some of the other families, primarily those with very young children, were still waving at the bus even though the windows were tinted and you couldn't tell from the outside whether anyone inside was even looking at you.

The Gismo was waiting in her hands, but she'd have plenty of time on the road to explore whatever Andy had put on it. For now, she just wanted one more look at her family. Looking out the window, she saw Adele say something to the boys. Andy nodded, and it looked like he might even be smiling. Jon kind of hung around, staring at the bus. He turned and waved at the bus. Instinctively, Brenda waved back, even though she knew he couldn't see her.

•◊•

Excerpt from the transcript for *Today in Sports* with Charlie Bannister, ESPN, September 6:

> Charlie: The most interesting series this week is definitely the Indians at the White Sox. The Indians have made a spectacular comeback in the second half, while the White Sox have had an equally spectacular meltdown. With the two teams virtually tied for second place in the AL Central, we're sure to see some of the best ball of the season with this series. Meanwhile, the rest of the division has settled into two separate and unequal factions. The Tigers are sitting pretty in first, with a comfy three-game lead, and the Twins and Royals are so far back they've already been mathematically eliminated from everything but dreaming of next year.

Chapter Twenty-One

•◊•

A S THE BUS PULLED AWAY FROM THE PARKING LOT, BRENDA TURNED ON THE GISMO TO SEE WHAT ANDY HAD DOWNLOADED FOR HER. She looked first at the music listings and was surprised to find all of her favorite bands—old songs by the Smiths and the Clash and the Jam plus newer things from the Black Keys and Arcade Fire. Andy never listened to this stuff. He had spent the last week down in the basement going through her old CDs and downloading music and putting it all on the Gismo. For her. Nothing he had ever done for her touched her heart more than this one beautiful, voluntary act of love.

She sniffed and wiped away a small tear. She had barely noticed that Doug Stone had sat down next to her. "You okay, Brenda?"

"Yeah, I'm fine," she said quickly. Even though Doug had become something of a friend, she didn't need to be seen crying in front of anyone on the team. Tears were a sign of femininity, of weakness. Some of her teammates and opponents still seemed to expect weakness from her. They studied her face whenever she gave up a hit or a run, as though waiting for the tears to fall, waiting for her to show that she wasn't strong enough to play their game. "It's just that my son downloaded a bunch of my favorite songs on here and gave it to me, and it was just a really sweet thing for him to do."

"Aw, what a great kid." Doug leaned a bit closer so he could see the Gismo. "Those are pretty new. How do you like it? I've just had this old iPod for years, but I've been thinking of upgrading."

"I don't know. I just got it. But it's one my thirteen-year-old liked, so it must be pretty good," Brenda said. Referring to Andy as a thirteen-year-old for the first time made her feel ancient.

"Do you know what the screen quality is like? I'd love to be able to stream some TV shows and stuff, but I feel guilty doing it on the team iPad."

"I don't know. You're welcome to look at it for a minute."

"Hey, thanks," Doug said, taking the Gismo from her. Brenda settled back for a moment and closed her eyes. After a few moments, she heard Doug say, "Wow" and jerked back to reality. "Wow what?" she asked.

Doug handed the Gismo back to her. "It looks like your boy has been busy," he said. "He's downloaded video of the starting lineups for the entire road trip."

"Are you kidding me?"

"No. Scroll through it. He's got Chicago, Detroit, LA, and Oakland. That's a lot of work. Poor kid probably didn't have time to download anything else."

Brenda took the Gismo back and started scrolling through everything that Andy had downloaded. Right in front of her was Chicago's starting lineup: Holmes, Tagiashi, Weymouth, Racino, Fernandez, Kowalski, Morris, Burt, and Parker. She hadn't yet faced any of these guys, but she and everyone else who followed baseball even a little knew first baseman Jorge Racino. He had one of the highest batting averages in the league and the highest on-base percentage. She started with him. Even watching film of him was intimidating. Whenever he swung the bat, he almost always connected with the ball.

She watched video on the Gismo all the way to the airport, on the quick flight to Chicago, and in her hotel room that night, using it instead of the team iPad and doing her best to memorize what she was seeing. Her studying seemed to pay off in the first game of the four-game series; she faced Burt and Parker in the eighth, striking out the former and getting the latter to pop out. After the game, Earl complimented her on doing her homework.

They split the first two games of the series, which was frustrating. The possibility of grabbing the wildcard spot in the playoffs had captured the team's collective focus. As a Cleveland fan, Brenda was no stranger to disappointment. She had rejoiced when the Indians started fielding competitive teams and cheered for them through all their aborted playoff and World Series bids. As a player, the excitement was different. Joining the Indians when the team was in the basement had removed some pressure—no one expected anything from them. Now that they were flirting with contention, the tension level in the clubhouse reminded Brenda of a squirmy little ferret run amok, nipping at random heels, causing small outbursts of chaos and impatience and occasionally leading to blow-ups.

Julio Ochoa was scheduled to start the third game in Chicago. Brenda remembered Ed talking about Ochoa when the Indians had signed him as a seventeen-year-old phenom about seven years ago. He was one of the few bright spots in a farm system that hadn't been able to produce many stars in recent seasons. Ochoa was ridiculously thin, although from what Brenda had seen in the dining room both before and after games, he ingested enough calories each day to feed an entire starting rotation.

Ochoa's pre-game ritual included a series of yoga-like stretches that were fascinating to watch. He would plop down in a corner of the field near the bullpen and contort his long, thin limbs into ridiculous poses that alternately resembled a crab, a back-hoe, and a swan. Brenda hadn't really talked with him that much, but he at least had the habit of smiling and saying hello to her. He seemed like a good guy.

Ochoa got off to a good start, pitching shut-out ball for the first six innings. The Indians managed to scrape out a single run and were leading 1-0 going into the bottom of the seventh when everything fell apart. Ochoa walked Racino and gave up a double to Fernandez. Then Ray Kowalski, the second baseman, who wasn't known for having a big bat, hit a three-run homer. Ochoa was clearly frustrated, but Munson left him in. Then the White Sox's right fielder Ben Morris came to bat. Ochoa lost control of the ball and beaned him in the side. Ochoa didn't have a reputation for head-hunting. To the Indians, it was merely a bad pitch. Morris thought it was intentional and glared at Ochoa as he took first base. On the next hit ball, a hopper that went straight at Dave McGall, Morris slid hard and broke up the double play, spiking Pasquela in the process.

Brenda was watching all of this from the bullpen. She cringed when Ochoa beaned Morris. She had yet to hit a batter and wanted to keep it that way. The idea of accidentally hitting someone with a hard little ball traveling ninety miles an hour made her stomach hurt. She didn't think she could ever do so on purpose. When Morris slid into second, she initially didn't realize what had happened. She saw Pasquela and Morris exchange heated words, heard Sparks yell, "He spiked him!" and saw both benches and bullpens immediately stand up. While she found it impossible to feel bad that it was Pasquela who had been spiked, her sense of fair play was offended.

The entire stadium was booing and jeering as Pasquela and Morris argued. The second base umpire seemed to smooth things out, and for a moment, it looked like the altercation was over. Pasquela went back to his position, but as Morris turned to leave the field, McGall said something to him. The two men started throwing punches, and both dugouts emptied. Brenda watched as the rest of the bullpen ran across the field to the fight. Without thinking, she ran with her teammates.

There were now two distinct places on the field: the place where people were fighting and the place where people were not fighting. The place where people were not fighting was rapidly depopulating.

Brenda's initial reaction was to stay away. In the time it took to take a deep breath, she had run through two syllogisms in her head: I'm a woman. Women don't fight. Ergo, I don't fight. Then: This is my team. My team is fighting. Ergo, I have to fight. All around her, her teammates and the opposing team were engaged in hand-to-hand combat. She thought she ought to be scared, but instead felt excitement. The players were throwing punches with wild abandon, taking out their frustration and anger with their entire bodies. It was intoxicating, and she wanted a sip.

The closest player to her was Harry Tagiashi, the White Sox shortstop. He wasn't much bigger than she, and he didn't appear to be fighting anyone, which, in the half a second Brenda had to think, seemed to be key criteria. She charged at him from the side and managed to knock him over through a combination of momentum and surprise.

"What the hell?" Tagiashi said as he hit the ground. Brenda ignored him and hit him in the side.

Tagiashi's face was half on the ground and she heard him yell something about stupid rookies.

She stopped pummeling. "What?"

Tagiashi got a good look at who had knocked him down and his eyes opened wide in a combination of shock and annoyance. "*Kuso!*" he said. "What are you doing?"

"Fighting you," Brenda said and laid a punch square in his stomach.

"Ow!" Tagiashi rolled over and pinned her. "I won't hit a woman."

"It's okay, I hit you first," Brenda said, trying to push him off. She managed to get one more swipe in at him and then it appeared as though Tagiashi levitated off of her. She scrambled to her feet and saw six-foot-three Art Groggins dump the five-foot-seven Tagiashi unceremoniously on the ground.

"What the hell are you doing hitting a woman?" Groggins said.

Tagiashi was livid. "She charged me!"

"Get out of here," Groggins snapped at him, then looked at Brenda. "Haversham, you're nuts. Get back to the bullpen before you're ejected."

Brenda stood panting, her heart racing and her stomach in knots. Every muscle in her body suddenly felt like mush. She looked around and saw that the fight had pretty much been broken up. The umpires were ordering players back to their dugouts and the two teams' respective managers and coaches were doing the same. She didn't see McGall or Morris and figured they must have been ejected. Tagiashi started the trek back to his dugout.

"I can't believe I got in a fight," Brenda said, half to herself, half out loud. "I can't believe I hit another human being."

"Believe it," Groggins said. "Now come on." He walked a few yards with her as he returned to centerfield and she returned to the bullpen. Just as their paths diverged, Groggins said, "Haversham, you're nuts, but you have heart."

"Thanks," Brenda replied.

"Don't mention it."

After the fight, Brenda sat in the bullpen, seething and flying with adrenaline. She went in as the stopper in the bottom of the eighth, facing Kowalski, who looked overconfident after his big blast and went down swinging. It only took five pitches, but when she saw Kowalski swing and miss for the third strike, she felt only relief. There was nothing left in her arm or her gut to muster for another batter.

They lost the game and left Chicago immediately after, arriving in Detroit in the middle of the night. As tired as she was, Brenda couldn't sleep, but instead sat up in her hotel room, replaying the fight over and over again in her head. She hadn't fought long or hard, but still every muscle seemed to hurt. When she was in the middle of it, she hadn't thought that she might be hurting another person; she was only focused on how the fighting made her feel—exhilarated. Her anger had come from a new source; she didn't have to conjure it out of memory. It hadn't required control or finesse or the call of the catcher. It was all pure, unadulterated fury. She didn't want to admit that she had enjoyed the release.

•◇•

Excerpt from the transcript for *Today in Sports* with Charlie Bannister, ESPN, September 10:

> Charlie: Those of you who tuned in to watch the Indians-White Sox game last night might have thought you accidentally tuned into the WWE. A dispute between Chicago's Ben Morris and Cleveland's Fred Pasquela and Dave McGall turned into a bench-clearing brawl. Apparently McGall and Morris fought in retaliation for Morris's alleged spiking of Pasquela, which took place in retaliation for Jorge Ochoa allegedly throwing at Morris. It's all very complicated and sounds suspiciously like how most Central European wars are started. Let's

hope the two teams sign a peace accord before they meet again later this month. The fight clearly put some gas in Chicago's testosterone tank, as they beat Cleveland 3-1.

Chapter Twenty-Two

•◇•

THE MORNING AFTER THE FIGHT, BRENDA FELT HUNG OVER AND GROGGY, AND HER STOMACH BURNED. She would have called it indigestion, but she hadn't eaten anything after the game. She lay in bed, staring at a single crack in the off-white hotel room ceiling. It seemed easier to will the crack to expand through brain power alone than it was to get up, get dressed, and face another game against another team in another city and another stadium of screaming fans. Having felt genuine, pure anger the previous night, the thought of mustering up an adrenaline burst of rage from memories of her divorce or thoughts of child abusers or war felt grotesquely false. She was tired, plain and simple.

"I don't want to do this anymore," she said aloud and let her own words linger in the room with her for a while, trying them on for size. What would happen if she quit? If she decided to retire from baseball that very morning? There were clauses in her contract about being unable to play due to injury. An injury meant she wouldn't be able to play, and right now, her spirit felt injured. *There's no crying in baseball*, she thought. *And no mental health days, either.*

"I need to get up. I need to get up," Brenda said. In the first weeks after Ed moved out, she had often started her days saying those very words, reminding herself that the boys needed her. But the boys were a couple hundred miles away right now, and so were Adele and Robin and everyone else she loved.

She glanced at the clock on the night table. It was 10:45. The boys were at school. She could call and leave a message and say what? After all her talk to them against violence and fighting, she felt like a hypocrite for having jumped into a fist fight herself. Her phone was on the nightstand. She called Robin and got her voicemail. Of course, she was at work. Brenda didn't leave a message.

The need to talk to someone who knew her and cared about her was growing. She scrolled through recent incoming calls and saw Charlie Bannister's number. Since their date, they had exchanged a couple of brief emails and he had sent Brenda her first text message. There was perhaps the beginning of a friendship there. She spent two nervous rings wondering if he was there and whether she really ought to be calling him or whether she ought to just deal with this herself. He answered on the third ring.

"Good morning, Brenda," he said.

"Hi," she said. "I'm sorry to call you so early."

"It's not early, and hearing your voice just made my morning."

This almost made her smile, but she was too tired to smile and hold the phone to her ear at the same time. "Do you have a minute?" she asked.

"Of course. Is there anything wrong?"

"Not really." She sighed. "I don't know."

"Did you get hurt during the fight? Because if you did, I'll head over to Chicago right now and start taking names and bashing heads."

There was something familiar and comforting about the way Charlie said this, as though long ago she had asked him to take on the role of bodyguard and he had happily accepted. With someone else, it might have seemed overbearing, but Charlie made it sound matter-of-fact and sincere. Brenda momentarily pondered whether Charlie or Harry Tagiashi would come out the winner in a fair fight. Not that she wanted or needed anyone to protect her. It was just nice knowing that someone found the idea of protecting her appealing.

"That won't be necessary," she replied. Calling Charlie suddenly seemed like a silly idea. They had been on one date. What made her think that he would understand or care what crisis of confidence she was having? "Look, I'm sorry to have bothered you. I just called to say hi—nothing important."

Charlie was silent for a moment. She could faintly hear him breathing on the other end of the line. "Okay," he said finally, but it was clear he didn't think everything was okay. "Hey, did you know I'm doing the show from LA next week? I'll be there when you're there. Would you like to have dinner on Monday? That's a day off for you, right?"

"I think so. I'm impressed that you know my schedule better than I do. I just show up when they say the bus will be there." She almost regretted saying this—it felt too revealing. But there was something about Charlie Bannister that made her want to reveal herself to him, even though doing so seemed daunting and a little frightening.

"Yeah, being on the road is tough," Charlie said. "Did I tell you I spent two seasons doing the play-by-play for the Brewers AA club? That was radio, so the only good thing was that no one could see the bags under my eyes. It's tiring, I know."

Brenda lay back on her bed and stretched out. "You have no idea," she said. She pushed aside the thought that she was lying on a bed half-naked talking to Charlie Bannister. After all, it wasn't as though he was lying next to her. She only had his voice, a rounded, warm baritone, telling her that he understood tired and worn out and not wanting to do anything anymore. She closed her eyes and listened.

"I remember there was this two-week road trip my first season that was just murder. We had a Friday night game that was postponed after a three-hour delay, a Saturday night game with an hour and a half rain delay, during which I had to keep talking so we wouldn't have dead air, and then they made up the rainout on Sunday with a double-header. So I didn't sleep all weekend, and then as soon as the double-header was over, I had to drive six hours in time for the game in Duluth the next day."

Brenda opened her eyes. "Ugh," she said.

"The whole way there, I kept asking myself why I was doing this."

"And what answer did you come up with?"

"I find the scent of boiled hot dogs intoxicating, and the sound of horsehide hitting wood is its own music."

"Very poetic," Brenda said.

"It's the truth. I love the game."

"I'd like to think that it was that simple, but it's a lot more difficult for me." Charlie didn't say anything for a moment.

"What's the truth for you?" he asked softly, and there was something about the tone of his voice and the words he used that opened the floodgates.

"The truth is . . . half the guys on the team won't talk to me. Phil Cipriani and Fred Pasquela seem to think their mission in life is to humiliate me and make me miserable. I still get called "Pork" by bloggers and radio hosts and half the people in the stands even though I think I've lost about ten pounds in the last month. Some asshole followed my boys home from summer camp and said horrible things about me to them. My arm feels dead, and there's a grassroots movement of people who think I'm committing a mortal sin by playing baseball with men. The truth is, this stinks."

"Holy cow. Are your boys okay?" Charlie asked.

She was glad that was the first thing he asked and reassured him that Andy and Jon were all right. "A little shaken up at the time, but they're okay."

"Good. That's the most important thing. Now, what I want to know is, if that's really how things are for you, why are you still doing this?"

She wasn't even embarrassed to say: "I need the money. I have to take care of my family."

"That's a fair enough answer, at least to start. But doing things for the money will only get you so far. You know that. I remember your answer to a question I asked at the press conference. You said you used to play ball with your dad but you never said you *liked* baseball. Maybe this is an obvious question—*do* you like baseball?"

Brenda didn't have an answer. She had always enjoyed playing it as a kid with her father. Playing baseball with the boys in the spring was the last time she had felt genuinely connected to both Andy and Jon. The game had momentarily brought them together as a trio, as a family without a father. "I like how the game can bring people together," she said after a few moments.

"Good, good. That's a great start," Charlie said.

"I don't know if it's enough to make me get out of bed today," Brenda said. Saying even this much made her feel very exposed, as though she had just disrobed in front of a stranger.

"Well, for today, focus on the mercenary part if you have to. Pretend that you won't get paid if you don't get out of bed. Then I want you to think about what else you like about the game. You can tell me about it when we have dinner in LA."

"Funny thing, I don't remember actually saying I'd have dinner with you in LA," she said slyly, consciously flexing her flirting muscles for the first time in what seemed like years.

"Come on, what else are you going to do in LA? Hang out with Fred Pasquela?"

"You really know how to sweet talk a girl, Charlie."

"Please say that again."

"What? You really know how to sweet talk a girl, Charlie?"

"That was the first time I ever heard you say my name. I like it."

Something in the gentle way he said this made Brenda catch her breath. It was the same way she felt the first time she walked onto the infield at Progressive Field—like a door had been swung open wide just for her.

They talked for a few more minutes, and when Brenda hung up, she felt slightly more hopeful about the day. Then she got to the ballpark and found that someone had taped a photo of her face to the body of a *Hustler* centerfold and put it in up in the locker room. It was hung up near the front of the room, just behind where Mark would typically stand when he talked to the team before the game. It couldn't have been up very long, because a few minutes after she entered the room, Art Groggins noticed it. He was standing in front of his locker, one foot on the bench in front of him, doing up his cleats. When he glanced up, Brenda caught his eye and he gave her a polite nod hello. Then his gaze rested on the centerfold. He looked back at Brenda and rolled his eyes, then strode over to the centerfold and ripped it off the wall. "Phil, what the hell is this?" he snapped.

Cipriani was a few lockers away and looked up with an overly innocent face. "What's what?" he asked.

Groggins walked over to Cipriani, crumpling the centerfold up as he did so. He shoved the balled up paper into Cipriani's hands and said, "Have a little respect for your teammates." As he turned away, he muttered, "Asshole," under his breath.

Brenda felt like she ought to thank Groggins but he didn't look as though he wanted to be thanked. Groggins was an old-school player, the type who didn't thump his chest or point to the heavens when he hit a home run but merely circled the bases, doing the job he was being paid to do. His type of play didn't often come up in highlight reels; he rarely had to dive for a ball because he was always in the right place to catch it before it got there. Brenda got the feeling that doing what needed to be done just came naturally to him.

Later, during the game, she watched from the dugout as Groggins hit a hard grounder to second. It was clear that he was going to be thrown out at first, but he never slowed down, running hard all the way to the bag. Far more than the smell of boiled hot dogs, she found this all-out effort in the face of certain failure to be inspiring. There was a kind of nobility to giving one's all to an endeavor at which one had no chance of succeeding.

Brenda kept that thought in the back of her mind through the rest of the Detroit series. They had split the Chicago series, but took two of three against first-place Detroit. Around her, she saw her teammates pushing themselves and giving a bit extra. Even guys like Pasquela, who had a reputation for being a little lazy, were hustling on every play. There might be nobility to giving one's all to a losing effort, but it was more fun to make that same effort and win.

The team arrived in Los Angeles late Sunday night, and Brenda slept in the next morning, grateful for a day without a game. It was getting more and more difficult to work up her anger in order to pitch. Early on, there had been days when she couldn't wait to throw, as though the anger within her would overflow without that release. Now she had to dig deeper and deeper to find that same rage to fuel her fastball.

She made it through the team workout, throwing lightly and doing calisthenics with the rest of the pitchers. The evening was her own. She called home before the boys went to bed, grateful for the three-hour time difference so she didn't have to stay up too late herself.

Jon answered, full of stories about fourth grade and eager to know what the weather was like in California. "Is it sunny?" he asked. "It rained here today and we couldn't go outside at all, not even after lunch. So they let us go in the computer lab and these two kids got into a fight because one of them said that the other kid went on a bad website and the other kid said he didn't, and then they started arguing and *then* they started hitting each other. Mrs. Prementine had to break up the fight."

"Wow," Brenda said without much enthusiasm. "Did they get in trouble?"

"Yeah, they both got on Red and had to go talk to the principal. And you know what? The kid really *did* go to a grown-up website, but it was Cleveland.com, which isn't like a dirty site, it's just boring stuff. Isn't that funny?"

"Yep."

"Are you okay, Mom?" Jon asked in a quiet voice that immediately made Brenda feel guilty.

"I'm fine, sweetie. I just miss you and your brother."

"Does your arm hurt?"

"No, not really," Brenda replied.

"Are you having a good time?"

She had to lie. "Yes," she said.

"You don't *sound* like you're having fun. Dad always says that if it's not fun, why do it?"

Brenda's stomach dropped, but she did her best to sound more upbeat. "That sounds like something he'd say. But sometimes you have to do things even if they aren't fun."

"Nope, don't want to," Jon said, and she could hear him giggling then saying something she couldn't quite hear. "Andy wants to talk to you."

"He does?" she asked, and wished she hadn't sounded so surprised. She said good-bye to Jon and heard the shuffle of the phone being passed. Then she heard Andy say "Hi, Mom" in a voice that had to be a tone or two deeper than it had been the last time they spoke. When had his voice started to change?

"Hi, Andy. It's good to talk to you," she said. She deliberately didn't use a term of endearment—she knew it would only make him cringe.

"I need to talk to you," Andy said. As he spoke, she could hear his footsteps going down the short hallway and then heard the squeaky door of his bedroom close.

"Okay," she said, wondering why he needed privacy to talk to her. "What's up?" She was afraid he was going to bring up the fight in Chicago but instead he said: "Dad asked me if I want to come and live with him."

A hole the size of Yankee Stadium opened up in Brenda's stomach. She could feel herself teetering on the edge, head spinning. She caught her breath, willing herself to stay calm. "When did he ask you this?" she said.

"A while ago, before my birthday, but I didn't want to tell you. He said he'd talk to you about it."

Brenda inwardly kicked herself for the couple of phone calls from Ed that she had taken perverse pride in not returning. "I'm glad you told me. Do you want to live with him?" she asked, although she wasn't sure she wanted to know the answer.

"I don't know," Andy said, and for one moment she heard his voice sound like a little boy again. "I mean, it'd be cool to be around him more, and he really seems like he's trying to be a good dad and stuff. And now that you're playing baseball, you're not around that much and . . . I don't know."

"I'm sorry I haven't been there that much lately."

"That's okay. I know you needed to work. And you really want to play baseball, so it's cool that you're getting to do something you want to do."

"Andy, sweetie . . . the only reason I'm playing baseball is so that I can give you and Jon a better future."

"You mean because you're making a lot of money now?"

"Kind of. I've paid off the house, and we'll be able to get a lot things fixed, and you and your brother will be able to go to pretty much any college you want and . . . we have some security. But I hate that it keeps me away from the two of you." There was so much she wanted to say that she just couldn't say to Andy, not now. Kids were supposed to be carefree, not worried about the future and financial stability. It didn't seem fair to give him those kinds of worries. "Please know that I love you and Jon more than anything else in this world, and I just want you both to be happy." She took a deep breath to prepare for the extra effort her words required. "So if you think you'd be happier living mainly with your dad, I'll support you. I'll always back you up."

"Thanks, Mom. I don't know what I want to do yet."

"Take your time deciding. And if you decide to move in with your dad and you don't like it, you can come back." She tried to sound upbeat when she said this, although inwardly she was praying that Andy would hate living with Ed. She didn't take time to question whether that wish was right or wrong—it just was.

They talked for a few more minutes, then Andy said he had to go because he was meeting some friends online to play a game. Brenda was left feeling empty and alone. She left a message for Alex Clemowitz, even though she knew it was after business hours. He was reportedly waiting for the new custody proposal from Ed's lawyer and for a date for the custody hearing. Brenda hadn't talked to him in a week. Leaving the message made her feel proactive.

Charlie had told her he would call her as soon as he was back from taping his show. He was taping the show at 8:30 in order for it to air live on the East Coast. She was surprised when he called her at 9:45.

"Hi," Brenda said, and for a moment she felt like a fifteen-year-old.

"Hi yourself. Is it too late to have dinner with you? I made it from LA to Anaheim in record time."

"Should I be impressed or flattered?"

"How about both?"

Charlie had a habit of saying things that made her stomach turn little tiny cartwheels. Brenda took a deep breath, trying to remember reality. He lived two states away. She had two boys at home who still needed her. There was no way this could ever be a permanent thing.

"Where do you want to meet?" she asked, suddenly cognizant that she was going on an actual date—a second date.

For only the second time ever, Brenda heard Charlie Bannister stammer. "Well, could I ask you to come to the eighteenth floor?"

"Is the Eighteenth Floor the name of a restaurant?"

"No, the eighteenth floor of your hotel."

"Why?" she asked, although she had a feeling she already knew the answer.

"Because there's where I'm waiting for you."

Again, she felt a cartwheel in her stomach and had to remind herself that life was already complicated enough without getting involved with Charlie Bannister. But she still said, "All right."

As she walked down the eleventh floor hallway and got in the elevator, she realized that eighteen was the top floor. Her arms and legs started to shake. She was as nervous as she had been the first time she'd pitched in a game. "He's just a guy," she muttered. "He's just another guy."

Charlie had told her to go to suite 1805. When she arrived on the top floor, she saw that it had less than half the rooms of every other floor. It was becoming more and more evident that Charlie had gone all out to make this a romantic evening, which made her more nervous. The nerves were tinged with a bit of annoyance. This was only their second date. It seemed like he was ratcheting up the commitment level just a bit too fast.

With each step down the tastefully decorated hallway, with its floral print carpeting and faux wall sconces between each door, she let herself get a bit more annoyed. This *was* kind of presumptuous. By now it was much later than she usually ate dinner, and she was ravenous. "Okay, I'll just have dinner and leave. That's it," she murmured as she knocked on the door.

Charlie answered almost immediately. She had to admit he looked nice in jeans, a white oxford, and a brightly colored tie that was done in a casual, loose knot. She hated that he somehow knew this was her favorite look on a man.

"Hi," he said with a nervous smile. "I'm glad you're here. Come on in."

She murmured a hello and followed him in. Charlie hesitated for a moment when she walked in, as though he wanted to kiss her on the cheek but wasn't sure if that was permissible. Brenda was glad he didn't. At that moment, she wasn't sure what she wanted. She took a deep breath and gave the suite a quick look. Off the short entrance hallway she could see a small formal dining room to the left and a living room complete with baby grand piano to her right. In front of her, a wall of windows showed her a balcony with a glimpse of the evening sky and downtown Anaheim. In spite of herself, she said, "Wow."

"Yeah, it's pretty cool, isn't it?" Charlie said.

Brenda walked into the living room and realized the suite probably took up the square footage of her entire bungalow house. She asked the first question that came to her mind: "Why?"

Charlie looked embarrassed. "You have a curfew. I thought it would be easier if you had dinner in the hotel, and I know you're rightfully paranoid about being seen in public with me."

"With anyone," she said quickly. "I already have enough people talking about me."

"I know."

He looked so kind standing there by the piano that she almost felt bad. What was she supposed to do in the face of such generosity and attention? Immediately jump into bed with him because he dropped a bundle on a dinner date?

"Would you like something to drink?" Charlie asked. "A glass of wine? I have a pinot noir and a sauvignon blanc."

A glass of wine or three sounded great. "The pinot, please."

She watched Charlie busy himself behind the small wet bar located in a corner of the living room. She also smelled a spicy scent coming from the dining room. Was it a curry? Clearly, Charlie had gone to great lengths to make this a special evening. She took another deep breath and tried to quell her growing annoyance.

Charlie handed her a glass of wine. "Just so you don't start thinking I'm going too far, I want you to know that there is no chef in the kitchen waiting to make us dinner and room service isn't sitting by the phone waiting for our order. However, there is a big bag of Indian take-out in the kitchen. I remember you mentioning that you like

Indian food and decided to just bite the bullet and order in a bunch of things and hope there's something you like."

This seemed both thoughtful and presumptuous. She wanted to like what he had done—she did like what he had done. But wasn't taking the liberty of ordering dinner the equivalent of ordering for her in a restaurant? That was kind of archaic. And it *was* awfully forward to rent a suite just for a dinner date. She didn't want to be the kind of woman who was so pliable that a little extravagance made her swoon. It was easier to be annoyed. She had gotten good at being annoyed and peeved and angry. There had been a time when she had also been good at joy and laughter and trust, but that Brenda seemed very far away.

Charlie had happened to pick some of her favorite Indian dishes (samosas and saag paneer and aloo gobi), and they talked about food. She asked him about taping in LA and answered politely when he asked about her flight from Chicago. She knew this was supposed to be a wonderful date. They were supposed to eat and talk and drink too much wine and sit on the couch later and kiss and maybe go to bed if they both felt ready to take that next step. She supposed she could go through the motions and do all those things, but what purpose would that serve? She could let herself fall for Charlie, and then what? She didn't need a long-distance relationship.

"Is something wrong?" Charlie asked.

She looked up and realized she had been sitting and staring at the half-eaten samosa in her hand for a good ten seconds. "No," she said. "Yes." Trying to articulate everything she was feeling was like trying to explain how she pitched. It was so much easier just to do than to think. "You know that this will never go anywhere, right?"

"I'm not sure what you mean."

"This is all very nice but you live five hundred miles away from me. Why even bother starting something that won't go anywhere?"

"Four hundred fifty, actually," Charlie said. "New York City is only four hundred fifty miles from Cleveland."

"I don't think that makes much difference. I'm not sure what you think is going on here, but I'm not looking for a one-night stand or a relationship or anything in between, so what's the point of all this?"

Charlie opened his mouth as though he was going to say something but thought better of it. He stared at the table for a few seconds, clearly trying to figure out what to say. Then he looked up at Brenda with a small smile. "You know, that's one of the very few times you've been completely honest with me."

"Do you think I'm kidding?" Brenda asked.

"No. I appreciate that you've actually told me something genuine about what you're thinking, because with the exception of your phone call the day after the fight in Chicago, I feel like you have a brick wall around you that's ten feet high."

"If you'd been through what I've been through, you might build a few walls too."

"Have you gotten a lot of petty comments from people openly wondering if you have your job because you know what you're doing or because of Affirmative Action hiring practices? Oh wait, that was me." Charlie said this without a trace of sarcasm. It seemed like he had been wanting to tell her that he had an idea of what she was going through but hadn't known how or when to say it.

"What am I supposed to say to that? I'm sorry you've encountered racist jerks like I've encountered sexist jerks? I didn't notice any mass protests when you took your job."

"How do you know? I bet you didn't even watch my show then," Charlie said playfully.

Brenda just sighed her agitation. She wasn't sure she wanted to be there any longer, but she was feeling a rush of adrenaline and anger that was making her want to stay. It was like the fight. "You're not as funny as you think you are, Charlie."

"I know," Charlie said, and added with a slight tinge of embarrassment: "And you aren't the first person to say that."

This wasn't going well. How were you supposed to argue with someone who wouldn't argue back? It was a useless exercise. Instead of defusing it, this only made Brenda's anger and agitation grow. If Charlie was really so all-fired-up happy that she was sharing genuine feelings with him then he should give those feelings more respect. Instead he was just being so darn *nice*. "Listen, what do you want from me?" she asked.

"I don't want anything from you," Charlie said, and Brenda noticed a touch of exasperation in his voice. "I'd like to get to know you better, and I enjoy spending time with you when you aren't looking for a fight."

"Who says I'm looking for a fight?" That was as annoying as having someone accuse you of being upset when the only thing making you upset was his presumption at telling you how you feel.

"You just seem kind of angry," Charlie said. She ignored that he looked concerned when he said this. Her anger was hers to own and hers to name, not his.

"You don't know me well enough to know my moods," Brenda replied. She felt that maybe she had him now, that maybe he would stop with the nice business and give her a good old-fashioned argument. This rush of anger was much more intense than the regular fury of anger she worked herself into in order to pitch. Having another person across from her made it feel like the genuine article, not forced. She didn't want it to end.

She could tell Charlie was trying not to take the bait. "Look, if you'd rather not be here, that's fine. I'm a big boy; I can handle rejection." He paused for a moment, as though giving her time to decide. "But I really wish you'd stay."

Brenda stood up and walked over to the window, looking out on the balcony. A few stars and the moon were visible despite the city lights. The anger felt good, better than any happiness she could remember.

She heard Charlie stand up and walk over just behind and to her side. She could see their reflections in the glass as she looked outside—Charlie's friendly and open face and hers looking thin and haggard and mean. She watched Charlie's reflection give her a gentle kiss on the cheek. It felt safe and even a little protective, not that she needed protecting. Then Charlie's reflection moved down to the side of her neck, and as he kissed her again, she closed her eyes. She didn't want to see herself enjoy it.

His lips and his tongue played ever so softly on her neck—just enough to pique her interest and make her want more. Brenda tried to grab the anger back. There was no future here. She didn't need another complication in her life. But the anger was out the door. As a tingle went down her spine, she involuntarily arched her back in pleasure. "Oh shit . . ." she murmured.

Charlie stopped kissing her and took half a step away. "I'm sorry. I'll stop."

She looked at him and suddenly wanted very much to have him continue doing exactly what he had been doing. Why not a one-night stand? It would be something else to get pissed off about later. She grabbed his arm with her right hand and pulled him close, giving him their first full kiss on the lips. She was not mistaken; this felt very good. "No," she whispered, her lips moving to his ear. "Don't stop. But don't call me in the morning either."

Excerpt from the transcript for *Today in Sports* with Charlie Bannister, ESPN, September 14:

> Charlie: Good evening, sports fans. This is the first day of our stay out west and I just want to tell you all: I *love* LA.

Chapter Twenty-Three

•◊•

Brenda stayed in Charlie's room just long enough to give herself something to regret the next day. He asked her more than once if she would stay the night, and being the one to say "No" and leave was a new sort of rush. It felt like power.

The next morning, she went downstairs to have breakfast in the hotel dining room as though she wasn't tired and a bit hung-over and hadn't missed last evening's curfew. As the only female and quiet besides, no one suspected that she might stay out too late on a game night. And she hadn't exactly been "out"—she could honestly say she'd never left the hotel. She ate alone with the newspaper and was only disturbed twice by autograph seekers.

Sparks, Groggins, and Landers were sitting two tables over. When the second autograph seeker left, Landers walked over to her table and plopped his big lanky body into the empty seat across from her. Brenda had always figured Landers must have been the class clown when he was a kid, and that air of mischief around him hadn't left.

"Morning Brenda," he said and leaned across the table as though they were co-conspirators in a serious prank. He paused a moment, obviously savoring what he was about to say. His hazel eyes actually twinkled as he looked at her and asked in a *sotto* voice, "How's Charlie?"

Brenda was chewing on a piece of toast, and she quickly put her hand in front of her face as though she was trying to be polite when really she was trying to avoid choking. "Excuse me," she muttered, as she finished chewing and swallowing. This gave her a second to calm herself. "Charlie who?" she asked, hoping she sounded more nonchalant than she felt. Landers and the rest of the team didn't need any more ammunition against her, and she sure as hell didn't want any sports writers or bloggers writing about her private life.

"Mr. *Today in Sports* himself. Tell me, did you slide down Charlie's banister?" Landers asked.

Brenda ignored the bad joke. "No. I did an interview with him a while ago but that's all. I haven't seen him since."

Landers leaned back a bit and said in a normal tone of voice, "Did you catch *Today in Sports* last night after the game? They're shooting from LA this week."

Brenda leaned back in her chair as well and took a sip of her tea. Well, she thought, if this is how he wants to play it, I can be just as laid back as he is. "Really? I didn't know that."

"Yeah, I guess they do this once in a while to boost their ratings."

Brenda knew she didn't have the credentials to pull off the "female-not-interested-in-sports" nod of disinterest, so she just murmured a polite "Is that so?" and glanced back at her newspaper. Her nerves were in turmoil, but she tried to calm herself. Obviously, Charlie taping the show from LA for the week wasn't a secret. And so what if Landers had even seen Charlie Bannister walk into the hotel last night after the taping? The hotel wasn't particularly close to the studio, but it was close to the ballpark. There was nothing connecting her with him. Landers was just trying to mess with her, like he always did. He was just the class clown lobbing spitballs from the corner of the room, trying to start something.

She was pretending to read the Arts section of the paper when she heard Landers say: "Hey, did you know I played in the Arizona Fall League with Carl Maladente back before both of our rookie seasons?"

Landers had gone from spitballs to heavy artillery. Okay, so he knew. "No, I didn't," she replied carefully, slowly lowering her newspaper. "Are you guys still friends?"

Landers smiled. He was always the first to laugh when Cipriani or Pasquela pulled a prank on her. Yet she recalled that when Ryan Teeset had told her about his suit being cut to shreds, he hadn't mentioned Landers as being one of the culprits. Around the clubhouse,

Landers just seemed to enjoy getting people's goat, but Brenda didn't get a malicious vibe from him. "Yeah, we're still friends," Landers replied. "We actually went out and had a couple drinks when we were in Baltimore a few weeks ago." Here Landers lowered his voice again. "And he mentioned that he and his family were taking a walk around the Inner Harbor when he saw an unusual couple."

Sparks and Groggins were still seated at their table, talking about something—Brenda couldn't hear what. She was too intrigued by the fact that Landers wasn't announcing the information to the rest of the room. In fact, he seemed to be trying to keep what he knew confidential. This gave her a little more confidence. He could just be waiting for the right moment to embarrass her, or maybe he was just curious. "Really?" she said. "Unusual how?"

Landers raised an eyebrow, as though he was expecting her to say more or give him a bigger reaction, but he kept his voice low. "You play poker, Haversham?"

"Not since college," Brenda said.

"You oughta play with us sometime," Landers said with a smile. "I think you'd be good at it." He stood up. "Make sure you get some rest before the game. I heard you broke curfew last night." With that, he went back to his table, where Groggins and Sparks were already standing up and getting ready to leave. Brenda noticed that they all left hefty tips for the waitress.

Since there were a couple free hours before the bus left for the ballpark, she took a walk, getting back to her room just after noon. She hadn't bothered bringing her cell with her; sometimes the electronic leash needed to be left behind. When she checked her voicemail, there was a message from Alex Clemowitz's secretary, saying that the preliminary custody hearing was scheduled for October 10. The secretary's voice was friendly, seemingly unaware that she was delivering news to make Brenda's stomach turn to knots and her heart start racing. The date felt both too soon and too far away. She wanted more time with Andy, just in case the judge decided to award primary custody to Ed. At the same time, she just wanted to get it over with. The waiting and wondering was giving her a near-constant stomachache.

She put the phone down after checking her voicemail and it almost immediately started ringing. Without even bothering to look at who was calling, she answered.

"Good afternoon," Charlie said.

"I told you not to call me in the morning," Brenda said.

"It's 12:10. I'm calling you in the afternoon."

This was infuriating. "I specifically said not to call me and now you're calling me."

"I thought you were just . . . I mean, it sounded kind of sexy at the time. I didn't think you were serious."

Brenda knew that if she were serious about not wanting him to call her then the obvious thing would be for her to hang up. But she didn't want to. She liked Charlie, but admitting this was a can of worms she had neither the time nor the inclination to open. And living in a constant state of perpetual annoyance helped her pitching. "Well, I was," she said. "Don't call me. I'll call you."

She paused but held onto the phone. After a moment, Charlie said, "I was afraid you were going to hang up on me."

"I don't want to be a jerk." That came out sounding too nice.

"*You* don't want to be a jerk, you just want *me* to be a jerk," Charlie said, as though he was clarifying a point of information. "Sorry, but I'm not an asshole. I don't spend the night with a woman unless I'm crazy about her, and I always call the next day."

Brenda was getting more and more frustrated even though she knew her feelings weren't particularly logical. "But I told you not to."

"What is with you? It's like you really wish I was some inconsiderate jackass."

"Yes!" she blurted out. For a second, she wished she hadn't said it, but that "Yes" felt like she had just opened the valves on the Hoover Dam. "Yes. It'd be a lot easier for me if you were a jerk. Then I wouldn't have to worry about this, and I wouldn't have to invest any emotional energy in it, and it would help me stay mad, and if I'm not mad, I can't pitch." She said this entire sentence in one breath and sighed deeply when she was done. She plopped back on the bed and closed her eyes.

She heard a low whistle through the phone, then Charlie saying, "Really? Is that how you do it?"

"It's not a magic trick."

"I just . . . I didn't know. "

"And now you do." Brenda didn't open her eyes, didn't feel like opening them for a long, long time because she knew that when she did, she'd still have to stand up and put on the uniform and sit and watch yet another game and try somehow to make the anger flow. "So there's your story. Run with it."

"What are you talking about? That's not a story—a lot of players play better when they're mad. It's all part of being in the zone."

"I don't think you heard me right. It's not that it makes me pitch better. If I'm not mad, I can't pitch. At all." It was futile trying to explain a mass of emotions that were more tightly wound than the core of a baseball. It felt histrionic and unreasonable. "So look, I can't get involved with you, I can't . . ."

"You can't what? Let yourself be happy?"

"And obviously going out with you is going to make me happy," Brenda said. "Let's hear it for the male ego." If her livelihood didn't depend on being able to work herself into an appropriate rage, she would have found the conversation almost comical. Was pushing someone away because you wouldn't be able to do your job with them around as clichéd as pushing someone away because of fear of commitment? Look, my life revolves around my family and a baseball. Anything beyond that muddies the water. I've got to go. The bus is going to leave."

She heard Charlie sigh the sigh of a man who has resigned himself to seeing something through to the end. "All right," he said. "Have a good game. I'm here if you need me, but that's a limited time offer."

Brenda couldn't bring herself to say "Thank you," she merely said, "Okay. Good-bye," and hung up. She didn't have time to feel guilty about being rude; she had a game to play.

She had been studying video of opposing lineups on the Gismo throughout the road trip, but hadn't yet faced the Angels in person that season. She still threw the ball down the imaginary tunnel when she pitched. But having watched video after video of hitters, she was starting to see their swings in a new way. It was almost as if she could see the line that their bat made when they swung. Their job was to swing the bat through the tunnel and hit the ball. Brenda's job was constantly to move the tunnel so they couldn't.

Anderson Sparks and the other relievers came out to the bullpen around the third or fourth inning. Brenda and Jimenez had been there since the game started. The Indians started out strong, scoring two runs in the first inning and three more in the second. Now in the fourth inning, the Angels were beating up on Hodges, the starter. They had already scored two runs, and with only one out and a runner on second, it looked like they could have a big inning. Out on the mound, Hodges looked tired and worn out in the smoggy Anaheim twilight.

Brenda was so engrossed in watching the game that she didn't even hear the first time Anderson Sparks said, "Whatcha thinking about so hard, Haversham?"

"Sex," Brenda replied.

Half a dozen heads turned toward her. From the other end of the bullpen, she heard Sparks say, "Really?" She gave him the same look she gave Jon when he announced that he had made a homemade parachute and wanted to test it by jumping off the roof. While Sparks hadn't necessarily been a friend to her, he hadn't been adversarial either. There was no harm in talking to him. "I was thinking Hodges ought to throw low and outside to Bimbo."

Bimbo was Billy "Bimbo" Birmingham, the Angels' DH, who had just come up to bat. Although he didn't put up the huge numbers that he had a few seasons earlier, Bimbo was still good for twenty-five home runs a year. When the Angels were in town shortly before the All-Star game, Sparks had come into a game in relief and given up what turned out to be the game-winning home run to Bimbo in the eighth inning. She could tell it still irked him.

"If you had ever faced the guy, you'd know that he never chases low and outside pitches," Sparks said.

From the other end of the bench, she heard Cipriani mutter, "Idiot . . ."

"I know he didn't used to, but for some reason, he's started chasing them." Even as Brenda said this, she felt a little lurch in her stomach. What if Bimbo wasn't really doing what she thought he was doing? The last thing she needed was to be completely wrong in front of the entire bullpen. Bimbo had fouled off the first pitch and then taken two for balls. Hodges threw a breaking ball that hit low and outside. Bimbo swung and missed for strike two.

"I didn't notice it before, but it looks like he's started crowding the plate a little too," Sparks added.

"Hmm," Earl said. "Good observation, Haversham."

Hodges didn't throw low and outside to Bimbo again. Instead he threw a high fastball that Bimbo smacked into the right field stands for a two-run homer, cutting the Indians' lead to one run.

The bullpen phone rang—it was the only thing that could stop all conversation and action in the bullpen. Cipriani went in to relieve Hodges and managed to get out of the fourth without allowing any more runs. Anderson Sparks was tapped to start the seventh inning. As he was leaving the bullpen, he stopped in front of Brenda. "Thanks," he said.

"Anytime. We're on the same team, you know?" Brenda said. She figured it couldn't hurt to reiterate that point.

"Sparks, get a move on."

"Right, Earl." He looked over his shoulder as he jogged out of the bullpen and said, "You got brains, Haversham."

•◇•

Excerpt from the transcript for *Today in Sports* with Charlie Bannister, ESPN, September 17:

> Charlie: I hesitate to say I have such powers, but apparently I've jinxed the Angels. Since I've been in town, they've dropped two games to the visiting Indians, and both in grand fashion. The last time these two teams faced each other, it was all Angels,

all the time, but now it looks like the Tribe has figured a few things out. Check out this at bat—reliever Anderson Sparks making Bimbo Birmingham look like a ceiling fan. Swing and miss—one, two, three times. Strikes him out to save a narrow Tribe lead, Cleveland wins 5-4.

Chapter Twenty-Four

•◇•

HELPING OUT SPARKS DIDN'T CHANGE THINGS MUCH AS THE ROAD TRIP CONTINUED. Before the first game in Oakland, she found a copy of the Bam! sports bra ad in her locker room with the double-D breasts of some centerfold model taped over her chest. After a month, this type of thing hardly fazed her. Brenda found that her burning hatred of Cipriani and Pasquela had simmered down to a dull, lukewarm sort of campfire—tended only because no one has the heart to put it out.

They had a Saturday afternoon game, which meant a Saturday night in Oakland to herself. At first, Brenda figured she'd be spending it like most evenings on the road—alone. But on the bus back to the hotel after the game, McGall and Landers asked if she wanted to go out to dinner with them and be their wingman.

"Wingman?" Brenda said. "You're professional baseball players on a playoff contender and you still can't get laid?"

McGall plopped himself down on the seat next to Brenda and Landers scooted into the seat in front of them. "Haversham! How can you be so crude?" McGall said. "This is a genuine matter of the heart. And it isn't for us—it's for young Master Teeset, who is smitten with a lovely waitress at the P.F. Chang's down the street from the hotel, but she won't give him the time of day."

"Maybe she doesn't like him," Brenda said.

"Au contraire, she likes him," McGall replied.

"Yes, she does," Landers added with a knowing nod of the head. "We've seen them interact, and there's definitely an attraction. She was flirting with him."

"She's a waitress. Flirting with you is how she gets tips. Haven't you ever worked in a restaurant?" Her question was met with two blank faces.

"That's immaterial," McGall said, with an almost palpable rise in his crazy level. "The point is, we know she likes Teeset. She even said he was cute, but she refuses to give him her number or an email address because—get this—she knows 'what ballplayers are like.' Can you believe that?"

"Yes, I can," Brenda replied. "Most ballplayers are known to be big sluts."

"Hey, hey, hey, hey—we're not talking about us," Landers said. "We're talking about Ryan Teeset, who is absolutely not a slut."

"I'm not even sure the boy has lost his virginity yet," McGall said.

"Unless you count that sheep back home at the ranch."

"That was me, and her name was Ginger, okay?"

"You know, Haversham, your face ain't gonna crack if you smile," Landers said.

"I'm waiting for you two to say something funny." She sighed, "Why are you even asking me to do this?"

McGall popped his eyes wide open—wide enough to make Brenda think this was a party trick he hadn't shown her yet. "Isn't it obvious? You're a woman. She's a woman. If you tell her Teeset is a good guy, she'll believe you. She even said she's a fan of yours," he added off-handedly.

"Now I know you guys are just messing with me. I don't have fans," Brenda said.

McGall laughed his donkey laugh, and Landers snickered the way he always did when he got somebody's goat in the clubhouse. "You don't get out much, do you Haversham?" Landers asked. "Do you ever look at the signs people hold up in the stands? Do you read the news? Look at the Internet?"

Brenda was tempted to tell them that she had stopped watching the news or reading the paper or visiting sports sites online because continually reading that one was a fat, no-talent whore got a little old after a while. She bit her tongue, though. Saying so would just let them know that sort of thing bothered her. "I'm too busy to watch the news," she said.

"Well, you've got more fans than you think," Landers said. "And I know for a fact that your jersey has outsold mine. Bitch," he added with a smile.

"She only had to sell two to do that, Greg," McGall said.

"Okay," Brenda said. "Against my better judgment, sure, I'll go out and be the wingman. But only because Teeset is such a nice kid."

"Of course he is," Landers said. "That's why we're doing this."

When they got back to the hotel, Brenda retreated to her room to call home. There was a missed call from Ed and texts from Charlie and Robin, all of which went unanswered. She hadn't pitched that day but still felt drained. Her arm was twitchy and sore, and she considered bailing on the guys. A phone call from McGall ("Where are you, Haversham? We're waiting in the lobby.") made her realize they wouldn't rest until she was sitting down to dinner with them at the table of the lovely P.F. Chang's waitress.

Ryan Teeset was blushing bright red by the time Brenda made her way down to the lobby. She could only imagine what advice McGall and Landers had been giving him.

"Thanks for coming with us, Brenda," he said quietly.

"Anytime, Ryan," she said. In his khaki pants and light blue dress shirt and emitting a faint scent of aftershave, it was obvious that he had taken pains to get dressed up while trying not to look dressed up. Landers had on the standard Dockers and golf shirt, while McGall looked like an art student, with beat up jeans and a dark red T-shirt that was tight enough to show off his lean, wiry physique.

"You ready to party, Haversham?" McGall asked.

"Absolutely not," she replied.

"Excellent," he said cheerfully.

The restaurant was only a few blocks from the hotel, so they walked. Brenda had gotten used to the sidelong glances the rest of the team received whenever they walked through a hotel lobby or airport. Some of the players, like Jimenez, were bona fide stars recognizable even to the casual fan. Others, like Groggins, who had been around forever, and McGall, who had two Gold Gloves under his belt, were sometimes recognized by baseball fans in other cities. Even in a small group, she noticed that the guys moved as a pack, apart from those around them. They all moved like men who knew every inch of their own bodies and exactly what they were capable of. Teeset and Landers were big enough to be pegged as professional athletes, crazy McGall was just about six feet. But it wasn't their size that made them stand out, each of them had a confidence to their stride that begged you to watch them. Brenda had always had confidence in certain parts of her life—her art, her intellect, but not her body. She envied how smoothly Teeset and Landers could swing and connect and send the ball sailing or how effortlessly McGall could dive, roll, come up with the ball, and throw it to first. And she marveled at their ability to do this over and over and over without any apparent need to psyche themselves up or work themselves into an angry fury in order to do so.

"You nervous, Teeset?" Landers asked as they stopped on a corner for a traffic light. "You're walking like a man going to a funeral, not one about to pick up the woman of his dreams."

"Yeah, pick up the pace," McGall said. "I'm hungry."

"I'm trying not to be in a rush," Teeset said.

"That's good. Women don't like if you come and go in a rush." McGall hee-hawed a laugh at his own joke.

"Come on, Dave. There's a lady present," Landers said in a mock scold.

"Haversham doesn't care. She's one of the guys. You even walk like a badass . . ." McGall said as the light changed and they began to cross the street.

Brenda stopped herself from telling McGall to buzz off. When the boys were little, she had often found the most effective way of dealing with their volatile, preschooler tantrums was to take herself out of the equation. Now that they were older, she still found this tactic useful. "If you say so, McGall," she said without breaking her stride, badass or otherwise.

They could see the towering faux Oriental pillars in front of the P.F. Chang's from down the block. Teeset was noticeably nervous. She moved into step beside him. "What's her name?" she asked.

"Lily," he said. He smiled a little when he said her name.

"When did you meet her?"

"The first time we played Oakland back in April. A bunch of us went out and she waited on us and she was so nice and pretty and funny, oh man . . ." His voice trailed off, and Brenda was reminded that Ryan wasn't that long out of high school. "I went back the next night and talked to her for a while, but she wouldn't give me her number or anything. But I think she was surprised when we went back last night."

"She probably figured she'd never see you again."

"I know. I mean, I know some of these guys have a girl in every city, but I'm not like that." Ryan turned to look at her as they walked. "I'm not like that at all."

"I know."

They were in front of the restaurant now. McGall was a step behind them with Landers bringing up the rear, talking to two young women who looked to be in their late twenties. Both were dressed for a night of clubbing in short skirts, heels, and low-cut tops.

"Greg! Are you adding to our party?" McGall asked.

"I'm trying to. Would you lovely ladies care to join us for dinner and maybe drinks later?"

The ringleader of the two, who was not as pretty as her friend but had the hard, hot mess look of a girl who knew how to party, considered the request for a moment. "Eh, I think we'll pass. Maybe if you guys played for a *good* team . . ." She and her friend snickered. They made Brenda ashamed to be female. No wonder so many men treated women like objects when so many women were willing to be treated like objects if the player was famous enough.

"I'll have you know that you're talking to the third baseman with the highest fielding percentage in the American League, a guy with two Gold Gloves, and a contender for the AL Rookie of the Year," she said and was surprised that her voice sounded as calm and measured as it did, because she could feel her nerves rattling around her stomach. "And they all play for a team that's a playoff contender."

"And what are you? Their only groupie?" The two girls snickered again.

"No, I'm the stopper. It's my job to stop people from making an ass of themselves. So why don't the two of you go off and have your standard meaningless one-night stand with some guy who won't respect you enough to remember your name the next day because you clearly don't respect yourselves?" She paused a moment, her heart pounding as though she had just run wind sprints across the outfield. "Good night," she said and went into the restaurant. She didn't need to know what happened next.

Ryan was right behind her, and McGall and Landers were on their heels. They were laughing like giddy schoolboys.

"Didn't I tell you Haversham was a badass?" McGall stammered in between loud braying guffaws.

"Yeah, but you're supposed to help us pick up women, not insult them," Landers giggled.

Ryan didn't say anything to her, just said hello to the hostess, who asked "Four in Lily's section?" in a melodic voice. The restaurant had a series of three dining areas, which didn't do much to reduce the noise. Looking around, Brenda couldn't see anything soft on the walls or the floor—it was all hard surfaces reflecting back the sound of dozens of people talking and eating. Not her kind of place, but it was where Ryan Teeset's dream girl was working, so there she was.

Lily was a pretty girl. Probably no older than Teeset, with a small, compact frame and long black hair pulled back. Brenda thought she might be half Caucasian and half Chinese. For a kid like Teeset, who grew up in an all-white, rural area, she was clearly an exotic creature. Brenda spotted her across the dining room—Lily's eyes visibly lit up when she saw Ryan. McGall and Landers might respectively be a whack job and an asshole, but they could read women. This girl definitely liked Ryan.

She took their order as professionally as possible. Landers and McGall kept up a steady stream of jokes, but to their credit didn't say anything overtly offensive. Ryan placed his order and then silently fiddled with his napkin after Lily took their menus and left.

"This was a stupid idea," he said, looking down at his huge hands, which were crushing the napkin into a tight little wad.

Brenda looked across the table at McGall and Landers. "Both of you be quiet." Amazingly, they listened. "No, it's not," she said to Ryan. "She likes you."

"I gave her my email address and cell phone number when I was here in April and again last night, but she hasn't used them."

"Of course she hasn't—she thinks you're one of those guys," Brenda said, with a tilt of her head toward their companions.

"Thanks a lot," Landers said.

"Face it, Landers. You're a man-whore," McGall said.

"You would be, but you're too ugly," Landers said with a smile.

"Edgy. I'm edgy."

The McGall-Landers Show went on for most of dinner. Near the end of the meal, Brenda excused herself to the restroom, which was at the far end of the next dining room. Lily was at the servers' station near the restrooms. Acting the matchmaker made Brenda feel old, but she persevered. She hoped someone might someday repay the favor if Jon or Andy were ever in love with a girl who wasn't sure about them.

"Excuse me," she said.

Lily started saying, "Can I help you?" even before she turned and saw Brenda standing there. "Oh, hello. Is everything okay?"

"Yes, everything's fine. But if you have a moment, I just wanted to talk to you about Ryan Teeset—the nice-looking, tall young man at my table."

"I know who he is," Lily said, and she lowered her eyes just for an instant when she said this, which made Brenda think that Ryan really might have a chance.

"I play baseball for the Indians too . . ." Brenda started to say.

"I know," Lily said. "Practically every woman in America knows who you are," she added with a smile.

"Not all of them," Brenda replied. "But this isn't about me. This is about Ryan. Look, I travel with these guys and work with them, and yes, a lot of them are big cheating half-wits who chase women. But some of them aren't. Ryan isn't. He's a kind, decent guy. And he really likes you."

"He lives in South Dakota. I live in California. I don't see much of a future." Brenda wasn't sure why she hadn't expected such a beautiful young woman to seem so pragmatic. It was refreshing.

"He's *from* South Dakota," Brenda said. "I don't think he's chosen where he wants to live permanently. And even so, all he's asking you to do is to give him a call or text or email him once in a while. Just start a conversation. You don't have to marry the guy. He only wants to get to know you. That's all. Just give him a chance."

Lily considered this. Brenda tried not to consider how her words might apply to her own life. "Maybe," Lily said.

"Thank you," Brenda said.

When she returned to the table, the guys peppered her with questions, which Brenda deftly ignored. She simply said to Ryan, "I did my best. It's up to her."

"Thanks, Brenda," Ryan said in his endearing drawl. He seemed to trust Brenda's word and didn't pester her with questions. McGall and Landers, however, kept up their standard banter. It got so bad that Brenda had to threaten to put Vicks VapoRub in their jocks if they said anything offensive when Lily brought the check.

Brenda noticed that Lily seemed to avoid their table during the meal, sending the bus boy over to check on things or refill drinks. But she did bring the check, gently placing it in the center of the table and saying, "I can ring this up whenever you're ready" before quickly retreating. Landers grabbed the check, certain that she had written her phone number on it. She hadn't.

"But since you picked it up first, Landers," McGall said, "that means you're buying."

"The hell I am," Landers replied. "Teeset's buying. He's the one who wanted to come here."

"We're dividing it four ways," Brenda glanced at the check. "I need sixty dollars from each of you."

"Sixty bucks?" Landers complained. "Are you giving her a one hundred percent tip?"

"No, twenty percent. And you're getting off easy. Do you have any idea how much you and McGall drank?"

"Not enough to get me drunk," McGall said. "Let's get another round."

"Drink on your own time," Brenda said. "I want to get home."

"Oh yeah, you're a fan of *Today in Sports*, aren't you, Haversham? Don't want to miss old Charlie Bannister at eleven." Landers played it perfectly, without tipping a hint to McGall or Teeset that he had anything on Brenda.

"Yeah," Brenda said in a nonchalant tone. "I watch it right after I watch my soap operas." She didn't dare look Landers in the eye but just threw it out there as an aside while she got her money out of her purse. The per diem money they received never failed to astound her. Having several hundred in cash at one time always made her feel like a drug dealer.

McGall laughed. "I think Haversham goes back to her room and reads, like, nineteenth-century novels and does embroidery. Either that or you've got something going on the side with Panidopolous."

"No, my doomed affair with you ruined me for any other man, McGall." Brenda was ready to go. She felt that she had done all she could to help Teeset's case with Lily, beyond that, having Landers and McGall acting buddy-buddy made her uncomfortable. She didn't trust them enough to believe it was genuine, and even if it were, she wasn't playing baseball to make friends.

There was no touching scene when Lily came to get the check. She didn't look deep into Teeset's eyes and say she'd call him, and he didn't stand up and profess his love in front of the entire restaurant. The one small part of Brenda that still felt some degree of optimism would have been delighted to see something like that happen. The rest of her knew better.

Ryan said he'd "just be a minute," so Brenda waited with McGall and Landers outside the restaurant. The two of them were screwing around on the sidewalk, telling jokes and planning their next move. Brenda remembered being in her twenties, when going out to dinner was the beginning the evening's activities instead of the entire evening's activity. She and Ed had been happy then. At least, she thought they'd been. The way things turned out seemed to call into question periods that she thought had been good in their shared life.

She had been overjoyed when each of the boys was born, but there were times when caring for them felt like a chore. She hadn't seen that in Ed, not when the boys were little. Maybe because he wasn't with them all day, every day, like she was. And yet that time seemed happier than most of the past year, when there had been too many days where she wasn't sure if she wanted to sit in a corner and cry or hit something.

Ryan came out of the restaurant and sheepishly looked at her and then at Landers and McGall. "Sorry I took so long," he said.

"Did you nail her in the bathroom?" McGall asked in that way he had of making everything sound like it was half joke, half sincere.

"Bathroom? No wonder you can't get a date, Neanderthal," Landers said. "You bang waitresses in the manager's office; sometimes there's even a couch in there."

"Goodnight, boys," Brenda said.

"Where are you going, Haversham?" Landers asked. "The night is young."

"But I'm not."

Landers and McGall gave her a chorus of mock disapproval. As she was leaving, Ryan murmured a "thank you" to her. Once she had extricated herself from the guys and gotten back to the hotel, the only thing that seemed appealing was going to bed. Sleep was one of the few things on which she could rely.

•◊•

Excerpt from the transcript for *Today in Sports* with Charlie Bannister, ESPN, September 18:

> Charlie: Welcome back to *Today in Sports*. I'm Charlie Bannister. With me, as he is every Friday, is former major leaguer Howie Wojinski for our weekly look at the world of baseball. Howie, good to see you again. What can you tell me about the American League playoff race?
>
> Howie: Nothing you don't already know, Charlie. Over the last few weeks, the Yankees have chipped away at the Red Sox lead and now have the AL East all sewn up . . .
>
> Charlie: Big surprise there. That never happens.
>
> Howie: In the AL West, it's still the Mariners' division to lose.
>
> Charlie: Which means all the excitement is coming from that bastion of small-market mediocrity . . .
>
> Howie: The AL Central?
>
> Charlie: One and the same, my friend.

Howie: Charlie, listen closely because I'm only going to say this once and I will probably never say it to you again, but Charlie, you were right.

Charlie: Call NASA. The world has stopped revolving on its axis.

Howie: About a month ago, you said you thought the Indians could take the second wildcard spot from the White Sox and I didn't believe you.

Charlie: You accused me of being a heavy drinker.

Howie: The way they played in the first half made their chances of seeing anything in October but trick-or-treaters look pretty slim, but their second half has been nothing short of remarkable.

Charlie: Amazing what can happen when you find a good stopper.

Howie: Again with Haversham.

Charlie: She's good.

Howie: Okay . . .

Charlie: She's really good.

Howie: Okay. Okay. You're right. She's proven herself. She's good.

Charlie: Thanks, Howie. It takes a big man to admit he was wrong.

Chapter Twenty-Five

•◊•

WHEN BRENDA FINALLY WALKED INTO HER HOUSE AFTER THE WEST COAST ROAD TRIP, IT WAS 3:30 IN THE MORNING. She grabbed an extra blanket from the linen closet and laid down on the couch to grab a couple hours of sleep. She awoke to find the boys already showered and dressed and sitting in the kitchen with Adele eating cereal. "Good morning," Brenda said as she half-staggered into the kitchen, almost embarrassed to be interrupting their breakfast.

Jon jumped out of his chair as soon as he saw her. "Mom! You're home! You're home!" he shouted. It made Brenda feel like a present under the Christmas tree. "I missed you," he said, snuggling into her side.

Brenda sighed and held him close for a moment, knowing that one day, probably soon, he would wake up and declare himself too old to be cuddled. "I missed you too, sweetie."

"Hey Mom," Andy smiled. "Welcome home. Again." Brenda walked over to Andy and gave him a one-armed hug, and to her relief, he didn't pull away. The thought of him living with Ed, of calling Ed's place "home" made her hold on even tighter. "Come on," Andy extricated himself from her arms. "You weren't gone *that* long." She was pleased to see that he had a playful little gleam in his eye as he said it.

"*Dobre rano, moja drahá,*" Adele said, getting up. "What can I get you?"

"Nothing, thanks," Brenda replied.

"No one wants me to make them breakfast anymore," Adele said in mock dismay.

"I *am* eating breakfast," Jon unfolded himself from Brenda and went back to the table. "I just like cereal. It has vitamins and stuff in it too so it's good for you."

"I'm not really hungry this early," Andy said.

"What about lunch? Can I make some sandwiches for you two?" Brenda asked.

"They have a burrito bar on Mondays . . ." Jon pleaded.

Adele spoke before Brenda had the chance, reminding Jon that if he wanted to buy his lunch today that was it for the week—he'd have to bring his lunch the other days. Jon didn't say anything else, but his look asked why he couldn't buy his lunch every day.

During breakfast, the boys caught her up on the first few weeks of school, reminding Brenda that Ms. Porter was Andy's Algebra teacher, not his Civics teacher and that Jon's gym teacher had once played a full season in the NFL and wasn't that cool? It was the type of information about their lives that she used to know. Ed had always been the clueless one who needed to ask things like whether the boys were still friends with the Amatti kids even though Vince Amatti had stolen Andy's hat and soaked it in ketchup or if Jon still liked That Little Indian Girl when the girl in question, Ani Patel, had moved away back in second grade. Ed was the one who didn't know the details of the boys' lives. Not her.

Adele stayed until the boys left for school, waiting at the end of the block for the school bus along with Brenda. As the bus pulled away, her mother turned to her and asked, "How are you going to enjoy your day off?"

"Sleep, maybe." This was the only off day until the end of the season, and Brenda wasn't sure if she had too many things to do or not enough. They started walking back to the house.

"I spoke to Robin the other day, and she mentioned she hadn't talked to you since Andy's birthday party," Adele said. Brenda nodded, trying to avoid the passive-aggressive trap her mother was laying out for her. No, she hadn't talked to Robin for a few weeks. Why would she want to talk to someone who was taking Ed's side?

They had reached the back door. "This is where I leave you, but I'll be back tomorrow night to stay with the boys while you're at the game," Adele said. She looked up at the clear September sky. "What a gorgeous day. Why don't you take your sketchbook to Euclid Creek Park like you used to?"

It isn't polite to tell one's mother that she's crazy, but Brenda was tempted. "I don't think so . . . I haven't really done any drawing for a while."

"All the more reason to start again," her mother said, giving her a quick kiss on the cheek. "It always seemed to make you happy."

Adele left, leaving Brenda alone. There was laundry and other chores to do around the house. There were also her mother's lingering words and unanswered messages from her best friend. "I hate it when Mom's right," Brenda said as she called Robin.

"Hey, stranger. Welcome home," Robin answered. She didn't sound quite as cheery as usual.

"Hi. Sorry it's taken me soo long to get back to you. I've had a lot on my mind."

"I know."

"I need to apologize for getting so angry with you about the whole thing with Ed and the custody agreement. I suppose I was angry because you're right."

"Aren't I always?" Robin giggled.

"Just most of the time."

"Brenda, I know you and Ed can figure out a reasonable custody agreement." Robin's voice had a little lilt to it as she added, "And if you can't, I'll help you kick his ass."

"That's an offer I can't refuse. Thanks. I've been kind of a jerk lately, haven't I?"

"You haven't been a jerk. You've . . ." Robin paused, and Brenda could almost hear her thinking. "You've had a lot of static around you the past few months."

Static. Somehow that summed it up. Brenda had been sitting on the ugly but comfortable easy chair in her room but now she felt the need to move. She stood up and went downstairs as they talked. "Static is a good way of putting it. But short of quitting baseball and doing . . . something else, I don't know how to get rid of it. You know, all I really want is one static-free day. Just one easy, good day where I don't have to struggle."

"I hope you get one," Robin said. She was silent for a moment, as if waiting for Brenda to say more.

"Thanks," was all Brenda felt up to saying. There was so much to say, but it somehow seemed a waste of time to say it. What would it help to tell Robin how the anger was the only thing keeping her career going and how miserable it was just walking into the ballpark because she wasn't sure what kind of humiliation the world had in store for her? Maybe someday those would be amusing stories, but not now. Nothing seemed funny now.

"Maybe you'll feel better after you talk to Ed," Robin said.

"That means I actually have to talk to him."

"Look, I know it's not going to be easy, but it's got to be better than going to court. You need to do this."

"Being an adult kind of stinks, doesn't it?"

"Yes, it does. Okay, I hate to say it but I have a client meeting that I desperately need to prepare for." They made quick plans to see each other later in the week and hung up.

Brenda was standing in the middle of the kitchen, not even sure why she had walked in there in the first place. She just felt restless. There were no more road trips—the Indians would finish the last six games of the season at home. If they won at least four of the games against the visiting Royals and the White Sox, they'd secure the second wildcard spot in the playoffs. When Brenda thought about being away from the boys for an extra month, she immediately said "No." But when she thought the word "playoffs," her inward answer was "Yes." The idea of the playoffs made her nerves dance almost as much as calling Ed did, but she called him.

"Hey, thanks for calling me back," he answered in his usual laid back manner, as though he wasn't threatening to shake up her life again. Brenda tried to detect any note of sarcasm in his voice and didn't.

"Sorry it took me a while," she replied.

"That's okay. I know you've been out of town and busy. I've been wondering if we could have lunch and talk about the boys and the custody agreement."

"You can talk to my lawyer," she didn't want to sound snappish but there it was.

"All right, I probably shouldn't have gone to my lawyer without talking to you first . . ."

"*Probably* shouldn't have?"

"Okay, I shouldn't have. And if you would have called me back anytime during the last few weeks . . ." His voice trailed off in frustration, and she could almost hear his mental reboot. "But that doesn't mean we can't figure out a new custody arrangement on our own. We can at least try."

Something in his voice sounded different when he said this. There was a sincerity she hadn't heard from him in years. And yes, she should have called him back. She considered the possibility that he was just scared of Alex Clemowitz—with Clemowitz's hourly rate, he ought to be. Brenda was doubtful they could hash things out on their own, but it had to be less painful than going to court.

"All right. Where do you want to meet?" she asked.

They made plans to have lunch on Friday, and Brenda spent the rest of her day off trying to feel normal and failing miserably. When the boys got home from school, Jon immediately asked if he could play with her new phone. Brenda told him that he could as soon as he finished his homework.

"I've been doing school stuff all day!" Jon whined. He was standing in the doorway of his room, backpack on the floor at his feet. "I just want to play for a while and *then* do my homework." Andy was sitting on the edge of his bed, bedroom door open, watching his mother and little brother square off.

"Get the things you *have* to do out of the way first, then you can play," Brenda said, trying to sound reasonable and warm. Jon tried to negotiate a few minutes on the phone before homework, and for a minute she thought that maybe she had been too stringent, but now that she had said "No," changing her mind seemed wishy-washy. Andy rolled his eyes and closed the door to his room. One tantrum and a few tears later, Jon made a dramatic entrance into the kitchen with his homework folder and workbooks, plopping everything onto the kitchen table without speaking to his mother.

Brenda went downstairs to throw some laundry into the dryer. She wondered if Jon acted this way at Ed's house. Was this why Andy thought he might want to live there? Maybe the boys were angels at Ed's house. Maybe it was her.

She felt guilty the rest of the afternoon and all through dinner, as though she ought to give her kids a treat because she had hardly seen them over the last two months. After dinner, Jon asked if they could play baseball.

"Now?" Brenda asked. The idea of picking up a baseball on her one day off seemed about as pleasant as picking up a tarantula.

"Yeah," he said.

"It's kind of late to go to the park. And it's a school night," Brenda said, glancing over at Andy for help.

"It might be fun," Andy said. "And it's still light out."

"I really don't want to play baseball. Why don't we shoot some baskets in the driveway? Or play Uno or Monopoly?"

"But you play baseball all the time," Jon said.

"And that's exactly why I don't want to play it today. That's my job, sweetie. Today is my day off from my job."

"But it's the best game ever," Jon exclaimed as though this explained everything.

"Guys, I'm really tired and jet-lagged. Please, no baseball tonight."

"You have the best job in the world, and it's like you don't even know it," Jon stomped out of the kitchen.

Brenda looked at Andy. "I'm sorry you're so tired. I know you got in late last night," he said, and she could tell he was doing his best grown-up imitation. "I'll do the dishes."

"Thank you, sweetie," Brenda replied, giving him a light pat on the arm. She went down the hall to Jon's room and knocked.

His voice came through the door: "Unless you're telling me we're going to play baseball, don't talk to me."

Brenda opened the door to his room. Jon was lying on his back on his bed, feet deliberately on the wall because Brenda always told him not to do that, and tossing a baseball back and forth between his hands. She sat down on the edge of the bed. "Jon, I'm sorry to have disappointed you. You have to understand that sometimes people want to do different things. Like the day Andy didn't want to go with your dad and you did. I'll play anything you and Andy want. Except baseball. Besides, it's too late to go to the park tonight."

Jon was quiet for a moment, silently contemplating the scuffed baseball in his hands. "How come you always act mad when you're home?"

"What?" she replied, although even as she said it, she knew what he meant. Some days the anger was simmering so close to the surface it was almost too easy to conjure.

"It's like you're always in a bad mood."

Saying this wasn't true would be a lie, and they both knew it. Instead, Brenda kissed Jon on the forehead, told him she'd try to be less grouchy, and left the room. What do you say when the nine-year-old is right?

The next day was a game day. The boys went to school, and Brenda knew she wouldn't see them awake until the next morning. That evening, she sat in the bullpen dugout and tried to like the game, to find some joy in the way old Art Groggins still hustled out a fly ball or how crazy Dave McGall could make stealing second look effortless. She closed her eyes and tried to focus on the sounds and smells of the ballpark. While she didn't find the scent of the hot dogs as intoxicating as Charlie did, she had to admit there was no other smell like it. The sounds were enticing—people calling for beer and food and the great vendor who patrolled the far end of the stadium shouting, "Peanuts!" in a voice that roared like a giant's. And when Josh Bandkins connected for a double to left center, the sound of wood colliding with horsehide carried all the way out to the bullpen. Charlie was right on that one.

Brenda had tried not to think too much about him, but as a relief pitcher, she had a lot of time on her hands to sit and wait and think. Charlie wasn't the handsomest guy she had ever seen. Looking around the bullpen or the dugout, Anderson Sparks was far better looking. So were Panidopolous and Groggins. And if she was going to start comparing physiques, young Ryan Teeset was built like an Adonis. So was Doug Stone for that matter. Charlie was a bit pudgy, like one of those chubby pitchers whom you'd never believe was a professional athlete if you saw him out of uniform. And yet she couldn't stop thinking about him.

Kansas City was in town for what Brenda referred to as the calm before the storm series. The Indians were walking all over the Royals, leading 8-4 going into the eighth. Cipriani had gone in to relieve Ochoa in the top of the seventh, and now, with one down in the eighth, the Royals had somehow managed to get the bases loaded. Cipriani had a habit of getting flustered when he made a mistake, and Kansas City capitalized on that. Earl told her to start warming up. She went to take some warm-up pitches and thought about the custody case and the possibility of Andy living with Ed. Some of the Frickers were near the bullpen, holding a sign that read "Go back to the kitchen." Brenda felt the rage start boiling up inside her.

"As usual, send a woman to clean up the mess," Brenda muttered to herself as she started the long walk across left-centerfield to the mound. As usual, the PA system was playing "She's a Lady." It occurred to Brenda for the umpteenth time that summer that she really needed to tell them what song to play when she came out—this had gone beyond insulting and was now ear-splittingly annoying.

"Strike him out. Just do this thing, just do this . . ." she repeated quietly to herself as she walked. She took a quick glance around the ballpark. It was packed, which was surprising for a Tuesday night against a so-so team. But the Indians were on the cusp of securing a spot in the playoffs, and that brought people out.

As Brenda walked by Pasquela at second base, she wanted to stop and ask if he hated that song as much as she did. Except Pasquela still hated her guts and would probably say something offensive. *Is it too much to ask just to be treated like a ballplayer? Like a person?* she thought. She glanced up around the stands and saw a group of men and two women on the third base side holding up signs reading, "No Women in Baseball." By now she was on the mound. She looked down at the pitching rubber and then at the glove of dear young Johnny Gonzalez behind the plate. "I just want a little respect. Is it too much to want it now? How soon is now, motherfuckers?" she muttered as she threw her first pitch.

•◊•

Excerpt from the transcript for *Today in Sports* with Charlie Bannister, ESPN, September 24:

> Charlie: My pick for game of the week is definitely Friday night, Chicago White Sox at the Cleveland Indians. They've been battling it out for the second wildcard spot in the playoffs. Cleveland just needs one win against Chicago to clinch it. To add fuel to the fire, the last time these two teams got together, they had the best knock-down, drag-out fight of the season. Folks, set the DVR on record because this is gonna be good.

Chapter Twenty-Six

•◊•

BRENDA WOKE UP AT 6:00 A.M. ON FRIDAY. She had watched the night before as her teammates completed a sweep of the Royals. If they took the first game against the White Sox, the pressure would be off.

The boys wouldn't be up for a while, and Brenda lay there in her bed, just listening to the occasional creaking of the house, the birds outside the window, a lone car driving down the street. The bed was by a small circular window at the front of the house, and lying there and listening to birds early in the morning always made her feel like she was a kid in a treehouse. She tried sinking back into the pillows and letting the early morning sounds carry her back to sleep for a few minutes, but the prospect of the series with the White Sox was too much.

She was ready for the season and the traveling and the time away from the boys to be over, and yet the thought of being in the playoffs had an appeal she couldn't deny. And there were some parts of playing baseball that she really liked. There was a certain satisfaction in striking someone out. She liked the quick rub of her finger against horsehide as she released the ball and watched it fly into Gonzalez's mitt. She had started to enjoy other things too: feeling her entire body engaged in launching the ball into the air, watching a batter swing at nothing, hearing the crowd cheer when she got the out.

"Playing ball a little bit longer wouldn't be so bad . . ." she said to the ceiling.

She had been able to score five extra tickets for Robin, Dan, and Lindsey plus Carl and his son, which was good, because the boys and Adele were going too. Everyone in Cleveland, it seemed, wanted to go to the game.

When she walked out with the boys to wait for the bus, Andy didn't protest that they didn't need her to wait with them (for that matter, neither did Jon). She stood in between her sons as they waited. Jon fidgeting on her left, Andy standing stoically on her right. She put an arm around each of them, and even Andy leaned into her.

"I'm sorry this was a tough summer," she said.

"I missed you," Jon said bluntly. "Even if you are grumpy," he added with a sly grin.

"I missed you too. Even if I am grumpy," she echoed. "The season's almost over though. Three more games."

"Unless you clinch tonight," Andy said without looking at her.

"Right. Unless we clinch." She looked down at Jon and over at Andy. He was already equal to her in height and his eyes met hers.

"It sucks having you away," he said and put his arm around her waist. "But you'd still better win tonight."

"Yeah," Jon added and gave her a hug. "Bring home a win, Mom."

Brenda felt a wave of maternal love wash over her. "I'll do my best," she said.

They stood silently until the bus arrived, and Brenda was pleasantly surprised when both boys hugged her good-bye first instead of the other way around.

She and Ed had made lunch plans at a restaurant by I-271 and Chagrin Boulevard, close to the edge of the city office parks where he worked. This was convenient for him but meant she'd have to bring her things with her and go straight to the ballpark. Typical Ed to think about what was easiest for him. She wanted a little extra time before the game to go through any new video of the White Sox lineup and preferred doing so in the film room at the ballpark.

Ed was waiting for her at the table when she arrived. It was one of those hyper trendy restaurants that catered to the office workers nearby and was always more crowded at lunch than at dinner. It seemed like the type of place Ed might take a date in order to impress her. Brenda wasn't impressed, but she was glad she had decided to dress up slightly instead of dressing down.

Ed stood up as she approached the table. It seemed like he was trying awfully hard, which gave her more confidence even though she felt a knot in her stomach.

"Hi," he said. "Wow. You look really great."

Brenda caught a glimpse of her reflection in the large tinted glass window near their table. The combination of playing baseball and a perpetually upset stomach meant that she had lost weight over the summer, and the team workouts and regular throwing had toned her arms and legs. For the first time since she was in college, she thought she looked pretty good too.

"Thank you," she said.

Their conversation started out awkwardly, but then Ed asked if Andy had told her about Carrie.

Carrie? Brenda scanned her mental database for any mention of "Carrie" in the past week. Nothing. "Is that her name?" she bluffed. "I've heard snippets about her." That sounded remotely true, although she couldn't recall any comment by either of the boys or Adele that would make her think Andy had a girlfriend or a crush.

"Yeah, I just managed to drag her name out of him last weekend. I don't think it's serious. From what he says, she barely knows he exists."

"He hasn't talked about her to me that much," Brenda said, happy to make a true statement.

"I'm not surprised," Ed said. "Besides Lindsey, which probably doesn't really count, it's his first real crush. A guy doesn't want to talk to his mom about that. He wants to talk to his dad."

"Is that why you think the boys should live with you?" There. It was out in the open, and Brenda felt better having said it. There wasn't any use in playing polite—if they were going to work this out on their own, they'd have to talk about it.

Ed ran his fingers through his hair. "That's one of the reasons, yes. I got to thinking this summer that maybe they should live with me full-time or at least half-time because they're boys and they're getting older and should be with their dad . . ."

"So you can teach them how to be men? If that's how you feel, why are we even here?" Brenda asked. She put her hands flat on the table and debated whether to stand up and just leave. But then the issue wouldn't get settled and they'd have to go to the hearing. And she was tired of running away from Ed.

"I didn't talk to you about it, and that was wrong. But you didn't tell me about the guy who followed the boys home, or about Andy getting into fights or getting caught shoplifting . . . When I found out you had been keeping that from me, I guess I went a little crazy. It just seemed like maybe they needed their dad." He paused for a second and looked at her with a mixture of sadness and embarrassment. "I'm sorry I didn't talk to you first. And I'm sorry for . . . everything."

Brenda actually felt her jaw drop a couple centimeters. Ed had a habit of apologizing for all the little things and none of the big things. Burned the hot dogs at the cookout on Memorial Day? Sorry. Spilled something in the living room? Sorry. Coming home late and accidentally denting Brenda's car because he was "a little" drunk? Nothing. Having a fling with a woman in his office? Nothing. And now here was a genuine apology, seemingly for all of it. Brenda felt her eyes well up with tears, and she almost looked away because she didn't want Ed to see her cry, but she forced herself to hold his gaze.

"Thank you." She had thought that saying what was on her mind somehow meant she wanted Ed back. Now it just felt like honesty. "What really hurt me the most through all of this was that you seemed completely unfazed. No remorse, no regret, no grief. It was like you took a pair of scissors and just cut your family out of your life, and then suddenly you decided you wanted to paste the boys back into your life and . . . Geez, I'm sorry, that's a really terrible metaphor."

"It's a lovely little metaphor," Ed said.

"I've just never been able to figure out why you did this." That, ultimately, was the question that had been nagging at her for the past year. Why? What was so horrible in his life with her that he felt compelled to leave?

"I wasn't happy. And neither were you."

"That's the biggest cop-out I've ever heard."

"You and the boys were like this little triumvirate, this tight little unit, and I felt like all I was doing was paying the bills and fixing things."

"So it's my fault? I pushed you away, yada yada yada . . ."

"No, no, that's not what I'm saying." Ed looked pained. "Look, I just feel like we started growing in different directions. And when the affair with . . ." He took a deep breath. "The affair with Martina was a symptom and I let it be the reason. It was so much easier to just hide behind the affair and let you throw me out rather than face up to the fact that we had grown apart or to try and do anything to salvage us as a couple."

Brenda half-expected the anger to start bubbling up inside her, but she felt surprisingly calm. There was no need to get mad when she was actually getting the information she had been looking for. "Why are you telling me all this now?"

"Because I realize I did something wrong and I'm trying to fix it. I'm not saying we should get back together—but it'd be nice if we could be friends. Or at least not enemies . . ." He again ran his hand through his hair—Ed always did that when he was thinking or was under the gun. It was a habit she used to find incredibly sexy, but now it just looked like the move of a man struggling for words.

For a moment, she struggled with what to say too. "I'm sorry I didn't tell you about the fights and everything else," she said finally, "I've been treating you like you're horrible and selfish and immature and now I'm not sure if that's because you are or because I just remember things that way. Just like the way you probably remember me as being a controlling, narrowly focused shrew."

"I think the word is 'bitch,' actually . . ." Ed said with a smile.

Brenda dipped two fingers into her glass and flicked water at him. Ed laughed, and for a moment everything felt like it did when they were dating, when the silliness and teasing seemed to be their own private form of foreplay.

"I tried to talk to you about this at Andy's birthday party, but I'm withdrawing the custody challenge," Ed said as the server came with their lunches. Brenda could only sit there across from him, not speaking, just staring down at the monstrous bowl of salad that had been set before her. It was as though a hundred-pound weight had been lifted from her back, and she just wanted to sit and savor the feeling of relief. The boys were staying with her.

She heard Ed's voice as though it was coming in through a scratchy, slightly off-station radio. "I do want them to start staying overnight at my place sometimes. I'm moving to a two-bedroom, so they'll have their own room at my place. Make it more like home for them."

"That's . . . that's a good thing. Wow. I'm starting to think you've been replaced by an alien Ed . . ." Brenda picked up her water glass and took a drink, half-wishing it were something stronger.

Ed grinned. "No more than you're an alien Brenda."

The rest of the lunch was a breeze. Now that Ed wasn't trying to take the boys, it was painless to come up with a shared custody plan they could both agree on. The boys would spend every other weekend, Friday through Sunday, at Ed's ("Plus an evening here or there," Ed added as a safety net, "In case we want to go see a movie or have a guys' night out.") and they'd switch off major holidays. It was as though this thing that had kept her tied up in knots for the past month had suddenly disappeared. She felt like she could breathe freely again. On her way downtown, she cranked the radio as loud as it would go and felt like a teenager who had just gotten away with something.

At the ballpark, she holed up in the film room, watching video of Chicago's batters, especially Jorge Racino and his .376 batting average, which led both leagues. When she went to her locker room, she found a copy of her Bam! sports bra ad taped to the mirror above her sink. A Post-It note was stuck to it with the words: "All that meat and no potatoes."

"Oh for crying out loud," she said to the note. The pornography and the lewd comments were somehow easier to take than this direct commentary on the inadequacies of her body. She took a good look at herself in the mirror. "Never had much in the potatoes category, but there's definitely less meat there," she murmured and felt a burst of confidence in her physical self that was neither fleeting nor shaky.

She opened her duffel bag and took out the photo of Pasquela (or was it Cipriani) naked from the waist down and one of the Sharpies she had learned to carry around for autograph seekers. Without thinking about what she was doing, for the first time since Ed left, she started to draw.

When she was done, she made a quick stop in the locker room to tape the two pictures to the wall near the television set and then headed for the field. Players from both teams were on the field, stretching or playing loose games of catch. There were always a few journalists hanging around the field at this time, generally the beat writers who were busy getting quotes or interviews or just shooting the breeze with each other or the players. Today there were also more national media than usual. As Brenda walked onto the field, one of the beat reporters for the White Sox stopped her and asked a few questions. When she was done talking to him, she took a few steps along the third base line and was stopped by one of the national writers (she couldn't even remember who he wrote for) who wanted to set up a lengthy interview. She told him to set it up with Stratagem because she knew she'd forget about it otherwise.

She continued out to the bullpen to throw a few pitches and loosen up her arm. Bandershoot, the reserve catcher, was in the bullpen and she asked him to catch her for a few minutes. She threw about three or four pitches when he pulled off his mask and asked, "You feeling okay? Is your arm sore?"

Earl was in the bullpen, watching Hodges warm up. She saw Earl, Hodges, and Bridges, who was catching, all turn their heads to her. One thing she had learned early on: Never say you're hurt. Never say you're sore. Brenda knew her right arm would need to be physically separated from her body before she could say she couldn't pitch without somebody muttering something about weak women.

"No, not sore at all. Just taking my time warming up, I guess." She knew this was an unacceptable answer as well and took a moment to focus on Bandershoot's mitt. The thought of Ed and the custody battle couldn't muster up any anger, but there was still Charlie Bannister to think about. He actually didn't make her mad. However the thought that perhaps she had thrown away something potentially good made her mad at herself. "You totally screwed that one up." she grunted as she threw. The shot of angry adrenaline worked; she could feel the velocity as the ball seemingly jumped out of her hands and into Bandershoot's mitt. Out of the corner of her eye, she saw Earl nod approvingly and then go back to talking with Hodges.

She threw sixteen pitches and felt fine. After thanking Bandershoot, Brenda started the long walk across left-centerfield back to the dugout. She was approaching third base when she heard a familiar voice say, "Excuse me! Brenda? Do you have a couple minutes for a quick chat?"

She stopped walking and looked down at the brownish-red infield dirt. The owner of that voice should not be standing right behind her when he had a live show to do that night in New York.

Brenda turned to see Charlie Banister. She heard herself gasp, "Oh!" and suddenly felt shaky and nervous. Not talking to Charlie for a couple weeks had made her hope she had gotten him out of her system; she wasn't sure if she was dismayed or not that this wasn't the case. She gave a quick look around. Anthony Fleetwood, Bandkins, Groggins, and Landers were in short left, playing easy games of catch and stretching. Just beyond them, McGall was running his customary wind sprints across center field. Teeset, Pasquela, and Stone were doing some stretches out in short right. Some of the White Sox were off along the first base line doing calisthenics and stretches. Members of the media and coaches and trainers moved among all these groups of players, giving the entire field the air of a beehive in full swing. One could either feel very exposed or very ignored out there. When she saw Charlie, Brenda felt exposed.

Without thinking about it, she blurted out, "What are you doing here?"

Charlie took a couple steps closer to her while still behaving like any other journalist talking to any other ballplayer. She noticed he didn't have a cameraman anywhere in sight. "I'm a sportscaster, and we're standing in a place where people play a sport," he said with a little grin.

"Don't you have a show to do tonight?"

"Yes, I'm doing it live from the ballpark. In case you haven't noticed, this is kind of a big game."

He was now just a couple steps away, and Brenda was suddenly seized by an almost overwhelming compulsion to hug him, which bothered her. "Yes, I've noticed."

"Are you ready?"

"I'm the stopper," she said slowly. "I'm *always* ready."

Charlie's smile turned mischievous. "Is that a come-on?"

"No!" she said. It was infuriating that he was getting to her, but she reminded herself that being infuriated was okay. After working out the custody arrangement with Ed, she had been feeling good—too good, perhaps, to do her job well. A little argument with Charlie might help, except that once again, it seemed that Charlie Bannister wasn't going to argue with her. "And this isn't the time or the place to be flirting with me."

"Nobody is listening to us or even watching this conversation. They're all too preoccupied with their own careers. And besides, I like that I made you flustered. It makes me think that I might still have a chance with you."

"You didn't make me flustered," Brenda said and tried not to stammer when she said it. And because he wasn't giving her the argument she was looking for, added, "And no, you don't have a chance with me. We never had a chance."

To her equal parts amazement and annoyance, Charlie smiled. "What's that line from Macbeth? Methinks the lady doth protest too much?"

"This is a hell of an interview, Bannister," Brenda said.

"I'm just getting started."

"Why are you here?"

"Ostensibly, I'm here because this series will decide the second wildcard spot in the AL playoffs and *Today in Sports* ought to be here to cover it. At least that's what I told my producer. The real reason I'm here is to see you."

"That sounds sweet, but the fact remains that you live in New York and I live in Cleveland." The echo of her own words to Lily the lovely P.F. Chang's waitress rattled around her brain, but she ignored it. "I barely have enough time to see my kids as it is without adding in a long-distance relationship."

"Is geography the only thing stopping you from taking a chance on me? We have telephones, Skype, email. Plus people move every day. The way I envision my future career, I can live anywhere. Remove that obstacle. What is it really? Caution? Fear? Join the club." He paused for half a second and gave her a look that made Brenda's heart stop. "At the risk of making a fool of myself and getting hurt more deeply than I ever thought possible . . . I'm in love with you. I realize you likely don't feel the same way, but I had to say this to you, in person."

For a moment, the rest of the world stopped. She didn't hear her teammates talking or the faraway muffled *thwump* of balls sinking into gloves or the breeze that rattled around 42,000 empty seats. Everything else seemed blurry and out of focus except for Charlie. Brenda tried to stay angry, but her stomach and spirits felt a little lift when Charlie said this, and involuntarily, she felt herself smile. It was like being poised on the edge of a cliff, about to dive into a clear blue ocean. And here was Charlie Bannister standing next to her, asking if he could jump in and share the adventure with her. It all felt very unreal and yet very natural at the same time.

After playing it safe for nearly forty years, she had spent the last six months doing things that scared her, and in spite of the harassment and the loneliness and the separation from her family, the chances she had taken had worked out. She was supporting her family on her own. She was playing baseball and doing it well. Perhaps this new bird could fly if she could only stop clutching onto her old life so tightly.

"There's always hope, Charlie," she said. Charlie looked hesitant, as though he wasn't sure how to read what she had said. "Let's try this."

Brenda had always thought that the tiny little laugh lines around Charlie's eyes when he smiled were one of his best features. She gazed at them now, a dozen or so adorable creases pointing at his eyes, which seemed to emphasize that he was looking right at her. Seeing that smile and those laugh lines on a regular basis might be kind of nice.

She heard Greg Landers' voice off to her right, loudly saying something to the effect of, "Over my flat white ass, you will!" and Bandkins, Groggins, and Fleetwood laughing. She saw the four of them crossing the infield heading toward the dugout.

"Hey Charlie! How's it going?" Fleetwood said, walking over to where they were standing.

"Hi Anthony," Charlie said, shaking hands all around. Brenda watched as he chatted for a moment with her teammates, asking some standard journalist questions and looking nothing like a man who had just bared his heart and soul. She noticed Landers tried to catch her eye, but she ignored him. If it were any other journalist, she would take this shift in conversation as an opportunity to leave. That's what any other player would do. Landers had an amused little grin on his face that grew wider and more amused the longer Brenda hung around.

Charlie was asking Art Groggins about doing a retrospective interview after his retirement at the end of the season. Brenda waited for a pause in the conversation then, forcing herself to sound as casual and natural as possible, said, "Hey Charlie, nice chatting with you, but I need to get going."

Charlie turned to her, his voice professional but his eyes soft. "Thanks for your time, Brenda."

"No problem." With her heart pounding, she added, "I'll have some time after the game to finish the interview."

"That would be great. Thanks very much," Charlie said, and she got another full dose of his cute laugh lines. Bandkins and Fleetwood had wandered away already. With all the self-control she could muster, Brenda turned and started to walk toward the dugout. She heard Groggins' deep bass voice tell Charlie to have the show call him and Charlie replying. Then she heard Charlie call her name. She stopped and turned, trying not to look too eager.

"Forgot one thing," he said, trotting a few steps to her but stopping far enough away to appear casual to any observers.

"What do you need?" she asked.

He extended his hand toward her. She looked at his hand, then at his face. He lowered his voice so that she had to strain to hear it. "I just wanted an excuse to touch you," he said quietly.

Brenda reached out and shook his hand, nodding as though she was answering a mundane question. "I'm glad you found one," she replied softly.

"Okay, thanks," Charlie said in a normal tone of voice and turned around. Brenda did the same. She hoped no one noticed that her legs were trembling as she walked away. Walking down the dugout stairs and into the tunnel leading to the locker room, Brenda felt as though she had a secret. It reminded her of when she first learned she was pregnant with Andy, but she and Ed didn't tell anyone for a couple months. Carrying that news around had been a private joy. She wasn't sure what to call what she was feeling now. In time, maybe she would call it love.

Brenda headed back to her locker room to review scouting reports and hitters on the iPad and didn't go back to the locker room until just before game time. When she walked in, she saw Hodges and Bandkins standing near the television, shaking with laughter. A few other players were in the locker room, and most of them glanced over at her as she entered. They were already dressed, so she knew that wasn't why they were looking at her. It had to be the pictures.

Pasquela, Landers, Sparks, and Cipriani were in their usual spots in front of the television, playing *Grand Theft Auto*. Other players were sitting by their lockers making last-minute adjustments to their cleats or gloves or doing whatever else they needed to prepare for the game. Other players were hanging out at the three round tables immediately in front of the main door where Brenda entered. She surprised herself by not feeling nervous or scared. "There's nothing he can do to you," she said to herself. "You're just returning something he left in your locker room."

Doug Stone was at his locker, and when he saw her, he chuckled. "You've outdone yourself this time, B."

Brenda was about to respond when she heard Pasquela's voice ring through the locker room. "Hey, Haversham!" he yelled, standing up. "I need to talk to you."

"I'm right here," Brenda replied. She gave a quick glance around the now-silent room. Every player in the room was watching them. No coaches, no trainers, no media were around. For half a second, this worried her, then she relaxed. Better to have it out with players only.

Pasquela picked up the two pictures and walked over to the table where she stood. He put them down on the table saying, "You gotta lot of balls hanging these up in here."

Brenda looked down at the two pictures. One was the picture she put in her duffel bag long ago of one of her teammates exposing himself from the waist down. From Pasquela's reaction, she figured it must have been him. She had turned the picture into a cartoon character, with the erect penis as the long, Pinocchio-like nose of a silly face. For not having drawn anything in ages, she thought it was pretty good. The other was her sports bra ad. She had attached a new Post-It note that read: "Don't lie, you know you love me." She thought pairing the photos together like that was pretty funny. "You've got a lot of balls putting those pictures in my locker room," she said.

She and Pasquela stood eye to eye, and Brenda felt a surge of misguided self-confidence. If she were a man, he would have hit her. She stood her ground with her heart in her throat. Every other player in the room was watching their confrontation, and she wondered how much it would hurt if Pasquela actually slugged her. For a long, long second all she could hear was her own heart pounding in her ears, then McGall started singing.

The collective focus of the room turned to McGall, who was jumping up and down on the circular leather couch in front of the television while he sang "Who has big balls?" to the tune of "Who Wears Short Shorts?" And just as quickly as the locker room had become quiet and tense, it shifted back to its standard noise and controlled chaos.

Brenda and Pasquela remained glaring at each other. The moment of potential violence had passed, but the pictures were still lying on the table. Brenda wasn't sure what to say. She didn't need to be friends with him; she just wanted a truce. She picked up the naked-from-the-waist-down cartoon and ripped it in half. Then ripped it in half again, crumpled it into a ball and tossed it on the table.

Pasquela pondered this for a moment, then nodded. He picked up the picture of her sports bra ad, ripped it in half and crumpled the pieces into a ball. McGall was still standing on the couch but was now expounding on the shortcomings of metal relative to punk like a music critic turned street preacher. Pasquela took both balled-up pieces of paper and threw them at McGall, yelling, "Hey McGall! I got your balls right here."

He walked away, heading toward his locker, without saying anything to Brenda. She didn't mind. That battle was over. Now that it was, she realized how shaken she was.

"He wouldn't have really hit you," a deep voice next to her said. She hadn't noticed that Art Groggins had come over to where she was still standing, her right hand clutching the table as though she'd fall over if she didn't. Groggins' presence made her relax her grip. He lowered his voice. "Pasquela can be a lazy little shit sometimes, but he wouldn't have hit you."

As always, Brenda was keenly aware of the constant stream of motion on the periphery of their conversation that seemed at odds with anyone's ability to talk privately. But Charlie was right—everyone else in the locker room was generally too preoccupied with himself to pay attention to anything else. "Why not? He wouldn't hit a woman?"

"He wouldn't hit a woman, but he'd hit another ballplayer," Groggins said pointedly, then added: "But other ballplayers have friends. A lot of people in here have your back, Haversham. Me included."

"Thanks, Art," Brenda said, almost overwhelmed with gratitude.

"By the way, you're a good artist," Groggins said and walked away.

Brenda watched him go and surveyed the rest of the locker room. McGall, Landers, Teeset, and some others were now watching some inane DVD and laughing like little boys. Anthony Fleetwood was sitting by his locker, Bible in hand, saying a quick prayer as he always did before a game. Doug Stone was sitting facing his locker in his quiet pre-game meditation ritual. Groggins had gone over to the corner and was stretching. Ochoa was doing more of his crazy yoga poses. Sparks, Cipriani, and Bandkins, in an attempt to meld saber-metrics with dating, were arguing about which supermodel had the highest Total Replacement Hotness. Hodges, who was starting that night, was silently psyching himself into The Zone.

She felt somewhat displaced and apart from the action, then she noticed Francisco Jimenez sitting in front of his locker, leaning back and watching the show just like she was. He gave her a little nod and a smile, and she nodded back. They were both just hanging out, doing nothing, and that was okay. She was their teammate.

When they went into the dugout at the top of the game, she didn't feel out of place. And when she went out to the bullpen after the first inning, she didn't feel that she was hiding out there.

Chicago came out swinging, scoring three runs in the first while Cleveland went down 1-2-3. Each time Ben Morris came up to bat, the stadium filled with boos. In the fourth inning, Hodges threw a pitch that Morris apparently thought was too far inside; he stepped out of the box, bat to his side, and glared at the mound. To his credit, Hodges didn't flinch. The face-off only last a few seconds, but it had enough shades of their last encounter with the White Sox to make both benches stand up. When Morris grounded out to second, Brenda couldn't help but say, "Serves you right, asshole."

Sparks was sitting in his usual spot near her on the bench and snickered. "You kiss your mother with that mouth, Haversham?"

"No, I kiss your mother, Sparks," Brenda said.

Sparks snorted a laugh, but that was it for conversation in the bullpen. The game was too tense, too important for goofing around.

Hodges was one of those pitchers who typically started off strong then would fall apart in the fifth or sixth inning. Tonight, however, he had his worst inning early on and then calmed down. The Indians scored in the third and fourth innings, and by the seventh inning, were up 4-3. Munson pulled Hodges and sent Sparks in for the eighth. Brenda was tense until Sparks got the third out with no runs scored. Jimenez, the closer, would go in for the ninth and that would be the ballgame. Brenda wasn't sure how she felt about not playing that night. A win was a win— it guaranteed them a spot in the playoffs, but part of her wanted to bring home a win, not just watch it.

At the top of the ninth, Jimenez went out to the mound and the stadium went crazy. He was the hero who had sent the Indians to the playoffs three seasons before. Now it was his turn to do it again. Brenda felt like a kid as she watched him take his warm-up pitches. Andy, Jon, and Adele were off in the family section somewhere along the third base line. She was glad the boys had the chance to see the game.

Jimenez was facing Burt, Parker, and Holmes. When he struck out Burt to lead off the ninth, the noise from the crowd was so loud Brenda could feel it seeping up through the concrete and into her legs. It was as intoxicating as the scent of boiled hot dogs. Parker flied out to Bandkins in deep right, and the noise somehow increased.

Brenda and the rest of the bullpen were on their feet, watching and waiting for the win. Then the bottom fell out.

Holmes, the top of the order, drew out a twelve-pitch at-bat, fouling off ball after ball before knocking out a base hit to left center.

The noise in the stadium quieted down considerably, but Earl kept saying, "He'll get out of it." The base hit seemed to take away some of Jimenez's confidence. Tagiashi was up next and fouled off three or four balls before drawing a walk and putting the go ahead run on base.

"He looks tired," Cipriani said. "Look how long he's taking between pitches."

"And he's rushing his motion," Earl said.

Brenda watched as Jimenez threw his first pitch to Weymouth, the next batter. She didn't see what Earl was talking about, but she did on the second pitch. It appeared that Jimenez was throwing the ball with his chest instead of his arm, as though he couldn't get enough power with his arm.

The bullpen phone rang and every head turned as Earl answered it. Cipriani turned to Brenda but didn't say anything. Brenda held his gaze for a moment then turned back to Earl, who was hanging up the phone.

"Haversham. Start throwing," he said. "And hurry it up."

Brenda grabbed her glove and went behind the bench to where Bridges was just putting on his catcher's mask.

"Let's do this," he said.

She took a deep breath and said, "Okay." She stood facing Bridges, aware of the fans who were now looking over the bullpen wall at her, aware of her heart pounding and her legs and arms shaking. "You can do this. You can do this," she said to herself and willed her nerves to calm down. She had only thrown two easy warm-up pitches, not even enough to loosen her arm, when she heard a collective groan from the crowd. Jimenez had walked the bases loaded.

"Haversham! You're in."

She walked back to the bullpen dugout. Cipriani was leaning against the bullpen railing, singing his own version of "She's A Lady." He stopped singing and smiled at her. "I needed a word that rhymed with 'bunt,'" he said.

Enough. "I'm not a lady, Cipriani," Brenda said. "I'm a ballplayer. Deal with it."

Cipriani looked at her, as though judging the depths of her soul. "Fair enough."

"And that isn't my theme song anyway." She could hear the first wavy, reverberating chords of The Smiths "How Soon Is Now?" begin to play over the PA system as her name was announced. "*That's* my theme song," she added over her shoulder and began the long walk out to the mound.

When she finally told the PA announcer what song she wanted played when she came into a game, she hadn't counted on how it would make her feel. Hearing a song she hated had always made her want to rip things apart. Hearing a song she loved made her want to create. Johnny Marr's keening guitar and Morrissey's plaintive crooning carried her across the field. The song wouldn't help her find the anger today, but it did pump her up, and she felt the familiar jumble of emotions and energy coursing through her veins.

She had had no time to prepare in the bullpen. Now, as she stood on the mound, Brenda searched for the anger. It was there. It was always there, bubbling just below the surface. She looked at Johnny Gonzalez's catcher's mitt sitting sixty feet and six inches away and tried to imagine Ed's face in its deep, creased pocket. But she threw a warm-up pitch to an Ed who was saying, "I'm sorry."

She tried imagining Charlie's face in the glove, but he hadn't disappointed her and she hadn't sabotaged a good thing.

She tried Pasquela, but could only see him yelling to McGall, "I've got your balls right here!" as she threw another anemic warm-up. She tried Cipriani, but his face would only repeat the words, "Fair enough" and nothing else.

Brenda was getting scared. She closed her eyes and let the noise of the sold-out crowd inhabit her ears and her head. Then she heard them. Some boos. Some jeers. Even a "Get out of baseball!"

The Frickers. Yes. They were always around and never failed to piss her off. She opened her eyes and took her first real look at the crowd. There was a group on the second level between first base and home plate. A couple of them were holding big placards that read, "No Women in Baseball." "Fuck you," Brenda muttered to the sign. Then she noticed two men a bit farther down who were holding a banner over the railing that read, "IroNy Shitts."

Brenda did a double-take. She squinted at the sign. If she looked closely, she could see that it was supposed to read, "Iron My Shirts," but the sign maker had bunched up the "n" and the "m" and written a lower-case "r" that looked like a "t." For all intents and purposes, the sign read, "IroNy Shitts."

And that's when Brenda laughed. For the first time all summer, she laughed.

She heard McGall's voice say, "Hey, Big Balls! What's the hold up?" and saw that he had joined her on the mound. Brenda was still laughing and could barely spit out the words, "Irony shits."

"What?" McGall looked around for a second and then saw the banner too. His donkey laugh was as melodious as the sound of wood hitting horsehide. "That's awesome, but dude, you've gotta pitch."

Brenda suddenly became aware of the 42,000 people sitting in the stands watching her. She saw Munson standing with one foot on the top step of the dugout. She saw Jorge Racino and his .376 batting average standing by the batter's box, waiting. And she had nothing. "Oh crap. I can't do this," she said.

"Sure you can. Just do what you always do," McGall said.

"I can't."

"Then do something else," he said as he trotted back to his position.

Brenda heard the umpire yell, "Batter up" and watched Racino step into the batter's box. He was broad and muscular and swirled the bat in a circle above his shoulder three times before each pitch. For some reason, Brenda found this quirk delightful. She couldn't stop smiling. As she stared down the alley at Gonzalez's mitt, Brenda realized she wasn't angry. Not at all. And yet she felt a great surge of energy and adrenaline running through her body. Her limbs and fingers and toes were tingling; even her hair felt electrified. She stared at her target and saw the familiar golden lines leading from her hand to the catcher's mitt, saw the rectangle demarcating the strike zone. As she threw the first pitch down that golden tunnel, she marveled at what she was feeling. She thought it might be joy.

•◇•

Excerpt from the transcript for *Today in Sports* with Charlie Bannister, ESPN, February 5:

> Charlie: Good evening, I'm Charlie Bannister and welcome to my last night as the host of *Today in Sports*.

> Howie: Good evening, I'm Howie Wojinski, and welcome to my first night as the host of *Today in Sports*.

> Charlie: Howie, your first day is Monday. This is still my show. And the powers that be told me that because it's my last show, I can say anything I want.

> Howie: And . . . ?

> Charlie: Anything I want.

> Howie: I'll miss your droll sense of humor. I hope it comes out in your writing.

> Charlie: It does indeed, but you'll have to wait until next spring to buy my book of essays. And

you'll have to wait about two years to read the graphic novel I'm working on with pitcher Brenda Haversham. I'll bet you didn't know she could draw, Howie. In the meantime, you can read me in *Sports Illustrated*, which I've joined as a senior writer. And no, just because I'm a *senior* writer doesn't mean I'm old.

Howie: You are just full of witty one-liners this evening.

Charlie: Howie, I'm full of witty one-liners and excitement and anticipation. I'm about to embark on a grand adventure. I'm going back to my first love, which is writing, and I'm moving back to my home state. I'm helping to start a series of baseball clinics for girls. Even though you won't see me on *Today in Sports* every night, I'll still be around and very very busy.

Howie: So you're not really retiring.

Charlie: No. Who said I was retiring?

Howie: Barney, the new intern.

Charlie: His name is Justin.

Howie: But he always wears purple, so I call him Barney.

Charlie: Howie, it's just not the same when you do it. [pause] Call him Justin.

About the Author
•◊•

Susan Petrone lives with one husband, one child, and two dogs in Cleveland, Ohio. In addition to writing fiction, she blogs about her beloved Cleveland Indians at itspronouncedlajaway.com. Her best pitch is a breaking ball.